THE WITCHES
OF AUBURN
BOOK ONE

The Gifts of
Our Mothers

HAZEL BLACK

Also by Hazel Black

THE WITCHES OF AUBURN SERIES

Gisel (Witches of Auburn 1.5) A Novella
The Sins of Our Fathers (Witches of Auburn, Book 2)

THE WITCHES OF AUBURN
BOOK ONE

The Gifts of Our Mothers

Brunswick House
New York

Brunswick House Publishing
244 Madison Avenue
New York, NY 10016
First Brunswick House ebook and print on demand edition: October 2017
The Brunswick House name and logo are trademarks of Brunswick House Publishing, LLC.
The publisher is not responsible for websites (or their content) that are not owned by the publisher.
Manufactured in the United States of America
ISBN 978–1-943622–12–2 (ebook edition)
ISBN 978–1-943622–10–8 (print on demand edition)

For my mother.
My favorite witch to ever come out of Auburn.

INDEPENDENCE

Helene

"I KNOW YOU'RE EIGHTEEN, BUT I still worry about you," my father said.

"I promise I'll be careful." He tilted his head down until he was at my eye level and raised his eyebrows. "Always. It's just a quick flight. After spending almost seven hours in a car . . ." I stepped back and stretched my arms over my head. "I need a little freedom."

He was used to giving the women he loved space. My mother had required it when she was alive. "I love you, Helene."

I paused, frozen by his words. Before she died, he'd rarely told me he loved me. My father was cerebral, not emotional, but since her death, the two of us had left very few things unsaid. It was only one of the ways things changed two years ago. The day I'd gone to school just like every other day, and come home to find out my mother had been killed in a car accident.

I could only hug him without responding—to do so would feel more like I was saying, "I'm sorry she died," than, "I love you," but I supposed he deserved both. I ran to the tree line behind our house that I'd taken off from since I was a little girl and disappeared right before launching into the black sky. It was like diving into an ocean with no water and no bottom, only waves of darkness and the currents of the night's breeze.

Weightless and finally free, I inhaled the air and soared over Auburn. The angles of the rooftops, the rectangles of land behind each one, the lone church, and the firehouse of the little town all made me miss my mother more. I banked east, leaving the thoughts of her behind with the terrain. The wind was at my back, and I used it to my advantage as I sped toward the tree house where I knew I'd find Isaiah waiting for me.

It was already ten, and the cicada and the crickets were the only sounds I heard as I flew close to the treetops. I dipped down at the sight of Isaiah's tree house and landed on the balcony outside. Candlelight glowed from the crack around the door.

I stood straight and inhaled the sounds of the woods to center myself before opening the door on the force that was Isaiah. He'd forever take my breath away. I didn't need freedom. Only Isaiah. I was still standing on the far side of the doorway when a shrill laugh echoed through the trees and climbed down my back with a chill. My gaze ran through the forest surrounding me as my mother's never-ending warnings to, "Never underestimate the Virago," rang through my memory.

A witch was rarely alone.

I pushed the handle and swung the door in until it hit his feet. He was lying on his back in the center of the floor. Isaiah's powerful body left little room for anything else. I raked my eyes over it, committing it again to memory for use when I went back to the

University of Vermont for good in a few weeks. This tiny separation—one night for freshman orientation—we'd survived, but it was hard.

He didn't say a word, not even when I closed the door behind me. I'd felt renewed in Vermont the last twenty-four hours. It was a fresh start without all the sympathy and sadness Auburn held for me. Watching Isaiah stare at the ceiling reminded me of what else this place held—my heart.

I climbed on top of him, straddling him while I sat up and stared at his beautiful face. He hadn't shaved. His dark hair climbed down his sideburns and dotted his face, which was softened by the candlelight. There was something missing in his stare.

I leaned down and kissed his lips.

Isaiah didn't move. He stared past me at the ceiling. The roof panels were closed. The sky was hidden. He was still mad. Our last conversation was the ugly culmination of weeks of bickering over my choice to attend college so far away. He refused to understand that I just needed some miles between me and Auburn . . . and the memories of my mother's death.

I lay flat on top of him and let my lips drag up his jagged beard until I reached his ear. "I'm back," I whispered and kissed his cheek.

Isaiah's gaze never faltered from the ceiling. I sat back, rested my hands on his stomach, and waited for him to face me. I ran my fingertips across the fabric of his shirt without him responding. I could run my hands between his legs to the spot on his thigh that always made him exhale my name. He'd close his eyes and forget he was ever mad.

"Isaiah. Look at me," I whispered softly, hoping to coax him out of whatever deep thoughts he was lost in. "I'm back and I love you today exactly the way I did yesterday." My palms drifted down the sides of his body. "You can't keep holding on to some collapse between us that isn't going to happen."

His chest rose, lifting me farther away from him. He'd never ignored me before. Anger and fear stirred inside me at the damage one night had caused.

He sat up, making me shift to keep my balance. My body craved his hands on me. I leaned into him and kissed him. Just a whisper of a touch, but when he reached up and threaded his fingers in my hair, I let the full force of my need for him unleash. I wrapped my legs around his back and tightened my body against his until we couldn't be separated. The deep heat that had been my anchor to this earth for the last two years, settled inside me.

He grabbed my wrists and clenched them in his grip as his gaze dragged from my eyes to my lips and landed on the space he'd created between us. "I have to tell you something," he said, and a biting chill descended on the room.

"Isaiah—"

"I've done something horrible." The intense blue of his eyes was soaked in devastation, making me want to pull my hands out of his grasp and move back.

"Tell me," I said. We would fix it together.

His hands touching me took on a different nuance. Gone was his warmth. It was replaced by the tortured look in his eyes. The something he had done was to us. I stared at him until the strength to ask the question finally surfaced.

"What?" The muscles in my arms trembled. My breaths were short. "Isaiah?" I could feel the tears coming. They were breaking free from the depths of my soul and dragging me into this conversation behind them. I pressed my lips together in defiance.

After a deep breath, I moved off him and leaned against the wall of the tree house, waiting. The enormity of my boyfriend was replaced by a small boy in front of me. He shrank with every particle of regret in his stare. A searing pain shot through my head. I reached up to touch it and halt the stabbing. My brain was grasping for some understanding of a situation that was incomprehensible.

"What have you done?" I prayed for murder, theft, anything but the truth I knew was waiting locked in his next breath. Because there was only one "horrible" thing that could possibly put that look on his face. The others could be forgiven.

"Last night, I went to Tina's bonfire. There were a ton of people there, and I drank too much. I didn't mean for anything to happen." He took a deep breath and ran his hand through his hair, still refusing to meet my eyes. "I didn't . . . we didn't mean for it happen. I don't know. Helene, I'm sorry—"

"Who?" I screamed the word in a voice I didn't recognize. My eyes burned with tears, and my heart raced with anger. I didn't need to hear the words—didn't want to know the details. I just wanted to know who.

My thoughts rushed from the unbelievable to the concept that maybe we'd never been what I'd thought we were. The inkling that my obsession with Isaiah had somehow clouded my judgment of him. Of us.

"Gisel." The name of my best friend—one of my coven of only four—spewed from his lips as if the sounds scorched his insides.

I stopped breathing and stared at my horrifically pathetic boyfriend. I wanted him to pull me into his arms and make this all stop. "No." It was impossible. I shook my head in denial of what he just said, but it only made the pounding against the walls of my skull throb harder. It centered right behind my eyes until I thought it was the sight of Isaiah that was causing it.

He would never.

She would never.

"I gave you everything." My mother would have killed me for telling Isaiah about the craft, but she was gone, and he'd become my life. "Even the secrets that weren't mine I shared with you . . ."

"Helene, it was awful. We were wasted. You have to believe

me." He choked up before adding, "We hate ourselves." The sight of him without his smile or the little laugh that slipped between every few words he spoke reminded me of another time. The night he first kissed me. The jokes had stopped, and the playfulness was silenced as he faced me in the moonlight and said, "I love you."

I shook the image from my mind. "I have to go."

"I love you, Helene."

My stomach churned on his words. This wasn't a prank. I stared at the floor next to me as visions of Gisel's naked body next to Isaiah's invaded my mind. "How could you?" I searched everywhere around the tiny room for the strength to hear his answer. "With Gisel?" I finally faced him.

"Helene." He reached for me.

"Don't . . . ever . . . touch me." The words were stifled by my thoughts. One by one, they pierced through the wall I was erecting to hide behind so I didn't have to face him or what he'd done. What *she'd* done. Images of the two of them ricocheted through my mind. Did they drive somewhere together? Did they do it in his truck? Was Gisel's hair tied back the way she always liked it to be when she slept? I faced my boyfriend one last time and asked, "Were you here?" The words threatened to break me, but I had to know.

"Helene, don't do this. You have to hear m—"

"Were. You. Here?" It was the only question I wanted answered.

"No." His single word was so broken and pained, I almost faltered. Almost. Instead, I pushed myself to my feet and turned toward the door.

"I don't want to see you *ever* again."

"Helene, I love you." I bent at the waist and held myself up with my hands on my knees. I inhaled deeply, trying to force air into my body that no longer desired to breathe.

"Stay away from me." I remained with my head dragging until the tears came. Without facing Isaiah again, I stormed out the door of his tree house and flew into the night sky.

I went straight up until the air thinned and my speed slowed. I flipped and careened to the ground, turning just before crashing at the edge of the crick that ran between the tree house and Auburn.

How could they?

I flew faster, tears blurring my vision as I zigzagged wildly through the trees.

Nothing mattered.

I was empty.

They'd ruined everything left that I believed in, including myself.

I pushed myself faster, not attempting to stop or change direction as I hurtled toward a tall oak only turning slightly before my side crashed into the trunk.

It wasn't suicide. That would have required me to choose death.

I no longer cared.

II

"WHAT HAVE WE HERE?" THE foreign voice played with my consciousness before I opened my eyes. It wasn't my father's. It wasn't . . .

I rolled onto my back, and the pain in my shoulder helped to block the memories of Isaiah from my mind. I would focus on the side of my body that impacted with the tree. Not on my heart that was unsalvageable. It was still dark out and the black sky didn't have a hint of dawn surrounding me. I waited for my eyes to adjust before searching for the voice again.

"You're hurt." I felt his breath on my cheek, but he was invisible.

"Who are you?" Blood dripped down the side of my head and onto the white tank top I'd worn to see my boyfriend. I pressed my hand against the cut to stop the flow.

"A friend." The way he half-whispered sent a chill down my

spine. "Don't be afraid." Blood soaked my fingers. "Hold still and I'll fix your shoulder," he said.

I flew to my feet before remembering not to divulge too much about the things I was capable of. "I'm fine." His silence made me feel rude. It was an absurd thought since I couldn't even see him. "But thank you."

"Please." His voice came from beside me and above my head. He was taller by at least six inches. "I promise not to hurt you. Unlike your boyfriend."

My breath caught. He'd been watching me . . . and Isaiah. He knew.

He placed his hands flat on the front and back of my shoulder, straddling the lump that was protruding from the top. "Just a moment, and it will feel better." He didn't apply any pressure, and yet, my arm bone shifted back into the socket. The pain lessened, and I inhaled the absence of it. "Better?" His hands remained on me. A warmth between each radiated to my swelling shoulder.

I sank into the energy from his touch.

"See? You're safe."

I might never be safe again. "I need to get home." Home to Lovie and Sloane who could hear me in their minds. The same way our mothers had communicated in theirs.

Lovie, Sloane. My inner voice was deathly level to match my demeanor with the hidden man beside me. Terror was never an emotion to be shared. His hands dropped from my shoulder and were replaced by the chilled night air.

Helene, where are you? Lovie responded. She was frantic.

There was not a plant out of place near me, but I sensed he was still there. I couldn't tell how close or exactly where, but I knew he hadn't left me. I could *feel* him. Lovie should be worried. My first step to the left faltered as blood rushed to my head. I reached out for a tree and landed in the arms of the man.

"I'll take you."

"No," was my only response. He tilted my body toward his chest. He had a peculiar smell that was thick but light and pleasant like the wind before a storm on a summer's day. I let my body relax as we launched into the dark sky. We'd both disappeared, which was a bit unsettling considering I had no idea what he looked like except his hands were large and he was tall and there was a hint of . . . honeysuckle.

That, and he was strong. I'd never heard of anyone flying while carrying someone before, but he seemed to do so without effort.

Just east of Auburn, I told him, "You can land here. I'll be fine."

He didn't answer. Just kept flying until we reached my yard. The back door to my house opened, and he walked through it as if he'd been there a hundred times. My father lay asleep on the couch with the baseball game on the television. He appeared weak and vulnerable compared to the force that was unseen with me.

We paused at the bottom of the narrow staircase before he leapt to the top stair in complete silence. My chest tightened as he carried me to my room, laid me on my bed, and sat beside me.

"How did you know?" I appeared. My shoulder was already a gray purple color.

"I heard you hit the tree," he whispered.

The kindness in his tone hurt me. I'd have preferred it if he'd killed me. I lowered my head in shame. Isaiah came back to me. His voice as he said her name—

"That's how I found you."

I shook my head and turned toward the voice of the man. "That isn't what I was asking."

"Oh. What?" he whispered.

I inhaled the honeysuckle scent. "How did you know where I live?"

Air rushed by me, and I reached out for him. "I have to go,

Helene. I'm not supposed to be in Auburn." He laughed at some joke I didn't understand. "It's your side of the crick."

"And my name. How do you know that?"

He exhaled and said, "You should go see a doctor tomorrow and get a sling. Although, I'm known for my medical aptitude."

"Show yourself."

"Not tonight." His voice flattened, and I knew there was no use asking twice.

He could fly and he could move things, but he wasn't a witch. Only a woman could be a witch. "What are you?" I asked, not completely sure he was still with me.

"Your friend." His breath brushed across my cheek as his lips touched the edge of my ear. "You don't ever have to be alone."

Then he was gone and a new voice was filling the space. "Helene," Lovie said as she and Sloane burst into my room. "We've been flying all over looking for you."

"What happened to your head?" Sloane asked in the tender voice she reserved for conversations of our dead mothers. She sat on the bed next to me. The devastation in her eyes mirrored my broken heart.

Sloane pulled me close to her chest, and I crumbled there. The sight of them. Their voices. The life we all shared had been shattered by one fourth of us. She should be here, too, but Gisel was no longer a part of me.

"He told me," I said to relieve them of the horror of having to admit what their expressions told me they already knew. I held on tight to Sloane and cried. "I don't know what happened." Lovie rubbed my back. "I can't understand how they . . ."

"It's unbelievable. If I hadn't heard it from Gisel—"

"Don't say her name. I can't ever hear it again." Lovie's expression twisted into regret.

"You won't hear it from either of us. We're here. No matter

what," Sloane said and lay down with me still in her arms. Lovie crawled under the covers next to us. That was how we stayed until my tears ran out and sleep finally took me.

THREE

I LAY AWAKE LISTENING TO the rain falling against my window. Sloane and Lovie were curled next to me with their eyes closed as if this were any other Monday. Even with them beside me, it felt like everything was gone.

I wanted him.

I needed him to come over and tell me it was all a horrible lie, that he'd never actually been with her because the thought of being without me was just that unfathomable.

I crawled out from under the covers, leaving Sloane and Lovie who rolled closer to each other without waking. This was a nightmare. I only had to find a way to wake up. I reached under my bed and found the shoebox that at first held my pearl embellished prom sandals but now housed every word Isaiah had ever written me. Notes, letters, cards attached to flowers. He was generous with his thoughts. I rummaged through them, tossing his sentiments onto the floor in disgust.

"You're beautiful."

"I love you."

"You're the reason I wake up in the morning."

"Please don't leave me and go away to college."

"Stay."

Did he think the same of Gisel? She was one of my best friends, a fourth of my existence. She'd spent hours with Isaiah and me, and I'd never suspected a thing. They'd only recently seemed to even understand each other, bonding over their futures in New Jersey while Sloane, Lovie, and I made plans to attend college out of state.

I shoved the letters back into the box and stared out the window to the second floor of Gisel's house. When we were little, we'd hold up signs to communicate with each other. This morning, I hoped I never saw her again. Rain fell against our houses. The scene on the other side of the glass blurred.

Helene, I'm sorry, Gisel's voice rang in my head. *Please forgive me. I hate myself.*

Tears streamed down my face, but I wiped them away harshly with the back of my hand and shut down the connection. I wouldn't cry over her, or him, again. I'd leave them both here. They could have each other.

I forced myself to look at her house through my window. Had they been there the night before? Did he drive her home? The rain was replaced by a fine mist. My father's car backed out of the driveway, and he glanced at our house one last time before disappearing down the road. I stared at the wet concrete until Isaiah's truck pulled in a few minutes later. He'd been waiting for my father to leave. A bitter taste dripped down the back of my throat, and I couldn't inhale. I didn't want to see him. So, I dropped a thick elm tree from the side yard across the pavement to stop him from entering.

"What's going on?" Sloane sat up in my bed and asked.

"He's here."

"Isaiah?" She was already pushing out of bed to come to my side. When she saw his truck, her eyes narrowed.

"He should leave." My voice was steady. I was discussing some-one else's boyfriend. Mine would never have done the thing he did. The Isaiah I loved was perfect. "I can't guarantee what will happen to him."

He stepped out of the truck, and the battered elm flew from the driveway onto the stone path between Isaiah and the door.

"I'll go talk to him."

I turned my back to the window. "Tell him to never speak to me again."

Sloane placed her hand squarely on my back. "Helene, are you sure?"

All I could do was nod, but it was all she needed.

Even with my back to the window, I could feel Isaiah's eyes on me. I didn't want to, but I turned anyway, watching as Slone strode from my back door toward him.

"She doesn't want to see you," she said.

"I can tell." He looked from me to the tree blocking his way. "I have to talk to her."

"What were you thinking?" Sloane wasn't yelling, but every word touched me deep inside.

"We weren't thinking. We were drunk . . ."

"Don't ever"—she pointed her finger at him—"ever make an excuse for this. You are disgusting."

"We love her. Both of us. That's never going to change."

I slid down the wall until I was sitting on the floor with my knees pressed to my chest, hiding from the reality of my life.

"The two of you. Completely selfish . . . you couldn't handle that she was leaving." Sloane's voice rose, and I wondered if Gisel could hear it next door. "You're such a pathetic coward."

"You're right!" He fought back. "I'm horrible. Every word she said about leaving sounded like it was about me, not this town. I couldn't take it anymore. She was going to find someone else."

"Now you've made sure of it." Lovie came and sat next to me as I listened. My bottom lip quivered as the wretched tears came again. "You have no idea what your pitiful weakness has destroyed. She will never take you back."

"Helene will *always* love me." My name from his lips was a knife twisted in my chest. I swore to myself this would be the last time I listened as he said it. "We're going to get through this. She isn't going to abandon Gisel or me." I shut my eyes tight. "Sloane, it meant nothing. I'll make her understand. Helene won't leave me."

Sloane's voice lowered. I strained to hear her say, "She's already gone."

"It isn't over," he said and a door shut. His truck backed out of the yard, and I was able to breathe.

I peered out the window at Sloane holding her middle finger high above her head as he drove away. The sun catcher that Gisel had made me at art camp when we were eight hung from the lock. It was a blue bird flying. I untangled the string from the position it'd been in for years and decided how to abstract myself.

"They behaved like animals," I said and stared at the bird. Lovie held still next to me. "Completely uncivilized."

"Helene . . ."

"Gisel's never been one to consider the consequences. I always loved that about her." Lovie was lost in concentration and staring at me. "She's gone too far."

I threw the bird on my bed. I found Gisel's black dress in my closet and her favorite Nirvana T-shirt in my clothes hamper. The earrings she'd loaned me to take to Vermont were in the pocket of my backpack. Every picture covering my closet door that she was in, I ripped down.

Sloane stormed into the room as I tossed the globe pillow from the head of my bed into the pile. Gisel had given it to me, but she'd always loved it. Every time she was in my room, the pillow was in her arms. I stared at it on top of the pile. She was everywhere. I'd be finding mementos of Gisel for years. How do you erase someone who's a part of your soul?

"What are you doing?" Sloane asked and eyed the items I'd collected.

"I'm returning these things."

She shook her head at me. "No. Helene, don't do anything today."

"Will it be different tomorrow?" I was completely void of hope. Lovie and Sloane had no answers. There should be some pill one can take to forget things. To erase the people that hurt them. "Is there a spell to make me forget?" They both only stared at me. Lovie began to cry. She could never just be a witness to someone else's pain. "Because that's what I want more than anything." I pushed Gisel's belongings into an old overnight bag. "There's so much I want to forget already. I'm only eighteen. How is that possible?"

"Helene . . ."

"I'll be back."

"We'll go with you," Sloane said.

"I think you should go home."

"Why?" Lovie asked and moved toward the door.

"Because this doesn't involve the two of you. I hate that you'll be a part of it."

"Everything that involves you and Gisel is a part of us, too."

"But that's the thing," I said. "I'm not going to be a part of *this* anymore."

Lovie stumbled back against the wall. "What?"

"She isn't my family. She isn't my friend. She's nothing."

"You don't mean that." The steely glare in Sloane's eyes stole me from my flight. "Helene, if you leave her, the coven will disintegrate. She's an Earth witch. She'll lose her powers." She held up her hands between us, as if I were a wild animal that she needed to calm. "We'll never be able to cast a spell. It will all be gone with you."

"You will still have your powers, and I'd rather not have mine if I have to share a life with her."

"But you'll have yours, too. There must be a reason beyond yesterday to stay."

"She chose a different path last night." I choked on the words. I didn't want to talk about this. I didn't want to see her. I just wanted to disappear and forget everything about this town. "And in doing so, she left me with no choice."

"Are you sure?" Lovie looked as if she might break.

"It's the only thing I'm sure of, and I don't want the two of you to be there. It isn't fair."

I walked past them to the stairs. I crossed the driveway to Gisel's house with Lovie and Sloane a half a step behind me. Before I could knock, Gisel opened the door and waved me inside without saying a word.

Had Isaiah been here? What words did he say?

Did either of you speak my name?

"I saw your father leave." The sound of her voice made me sick.

"Thinking about having sex with him, too?"

Gisel closed her eyes and reached out for the chair to steady herself. She was wearing old shorts and a T-shirt without a bra. The outline of her breasts made my stomach turn. Had he touched them? Her eyes were swollen and red like the tip of her nose. I didn't care that she'd been crying.

"There must be something else you can take from me," I said.

"I'm sorry. My God . . . so sorry. I wanted to tell you. To explain—"

I held up my hand. "Please stop speaking." I wouldn't scream at her or try to physically injure her. "I brought your stuff over."

She surveyed the bag in my hand. I flung it on the table. "Why?"
Gisel looked behind me at Sloane and Lovie. "What's going on?"
She faced me again. "What are you doing?"

"I'm leaving you. I can't be . . . with you anymore."

"Helene, I'm sorry. We drank too much tequila! We're sisters."

"If we were sisters, you wouldn't have done what you did—tequila or not."

"We can get through this."

"I can't."

"But, but . . ." Gisel's gaze darted around the room as she sputtered. "They'll come for us. The Virago will come for all of us." She motioned to Sloane and Lovie. "You think just because you'll still have your powers, the Virago won't come? Without the coven, none of us will be safe."

With little effort and no emotion, I said, "I'd rather know darkness than mistake it for light."

"You can't do this to me. They'll come for me first," she shrilled. "I'll lose my powers. I'll lose everything without you."

"I lost everything with you." I stared at Gisel until I thought she might break in front of me.

"The three of you are leaving me here alone without any powers? It isn't fair!" she screamed at us.

"What is going on?" her mother asked as she walked into the room. Clara stood at the end of the table like a hawk poised to pick us each from our small place on the earth.

Lovie seemed to shrink in front of us. Her heart couldn't take this type of hate. She wasn't created to fight. "We're trying to figure that out," she said. Lovie was kind, but not weak.

"Figure what out?" Clara looked to each of us and her own daughter with disgust.

"Mama. I've done something terrible." Gisel fidgeted in her mother's glare. "Two nights ago, while Helene was away . . ."

"What?" Clara screamed at her daughter. We all jumped as her anger ricocheted around the room.

Gisel's lip quivered as she fought through her fear to say the words I couldn't bear to hear. "Isaiah . . . and I."

Clara froze in her daughter's profound guilt for only a heartbeat before her face twisted into a sneer as she turned to Lovie, Sloane, and me. "The three of you are disgusting. Your mothers left you here without an ounce of honor between you. It was a curse my daughter and I were born into this coven."

"Mama!" Gisel wailed, but Clara didn't falter in her razor-sharp focus on us. "Leaving her behind over a boy! A pathetic little man without any power at all. You'd give up your own for that?"

Gisel touched her mother on the arm, and Clara pulled it away. Gisel was thrown against the wall, her head hit the shelf, and she fell to her knees in front of us. Sloane leaned back on one leg, her defensive stance I'd seen so many times before.

"Thinking you get to decide the fate of my daughter. You have no idea what it means to be a coven."

We stood facing the most terrifying witch we'd ever known. She was stern and cold and had been the stand-in for our mothers when they died and left us here with only her to guide us.

"You think you know loss? What this universe can do to you when your soul walks out the door one day and leaves you behind? You've learned nothing from your pain. You'll abandon this town and your sister and the coven you were born into?" Her frigid blue eyes tore through each one of us as she said, "Each of you, and every daughter to come, will know the pain you've caused today."

Heat rose up behind Clara. I covered my eyes to still see her as the rest of her hate-filled words overflowed from her mouth. The rhyming lines that would twist our futures into recurring scenes from our past were chanted over and over until darkness fell upon the kitchen, and a putrid dread overcame us.

OBSTINANCE

Ever

Twenty Years Later . . .

MY EARS POPPED AS THE plane began its descent. Below us was a sea of buildings and highways surrounding Philadelphia. The crisp cabin air slipped down my neck. I couldn't wait to get off the plane. I pulled my hood over my head and tightened the strings. Instead of my mother's typical glare, she seemed almost sympathetic.

What if I hate it? My voice was silent and only a fraction of the secrets we held between us.

Oh, Ever. You won't. She was certain. She'd fled Auburn right after high school and was bringing me back here to the same school, the same town. *Auburn's in your blood. It's been waiting for you to return. For all of us.*

We banked right, and I could see the Delaware River and the

Ben Franklin Bridge across it. We'd be on the ground in minutes. A muffled announcement came over the speaker as the flight attendant came down the aisle to collect the last of our trash. Traveling in a plane was inferior to flying, but my mother hated flying long distances these days. The aircraft shook and rumbled as if in agreement with my assessment.

It's time we lean on each other. My mother was talking about my aunts—the ones who weren't related to us but had been our family since the beginning of time. They appeared on the day I broke my arm in third grade, brought cupcakes for the opening night of my first school play, and were there when the police officer told us my father's tire had blown and his car rolled into a ravine, killing him instantly.

We'd barely shut the door, and they were there. Lovie was in her robe. She'd flown to us without putting her coffee cup down. She'd been in Hawaii at the time, six hours behind us, and clearly not prepared to fly to Vermont. Sloane didn't cry. She held the rest of us up. My mother'd been swallowed by their love and understanding on that awful day. I'd been numb.

The lights turned off in the cabin. The flaps on the wings ground into position. My mother caressed my arm through the fabric of my sweatshirt, and I lowered my eyes to the embroidered falcon on my chest. I should have been flying somewhere below this plane. I could have come alone and met my mother in Auburn, but *that* was out of the question. The plane roared to a stop just shy of the end of the runway.

With every step toward baggage claim, my mother relaxed, but the prickly details of the unknown still plagued me until my aunts came into view. Lovie and Sloane were waiting by the turnstile, completely oblivious to the stares and looks they were garnering. Their bright eyes and richly colored hair, the two of them with my mother were some type of irresistible element one couldn't help but be drawn to.

"Helene!" Lovie said and embraced her. Energy burst from them like a sparkler. It was beautiful and seemed too hot, but even as a child, I knew it would never burn me. I only had this feeling of security when the three of them were together. It would come upon me as they approached and grew stronger the closer they got. It made no sense, but it wasn't supposed to by earthly standards.

Sloane gently took my mother's bag from her shoulder and held it in her arms. "Geesey," she said, and I knew it was a word from their childhood language. They used it for hello and I love you and for when the stagnant silence of mourning left us without any words to say.

"Ever, come here," Lovie pulled me tight against her body. "We've missed you." She meant her and her daughter, Maya. Lovie let go and melded into my mother and Sloane's conversation. The three of them went on as if they were alone in the world. I'd thought they were two months ago when Lovie's husband died. They'd stayed up the entire night talking about the past and what was to be done about the future. Maya, Ruby, and I—the daughters that discussions were hushed around—were left by the empty fruit bowl on the patio, listening to our mothers decipher death.

Our luggage circled the conveyor belt, and I resisted the urge to telekinetically retrieve our enormous suitcases. Instead, I behaved and hauled them off, placing each one on the floor between my mother and me like the rest of the passengers. Without hesitation, Sloane and Lovie raised the handles and rolled us all toward the exit. I followed them until we stopped at the median for the rental car shuttles to pass.

The elderly woman next to me rested against the concrete divider, and I looked around for an escort or family member to help her. She slipped me a knowing smile, as if she'd read my mind, but then I realized she was admiring my mother and Lovie and

Sloane. The way they rested near each other gave the impression they were touching, when in fact, they were only connected by each other's souls.

The woman stepped off the curb and dragged her suitcase behind her. When the shuttle bus continued to speed toward her, not yielding to let her cross, I stopped it. It screeched to a halt two feet from the woman's floral tapestry bag. Grateful for the break from the mundane, I shut down the engine entirely, leaving the traffic behind the bus to honk and wonder why they were no longer moving. I silenced their horns and watched as they beat on the steering columns that were betraying them. The shuttle driver examined the dash and pedals of the vehicle as the elderly woman continued to walk the pavement with her head held high.

"Ever," my mother chastised me under her breath, and I released my hold on the components of the cars. "We are not invisible."

"Oh, Helene, she's strong," Lovie said.

My heart stopped at my aunt's tone. It was more than adoration. There was a hint of desperation, too.

I turned to my mother. "Why are we really in New Jersey?" I asked, but she was lost in her mind and surrounded by vehicle exhaust in the parking garage.

They ignored my question and stayed in their own little world the entire drive to Auburn. Lovie exited the highway onto a road with two lanes in each direction. It had the requisite fast food, hotels, and gas stations lining the shoulders of it, but within minutes, we were away from civilization and driving through fields that covered both sides of the street. Southwest, southeast, southwest, we zigzagged through the countryside as I followed the directions in my mind.

I knew I'd fly this path again as soon as I had a moment of freedom in my new home. We crossed the crick, as my mother called it. "Is crick spelled c-r-e-e-k?" I asked, and the three of them laughed as though I was the one who was funny. A sign read "Welcome to Salem County. A nice place to live," and the realization finally hit me like the heat from a fire—we were never going home to Vermont.

Lovie's minivan climbed the hill leading into Auburn and turned into the driveway of the house sitting at the edge of the high ground and almost completely obscured by trees. The two-story with a third set of windows in the attic appeared as if it might topple over and roll down in a strong wind, but the dulled paint and cracked wood made it clear the house had weathered many storms.

Ruby and Maya were sitting on matching Adirondack chairs circling a fire pit. My eerie nervousness was replaced by excitement at the sight of them. Wherever they were was home. The fire died out as Lovie cut the engine of the car, and I rushed to get out first. I wanted to see the yard without my mother's longing for my acceptance hovering over every inch of it.

I hugged Maya. She was wearing the teal sarong I'd bought the last time I was with her in Hawaii. It had been shipped with every other item in my possession. She held me close as the scent of coconuts wafted from her skin. The lawn stretched back behind an old garage and into the woods. Trees on both sides of the house blocked most of our neighbors' views. The parcel was the perfect location for a bunch of witches to reside.

"Come see our room," Maya said with great anticipation. She pulled me toward the house as Ruby flipped me the piece sign. When I was close enough that our mothers couldn't hear, Maya added, "I hope you don't mind. We went through the boxes you shipped and used some of your stuff to decorate." I'd assumed they would. There were no boundaries between the three of us.

"And we've been wearing your clothes for two weeks," Ruby added. I'd assumed that, too. "At least the ones we could fit into. You should eat some bread."

"I'll consider it."

Ruby was wearing ripped jeans. I knew without asking she'd done the damage herself instead of buying them already distressed. To have purchased them torn would have been inauthentic to her. A T-shirt with What Happens in Vegas written across the front was tied in a knot on the side and a sliver of her taught belly could be seen. The outfit was definitely not mine. Nothing I owned was ripped.

I followed them into the house and purposely ignored the downstairs. The entire residence, the town of Auburn, and the creek that bordered it were too much to take in. I reserved my attention for the space that would be my own. On the second floor, we passed three bedrooms, one for each of our mothers, and then walked through a fourth bedroom that was set up as a spare. Ruby pulled open the closet door, and Maya and I followed her up a narrow staircase to the attic.

A small bathroom with a standing shower was to the left, and the rest of the top floor had been converted into a large bedroom with beds in three corners of it and a love seat in the fourth.

The house faced northwest with the window by Ruby's bed looking out to the street. Maya's window had a view of the creek running below, and mine opened to the backyard. They'd decorated the corners in our favorite colors and hung tapestries from the ceilings above our spaces. Each bed had a trunk at the foot of it and drawers under the mattress, and one entire side of the attic was a shallow closet, just deep enough for a hanger, but wide enough for all three of us.

Ruby and Maya looked at me.

"Do you like it?" Maya asked. I wasn't sure if I did, but her desire for me to be happy pleaded from her tanned body, and I couldn't hurt her. "Ruby came weeks before me, and the room was still bare when I got here. I had to *force* her to participate." Maya's dark brown eyes shone with excitement. Ruby and I could never disappoint her.

"It's great." I surveyed the space again. It was cooler than my room in Vermont had been. It just wasn't mine, and I'd never shared a room with anyone before.

"Think of it like a home for wayward girls," Ruby said. I laughed even though it crushed Maya a little.

"It kind of is, isn't it?" The three of us looked at each other in silence. Miles and time zones and completely different lives had never separated us. We were born alike, and we'd forever be connected, even if our houses were not.

"Oh, it's beautiful," my mom said as she ascended the last step and peeked into our oasis. "Ruby and Maya, you did an amazing job." She paused for my reaction. "Didn't they, Ever?"

"They did."

"What do you guys want to do tonight? Cookout?"

"I want to fly. I've been sitting too long on that plane. I need some space."

"I don't want you to go alone." My mother had never been stern with me in Vermont, but in that moment, she had nothing but an uncompromising mom tone.

"Why? I flew from Vermont to Canada alone last year." No one was better with directions than I was.

"Because it's your first night here, and you know nothing about New Jersey. I want you guys to stick together." She wasn't backing down. "Things are different here than in Vermont."

The famed Virago that I'd heard stories about since I was a little girl, but had never actually encountered were here. My mother never joked of them. It was always a fearsome and elaborate lecture, but I'd stopped being afraid of fairy tales when I was little. For me, the Virago was just that—make believe.

"I want to fly, too," Maya said.

"I'll fly, but then I want to eat," Ruby added.

Thank you, I thought, and Ruby and Maya nodded having heard me in their heads.

It was almost dark, but we were still careful not to make a sound as we headed out of the house and into the trees. We hadn't met our neighbors, and letting them in on our secret wouldn't exactly make the best first impression.

We disappeared behind the tree line and took off. A witch couldn't be too careful with the trail cams, drones, and security cameras that littered the earth. "No place can be assumed to be private anymore," was what our mothers drilled into our heads. While our friends' parents were constantly talking about internet safety our mothers were teaching us to avoid all the protections theirs had put into place.

After the initial bend in the road, Auburn appeared to be about a block long. Backyards, an above-the-ground pool, some leftover Christmas lights that were still lit in August all worked to give the small town personality. I just wasn't clear on what it was. We took our time. I wanted to see the neighborhood, but almost as soon as I started the flight, Ruby's laughter was inside my mind.

Oh look, in the time it took me to inhale, we've exited Auburn.

It can't really be a town. I needed to check the boundaries on a map again. I glanced back over my shoulder at the miniscule street we'd just left behind. Do people name streets towns?

It is. Maya thought. *According to my mom, it's our town.*

We took off and left Auburn behind, passing over the creek that ran west all the way to the Delaware River. There was a small development and several pastures. Cattle and horses turned their noses to the sky as we soared by, hidden from their sight but visible to their other senses.

We reached a park, and I heard Maya crying. Ruby and I stopped at the same time on a trail near the back. Maya landed and met us where we all appeared in the waning sunlight on the hill.

"What's wrong?" I asked Maya who was drying her eyes with the back of her hand. Her dress blew against her thin frame in the breeze that was strong in the park but had been completely absent at our house. I tilted my head and let the wind blow my hair off my face and away from my shoulders.

"Everything I've ever known and loved is in Hawaii, waiting for me to come back." Maya was still reeling from a life without her father. "I can't stop thinking he's there. Everything in Hawaii reminded me of him."

"Maybe that's why your mom brought you here. Maybe she couldn't take the memories," Ruby said, but I knew it would take more than moving to forget.

I walked forward as they spoke. Ruby and Maya followed me. We strolled the path as if we'd walked it a hundred times before until we reached the pavilion on the far side. There were elementary school girls practicing cheers next to it and cars driving in and out of the entrance. The sign read Marlton Park.

Two women wearing yoga pants and tank tops walked a dog on a leash. They moseyed toward us, taking up the entire width of the path and talking far too loudly. "I could have cursed her. Who does she think she is? Telling me I had to bring in cut vegetables instead of cupcakes for Piper's birthday," the short one said with her arms flailing in front of her.

The one still wearing her sunglasses nodded in agreement.

"If there wouldn't be so many *annoying* questions, I'd lodge a sharp carrot stick right in her esophagus—"

The silent woman's steps faltered, and she grabbed the arm of her irate friend. Even through her sunglasses, I knew she was staring at us.

"What, Heather?" the other woman asked, annoyed her train of thought was interrupted. She followed her friend's gaze to us and gasped as if we were an enemy raised from the dead.

In unison, they took one step back and pulled the dog closer to them. As the women's feet touched the ground, they all disappeared, and an angry collision screamed through the park. Tires screeching, metal grinding, and then . . . silence.

Ruby, Maya, and I turned to see a truck with its airbag deployed crunched up against the tree in the middle of the parking lot. The roots were still in the ground, but the top half of the tree was now lying across the roof of the vehicle.

Where did they go? I asked.

I don't know, but they're still here. Ruby leaned back on one foot and raised her hands in front of her.

The crowd tore into motion. Yells for help, paramedics, or a doctor came from the scene. The little girls cheering were corralled under the pavilion and their view was blocked. The rest of us gathered around and watched the chaos of the truck's driver being helped from the cab and standing without assistance.

"At Marlton Park," the dad next to me said and shook his head. He loaded his two daughters into the back of his car that was behind us as a woman came over to talk to him.

"Can you believe this?" she said. "You're not safe anywhere!"

Fur brushed against my leg. I followed its invisible motion with my eyes as the animal's scent diminished.

The driver of the truck was shaken but unharmed. No one else had been hurt, but still, there was a lot of noise. The town's response was swift. Two fire trucks, a police cruiser, an ambulance, and a county marshal were all added to the landscape within minutes.

"In Vegas," Ruby started, and I waited with delight for her take on the chaos we were witnessing. "A person gets shot dead at the doorway to a casino and no one even misses their dinner reservation."

Lights flashed everywhere around us. "You're not in Vegas anymore," I said.

I looked back at the spot where we'd landed. It was near the top of an almost flat hill, which was completely silent. Ruby and

Maya stood next to me and examined the landscape, too, before Maya sighed.

"I miss the ocean." Maya sounded like she was going to cry again. I pulled her close to me.

"I miss the mountains," Ruby added.

I stayed silent. The only thing I missed was my dad, and after six years, I was ready for a change.

SCHOOL STARTING AFTER LABOR DAY was strange for all three of us. We'd have been in full swing by the end of August in our old towns, but since this was New Jersey, we were still sitting around our attic waiting for the torture to begin.

"Let's go to the shore for the day," Ruby said.

Maya sat up. "I'm in."

"I'll go." I'd pretty much go anywhere. "Do you think they'll let us?"

"Let us what?" my mother asked as she walked into our room.

I wasn't sure if I should say the beach or make up a safer, closer destination. Without any indication from Ruby and Maya, I answered, "Go to the shore."

My mother stopped moving around. "That's a wonderful idea. We should all go."

"We were thinking of going alone." I didn't want to hurt her feelings, but we'd had plenty of family time since we'd landed.

"How about we all drive down together and then we can split up? You won't even know we're there."

Something crashed to the floor below us and was followed by Sloane screaming obscenities at it. "Sure," I said, and my mother left us alone in our room.

"It's still the shore. The ocean. It's going to be heaven." Maya rushed around our room and changed into her bathing suit as she tore through the tote bags in the trunk at the end of her bed. She was used to being a block from the water, not the width of a state, even one as narrow as New Jersey, and I could feel the excitement pouring off her. "Ahhhh. Let's go!"

Ruby and I shot to our feet. Maya wasn't kidding. She ran around us, packing sunscreen and towels. We followed her whirlwind to the kitchen where she added grapes and water to her bag. Sandwiches were made and batteries were placed in the old boom box on the kitchen counter. Maya willed us into the SUV along with the boogie boards she'd found in the shed out back. She was our undertow, dragging us out to sea.

"We have to make one stop on the way," Lovie said.

"What do we need? I packed everything." Maya was losing her patience, and we weren't even on the main road yet.

"You'll see. It'll only take a minute. We're just about there," she said, and Sloane made a right at the stop sign in Woodstown.

We parked in an empty spot on the horseshoe drive in front of Woodstown High School. As far as I could see, the building was brick everywhere. Stately. The doors were heavy and unlocked, but were new compared to the rest of the school.

"How old is this place?" Maya asked as we entered and climbed the center stairs to the main hallway, which seemed to have been trapped in time way before the three of us were born.

"Over a hundred years," my mother said. She tilted her head back to take in the ceiling and then looked left to the far end of the hall. I felt a group sigh from the three of them. A peace descended on our mothers. They were home.

As for Maya, Ruby, and I, we were appalled. It just felt old. Even the beige color of the walls felt dated. There was no historical romance hidden in the endless shades of brown within the halls of the structure.

"In Hawaii, I could see the ocean from the windows of my school."

"Here, you might be able to see the smoke from the nuclear power plant—"

"Ruby!" Sloane hissed, silencing her daughter.

My mother led the way to the office. Before opening the door, she whispered to the three of us, "Try not to stand together. You're less remarkable alone."

We followed her through the door into the main office.

"Can I help you?" The secretary asked before recognition covered her face. "Why, Helene, how are you? And Lovie . . . and Sloane!" She stood and took a half step back, stunned. "Wow! What are you all doing here?" She stumbled into the table behind her.

"Hello, Trish. We've recently moved home and need to register our girls for school." Her shocked eyes tore from my mom and flicked between Ruby, Maya, and me.

"Oh my Lord. Would you look at them?" She turned back to my mom as if the rest of us didn't speak English. "You haven't changed a bit. None of you. The three of you still together . . ." Trish shook her head and blinked her eyes at us. "The only thing missing is Gisel."

None of our mothers responded.

"I saw her over the summer," Trish continued. "At Kevin Flitcraft's daughter's graduation party. Can you believe any of us are old enough to have high school graduates?" I'd never heard of Kevin Flitcraft or Trish or Gisel. "When did you guys get back? It's been . . . how long's it been?"

"Too long." My mother overwhelmed Trish as she stepped behind the counter. "We've brought their proof of residency, birth certificates, and transcripts. Is there anything else we need?" She enticed Trish to her desk and opened the file folder with all our information in it. "It's organized by child."

Trish sat in her swivel chair and stared at each of us again. She shook her head a bit while I inched toward the door, putting Lovie between Ruby and me.

"Hey, Trish, we're going to give the girls a tour of the school," Sloane said instead of asking.

"Well, of course. Not much has changed since you've been here."

"Clearly," Ruby said, and her mother glared at her.

"I'll get all this paperwork together while you're going around. Stop by before you leave in case I need something else and we can talk about the girls' schedules."

"Thanks so much, Trish," Lovie called as she opened the door and the empty hallway beckoned us into its safety.

"Oh wait. I already have a question," Trish yelled. My mother stayed behind as the rest of us paused at the banner hanging in the hallway with what appeared to be an aerial picture of the entire student body in the shape of a one hundred.

"One hundred years wasn't an exaggeration?" I asked, nodding to the banner.

"This place is hell." Ruby was still not impressed. "And we're a spectacle."

"A small distraction. Trish will spread the word we're back," Lovie said. Ruby and I read the bulletin board full of activities we probably wouldn't join. "Try not to walk together through the halls," Lovie added, confirming we were freaks. It was true that separate it wasn't as pronounced, but when all three of us were together, people noticed. It wasn't necessarily our bodies or the color of our hair, but our energy.

I'd been without Ruby and Maya for most of my life, but when they visited, everything was more potent. I could hear better. I could fly faster. My powers fed off them somehow. According to my mother, it was the strength of the coven. The one conceived the year we came into the world.

We followed Lovie and Sloane up the bland side stairs to the second floor. Foreign language classrooms lined the front hall of the top floor. The two-tone brown and white walls were as depressing as the gray carpet. My mother joined us without a word. She ran her fingers over the vented metal of a locker on the end of a row. She lingered there with her head hanging low. She closed her eyes and inhaled. Her shoulders rose. I couldn't tell if she was gathering strength or about to throw up. The sight of her slumped over scared me.

"What language have you been studying?" Maya asked Ruby.

"Latin."

"They don't have that here." Sloane spoke without any apology. It was the new way things were going to be. "You can take Spanish or French."

My mother stepped away from the locker and turned to us. She was smiling, but the expression didn't touch her eyes. Pain still lingered in her stare.

"Great," Ruby said. "What about Italian? German?" Sloane just gave her a small, tight smile of negation. "Seriously. Can we all just go back to Vegas? My school was state of the art. This one is . . ." Ruby's inability to find the words was terrifying.

Sloane locked arms with Maya and me, and we all faced Ruby. "This school is old and it's small. But there's a great deal of history in these walls." She stared at my mom with a sympathetic expression.

"It doesn't matter what school you go to, as long as you're together."

Ruby eyed the lines of rectangle panels in the ceiling and shook her head. She relented from her stance and slipped her arm through mine. "If I promise to stop complaining, can we go to the beach now?" She led us to the stairs at the end of the hallway without waiting for an answer. Then, as if we all silently agreed to just let Ruby have her way, we followed after her.

Lovie stopped by the office, and my mom and Sloane giggled the entire walk to our car as they interjected stories of their years in the building.

"Remember the time freshman year when you snuck out and drove your dad's car right past my mother?" my mom asked.

"Or when the three of us landed at the Schalick football game and walked out of the woods to find Vaughn Eller staring at us?"

They practically howled with laughter. "He looked like he'd seen a ghost."

"Well, what was he doing behind the baseball fields anyway?"

"Maybe he was flying, too?" Maya said. Sloane and my mother spun around on the step below us.

"Men can't be witches, Maya," Sloane said. "You know that."

My mother hopped off the last step and opened the door to the outside. The sunlight blocked my view of her as she disappeared into it, and Sloane followed her out.

A bizarre quiet descended on the six of us as we drove away from Woodstown High School. I listened to reggae music through ear buds and drew for the majority of the hour ride to the shore.

The pages of my journal had no lines, only a single feather making up the watermark on each page. I darkened the edge and added all our initials into the feather's design. I was almost done when Sloane parked the car on 55th Street in Ocean City. Maya was opening the back hatch and pulling out her boogie board before I stashed my pencils in my bag.

"I wish I could have brought my long board," Maya said and left the rest of us to carry everything else. She climbed the dune, dropped everything, and ran into the water as we drug our feet through the soft sand behind her. After we'd set up the chairs and doused each other with sunscreen, Lovie followed her daughter into the surf. They seemed more like twins than mother and daughter as they swam out past the breakers.

Ruby and I walked to the edge of the ocean and let it wash over our feet. It was warm still. The summer might have been ending, but no one had told the ocean.

"What are you wearing?" Ruby's words, and her tone, stole me from the serenity of the water.

My attention fell to my aqua bikini. The only thing I had on. "What?"

Ruby's bathing suit was a one piece, sort of. The plunging neckline fell all the way to her pelvis. It was open wide across her chest and the back was made up of a series of straps that I'd never be able to figure out how to put on.

"You look like you're headed to swim team practice."

"This is my sexy suit."

Her mouth hung open in disgust. "Oh, Lord."

"What?" It was a regular two-piece. The suit had no ties, or straps, or strange openings, but it never fell down. "Why are you so nasty?"

Ruby stared at the sky and sighed. She shook her head and finally said, "I'm sorry. I just don't want to be here."

"None of us do. Don't take it out on my swimwear."

She eyed my torso again and laughed a little. "You can do better than that."

"No. I really can't. Love me."

Lovie rode a wave until she was only a few feet from us. She stood, straightened her suit, and said, "Maya's all yours. Keep an eye on her, or she might swim back to Hawaii."

"We will." Ruby's words lacked their usual bite. It was a rare moment of sympathy. I felt it, too. It was mixed with confusion and, depending on the day, anger regarding why they'd assembled us all here.

Lovie walked back to our mothers and lay on the blanket beside them without even drying off. She was petite compared to my mom and Sloane, and she was still dark tan and a little soft. Even though Lovie had been born and raised in New Jersey before moving to Hawaii, she looked like a Pacific Islander.

"She's pretty," Ruby said.

"They all are." Our mothers sank into the comfort of each other's presence. "Does your mom ever date?" I asked Ruby.

Without hesitation, she answered. "Never." Sloane was apparently just like my mother when it came to relationships.

"My mom cried for two months straight after my dad died," I said. The sound of her sobs still stormed through my mind. I couldn't go through all that again. Not ever. "I hope she never meets someone else."

"That's selfish of us, though. Don't you think?" Ruby was again without the disagreeable remarks. "They should have someone." Her lack of sarcasm and abundance of empathy concerned me. It wasn't our normal, and it had me a bit on edge.

"Look at them." They were laughing at something Sloane had said and watching us. I waved to put my mother at ease. "They have each other."

We dove into the water and swam out to Maya who was floating well past the breakers. As the waves came, she let her feet rise first before her body followed toward the horizon. She rolled over on her stomach with her head tilted toward the sky and somehow could float like that, too. Maya was unsinkable.

Ruby dove under the water and came up next to Maya. She

submerged again and performed a tilted handstand until her legs fell over with the coming wave. Ruby popped back to the surface smiling. She treaded water next to me. Her eyes were bluer than the water and brighter than the sun. "How did you know Harry was the one?" I asked. Ruby was the only one of us who'd had sex. I'd met him once while we'd visited Nevada, but they were just friends back then. I almost fell over when she told us they'd done it.

"I don't know." She stared south along the coastline as she spoke, and I regretted bringing him up.

"We don't have to talk about this." God knew there were plenty of other depressing subjects to discuss.

"It's okay." Ruby tilted her face to the sun. "It's just that I know he's going to find someone else. I get it. I just keep waiting to hear about it or see it online." She paused as a wave swept us up and over it. "I'm bracing myself for it like the direct hit of a hurricane. Each day that it doesn't happen, I feel relief, but I still know it's coming."

"How did you guys leave it?" Maya asked with the gentleness of a breeze.

"We didn't. I barely had time to pack. I pretty much told Harry I loved him, and my mom told me we were moving."

I'd lost track of what was going on while we were immersed in the chaos of Maya's father's death. Ruby came right after the funeral, but I didn't know I was coming until later. Weeks later.

"Is that why you hate it so much?" I asked, and they both moved closer to me in the water.

"Yeah. I had sex with Harry—my first mind you, which is kind of a big deal. I told him I loved him that night. It was June tenth." I looked to Maya, knowing exactly what happened June eleventh. "The next day, we flew to Hawaii. My mom didn't say why we were going, but we landed just in time for the Coast Guard to tell us Maya's dad was missing at sea."

I let Ruby's words sink in. My mother had been just as abrupt when she announced our unplanned trip to Hawaii.

"As soon as we got back to Vegas, my mother said we were moving. There was no discussing it with her."

I kicked until I was close enough to Maya and Ruby that our mothers couldn't judge our expressions from the beach. "Something about your dad's death freaked them out enough to bring us here."

"What though? They'd each lost their own husbands." What a dismal history the three of them shared. They weren't even forty and all three widows.

"I don't know," I began. "My dad died six years ago, and my mom mourned your fathers the same way."

"Mine, too," Ruby chimed in. "We came home from Hawaii and started packing. My mom drank her way through it. After two days, she sobered up, gave me a hug, and told me we'd figure it out."

"Figure what out?" None of it made sense. He was Maya's dad.

"At the time, I thought she meant life, but now that we're here, I don't know."

The waves around us grew. They were much smaller just a few feet away. Maya laughed as she floated over them.

"Maya, are you doing that?" Ruby asked her. Her voice was terse. She was her annoyed self again.

"Me?" Maya exaggerated. "I do love them big." She dove into the water between us and swam around like the fish we'd always known her to be.

Maya's bathing suit was mismatched and faded. For Maya, the suit was necessary to get to the water, not a fashion statement.

I turned to Ruby and raised my eyebrow. "How come you're not torturing Maya about her suit? At least mine matches."

"Her dad just died." Ruby laughed. These were the things we laughed about now.

VI

THE DENIM SKIRT WITH THE frayed hem that Ruby had selected for me rode up my thigh in the car. I was fine with the skinny jeans I'd lain out on my bed, but when I came out of the bathroom, they were missing and this tiny skirt had been placed in their spot.

I'd raised my eyebrows at her across our attic. "Really?"

"Come on. Work with me," she'd said. She tilted her head at Maya, who was wearing flip-flops and a dress the same material as a T-shirt. It was more like a bathing suit cover up, but Maya's entire wardrobe revolved around going in or coming out of the water. At least it had until now. "You'll thank me later."

"What if I have to run somewhere?" I'd asked, inspecting the short skirt again. I was thankful she'd let me keep the vintage Pink Floyd T-shirt with Learning to Fly written across the chest.

"It's the first day. The only thing you have to do is make the right impression. That skirt says something."

"I'm for sale?"

Ruby glared at me. "It says, 'Only real men should play with fire.'" She ignored my eyes rolling back into my head.

We climbed into the back seat of Lovie's minivan, and Maya took shotgun. Ruby crossed her legs and the chunky black wedge sandals she was wearing loomed over my side of the car. Her dress was black-and-white striped with a deep V-neck. To break up the tailored look, she carried an army surplus bag across her body.

"Do you always wear a dress on the first day of school?" I asked. This was our first one together.

"I don't *always* do anything."

"Of course."

When we reached Woodstown, Lovie began to chat on about the town and the surrounding areas that also sent students to Woodstown High School—the sending districts as they were called—Auburn was one of them.

"Some years, Auburn sends no kids, and some they might send five."

"How many of us are there this year?"

Lovie looked at the three of us, "According to Trish, three."

We got out of the car, shut our doors without saying goodbye, and walked across the side lawn of the high school.

"Are we going in the front or the side doors?" Maya wrung her hands as she spoke, and her nervousness was starting to creep into my own. I took a small step back, unwilling to let this town get to me. It was the first day of school. That was it.

"Does it matter?" Ruby asked. She hid her nervousness behind anger. I liked it.

"Probably. It's the first time we're ever going to walk through these doors. It must mean something."

"I think it's a new adventure." I tried to put them at ease, settling somewhere between Ruby's anger and Maya's anxiety. Hopeful. "A fresh start."

Ruby stopped walking and stared at me. "I hate the New Jersey you."

"Maybe . . ." I slipped my arms through their elbows and moved us toward the front door again. "If we just give it a chance, we'll like it."

"I feel like we've been over the extensive number of reasons for why this sucks, but since we only have a few minutes, I'll just review the worst one." Ruby kept moving as she spoke. "We are new here, and no one else is."

"They're going to love us," I said dismissing her.

"What's not to love?" Maya chimed in. She stared up to the top of the building that was more enchanting in the morning sunlight than it had been the first time we'd been there.

We climbed the four stairs to the front doors of Woodstown High School the same way our mothers had decades before us. I wondered if they'd been nervous, but dismissed it. They grew up in Auburn. We were surrounded by strange faces, all of which were looking at us with curiosity. There were people on the stairs inside the foyer, in the hallways, and at their lockers. Teachers and administrators were everywhere. This was where we separated.

Two men who appeared to be security guards stood near the stairs and bathrooms on the first floor. They wore matching khaki pants and red shirts. A sense of authority surrounded them.

As I walked past the bald one, he stared at me until my feet stopped moving.

"Sorry," he said. "Are you related to Helene Paulsen?"

"She's my mother."

"I can tell. Something about you reminded me of Helene." The guard seemed more like a teenager than an adult as he broadly grinned at some reference I was missing since all my past experiences took place in Vermont. His shoulders shook a little before he said, "Your mother and I had some good times growing up." I wasn't sure how to react or if he meant good times or "good times." He appeared innocent, almost like an uncle, so I hoped he meant the former. Still, the conversation was weird. "How's she doing? I heard you guys lived up north somewhere."

"Vermont." I didn't want to conjure any more memories for him. "She's Helene Ayars now and she's fine." I glanced toward the staircase. A student who was bigger than the security guard I was talking to was coming up. His hair was dark, almost black, and he had interesting eyes, but I couldn't tell if they were a dark blue or black. I stared until I decided they were blue.

He wore long shorts and a Woodstown T-shirt that read: Sweat Orange Bleed Blue. I liked the cadence of the words, and I wouldn't forget the school colors after seeing them stretched across his chest. He stopped on the stairs. The students behind him didn't say a word, only stumbled to move around him without touching him.

"Well, have a good day." The security guard drew me back to the doorway we were standing in.

"Thanks," I said and walked through it. My heart was pounding against my chest as I took the first step toward the blue-eyed bear. When I passed him, I grabbed the handrail to steady myself. His presence overwhelmed me—pure, undeniable strength. When I was on the step below him, I remembered to breathe.

"Thank you, Ruby, for this skirt," I whispered.

I was grateful until the moment I was sent from homeroom to the vice principal's office and advised of the dress code that required skirt lengths to reach my knee. Then I wanted to curse Ruby.

"This isn't even my skirt," I tried to explain. The man on the other side of the desk was unmoved by my brilliant excuse. "In fact, I didn't even want to wear it." His eyebrows furrowed with confusion. "Right." I gave up. "Well, thanks for the information."

"I understand this is your first day. Our conversation is only a warning."

"Thank you."

"Next time will be a detention."

"Thanks." *Ruby!*

Honors English III was a list of titles and expectations. It was in the basement and brought me down to its level. Primary schooling had been a series of books I couldn't care less about. The only one I loved was *The Great Gatsby*. The only one of interest on this class list was *A Tale of Two Cities*. It was going to be a long year. As Mr. Kranz said his final words, I took out a red pen and crossed Language Arts off my schedule.

I found the physics lab by the Ag room where my mother had said it would be and sat at a table in the back. I wished it were chemistry. My mother and I were both shocked by how much I'd loved it last year. The study of what something was made of and how it could be changed, was fascinating to me. This year, it was physics, and I had little interest in the study of matter and how it moved. Probably because I could fly. I held my phone in my lap and read absolutely nothing on it. I had no new emails, no apps of interest, and had disconnected all my social media when I moved. I didn't want to put it away, though. The phone separated me from the rest of my classmates, who were more than happy to see each other after the long summer. They chatted away about the shore, their jobs, fall sports, at least ten people I didn't know, and the football game this Friday. I kept my eyes low and my short skirt under the table.

The seats around me filled in quickly as the teacher finally looked up from her laptop and addressed us.

"Have a seat. I know you've missed each other, but everyone needs to find a seat and instead of picking one near your friend that knows nothing about physics, how about diversifying?"

The seat next to me was taken by a brown-haired boy who smelled like candy.

I'll take it.

He never introduced himself, just silently unwrapped a yellow Starburst and slipped it in his mouth before offering me one. It was as close to a hello as was necessary. I shook my head. Apparently, we were both incapable of speech.

"Hey," the guy in front of me said and drew my attention away from the candy. "You're new."

"I am." Internally, I was willing the teacher to begin class and end the coming conversation. The guy looked from my eyes to my chest and then leaned over and peered under the desk. He rose back up smiling, satisfied with his inspection. I was in shock. "You're perfect."

"For what?" A cold air surrounded me in his stare.

"Me, but we'll get to that. I'm Billy." Billy didn't care who heard him. He was oblivious to everyone around us. "Billy Roberts." He bounced his eyebrows at me.

I was at a loss for the expectation of my participation in the exchange. "Ever," was all I had to offer as I dropped my eyes to his Woodstown soccer shirt and then my desk. I wasn't used to, comfortable with, seeking, or pleased with his attention. I'd spent my entire day trying *not* to be noticed, and Billy was ruining it.

"Ever." He tilted his head to the side as he said it. He was piecing it together with his other observations. Based on his intrigued expression, he liked my name. Goose bumps dotted the skin of my arms. I crossed them at my chest. "That'll work. Thanks."

"Billy—" the girl at the table in front of Billy said, and he silenced her with a raised hand. He never turned away from me. I was left in the shunned girl's line of sight, and her eyes narrowed. I shrugged, not knowing what else to do. Billy was more than unusual. He was foreboding. Even as he peered into my eyes and smiled.

"Interesting name." I longed to be far away from his sandy-blond hair, his unnaturally white teeth, and the rapid speed at which he chewed his gum. What was more unnerving was the way he stopped chewing at intervals as if policing himself somehow. I listened. I inhaled . . . and I wanted to leave, which seemed ridiculous because we were in Woodstown High School, and he'd only told me my name was interesting and that I was perfect.

The teacher stood in front of the room. She made Billy and three other students throw their gum in the trash. The word prison slipped into my head, but was replaced by the eerie feeling connected to Billy's presence in front of me. I couldn't shake it. No matter how hard I focused on the syllabus, grading scale, assessments, and every other bit of minutiae associated with the class.

Physics lab ended, and Billy left without saying goodbye. He walked away with an easy step. His tall build shrunk as the distance between us increased. Something told me I was only going to remember two things about Billy Roberts—his almost black eyes, and the malignant feeling I had near him. I took out my schedule and marked a red marker line through lab.

Honors Physics was infinitely more pleasurable. We had assigned seats and mine was in the second row, right behind the blue-eyed bear I'd seen on the stairs. He walked in, and I let myself feast on the sight of him.

How's it going? Maya asked Ruby and me.

Better was all that I responded. Ruby never thought a word.

I focused in front of me. I put three notebooks side by side and measured the width of his shoulders against them. He was magnificent.

"Hi," said the guy next to me, who I hadn't noticed was the same guy with the Starburst in lab.

The bear swiveled in his seat upon hearing the statement, and suddenly, I was speaking to them both.

"I'm Ever." I waved.

"I heard," the boy next to me said. "Unusual name."

I'd stopped making excuses for the name when I was five. My mother loved it. I preferred it to Kathie or Jill or Kate. A name was a funny thing. It was the first thing a person found out about you, and you had no input in. Although, the first thing would be your skin color, and a person had nothing to do with that, either. I wandered around in those thoughts.

"I like it. I'm Mick," he offered without my asking.

I faced the bear. "What's your name?" I couldn't care if that sounded cool. I wanted to know his name more than I wanted to make a good impression. There might have even been some compulsion to know it. His closeness made me unclear on almost everything. As opposed to the razor sharp diseased feeling I'd had in Billy's presence, this guy made me want to lay in the sun next to him.

"Ike." He barely moved his lips when he said it. I wouldn't have missed it. My sight was glued to them. One syllable with a hard *K* sound. He looked down at my three notebooks in a row and back up at me. I gathered them into a pile and shoved some air into my lungs. "Kennedy," he added and glued me back to his existence.

"Nice name." I should have said something else, preferably something witty and memorable. Naked energy was strumming just below the surface of my skin. It replaced my mental capacity with my knee uncontrollably bouncing beneath the table.

"Okay . . ." Mick said next to me, and the teacher walked to the front of the room.

Ike turned around, leaving me with only his shoulders to stare at. It was actually perfect. I could drool over him and still appear to be listening to the teacher. There was nothing—no one—like Ike in Vermont.

I wanted to know where he lived. If he liked chemistry better than physics like me, and if he had a girlfriend, but only if he didn't have one. Otherwise, I wanted to live in ignorance as long as his shoulders sat in front of me.

The teacher surveyed us for our graduation years and Ike raised his hand when he asked how many seniors were in the room. Besides myself, there were four other juniors in the class. They were all boys.

Assignments, expectations, grading, homework policy. Was there anything more boring than the first day of school? I knew the answer. The only thing more boring would be the first day without Ike Kennedy . . . I bit my lip.

The bell rang and half the people tore out of the room. I collected my notebooks from their tower and took my time zipping everything in my backpack. It was new and navy blue, and when I looked at it, I only saw the color of Ike's eyes.

"So . . . are you going out after the game?" a girl who sat across the aisle from us stood in front of Ike's desk and asked him. She clearly knew him; although, this was Woodstown and the security guard and the secretary went to school with my mother, so these two could be cousins. "I want to go where you're going." She placed both hands on the table in front of him and leaned down until Ike—and I—could see right down her shirt.

Subtle.

Her stance and the way she lingered on her words made it clear they weren't related. I leaned back in disgust. My vision of Ike wasn't ready to include his girlfriend or whatever this girl was. I crossed physics off my schedule and left to find Honors US History II.

History was a blur. I was fatigued from the morning's classes, but when I put the line through my schedule, I perked up a bit, knowing I was finally going to see Ruby and Maya. Lunch was next, and I was starving.

It was the only time we were allowed to eat or drink throughout the day. In my Vermont school we were allowed to eat whenever we wanted and as long as we didn't pull out a foot-long sub in health class, it was never an issue. Something had happened at Woodstown because food and drink were the enemy. You could take out your phone before a piece of gum.

My stomach growled as I stood in line with my tray. I never realized how many snacks I had a day until I wasn't allowed to have any. Maya waited two people ahead of me, and Ruby was a dozen behind me. We tried to blend in. It was impossible since we were new, but at least we weren't drawing attention because of anything else.

Maya found three seats at the end of a table mixed with girls and boys who appeared to be about our age, but I quickly realized they were freshmen from the sending district of Alloway. Their newness to the school must have attracted me.

I scanned the tables and the line for the grizzly from physics, but I never saw him. I wanted to hear what Ruby and Maya thought of him.

"So. Are we surviving?" Maya asked and opened her milk carton.

"I think they call it living here." Ruby lifted the top bun off her cheeseburger and inspected it as if it might move. "We are seriously screwed. Like . . ." she shook her head slightly, "every single person I've met today has lived here their entire life. As have their parents. And their grandparents. And—"

"We get it," I said. I had a similar assessment from my morning. There weren't a lot of transients in Salem County.

"I think it's . . ." Ruby and I waited for Maya to somehow make this better, "charming." She exhaled as if finding that word had taken a lot from her. "Just because everyone here has known each other forever doesn't mean they're no fun."

"Oh, I think it does," Ruby said. We laughed, but just a little.

We ate in pleasant silence. All three of us were lost in our own first days inside our minds.

"Well, I met someone interesting." Maya's face lit up with

excitement as she spoke.

Ruby stopped eating and focused on Maya. "What's his name?" I'd been thinking the same thing.

"*Her* name is Gwen, and she's sweet."

That guy is staring at you.

I turned to see who Ruby was thinking about. Billy smiled as the three of us looked at him.

I know him.

Obviously.

Do you like him? Maya chimed in my head.

No. But I don't know why.

The bell rang, and one by one, we rose and threw away our lunches. We purposefully kept some distance between us as we spilled into the hall with the rest of the cafeteria. I had not one other period with them. I would take it for lunch, though. I took out my schedule and crossed lunch off with my red pen. Halfway done. Spanish IV was next, and it was multi-grades, which would make it more interesting.

"*Buenas tardes. Bienvenido, señorita,*" the teacher said as I walked through the door. She was sitting on the edge of her desk and appeared genuinely happy to be there. The opposite of me.

I hadn't spoken Spanish since June, and was a bit rusty when I replied, "*Gracias. Mi nombre es* Ever."

"*¿Ever? Que adorable. Por favor tome asiento.*"

I took the seat farthest from the front. The other students filed into the room and into desks arranged in four rows facing the white board. They were each greeted in a similar way, but few spoke back. Their Spanish must have been rustier than mine.

I liked my seat. I could openly watch everyone without anyone noticing. The girl sitting in front of me was petite with curly brown hair that stuck out as wide as her shoulders. She placed a notebook on her desk and revolved completely around to face me.

"You're one of the new girls, aren't you?" Her expression was kind in a curious way. She was strumming with anxiousness. This girl, who'd already said hi to at least four people around us, was nervous to meet me.

"I am," I said, and the rest of the students surrounding us turned at the conversation opening.

"Where are you from?" Before I had a chance to answer she said, "At lunch everyone said Las Vegas, but then I heard Hawaii." She shook her head as if the confusion was the most frustrating thing to happen to her today. "You look like you're from Italy, though."

"I just moved from Vermont." The girl lit up. She liked having information, and I was willing to feed her as much content as possible *not* to have to repeat this conversation with the other seven hundred students in the school. She pulled her dark curls back into a ponytail and snapped a band around it as if she was rolling up her sleeves. "My mother wanted to move here to be closer to family. She's from New Jersey."

"I'm Gwen," the girl next to me said with a quiet calm. Peace surrounded me in the one moment Gwen mercifully took all the attention away from me.

"Ever."

"That's an awesome name," the girl in front of me said. She grabbed Gwen's arm and added, "I saw Ike this morning. He's so freaking hot." She closed her eyes and shook her head as she said hot. I felt like I was reading her diary. She was so open with every emotion.

"Not if he's your brother. You think he's hot. I find him repulsive."

"Well, you're wrong."

Gwen and I endured Spanish and walked together to our next class, art. She sat next to me and introduced me to everyone around us. A guy named Paul who was almost the same size as her brother teased Gwen as if they were related.

"I'll tell your mother," she finally warned, which stopped his words so fast it was comical. "Paul, have you met Ever?" I waved in silence. "Paul is my brother's best friend, and he is at our house *all* the time." There were no strangers to Gwen at Woodstown High School.

Sadly, I crossed art off my schedule and left Gwen to forge my way to pre-calculus alone. I drew on the cover of my notebook as Mr. Lange reviewed his expectations. The picture was a falcon sitting on the edge of the high school with the front lawn and East Avenue behind him. I stared at it until I thought it could fly. Until I could see it soaring through the sky.

"I hope you're as interested in the fundamental theorems as you are art, Ms. Ayars," Mr. Lange said. I flipped the notebook over and sat up straight to apologize for my obvious disinterest in everything else he'd said. His eyes were kind.

Then I was off to chorus, which was swift and painless and my last class of the day. When I walked out, Ruby and Maya were sitting on the concrete stairs by the tree in the side yard. It felt like my hundredth day at the school instead of my first. I'd already learned all that I needed to know.

I inhaled the silence. No more hellos. The introductions had ended. Tomorrow would be easier. There'd be the business of school that'd begin, and by lunch, everyone should have heard about the three new girls and where they were from. According to our mothers, we were from here.

I dropped my bag and turned to sit, but then spotted Billy Roberts leaning on a car parked across the street. He stared at me as if he were waiting for me to drive away with him. I shook my head slightly, denying it to myself and dismissing the lick of cold that snaked around my arm. He must have been waiting for someone else.

I sat between Ruby and Maya on the step. Maya rested her head on my shoulder.

Gwen walked down the hill to the left of us. She looked back over her shoulder and said, "Welcome to Woodstown. It's not as bad as it seems." The wind picked up above us and swirled until the freshly fallen leaves circled us.

"There's something wrong with the wind here," Ruby said with her usual tone of intolerance.

A little bug with metallic colored wings landed on my thigh and Maya flicked it away. I looked up and Billy was gone. "It's the wind that's the problem?" I asked.

A cool breeze blew from the west. The leaves settled at the base of the hill, and the three of us exhaled.

VII

"WAKE UP, YOU THREE." LOVIE'S voice was so beautiful that even as an alarm clock, it sounded like a song. "We have work to do."

"No work on Sunday," Ruby yelled and hid her face under her pillow, not as impressed with Lovie's voice.

"It's going to be fun. A little witchcraft on our day of rest. First we're going to church, though."

Ruby lowered the pillow. "What?" She was horrified. "Does my mother know about this? We never go to church. As a rule. It's kind of our religion."

"We live in Auburn now. There's a stop sign, a fire house, and a church." Lovie yanked the covers off Maya. "We're going to church. Today and every Sunday."

"We haven't gone yet," Maya said.

"We gave you some time to settle in. There's been so much . . . change recently." Lovie floated over the words, not letting any of them stick.

"Why do you guys want me to hate it here?" Ruby spewed as she got out of bed.

"We want you to love it. Church is good for your soul."

"I left my soul in Vegas."

That should be a bumper sticker, I thought, and Ruby just glared at me.

We brushed our teeth and got dressed in our "Sunday best" as Maya described it. It was still warm enough for sundresses, but our moms made us put on cardigans, muttering something about exposed shoulders in God's house. We didn't argue. We did, however, look as if we were the three remaining members of a defunct family a cappella group that just couldn't let go of the dream, but Ruby's sneer made it obvious we weren't going to entertain.

"Try not to stand together," I said to Maya and Ruby as we stood side by side, observing ourselves in the mirror. Ruby huffed at the entire situation.

We followed our mothers up the hill to the small church in the center of town—street. There were maybe twenty other people sprinkled throughout the pews. They were all thrilled to see our mothers. Every single one of them stopped by to dote over them and talk about our grandmothers. A few mentioned the woman named Gisel that Trish had commented about. On the third time, my mother winced at her name. It was an unusual crack in her polished demeanor. I'd ask her who Gisel was the next time we were alone.

After the service, I was introduced to Edna Schrufer, who snuck me two extra cookies and a smile. Those and some orange juice later, and we were released back into the sunshine. We walked like a flock of ducklings down the sidewalk to our house. Shades were opened. People stopped in their yards. We were noteworthy. Exactly how I hated to be.

Our mothers rewarded our godliness with a brunch that consisted of chocolate chip pancakes. All of our favorite since we could chew. Our chefs were pleasant and kind, attentive and generous, and I was sure they were up to something.

"Go change so we can get started," my mom said to the three of us.

"Start what?" I asked.

My mother looked at Ruby and Maya, avoiding making eye contact with me. "We're going to see if you three can cast a spell."

All six of us stopped moving. Spells had only been talked about as part of other witches' lives, not ours. I'd never seen one cast or heard of the effects of one. Like falling in love, my mother had always spoken of spell casting belonging to my distant future. I had flown since I could remember what the sky looked like. Disappearing and communicating in our minds were the games my mother and I played on the floor of my bedroom, but for some reason spell casting was never a given.

Ruby stood and clapped her hands together. "All right! Now we're talking. Finally!"

"Go get dressed," Sloane said, dismissing her daughter's enthusiasm.

We filed up the staircases to our room and hung our dresses in our closet. We didn't say a word until Ruby divulged, "I've been trying to cast spells for years, and it never works."

"What have you been trying to do?" I asked, a little afraid of the answer.

"Get rid of this red hair." Maya and I laughed. "What? You guys don't know the burden of it."

"Ruby, you won't be Ruby without your red hair. It's gorgeous, and it's you."

"Ruby, the girl with the red hair who likes fire," she said deadpan. "I am drowning in the predictability of it."

We met our mothers in the kitchen. The doors were locked. The shades were drawn. This was not to be shared with the rest of Auburn. Our moms stood on the side of the table with a notebook open in front of them, completely oblivious to our presence.

"We're here," I said and stood between Maya and Ruby. It was never our intention, but at some point over the years, I'd become the middle of our threesome. Maya was sweet and mild. Ruby was abrupt. I balanced perfectly between them.

"Okay. We're going to start with something small."

"Like my hair?" Ruby chimed in.

"You're *not* changing your hair color." I cringed just a tiny bit at Sloane's harsh tone, but Ruby was unfazed.

"Just going on the record here, if this works and we're able to cast spells, I'm changing my hair color."

"I'd like a boat," Maya said. She was still mourning Hawaii along with the loss of her father.

"Blondes have more fun."

"Ruby!" her mother yelled. "Spells are not a wish list. You are witches, and there comes a great responsibility with that birthright. You can't wish for big boobs or eternal life. Spells are never to be cast frivolously or in anger or revenge." The last sentence struck all three of our mothers as Sloane said them. "They can't be reversed." My mom stared down to hide her reaction from us, but I saw the significance of Sloane's words in my mother's defeated posture. "Every life has a course. We can impact the natural plan for one's life, but it isn't to be taken lightly. Destiny doesn't take kindly to interference. We risk consequences that we can't foresee."

Maya, Ruby, and I were quiet, but I knew Ruby was wondering what life-changing ramifications her hair color would have. Thankfully, she didn't ask. We had nothing to add that wouldn't get us in trouble.

"Spells are used to permanently change the world," Lovie started with a serene voice. She was trying to calm everyone in the room. "Because of their serious nature, we can only cast them with a full coven." They regarded each other for one silent moment.

"What was the last spell you cast?" Ruby asked Lovie.

"It was a lifetime ago." Lovie looked to Sloane and my mom before saying, "The last successful spell we cast was to help find two lost friends. Their boat had capsized at the shore and they were stranded, but no one knew it." I'd never heard the story before.

"Ever, you met one of them." I stared at my mother confused. "He's the security guard at your school. We grew up together, and he was supposed to die the day of the accident." Her words trailed off, and then she added, "But then we changed his course, which in turn altered the life of every person he has come in contact with since, even if only just a little."

The enormous responsibility sank in. Every life had a course, and we were about to learn how to alter it. No wonder they took us to church first.

"So, what do we start with?" Ruby was the first to move on.

Lovie pulled a small blue bird figurine off the windowsill above the kitchen window. "We learned spell casting on a bird just like this." She set it in the middle of the table.

My mother turned the notebook around on the table to face us.

"There's nothing on there." Ruby gently advised them as if they were losing it.

"Look again," my mother said. Words appeared on the page in my mother's handwriting. It was written in verse. "Read it a few times in your mind."

One blue bird as still as can be
Bring him to life to fly with me

"Now concentrate on the figurine." We beheld the little blue bird. "Focus. See it alive. Believe what you can do to change it. Breathe in your power." I focused on the statute. It would soon be alive. "Now recite the spell. Over and over until it becomes the new reality of the world."

"One blue bird as still as can be
Bring him to life to fly with me

One blue bird as still as can be
Bring him to life to fly with me

One blue bird as still as can be
Bring him to life to fly with me

One blue bird as still as can be
Bring him to life to fly with me . . ."

My mouth was dry. My lips, too. I wanted to stop speaking because this clearly wasn't working, but I dutifully continued. I concentrated on the bird. I could see it flying. I kept chanting until I finally closed my eyes and let it go.

After thirty times, Sloane saved us with her harsh proclamation of, "It isn't working." My mother uttered a loud sigh while Lovie's head hung in despair. Ruby, Maya, and I just wanted to be left alone.

"Is there some camp we can go to for this?" Ruby asked. "Not that you guys aren't great teachers, but it feels like we're missing an important part." She was right. Something wasn't working. "Like, are we supposed to cook a toad at the same time as we chant? Maybe we're supposed to sing?"

"You guys can go," my mother said, sliding the book back toward her before flipping the cover closed. Guilt washed over me as I tried to figure out what we'd done wrong. I felt defective in some way.

VIII

WE DROPPED OUR BACKPACKS ON the wooden kitchen table. The leaves were always in it leaving room for homework, food preparation, and eating all at the same time. I did my pre-calc first. Maya said I should save it for last since I loved it, but I couldn't. I was busy leaving English for last for the opposite reason. I pushed my copy of *A Tale of Two Cities* away from me on the table. The book itself looked thirty years old.

When I finished my Pringles, I ate all the orange slices Lovie had cut for us.

"Good Lord, you guys are eating like you're pregnant." We stopped chewing and stared at her. She leaned down to the table and said, "You're not, are you?"

"No!" Maya answered for all of us.

"Something tells me you guys will know before us," I said. They seemed to know more than us about everything. Like the fact that we were moving to New Jersey and that we were all going to live together in the same house. "Lovie, if this is Sloane's old house, what house did my mom live in when she was growing up?"

"She lived across the street." Lovie gazed around the room and out into the living room. "And I lived next door to here." She'd suddenly lost her aloha peacefulness. She stood and ran water over the dishes in the sink. She didn't pour soap in or load them in the dishwasher. She just added the noise from the running water to the conversation we were trying to have.

Ruby looked me in the eyes from across the table. *What the—*

I shook my head and sighed. Of our three mothers, Lovie was the least skilled in secret keeping, but even she was strong enough to just shut down rather than divulge anything interesting. I was bored with the whole thing.

"I'm going flying." I stood from the table and inhaled deeply. Relaxation touched every inch of me as the decision sank in. Yes. I needed to fly away from here.

"Alone?" Lovie asked.

"Yes. Alone." I met her at the sink and rubbed her back. "I'll be fine. I'm starting to get my bearings around here, and I flew by myself in Vermont all the time." She still hesitated. "I promise. It'll be good for me to have some time with my own thoughts." At this idea, Lovie perked up. She understood the need for quiet. She was the one who was always reading or listening or cooking. She was peaceful in a house filled with women. If anyone could relate, it was Lovie.

"Be back by seven, okay?"

According to the microwave, it was five thirty. "Thanks."

I walked out the door without turning back. I ran toward the woods behind my house and just before the tree line, I disappeared and flew into the air.

I swirled around above my house for a few minutes. From the sky, the miniscule town of Auburn was even more striking. Two lines of houses that faced each other, a church, and a fire house on a small hill in the middle of nowhere. *The middle.*

I followed Oldmans Creek to Harrisonville Lake and headed south. Houses dotted the ends of farms all the way to Route 40, which I followed straight to the school. I wished I could fly every day rather than being driven by my mother or one of my aunts. The football players were walking across the bridge from the field. I flew lower until I found Ike in the crowd and landed right next to him.

Ike paused in his step. I looked around to see why he'd stopped, but then he kept moving as the players around him surged forward.

"It's a sick ride," Paul said to him when they reached the top of the hill. "I can't believe your parents let you get it."

"I can't either."

"My parents won't even let me on it, let alone ride one around town every day."

"I started asking for it in eighth grade. I got nothing below a B since I started high school. All to have a *chance* of getting it."

The entire team stopped and congregated around a motorcycle in the lot behind the gym.

"So worth it," Paul said and bent down to examine some part of the bike.

"I know." Ike was genuine in his acknowledgement of how lucky he was. He could have bragged about the bike, or played it cool, but he was fine being one of them. He had nothing to prove.

The football team filed into the locker room, and I waited outside the gym. I sat on the curb next to the bike and studied every inch of the shiny chrome, trying to reconcile the stereotype of someone who rode a motorcycle against what I knew about Ike. A junior at my school in Vermont rode a motorcycle. He rarely spoke to anyone. I waited every day to hear he'd gotten on it and just ridden away without saying goodbye, but he was there, every morning, not saying a word.

I didn't realize I was waiting to follow Ike home until he emerged from the gym, and I stood ready to go. In all my years of being invisible and flying around, I'd never followed someone. I didn't need my mother or anyone else to tell me it wasn't a good idea, but when Ike settled onto the seat and started the bike, my heart raced in my chest. I was going wherever he was headed.

Ike was careful through town. He fully stopped at every stop sign and looked both ways at intersections. When he cleared the thirty-five miles per hour section of the road, his ride changed. He went much more my speed.

I flew low, right above him and stayed close to his shoulder the way Ruby and Maya were usually behind mine. I was careful not to touch him or spook him in anyway.

Ike leaned down and accelerated more. He was racing over the country road toward the town of Alloway.

I pulled up and followed him from the air. When he reached Lakeview Drive, I dropped back down and flew next to him as he crawled around the circle and into a driveway. He parked the bike and stepped off it at the exact moment a woman walked out the garage door.

"Did practice end early?"

I didn't have my phone or a watch to know exactly what time it was. I should have left to go home because of it, but the woman intrigued me almost as much as Ike did.

"No," he said and laughed at some joke between the two of them.

"Well, by my calculations, you shouldn't be home for another four minutes. If you'd been doing the speed limit, that is." Her hair was a dark brown, almost black, and hung past her shoulders. It was the only physical characteristic she and Ike shared. Her eyes were hazel, not the rich blue Ike's were. "I'll take it away." She raised her eyebrows at him. Love flowed from her decisive glare. "Just because you turned eighteen does not mean I can't."

"I'm fine. Very careful," Ike swore, and she clasped his face in her hands and stood on her tiptoes to kiss his forehead. Her long tank top swirled around her as she moved in her short denim shorts and flip-flops. She was as little like a typical middle-aged mother as my own, or Lovie, or Sloane. The thought of them as middle-aged was comical.

She stared sternly into his eyes and said, "Don't be that kid."

"What kid?" He was undaunted by her stare.

"The one that has the accident." Ike stepped out of her reach. "The one that makes the *whole* town talk about how ridiculous it is that his mother lets him get a motorcycle and then he crashes it."

"Are you more worried about me having an accident, or you being wrong about something?"

She stood straight. "I won't go on without you," she said, and the weight of her words stole the breath from my chest.

"I'm fine," Ike said. "I promise I'll be careful. I know you're putting a lot of trust in me."

"Why can't you just drive a car?"

He laughed at her as though they'd had the same conversation a hundred times before. "I like flying."

"I hear you," his mom said at the exact moment I thought it.

Mrs. Kennedy handed Ike a mum and motioned to the side yard for him to carry it out. I followed him as his mom came out with a mum of her own. "Gwen said homecoming's in a few weeks."

Ike rolled his eyes as if any sentence with the word "Gwen" in it required him to do so. "I bet she did." He seemed younger with his mom—less of a grizzly.

"Any thought on a date?" He closed his eyes at the question, as if this too were a conversation they'd had dozens of times before. "What about that nice girl we saw at the custard stand last weekend?"

"Maybe." He answered too fast. Even to the invisible outsider stalking him, it was clear he wasn't entertaining the idea even for a second. I leaned against the corner of the house closest to the flower bed they were working in.

"What was her name?" I liked his mother, or maybe I just liked Ike more when his mother was around.

"Her name is Grace, and I don't think it's going to work out."

Mrs. Kennedy stopped planting the mum and stood to face her enormous son. "Why? You seemed to like her just fine at the end of the summer."

"Things have changed."

She smirked as if she knew more about his reasons than he did. She reminded me of my own mother. "Sure they have." Mrs. Kennedy brushed by her son and disappeared into the garage.

Ike stared at the ground. I almost moved to see what he was watching, but then he turned and stared directly at me. My eyes darted down to make sure I was still invisible. I was, but the coincidence of his gaze was unnerving. He walked over until he was standing directly in front of me.

I held unbelievably still as he reached out and touched the corner of the house next to me. I let my sight linger on his hand and his forearm until it reached his shoulder only inches from my own. If I'd been breathing, he would have felt it on his neck.

Without a word, Ike tilted his head down and looked directly into my eyes. I fought for silence and let out a miniscule amount of air so I wouldn't pass out at his feet. I couldn't tell what he was thinking. There was nothing in his stare to give me a hint of what was going on.

"Are you coming in?" his mother asked. She was standing near the garage and seemed as confused as I felt. "What are you doing?"

"I thought I felt someone," Ike said, and I stopped breathing again.

I didn't turn to his mother. My heartbeat pounded against the entire front of my chest.

"Felt?" she asked, and her voice seemed closer and a bit . . . worried.

Ike shook his head, taking a step away from me. "Saw something." I waited as his eyes lingered on my hiding spot for another second before he followed his mother into the house. I stayed still for a long while after they both disappeared inside.

Then, without bothering to take a few steps, I launched myself into the air, racing to my house. I was halfway down the Woodstown-Alloway road before I let myself think about what had just happened.

It was impossible, a strange and eerily timed coincidence. It was what I deserved for eavesdropping and following him like some lovesick groupie. I didn't belong in his yard, and I wasn't going back. Ever.

Yet, when I went to bed that night, I closed my eyes, and I could see Ike. The way he'd smiled at his mother and the way he'd stared at me—or at least, in my direction because he couldn't see me. I turned over in my bed a hundred times before finally quieting my mind. I fell asleep thinking of him and fell *back* asleep after Ruby poured a half glass of water on me to wake me up. I ran to the bathroom, brushed my teeth, and threw on clothes. I dragged the brush through my hair and ran down the stairs, skipping five at a time. My mother was waiting for me with a bagel and the car keys in her hand. Ruby and Maya were already in the car.

"We're going to have to set up some rules regarding your flying," she said as we drove out of Auburn. I kept my sight focused on the endless fields outside the car windows. If I ignored the subject, maybe it'd go away. "I know you hear me, Ever. You can't fly on school nights and then not get up on time the next day." I just kept staring out the window. "It isn't fair to Maya and Ruby and me."

"Why not? What are you doing that's so important you can't take a few extra minutes to wake me up?"

"We're fixing up the house and figuring out what we want to do for work." I was skeptical. None of our mothers ever seemed to really work. Somehow, they'd always had everything they required without a lot of money. They had different needs than the rest of society. "We're also doing research. We want some things to change now that we're home, and the answers lie somewhere in this county." She scrutinized me for a moment before asking, "Do you hate it here?" Ruby and Maya stayed completely silent in the back seat.

I shook my head at my mother. "No. It's okay." I didn't want to add to her torture. "Even when Dad was alive . . . I always felt like we were waiting for something." I watched for my mother's reaction, but she was solid as she drove. Her eyes focused on the road in front of us. "Now I think we've always been waiting to come back here."

Her spine straightened, and her chin tilted up. I'd hit on something. Something that was unknown even to her until I'd just said it. I was afraid to go on. Dismayed by what it might mean.

"It's a part of us," she said and relaxed again behind the wheel. "It's a part of you."

"Give it a chance. It's more than just a street. It's the home of our coven."

"I'm giving it a chance. We all are." Thank God for Maya and Ruby. They made anything a possibility, even eleventh grade in New Jersey.

We turned onto North Main, Elm, and then Broad Street. My mood changed with my proximity to the high school. I could have stayed in bed all day and flown all night. Two more years of this, and I'd be free to do exactly that.

"Are the kids being nice to you?" my mother asked. I couldn't think of a person who hadn't been at least polite. No one had been cruel. "Boys?"

"Nice enough," I admitted as she drove.

"Did you guys meet Billy Roberts?" I asked Maya and Ruby. I knew my mother was listening as she drove. She was never *not* listening.

"I've seen him, but I haven't met him," Maya said.

"I did. I wasn't impressed," Ruby added. I knew she'd feel the same way about him that I did. Maya gave people more chances than Ruby and me.

"I don't recognize the name," my mother said, confirming her participation even if it wasn't requested. "Reed?"

"Roberts," I corrected her, to which she only shook her head.

"How about Gisel? What do you know about her?" I peered at my mother as she looked in the rearview mirror.

Her good morning cheer never left her face. "Why do you ask?" But the lightness was missing from her voice. "Where did you hear that name?"

"In the school office and at church." The same places she'd heard them. I waited for her response. I knew she was hoping she'd run out of road before this conversation went further.

"I graduated with a Gisel, but it's a pretty popular name." She turned down Lincoln Avenue and fought for a place near the sidewalk to drop us off.

"No it isn't," Ruby chimed in. I stifled my pleased reaction to her statement.

"Did you like her?" I asked. I stared at a house on Lincoln Ave as my mother pulled to the side of the school. When she stopped the car outside of the side entrance with the word "Girls" carved in stone, I didn't open my door. We weren't done talking yet.

"The Gisel I knew?" I nodded and stayed still while Ruby and

Maya got out. "Yes. I loved her very much."

Groups of students hurried by us, heading for the building doors before the late bell. We were both busy making sure I had my backpack, hoodie, and the water bottle I'd have to hide all day. I looked up to Ike staring in my car window. As soon as I saw him, he winked without smiling.

My breath caught, and then I remembered my mother was next to me.

Sulfur, number sixteen, S. Tin, number fifty, Sn. Scandium, number twenty-one . . .

I recited the periodic table of elements in my head to throw off my profound ecstasy. It was unnecessary because when I was brave enough to face my mother's curiosity, she was lost in her own trance.

"Do you know him?" Her words were as stunned as the rest of her.

I'd never seen her this way. "His name is Ike." *With a hard K.*

"Kennedy?" She watched as he followed the crowd to the door. "How did you know?"

"He looks exactly like his father did at his age." She warmed to despair.

I was torn between hugging her and fleeing from the car. "Oh."

When Ike was out of sight, she snapped her attention back to me. "Ever, listen to me. You are to stay as far away from that boy as possible. Do you hear me? The whole family is awful." My head shook a little, and my mother grabbed my upper arms. "Do you remember everything I've told you about the Virago?"

I leaned back to the car window behind me seeking distance between my mother's words and myself. The Virago. The dark ones. Witches gone wrong. They'd abandoned balance and conservation for power.

Without a word, I left my mother on Lincoln Ave. Her lectures from my childhood drummed in my head. "They are outcasts and bitter, but it is in their blood to be whole. Our nature is to connect. That is not buried just because they're alone. Some have lost their powers, all have lost their covens. They are the enemy because they cannot exist while we remain united." Since my drive to school, the Virago had become important.

My mother's reaction had increased the intensity of her warnings. One of our instincts was wrong about Ike and his family, and neither of us had ever been wrong before. The realization was more frightening than the first day at a new school. It was the first day of a flawed world.

It took less than a week to realize choir and lunch were my only times "off" during my school days, and that was only because I liked to sing and I loved to eat. By week two, I could navigate every hallway in the school, and I'd figured out which shortcuts worked the best to get to the other side of the building.

Almost every morning, exactly like the very first morning, I passed Ike Kennedy in the stairwell. Like clockwork, he was on the same step coming up as I passed him going down. Every single time, he stared at me until I thought he'd swallow me whole. He never smiled. Although, one day I thought he was about to, but no. He didn't.

Whenever we were actually together, like in physics when he was only twenty-six inches from me—just an estimation—he barely noticed me. On the stairs, though. That was our time.

The clubs had also officially begun, and we added chess club twice a month to lunch and chorus as our respite from high school. Maya wasn't as much a fan of chess as Ruby and I were, but she liked to be with us, and it was one of the only activities we didn't have an unfair advantage in. It also met during the down time at the beginning of the day, so she had nothing better to do.

My father had played chess with me. After the time I'd "accidentally" moved the goal over four feet while taking a horrible shot in youth soccer, he'd searched for more intellectual outlets for me to pursue.

He brought home a chess set from his trip to London. It was a Battle of Hastings themed set with a leather board. King Harold II was carved from off-white marble and rode a horse. The figures were almost as fun as the hours I spent with my father. That time seemed like a hundred years ago.

Mick was my opponent most days. Today, he was wearing a Woodstown sweatshirt I'd never seen on another student. It was blue with orange letters embroidered across the front.

"Where did you get that sweatshirt?"

Mick glanced down at it. "My dad." He set up his pieces. "It was his."

I stared in shock at the sweatshirt. "Like, he wore it when he went to school here?" Mick was unfazed. "Did everyone's mother and father go to this school?"

"Your mom went here."

"I know, but it doesn't seem it." I sat back and thought of my mother. She was different since we'd moved home. She melded into the Jersey landscape. "Maybe it does."

"It isn't that big of a deal. Everyone just knows everyone." Mick offered me a Blow Pop, which was pretty much contraband in this building, but I thought we might be able to get away with it during chess club. We deserved some joy.

I reached out my hand, and he gave me a watermelon one. "What's with all the candy?"

"My mom told me I talk a lot when I'm nervous, so I try to have something to chew on."

"Oh." I liked a guy with a plan. "Are you nervous often?"

"I don't know. I didn't know I was at all until she told me."

Mick focused on the board signaling he didn't want to talk about it anymore.

I moved my pawn to king four and put the Blow Pop in my mouth. When our teacher looked up, I smiled ridiculously with it in there, and he didn't tell me to throw it out. Mick cracked the lollipop between his teeth. His anxiousness seemed misplaced since I'd only just taken the first move. I leaned in closer to the board and asked, "Everything okay?"

"Billy Roberts was asking me about you yesterday," Mick blurted out. His shoulders relaxed at the divulging of the information.

"He did? Well, what did he want to know?" After the first day, Billy hadn't said a word to me, which was a relief. I didn't want him asking about me, and the thought set me just the tiniest bit on edge.

Mick shook his head, insinuating the questions were unbelievable. I hung on his every word. "He asked me where you live and if I've ever been to your house?"

"Really?"

"Which I haven't, so that's what I told him."

"Of course. You know you're welcome to come over anytime." Mick exhaled loudly as if he'd been holding his breath until I responded. He was more at ease. I was not. Billy's interest tensed the muscles from my neck to the tips of my shoulders. Why did he want to know where I lived?

"He also told me to back off you in lab because he wants to be your partner. It's cool if you'd rather partner with him. I just asked you because we were sitting next to each other in class."

"No." I shook my head. "I want you to be my partner. You're smart and funny and a great partner." I hoped I wasn't laying it on too thick. I didn't want Mick to get the wrong idea, but all of those things were true about him. I just wasn't interested in him beyond a friend, and lab partner, of course.

Maya glanced over from her chess game. She liked Mick. Maya

liked everyone in the world who was kind and nice.

We're just friends, I thought to her.

I know.

"So, Mick. What's Billy's deal? He seems . . . different."

Mick stiffened again before my eyes. He sat back in his chair, distancing himself from my question. "Billy's lived here his whole life, too. He . . ." Mick's words trailed off as his gaze darted around the room. "He's always at the start of trouble, but somehow missing when things get out of hand." I concentrated on Mick's words. "Does that make sense?"

"Yes. It does." It almost verbalized what I thought of Billy, but there was still something missing. A feeling that wasn't as easy to describe with words. "Hey, Mick." He broke his concentration on his next move and faced me. "Since we're talking about people, what's up with that guy, Ike, who sits in front of us in physics?" I wanted to know if Ike Kennedy had a girlfriend. It might have been *needed* to know.

Ike was the coldest fortress I'd ever encountered. If I wasn't hanging on every breath he took, I might have missed the few times he ever acknowledged that I was alive, which was always when we were moving in opposite directions.

Mick tipped his head and thought for a moment. "He's actually a lot nicer when you're around."

"Really?" My voice was low. Shock masked its usual tone. "He never seems very nice."

"I think this is nice for him."

I let the subject drop after that, but I didn't stop thinking about what Mick had told me.

Ike wasn't in physics so I was able to pay attention to Mr. Slopey during the few minutes I wasn't wondering where he was. Lunch was a reprieve, but the rest of the day was flat beige like the walls without Ike Kennedy to pique my interest. I longed for Maya and Ruby. My mother would call my need for them the power of the coven. I would say it was friendship.

Instead of paying attention during chorus, I reveled in their presence and thought of how I'd never have survived without Ruby and Maya after my father died. In the early days, we spoke every night because I couldn't sleep. Since moving here, I got to see them every day. They hovered above me as I organized my backpack and found my Spanish homework still lying against my notebook.

"Shoot. I've got to hand this in." I pulled out the paper and showed it to them. "Don't wait for me." *I'll fly home.*

Are you sure?

Yes. I feel like flying. There wasn't a thing I was surer about.

I left the paper in the center of Mrs. Gorman's desk and paused in the hall as students rushed by me to catch buses and rides. Some were collecting hockey sticks or shin guards and trudging past me with multiple bags. The locker my mother had leaned on the day we'd visited was to my left, and when the hall emptied, I rested my hand on it, too.

Nothing moved me. There was no clue as to why my mother had chosen it to rest against. I stayed with my hand on it and my eyes closed until images of my father invaded my mind. He was dropping me off for the first day of third grade, then taking me to my first movie, and lifting me into his arms when I'd fallen off my bike and cut my knee so badly that blood was dripping down my leg. I took short breaths. My chest was tightening around the memories. I couldn't let them slip away.

The birthday card I made him that he'd kept in the drawer next to his bed. The way he sang, "Forever you'll be my Ever," when he woke me in the morning. Warmth flowed from the hand on my shoulder, and I forced open my eyes. Ike Kennedy stood next to me, completely disturbed by my pain. He used his thumb to wipe a tear from my cheek, but even his enormous hand touching me couldn't steal me from the memories. I might have died of embarrassment if I could've shaken the intense feeling of loss.

"Hey, are you okay?" His voice saved me from the devastation in my mind.

I was afraid of what I might give away if I let myself speak, so I nodded and dropped my gaze to the floor to avoid facing him.

"You don't seem okay." He was practically whispering. His gentle stance and quiet words were throwing me off balance. I was trapped in a historic haze by this locker near my Spanish classroom.

"What's going on here?" Billy Roberts walked up and stood too close to me. His locker was next to the one I'd been touching.

"Nothing." Ike never took his eyes off me as he spoke.

"Great. Ever, are you and your pack going to the bonfire to-morrow night?"

"Not sure," I managed to get out with Ike still watching me.

Billy looked from Ike to me and back at Ike again. He was con-fused, and so was I. The only person who seemed to be unaffected was Ike, but that was him in every situation.

"Let me give you a ride home," Ike said.

"Don't you have practice?" Billy's expression was smug as he asked. "I'll drive you," he directed to me.

"I don't need a ride. I'll catch the bus." I needed to fly now more than ever.

"Long gone," Billy said. It was just the three of us in the entire top floor of the building. He took a step toward the door. "Let's go," he said playfully.

I had no legitimate reason not to take the ride and no way home that I could share with either of them. It was yet another moment I felt trapped with Billy, but he'd done nothing but kindly offer to drive me home. Without wanting to discuss the logistics further, I dragged myself away from Ike's attention.

Billy and I walked out of the school and down the hill to the student parking lot.

"Don't you play soccer?" I remembered he did as soon as the soccer team passed us on the sidewalk.

"Not today." He offered no other explanation; he just kept us moving as though we were outrunning something I couldn't see.

"Really, I can get a ride."

He stopped and said, "I know, and you are getting a ride." There was a force behind his words that stole my participation in the decision. Suddenly, I really didn't want to get in a car with him, but I didn't know what else to do.

Billy's car was the first in the lot.

"What time do you get here in the morning?" I asked.

"Early enough to greet everyone." His expression was devious. He opened the driver's door of an old BMW and pushed the unlock button so I could open mine.

Billy Roberts is driving me home.

Really, Maya thought back.

Ew, was all Ruby responded.

"So, where do you live?"

The football team was running over the bridge to the field. I searched through the bodies for Ike, but I couldn't find him.

"Auburn."

"That's a new one."

"I hear you." I sat back in my seat.

"Seriously, I've lived here my whole life and never known anyone from Auburn."

"I don't think a lot of people are *from* Auburn."

"Is it even a town?"

"It is." I was tired of the questions. "Where do you live?"

"In Woodstown. I never even drive through Auburn. It's on the way to nowhere."

"All roads lead to Auburn," I absently spoke and stared out the window the rest of the ride. We stopped at the intersection before town, and I said, "This is Pointers-Auburn Rd." I pointed to the road in front of us that would eventually become Main Street, Auburn. "On the other side of it are the Pedricktown-Auburn Road and the Pennsville-Auburn Road." He was nodding. Catching on. "And of course, we're on the Woodstown-Auburn Road. All of them lead toward Auburn. For being in the middle of nowhere, it is clearly the middle."

My defense of this tiny street-slash-town shocked even me. We turned right. I blinked, and we were halfway through Auburn. Right before the hill, I said, "It's the last one on the right."

Billy made a right into my driveway and drove up the steep hill to my house. Maya and Ruby were waiting for us. They weren't in the middle of doing anything like putting the kickstand down on a bike or kneeling to plant a flower. They were standing completely alone facing the driveway.

Billy tapped the brakes in shock at the sight of them. I was at ease.

"What are they doing here?"

"They live here, too."

His eyebrows rose, and for the first time since I'd met Billy, he seemed not in control of the situation. Without taking his eyes off my coven, he asked, "You all live here?"

"Just until we find places of our own. Our mothers were child-hood friends, so we're staying together for now."

I'd said too much. Billy's gaze fell to my shoulder as he digested each word. When he looked me in the eye, a chill ran down my back, but I didn't flinch in the coldness that surrounded him.

"Well, gotta go. Thanks for the ride." I stepped out of the car. Maya and Ruby continued to stare at Billy until he drove back down our driveway.

"What was that about?" Maya asked. "And why did you ride home with him?"

"There's something wrong with him."

They followed me into the kitchen before Ruby said, "Probably several things."

"It's like he knows things that he shouldn't."

"At least he's not a witch."

IX

"THERE'S GOING TO BE DRINKING." Sloane stopped at the four-way stop at Seven Stars.

"Why do you call this Seven Stars?" Maya asked.

"That's the name of the house." Sloane pointed at the old brick house on the corner.

My eyes traipsed up the side, over the patterned brick that had the year 1762 in the design on the other side, and stopped at the attic window. "Do you guys see that?" A mannequin with a long gray wig leaned over something near the window. The area was barely lit and wholly terrifying.

Sloane leaned over the steering wheel and look up through the front windshield. "They are still doing that." She sat back satisfied. "Even when we were little girls, there was always someone in the window, watching over the crossroad."

"Freaks," Ruby said.

"Not at all," Sloane dismissed her. "I think we should hang out with them." Sloane sped away from the stop sign.

"I always feel like someone is watching us here." Had the statement been made by Ruby, no one would have even noticed her latest criticism, but because Maya had said it, there was some weight to her observance.

"Why do you say that?" Sloane feigned lightness in her words. I could see the stress Maya's declaration had caused in the defined lines between Sloane's eyebrows.

"It's just a feeling."

"That's nonsense." Sloane focused on the road again. "Back to the drinking. It's probably not going to be beer since it's easier to just steal a bottle of liquor from their parents' stashes." I was trying to pay attention to the directions she drove, but everything looked the same. "And weed, of course. Is that what you call it now? Weed?" Maya was next to me in the backseat and she, too, was listening to Sloane. "Hooch? The green good stuff? Gon-ja!" She exaggerated both syllables of the last one before surveying all three of us. "You can tell me."

"Why do you assume you know what this is going to be like?" Ruby asked her mother. I'd been thinking the same thing.

"You saw the inside of the high school." Sloane was leaning back in her seat with her arm out straight to reach the steering wheel. "Nothing changes around here. We used to drink in a bunch of fields, too."

Ruby's top lip curled in disgust. Nothing made a parent seem older than when they pretended to know what their child's life was like. "Oh sure, you idiots are big on prescription drugs now." Sloane shook her head as she drove. "But the parties haven't changed much. I guarantee it. If a fight breaks out, leave. It never gets better after a fight. Ruins the whole thing."

"Okay, I think that's enough parental wisdom for one night," Ruby said.

"Don't drink anything someone has poured in a cup for you, including water, and don't smoke anything." She nodded, pleased with her own advice. "But if you're going to smoke, make sure it's something that grows from the ground."

"Kill me," Ruby said under her breath.

"Be home by midnight."

"Really?" Maya finally joined in. Her curfew in Hawaii had always been eleven.

"Yes," Sloane answered Maya. "Never forget." She raised her finger in the air at us. "You're not the only witches out there."

"I've heard that my whole life and never met another witch," Maya said.

"That's because you didn't live near your coven. If a witch is alone she keeps to herself, or . . ." Sloane stopped the car on the dirt shoulder behind three pickup trucks.

"Or what?" I asked.

"Or she lives in the dark," she rushed out. "Now, go have some fun. Meet some people and be safe."

The three of us got out of the car and stood shoulder to shoulder facing Sloane in the driver's seat of the minivan. We weren't moving until she left. She rolled down the window and said, "Try not to stand so close to each other."

She drove away, leaving the three of us in the center of nowhere. I wasn't even sure if we were still in the same county. The roads were all the same, and without the creek, it was harder to navigate. Flying home should be an adventure. It was the perfect deterrent to drinking.

"Okay. It's time to go meet some people," Maya said with fake enthusiasm.

We climbed the steep hill behind us that leveled into what could have been a backyard, but the only house in view was at least an acre away. To our right was a bonfire. It was small with only a few people nursing the flames. The sun had set hours ago, but the sky was bright from the moon. October nights were some of the most beautiful to fly. Gone was the oppressive humidity of summer, but the winter chill was still at bay.

Directly in front of us, six guys played football. Ike was one of them. My sight fixed on him as he ran in the opposite direction and caught the ball that was thrown to him. People lined the sides of the makeshift field. Everyone had a cup in their hand. Some were smoking. Music blared from portable speakers on top of a truck cab parked next to the bonfire.

Ike was tackled by two players and still drug them to the goal line. I watched in delight as they hung off him while he celebrated his score and realized I'd been holding my breath. There was something magnificent about him, even if it weren't obvious in his personality.

"Oh, game on," Ruby said and tipped her head toward the volleyball game to our left. Each team had five players on it, most of which were shirtless boys. They wore shorts and jeans, boots and bare feet. There wasn't a lot of reason that went along with the cliques of the school. They seemed to intermingle randomly, but I thought that was because most of them were related in some way or had known each other their whole lives.

Ruby left us to watch the volleyball game. I wanted her to find someone to take her mind off Harry. I'd had no one in Vermont it hurt to leave behind the way Harry's absence was killing her. I'd had a boyfriend, but he was easy to abandon, which made me wonder if I'd ever feel about someone the way she felt about Harry. Closeness eluded me every time I kept my craft a secret.

Truthfully, the only thing outside my family and coven that would pain me to lose was flying. It was the only thing I ever wanted to do. I wasn't sure I could love a person who didn't know about it, who couldn't do it *with* me. It'd be like having a heavenly singing voice and never sharing it with a soul. Just singing to myself every day. Would a person ever really know me if they didn't know about that?

"Hi, Gwen." Maya saw her first. She was standing behind a group of people and between two trucks parked by the fire.

"Hey." Gwen barely looked up.

She was holding back the hair of a girl who was bent at the waist with her head between her legs. I stood still, waiting for the girl to throw up. I didn't recognize her from the back of her head. Gwen never took her eyes off the girl as she dry-heaved one more time.

"I think I'm okay. Too much vodka." She was the girl from physics who wanted to be wherever Ike was. "It tasted like peppermint." I waited for him to come help her. If she was his girlfriend or something similar, it would make sense Gwen was close to her, but he should be here taking care of her. Even if he lied to his mom about her.

Ike was standing near the end zone with his hands on his hips, watching me. Heat fell down my chest and over my thighs. I inhaled, and the girl dropped her head and dry heaved again.

She should go home.

I agreed with Maya.

"Oh look. Grace's wasted and throwing up. What a shock." Billy's words weren't just cruel. They reeked of a vengeful need. It seemed like a poor time to get someone back, but maybe Billy wasn't into a fair fight.

"Leave her alone," Gwen said and glared at Billy.

"Why? Because she's drunk? If we all left her alone while she was drunk no one'd ever talk to her."

Gwen's cheeks flushed red. She trembled with anger as the fire behind her surged higher.

Who did that?

I turned to find Ruby. She was cracking up at something two guys had said next to the volleyball game. She was completely unaware of us and the fire.

I don't know, Maya answered.

Grace leaned over again, and Gwen rubbed her back. "I'm serious, Billy. Leave her alone." She was good. Like her brother, and nothing like what my mother had said about their family.

"She should want me to stay. At least I'm not going to have sex with her and never call her again."

"Shut up, Billy!"

Wind tore by us as the flames intensified and formed an umbrella with us beneath them. Maya and I moved back. Anger swirled around us. Gwen cowered under the flames that she'd been too angry to notice a second before. She moved herself and Grace away from the fire. My mother's claims of the Virago seared through my mind. Gwen wasn't dark, she was afraid of a little fire.

"She knows she's a whor—"

"Give it a rest, Billy," Ike said from my side. I hadn't seen him coming.

"Aw. Thinking about rekindling that one-night from over the summer?" My eyes never left Ike as Billy spewed all his nasty words about the girl who couldn't stand up between us. I hated Ike anywhere near this. I wanted him to be above the ugliness surrounding this drunken girl and her attacked reputation. "It's always one night with Grace."

"Enough," Ike said to Billy. Grace found some reservoir of strength, straightened, and stumbled toward the house with Gwen following her. The fire roared on behind us while anger ignited between Billy and Ike. They were going to fight, or explode.

I wasn't interested in waiting around to see which one.

I'm going to pee in the woods, I thought to Maya.

"Do you want me to come with you?"

"I think I can handle the forest." The unresolved hatred between Ike and Billy hadn't dissipated. They stood glaring at each other in front of the flames. "Probably better than the fire."

I walked past the volleyball game. The teams were exactly the same as when we'd arrived. They were in a serious battle that contained none of the anger of the bonfire. I stepped into the woods and the remnants of the dead leaves of the past autumn sank beneath my feet.

I bent down to avoid branches that were chest high and pushed more out of my way as I walked farther into the darkness. The sky was hidden by the treetops, which were still full of leaves, and the deeper I went, the darker it became. It was nighttime in the forest hours before the fields.

I slipped behind a tall maple and lifted my dress to my waist. Without another option, I pulled down my underwear and squatted by the tree.

"Sorry," I said and patted the bark with the hand I was leaning on.

Footsteps crunched near the entrance of the woods by the party. Just two at first. I continued to pee. It was probably someone doing the same thing as me. The steps paused, and I did, too.

Three more steps came toward me. I held my breath and listened. I could hear him breathing. I disappeared.

"Ever." It was Billy. "I saw you come in here."

I'll bet you did.

I stared into the thick leaf cover above me and watched the bats hanging and waiting to fly. I caused the tree's branches to shake, but the bats were slow to respond. Billy's footsteps grew closer. I closed my eyes and concentrated on every branch shaking within twenty feet of me.

Hundreds of bats called out as they descended from the trees and swarmed around Billy.

"Ah! What the—" I finished and listened to him running from the woods.

I took my time straightening my dress. I was in no rush to return to Billy's vicinity. The farther I stayed from him, the happier I'd be. I followed the same path out that I'd taken in.

Ike was leaning against the last tree of the line. He was facing out toward the volleyball game, standing guard and watching over the woods. I walked up and stood next to him without a word, as if I belonged right there.

"Everything okay?" he asked. He wasn't surprised. He'd been waiting for me.

"I'm not sure." I didn't know what to make of Billy, except that he was cruel and horrid to Grace. An awful history between them must not have been left in the past. He also thought it was okay to follow girls into the woods. Billy didn't play by the rules.

Ike took up all the room between us. I had stopped so close to him that I could smell soap, cigar smoke, and a hint of gasoline coming off him. "Is New Jersey anything like Vermont?"

I looked past his head at the trees that towered over us. "Parts are very similar." My gaze fell down the tree trunk and the branches to the jet-black hair on top of Ike's head. I lingered through it, wishing my sight were my fingers, until I found myself staring into his navy blue eyes. "And some things are completely different."

Ike pushed the stray hairs off my face. His hand was covered in dirt and rough. I reached up, pulled it down, and laid it flat between us. I ran my thumb over the creases that formed a slanted E in his palm.

"Ever," he said, but not in a way that suggested he was talking to me. "You shouldn't be in the woods alone."

His concern surprised me and caused a nervous laugh. "I'm not afraid of the woods."

Ike leaned against me and rested his arm above my head on the tree behind me. "Something tells me you're not afraid of anything."

"Fear is a wasted emotion."

"Spoken like a crazy person."

"Or the daughter of a marine." My father and I sailed through every adventure without slowing down to be afraid. "Give 'em hell" was his favorite saying.

"Your father's a marine?"

"Was." With that one word, the weight of loss returned and pressed against my shoulders.

"Do you feel that?" Ike asked and leaned closer to me. It wasn't loss, but something more evil. The two of us were being pushed against the tree until the bark scraped at my back through my clothes. I tried to push Ike away. His arms were flexing against the tree as he tried not to crush me. A defeated groan came from his mouth as he moved closer still and the bones in my neck and back ached. A branch cracked above us. Ike and I looked up as it fell straight toward us. I closed my eyes and redirected it toward the clearing. "What the . . ."

Ever, come here.

The pressure broke. Ike leaned over with his hands on his knees trying to catch his breath. I stepped away from the tree and Ike. I scrutinized every inch of him for an explanation as to what had just happened. "I have to go."

"What was that?" Ike was still eyeing the branch on the ground and the broken remnants above us.

Now! Ruby demanded.

I jumped a little. "What was what?" I asked. Without answers, I'd contribute to the questions.

Confusion covered his face. "I don't know."

Why did it always have to be so intense with him? I just wanted to touch his hand or lean into him while he kissed me. Something a non-witch would do. Without bats and disappearing and strange winds and fire. I just wanted to be . . . with Ike.

Ever!

"I'll see you later," I said, not knowing what *that* was and not willing to give him any time to speculate before I walked away like a normal girl would.

Ruby was scanning the crowd, searching for me. She hadn't moved from the volleyball game, but instead of friendly competition, the game had taken an ugly turn. Maya and I joined Ruby at the exact minute one guy head-butted another.

"It's time to go," Maya said and inhaled.

"You have no idea." Ike was examining the branch that had almost fallen on us.

"And tonight had so much potential." Ruby walked toward the hill. Maya and I followed her over it and out of sight. We took three steps down the road and disappeared.

We flew in silence with me between them. I sped in front, and they flanked my sides, resting in my draft. It was the way we'd always flown, except for when our mothers were with us. When we were young, we'd line up diagonally in the sky behind them and follow as they turned, and dropped, and navigated over the earth.

On my twelfth birthday, I'd challenged my mother to a race even though she still treated me as if I was adorable. I beat her, and she started talking about the Witch Olympics. She was always the fastest witch she'd known, and now I was faster than her.

I held back. I didn't want to lose Ruby and Maya, and I wasn't completely sure of where I was going. We were just north of Woodstown when I picked up the creek again. I followed it straight to Auburn.

"Nice job," Ruby said as we landed in our backyard.

"Thanks."

We followed Maya into our kitchen. Our mothers were sitting around the kitchen table playing rummy and drinking merlot.

"You guys are home early."

I searched through the large cabinet for Oreos. There weren't any. "You told us to come home when the fight broke out."

"You did?" my mom asked Sloane, who was pleased we'd listened, but Sloane just smiled, so my mom turned to me. "Did you have fun?"

"Um . . ." I opened the freezer and found the cookies and cream ice cream.

"It was interesting." Ruby chimed in, saving me from figuring out what I thought about our night.

"Give this place a chance," Lovie said and drew a card from the deck. "You're going to love it as much as they'll love you."

"Who are 'they'?" I asked, but the three of them were already lost in their hands as Lovie dropped three kings on the table in front of her.

I filled a bowl with ice cream and followed Ruby and Maya up the two flights of stairs to our room.

"Who was even fighting?" I asked, and they both shrugged.

"The guy who head-butted the tall one is in my oceanography class," Ruby said.

"Does he seem like a fighter?" I put a spoonful of the glorious awesomeness in my mouth.

"What does a fighter seem like?"

I thought about it. "Angry. Repressed."

"That's the vibe I get from Gwen's brother," Maya said and immediately stole my attention.

"Ike?"

"Yes. He always seems so distant. Don't you think?" I didn't think that at all. I felt like every minute he was anywhere near me that he was close to me. Inside my head even.

"No, I don't get that feeling from him at all."

She shrugged. "I like Gwen. So, I'll give him a chance."

I fell asleep next to the empty ice cream bowl on my nightstand. It was hot in our room, and I kept rolling over to stick my foot out from under the covers on my bed. I finally rested until I realized I was in the woods by the bonfire again. I was dreaming, but that was impossible. I'd never had a dream before, but I was there. Right by the maple tree I'd peed next to. I walked toward the tree line, hoping to find Ike again. I wanted to be with him even if it was in my dreams. He was standing there, but instead of the clothes he'd had on at the bonfire, he was dressed in a Marine uniform. The way he stood still, breathing through his slightly open lips, suggested he was waiting for me to say something, but I didn't know what.

"Ike?"

"Tell me, Ever," he said, but I didn't understand what he wanted. "Tell me."

I turned my attention over my shoulder, needing Ruby and Maya with me, but they were nowhere to be found. I turned back, and Ike was gone.

I rolled over again and opened my eyes.

I studied the ceiling of my room until I was certain I was awake.

It was a dream. I had a dream.

I was sure of it. I reached over and grabbed my journal off the floor next to my bed. I wrote, "Ike, woods, waiting for me to tell him," and dropped the pad back on the floor. I lay back again, chasing him in my mind. If I could fall back asleep, maybe I'd dream of him again.

I didn't wake again until morning, and if there had been more dreams, I wasn't aware of them. The light hit my side of the room first. It poured through the small window above me and covered my bed with sunshine. Instead of shunning it and hiding under my covers, I let it cover my face for a moment before I slid out of bed and tiptoed downstairs.

"Morning." My mother was standing at the counter pouring

a cup of coffee. "You're up early." Her eyes lingered on me, but I didn't feel scrutinized, only loved.

"You, too. You used to love to sleep in." I smiled as I reached into the cabinet and picked out my favorite glass from our house in Vermont. It was blue with flowers engraved all around it. I filled the glass with milk.

She shook her head. "Not so much here. There's something about being home that won't let me miss a minute of it."

I watched as she gingerly sat and gathered the cards that had been left all over the table the night before. I could feel the peace and love in her more than I'd ever known. Vermont was her hiding place. Auburn was her home.

"Mom, how come we don't dream?"

She left the cards in a pile and studied me as I took the seat across from her. "Why do you ask?" She was gauging my response, and I wasn't ready to share the dream with her. She hated Ike, and something about the dream coming to me made me possessive over it. At least for the time being.

"Some people were talking about their dreams last night, and I wished I could dream. They sound fascinating." Mine was. "I was just wondering why we never do."

She paused for a moment before answering. "No one is sure why people dream, or why witches do not. It isn't a hard rule. *My* mother always felt that our connection to our subconscious was much stronger so our need to dream wasn't as prevalent." She shuffled the cards in her hand. She had something else to say. I could feel her holding it back, and I didn't speak a word, hoping she'd share. "I used to dream when I was pregnant with you."

"You did?" She'd never told me, not even when I was little and used to whine about how I wanted to dream.

"Yes. Every night. They started before I knew I was even going to have you."

"What did you dream about?"

"You. Every single time. I dreamed of you." She leaned across the table and grabbed my chin between her thumb and finger the same way she had my entire life. "I think it was more of me seeing you because you are exactly the same young woman as the one in my dreams."

"Was Dad ever a part of them?"

She lowered her head. Even after all these years, the mention of him hurt her. "No. It was always just me and you, which dismayed me as much as enchanted me."

"Have you ever dreamed of anyone else?"

My mother stared at me. She was less forthcoming in New Jersey. More guarded and I didn't know why. "The night Maya's father died, I dreamed of Lovie and Sloane, but that was the only other time. Otherwise, never," she rushed out, and I thought she was lying. It was the first time I could ever recall her lying to me. "Maybe someday you'll dream of your daughter."

"Maybe," I said and tried to make sense of Ike's intrusion the night before.

X

MR. SLOPEY LET US PACK up early, citing the throbbing headache we'd given him with our lack of aptitude for physics. I was finishing copying the notes off the board while the rest of the class was talking, grating on Mr. Slopey I was sure.

"Are you coming to the game tonight?"

He spoke.

Ike Kennedy had turned toward my table and asked a question.

"Me?" Mick asked with his finger pointing toward his chest.

Ike glanced from me to Mick and without even the hint of a smile said, "No."

Mick walked away. He tripped on two chair legs on his way to the back of the room.

"You're very gruff," I said, and Ike focused his attention back to me.

"Gruff?"

"Yes. You make people nervous."

"Are you nervous right now?"

Nervous wasn't the right word. He did make me hot, though. "No, but I know you're not as abrasive as you seem."

"Abrasive? And gruff?" He leaned toward me, leaving only inches between us. I held my breath until he blinked and looked down at my lips. "You make me sound like I'm a monster."

The bell rang and Ike stood next to my table.

I gathered my stuff and faced him, and then I realized I had to tilt my head back in order to look him in the eyes. "You're enormous. And for some reason, you don't smile that often. It gives people an impression of you that's unwarranted, but when you speak like that, it makes you seem gruff."

"Again with the gruff." Ike grinned on purpose. It was far from effortless. His eyes were forced open wide, and he was on the verge of laughter. "No one's ever called me abrasive before."

"Maybe they're too scared to."

"Maybe you should be scared." The closeness of his body was causing something inside of me close to fear. I was holding my breath and realized I was anxious. Like, I-wanted-to-rip-his-clothes-off anxious. Heat rushed to my cheeks, and I was sure I was blushing. "I was kidding."

"I know. You're hilarious."

"Can we start this over? Are you going to the game tonight?"

"Yes. I think I am. It's home, right?"

He nodded. "Paul's parents are away. The team's going to his house after the game." He cocked his head a little to the side.

"Is this a declaration or an invitation?"

"Are you always this difficult to talk to?"

I wasn't sure how to answer. I'd never been told by anyone else that I was difficult, but no one had ever made me feel the way Ike Kennedy did. "Possibly."

I was speechless the rest of the day. I kept going over the conversation in my head while the witty and intriguing things I could have said came to mind. I was still pondering it as I lay on my bed after school. The fall breeze blew through my window and ruffled the tapestry above my head.

Ruby sifted through all the shoes at the bottom of our closet, and I asked her, "Did your mom like Harry?"

She didn't even pop her head out. Just kept searching for whichever pair was eluding her. "She always seemed to like him until we were moving here. Then she just wanted him gone." Ruby stood with a pair of black suede booties in her hands. They had studs on the sides of the heels.

"Nice shoes."

"Do they match my orange and blue?" She wasn't really asking. If they didn't match, that was the intended look. Ruby didn't make fashion mistakes.

"They're perfect. Of course."

"Is this about Ike?" Ruby's question took me off guard. She walked over and towered above me. "Because I'm assuming that's the sudden interest in Woodstown football."

"My mom specifically told me to stay away from him. She said his family was part of the Virago." Ruby's eyebrows rose. None of our mothers had ever mentioned anyone of the Virago specifically. She recognized the severity of the statement. "But I don't feel a bit of darkness when I'm near him or Gwen. How can that be?"

"I don't know." Ruby was uncharacteristically quiet. She always had an answer.

We picked up Maya in the kitchen. Sloane was already waiting outside to take us to the game.

"When should we expect you three home?" Sloane asked and

pulled out of our driveway.

"I think we're going to a party afterward." Ruby said it as if it weren't noteworthy—we'd all attended *lots* of parties the year before in our home states. In reality, we'd only been to a few between us.

"Whose?"

"Paul Wentzel. He's on the team." Ruby, Maya, and I watched for Sloane's reaction. We could all predict it. Either she dated, knew, was in a band with, or was somehow related to Paul's mother or father. The connections in this town were endless.

"Oh," was all she said. She eyed me and Ruby in the rearview mirror. "Is Paul's dad Mike Wentzel?" Satisfaction from the predictability filled me.

"Don't know," Ruby said.

"Well, if he is I'm sure Paul is a hell raiser. His father always was. How are you planning on getting there? Where does he live?"

"On Stewart Road," I said. Maya and Ruby stared at me in shock that I knew.

"Oh yeah. His dad is Mike Wentzel. You three need to be home by midnight, and if you're even a second late, I'm coming to get you. Call if you need a ride. Do *not* drink and fly."

"We know. We know," Ruby said.

We rode the rest of the way to the stadium in silence, and by the time we got there, the stands were almost full. We walked along the home side, searching for seats until Gwen stood and called Maya's name. She waved us up to where she was sitting as the girls around her scrunched together and made room. Ruby took the seat to Gwen's left; Maya and I sat on the bench below them.

Pitman kicked off, and the crowd around us came to life. The cheerleaders and the band were in sync as they kicked off their own game. I studied every play for Ike. I knew from the jersey he'd worn to school that his number was fifty-one, but even without knowing, he was easy to find. He was the biggest guy on the field for either team.

The offense took over, and Ike came out to the sideline. He poured water into his mouth through his helmet guard, a coach talked to him as he pointed to the field, and other players tapped Ike's shoulders or back as they walked by him. Even without being part of the play, he was the epicenter of the team.

I wanted him to see me. It was important that he knew I was there. He had, after all, invited me, but I knew there was no chance of him paying attention to anything but the game.

"Who are you texting?" Gwen asked Ruby after the rest of the stands erupted over a touchdown while Ruby sat still on the bleacher with her head in her phone.

Ruby sighed. "No one."

"Harry?" Maya asked.

Ruby checked her screen again. "It's different now. The end is near."

"Boyfriend?" Gwen listened to Ruby with complete understanding.

"In Vegas. It's like we both know it's over, but we still miss each other." Gwen rubbed Ruby's shoulders as if they'd been friends their whole lives. "Or maybe we miss *it*."

Ike took the field with the rest of the defense.

"I have no clue what's going on," Maya said.

I knew everything that was happening. I'd watched every Minnesota Vikings game since I was three. Until I was ten, I watched them with my father. After he died, I watched them alone just to feel close to him. My mother tried to watch football with me, but she felt like an outsider. It had been something special between my dad and me, and no matter how hard she worked, she couldn't fill all the holes he'd left behind. Some of them I just had to wallow in all by myself.

Grace sat behind Gwen. She leaned forward and said, "What's

going on with your brother?" Her words flew over Gwen's shoulder and slapped me in the face.

"I don't know." Gwen was shaking her head, dismissing Grace immediately.

"Everything seemed fine until school started. Now nothing."

"Don't ask me. I have no idea what he's doing." Gwen held her hands up in frustration having been asked about Ike too many times before. "Believe it or not, Ike doesn't tell me a lot about his love life." I laughed, not because it was funny that Ike kept it to himself but because the phrase "love life" anywhere near him struck me as ridiculous. Grace found no humor in the situation. She stared at me, but her mind was lost in thoughts that didn't include me. She was considering Ike Kennedy.

Join the club.

"Now with her." Gwen tilted the top of her head not so inconspicuously toward Chrissy, who'd just entered the bleachers. "I know exactly what's going on." Chrissy swung her hair out of her face when the wind hit her. She coyly held down her cheerleading uniform as if the entire grandstand was hoping to see it blow up. She and another cheerleader were selling fifty-fifty tickets. Chrissy was practically a professional head shot walking toward us. "In ecology today she told me to 'get a grip.' That Dave Anzaldo was 'way out of my league.'" Gwen held the stare of death until Chrissy tripped on the concrete stairs in the middle of the grandstand and Gwen relaxed.

After that, my attention stayed glued to Ike the entire game. If he was off the field, I had no idea what was going on. I couldn't tell what happened in any play he wasn't a part of.

The game went into overtime, and I cursed it. I wanted to be at Paul's with Ike, not just watching him from behind the soccer team in the stands. It was already ten. If the game didn't end soon, I wasn't going to see him at all except from twenty yards away.

A crisp wind blew in my eyes. I tilted my head to the side and left the vision of Ike. Billy was staring at me from the seats below. He didn't look away when I noticed. He didn't blink or say a word. I was certain he'd seen me watching Ike, and Billy knowing anything about my thoughts on Ike, sent a chill down the back of my neck.

Nitrogen, number seven, N. Nickel, number twenty-eight, Ni.

I wouldn't give anything away to Billy.

Woodstown scored, and the game ended. Everyone going to Paul's rushed to their cars. We were all thinking the same thing. I was pretty sure Grace was. I wondered what else she and Ike had done over the summer. If she'd ridden on his motorcycle yet. If he took her to the shore. I wanted to know all of it, but I didn't have the heart to ask anyone.

The football team crossed the bridge, and somehow, we ended up climbing into Billy's BMW. My claims that I had a ride were ignored as Gwen shuffled Maya and Ruby into the back seat. I tried to sit back there with the other eight thousand people, but I landed up front with Billy. He turned up the music in the back and waited in traffic to exit the stadium parking lot.

"So. You like football?"

I kept staring out the window.

"What's your favorite team?"

I tuned to Billy. He wasn't going to leave me alone. "The Vikings." My voice was low. I hoped it conveyed my lack of interest in this conversation without my saying it. I returned my attention to the houses lining Millbrooke Avenue.

Instead of heading straight to Paul's, Billy drove the opposite way through town.

"Where are we going?"

"Wawa. I'm hungry. You?" I shook my head. I wanted to get to Paul's, not satisfy Billy's appetite. "Don't worry. It'll take a while for the team to get anywhere."

He annoyed me. Even the way he rested his elbow on his knee against the car door irked me. I wanted to be away from him. He maneuvered the car around two police cruisers and an ambulance with their lights flashing. The chaotic rhythm of the lights bounced against the dark woods on the side of the road where two officers stood talking.

"There must have been an accident," Gwen said from the back seat.

"Or a deliberate act," Billy half mumbled. He sped up once we cleared the scene.

After what felt like an hour of wasted time, Billy parked in the next open spot on Paul's lawn. Our "conversation" left me feeling exposed. If it weren't for Ike, I'd have flown home as soon as I got out of the car, but I wanted to see him more than I wanted to be away from Billy.

I let everyone walk ahead of me into the house. The kitchen was crowded. They moved Paul's mother's barn door napkin holder onto the counter next to the yellow toaster and were setting up a beer pong game on the table. Her possessions had been pushed aside as I'm sure Paul's guilt was also.

I waited in line to use the bathroom on the main floor. Paul breezed by me, putting a shirt over his head as he moved. He'd just showered and changed from the game, and for the first time, I noticed how big he was, just like Ike. I shook my head. No one was like Ike. I caught myself smiling as Grace exited the bathroom. The smile she gave me back fought against the unkind muscles of her face. She seemed to hate me, but I'd done nothing wrong.

When I finished, I scoured the house for Ruby and Maya and found them on the couch in the basement. Ruby was dominating in *Call of Duty,* and Maya was nestled among the four guys, watching her play. I headed back to the kitchen, and Billy met me in the middle of the dimly lit staircase.

"Want a beer, Ever?"

"I'm good. Thanks."

He leaned closer to me and placed his hand on the wall behind my head. "Anything else I can get you?" Billy's black eyes bore into me. It felt like his soul was black, too. "Water? Want to smoke?" He leaned closer. His breath swept across my cheek and against my ear. I shivered from a chill. Billy laughed. The sound was colder than the air.

I swallowed. "No thanks." I continued up the stairs and away from him. I walked straight outside and inhaled the fresh air as soon as I passed the smokers. I escaped to the tree line behind Paul's house. I preferred the woods to Paul's staircase. The predators I couldn't see to Billy's hollow kindness.

When I was almost out of the yard, Ike rode up on his motorcycle and parked in my path. I stopped. My heart possibly stopped. Everything around me might have also. I'd been waiting for his arrival more than I'd realized.

He took off his helmet and studied me as if I were bleeding. "You okay?" he asked, and I hung on every syllable, stuck between getting lost in the sound of his voice and trying to figure out why he would think something was wrong. Then I realized I was walking alone into the woods.

"Just cold." It was a stupid answer. Cold people went inside, not outside. I exhaled loudly as my frustration took over my body.

"Here." Ike climbed off his bike and took off his hoodie. He handed it to me. "Take this." I stared at it in his hand. When I finally looked up at his face, he said, "I'm hot," with a naughty smirk. "And sweet. Don't you think? Like, not gruff at all?"

"Yes." I stood still frozen in front of him. My eyes were glued to every inch of his chest in his T-shirt. "But I can't. Thank you."

"Of course you can." Ike pulled the sweatshirt over my head. When my eyes cleared the opening, his body was everywhere in front of me. If I tilted my head up, he would have kissed me, or so I thought. My mother's warning kept my head down. She would kill me for being anywhere near him.

I really can't do this.

"Yes you can." My head snapped up. The way he phrased it was in answer to me, but that was impossible. Ike stood perfectly still, and I pushed my arms through the sweatshirt. I rolled the sleeves and straightened the waistband. It covered the tops of my jeans completely.

"I think it's . . ." Ike was practically smiling, as if he knew everything I was going to say before I said it. "Going to upset some people."

"What people?" He leaned back. His eyes narrowed as he amused himself.

"I think Grace, at least." I straightened the sweatshirt and inhaled Ike's scent from it. "I suspect there are others." The more I inhaled, the less I cared who wanted him.

"Oh. The *others*." He lifted my hair out of the back of the sweatshirt. His hands near my neck lit me on fire. I held my breath. "Let me worry about them."

The noise from the party spilled out of the kitchen as the back door opened. It was Ruby. She held up her phone alerting me to the time.

"It's late," I said.

"I'm spending the night. I had to ride home and get my stuff."

"Oh." The brilliance that came out of my mouth around him was outstanding.

"I saw you at the game." Paralysis set in. "Sitting with the soccer team."

"I was sitting with your sister. You'll have to discuss our seat location with her."

"Maybe I will."

"It was a great game." I let my eyes linger on his chest again. I imagined resting my face against the right side and sighed before moving it over the left in my mind. There was plenty of Ike to explore. "Impressive."

I knew Ruby and Maya were staring at me without turning around.

We have to go, they thought in unison.

"I have to go."

"Already?"

It actually hurt to nod my head. I was in pain from having to separate from him. Watching him all night had solidified my need to be near him, but it felt like I was always leaving him.

"What are you doing tomorrow?" he asked. "Oh." Ike shook his head in disgust. "Forget I asked. I have to work, and then I'm supposed to go out with Paul and Ty."

"Where do you work?" *What do you do? What size shoe do you wear? What scares you?*

He laughed a little before answering. "The Hitchner farm."

Ever!

"Okay. Well, have fun. I'll see you Monday."

"Yo!" Paul yelled to Ike out the kitchen window. "Get in here."

All I could think was that Grace was in there and I didn't want Ike to go, which was infantile. They had a history. Ike and I had a few conversations. He loaned me his sweatshirt, offered me a ride home, and routinely took my breath away. But when I was with him, it felt like there was only him and me—no one and nothing else.

I met Ruby and Maya, and Ike entered the house through the back door without another word to me. The three of us walked behind the row of cars and disappeared into the night sky. We raced home, flying faster than we ever had before, but we weren't about to screw up our curfew. We landed in our yard at exactly midnight. Maya sighed with relief.

We closed our mothers' doors as we passed so if they woke in the middle of the night they'd know we were all tucked in. We knew the three of them were lying in bed awake, but it was a nice system.

The windows in the attic were all open. The curtains billowed out on the west side as the air blew in. It was the crisp fall breeze that we'd just flown home in. Our attic was so high it blew right through it.

I brushed my teeth and waited, still dressed, on the edge of my bed. When Ruby and Maya switched off the lights, I whispered, "I'm going back."

Maya turned the light on next to her bed. "What?"

"I'm going back to Paul's. I want to see him again."

"You're crazy," Ruby whispered. "Do you want me to come with you?"

Maya's head snapped in Ruby's direction.

"No. I won't be long."

"You think he's with Grace, don't you?" Maya's question hurt me, but it wasn't invalid.

"I don't know what I think, but I need to know. I really like him. I can't do this if he's with her."

"Oh, I get it," Ruby said. "Go. Be quiet. I'll stay awake until you get home so just call me if you need anything."

I loved them, both of them.

I moved to the window by Ruby since none of our mothers slept beneath her and climbed out. Without even a step, I disappeared and flew into the night. I was back at Paul's faster than when we'd flown home since I didn't have Maya and Ruby to hold me back.

There were only three cars left on the lawn. Billy's was one of them. Ike's motorcycle was where he'd parked it. I waited for the back door to open and before it hit the jamb, I breezed through it. I leaned against the kitchen counter and watched as Ike dominated a game of beer pong. He was good at everything. The thought of the other things he was good at caused me to inhale and close my eyes.

When I opened them, Billy was peering in my direction as if he could see me, but when Grace stumbled into the kitchen, his attention focused on her. He was a hunter sizing up his prey. Grace's intentions were the same as Billy's, except her interest rested solely on Ike.

The game ended, Ike stepped back from the table, and Grace walked over and leaned against the front of him. My jaw pressed together. He put his hand on her back and steadied her, which made my stomach sink. I swallowed down the reality of how much I wanted him. He wasn't just a distraction in physics. He'd somehow become more.

Grace stood on her tiptoes and kissed Ike's cheek. He stared at her, and I waited for the words he'd say.

"I'm going for a ride." He grabbed his helmet off the counter.

"I'll come with you," Grace said, but Ike kept walking to the door without another word in her direction.

"I'll give you a ride," Billy said. He handed Grace a beer from the table, but her eyes stayed on Ike's retreating back.

I followed Ike outside. I wasn't sure how much he'd drunk, and I didn't want him on a motorcycle. I thought about showing myself and telling him just that, but Paul stopped him with the same line of questions.

"I'm good. I swear. Just going for a ride. I won't be long," Ike swore.

"You're sure?" Paul asked, moving closer to gauge Ike's steadiness.

"I swear." Ike looked and sounded fine. Slightly detached from his surroundings, but fine. "Grace isn't staying here tonight, is she?"

"I don't think so, but I can probably arrange it if you want." Paul's expression was conspiratorial.

"Actually, no."

My heart jumped. Life bloomed inside me. He didn't want her, and I knew without him saying a word it was because he wanted me.

Ike climbed on his bike. I promised myself I'd take off with him and then go home. I wasn't going to turn into a stalker. At least not more than I'd already become. I needed to get ahold of myself because none of this was how I would have behaved in Vermont. Although, there hadn't been an Ike Kennedy in Vermont.

He rode out of Paul's driveway and traveled northeast. At Whig Lane, he made a left and headed west. He rode without speeding, and I stayed just above him. He followed Point Airy Road, clearly staying far away from his own house, and when he reached Auburn Road, he made a right.

I was supposed to leave him, but I'd lied to myself. I could no more leave him in that moment than I could if we were alone on an island somewhere. I wanted to be with Ike more than anyone.

He slowed when he crossed into Auburn. His bike was quieter, and he stopped two houses from mine. I searched my mind for the resident's name from the people I'd been meeting at church. I'd never told him where I lived, and I didn't know who lived in the house we were in front of. Ike walked his bike in the silence of the night until he was directly across the street from my house.

He looked up to the tops of the trees and our attic as though he'd been invited in a thousand times before. I watched him as he stared at my house. I was only a few feet from him and completely enthralled by his presence.

Ruby, I thought.

Yes.

Turn on your light.

My gaze never left Ike. He leaned back in shock, and I knew the light was on in my bedroom without looking up.

What's going on?

Stay away from the window. I'll explain in a minute.

Ike was watching the window. He took off his helmet and rested it on his thigh. I stared up at it, too.

"Come to the window, Ever." I heard, but the words weren't spoken. I watched Ike, confused. I waited for him to say it again, but he only stared at my window.

Turn it off.

On. Off. On. Off. What am I?

I silently laughed next to Ike. The light went off. My room was dark again. I heard—no I felt—Ike sigh next to me.

"This is crazy," he said and shook his head. I knew how he felt. I was watching him watch me. I tried to untwist that in my head as Ike put on his helmet and started his motorcycle again. He drove away, leaving me alone to stare at the dark room above us. I flew to the window and climbed in.

❦

"Ruby and Maya said you guys had fun last night, and that Woodstown won," my mother said and sat on the edge of my bed. She overflowed with love for me. The three of us liking our new hometown meant more to our mothers than we'd ever understand, but even without comprehending it, I knew mine only wanted me to be happy.

"It was a great night." I tried to downplay my emotions. I didn't want her sensing my feelings for Ike.

"I used to love the football games here. Does the band still play during the game?"

"They sure do. We sat in front of them." She laughed. "This whole town is really into their football."

"We've been playing a long time."

I stood and stretched. "What hasn't been going on here a long time?" I grabbed my phone off my nightstand.

"Ever." Her voice was strained. The room filled with tension and anger. "Is that Ike Kennedy's sweatshirt?"

I looked down at the sweatshirt I knew had his name written across the back. "Yes," I said weakly and then garnered some strength. "Paul gave it to me to wear when I was cold last night." The lie fell off my tongue. The universe was helping me protect us.

"I told you to stay away from him."

Something about her taut jaw and flaring nostrils told me not to question her on this even though I wanted to scream, "Why?"

"I am. I promise. Just not his sweatshirt." I took it off to put her at ease. "I'll give it back to Paul on Monday."

"See that you do." She stood and left without a word of kindness or understanding. I hugged the sweatshirt. He hadn't just lent it to me; he was here. Just knowing that Ike knew where I lived made my whole room feel different.

XI

BREAKFAST WAS PANCAKES AGAIN. RUBY and I stared at each other across the table as an eerie chill swept around our ankles.

Sloane put the syrup down in front of Maya and said, "A woman was found in the woods last night. She'd been beaten."

"That's horrible," Maya said.

Ruby buttered her pancakes and then doused them with syrup. Her mother grabbed the bottle out of her hands and sat on the table between us.

Sloane looked from Ruby to me and back at Ruby again. "No one goes in the woods." She stood, leaned on the table, and pierced each of us with her stare. "Stay out of the woods." When none of us spoke, she said, "Do *not* go into the woods."

"We got it," Ruby said and ate the first bite of her pancakes.

"I don't feel like you're listening."

"Well, we are so maybe it's a self-esteem issue," Ruby said, and her mother held her within the glare of death.

"This was the fourth attack." Sloane's words slowed into a new tactic.

"Why didn't you tell us about the others?" I asked. A woman I didn't know was attacked in the woods on the other side of town. It was tragic, but so were the other three, and we never heard a word about those.

"This woman was a witch."

Silence engulfed the room. My mind scrambled around the idea a witch could be killed and left on the side of the road. Where was her coven? "Why didn't she fight back?"

"She probably did."

"But how?" Maya's voice was just this side of a cry.

"We can't defend ourselves against everything and everyone. There are other powers in the world that are as great as ours." She paused to look at each one of us. "Now do you understand why we don't want you in the woods?"

The woods had been my home in Vermont. There wasn't a mile of it I hadn't explored. Alone. We didn't mention the attack again, but Maya was quiet the whole way to school. I knew the violence was weighing on her sense of security.

Mick dropped his bag on the table next to me without looking up. He sat in his chair still engrossed in his phone. He slid a picture back and forth across the screen. He enlarged it, returned it to its normal size, and finally showed it to me.

"This is my stepbrother." He pointed at the guy in the picture. He was wearing a dress, wig, and makeup. He actually made an attractive woman. "He's going in the men's room." Mick held his stomach while he laughed. "He's protesting."

"What is he protesting?" I asked. I didn't want to offend Mick with my analysis that was slowly moving through my mind. Ike turned in his seat and faced us both.

Mick stared at the picture again with a confused expression. "I'm not exactly sure," he admitted. "What's your username? I'll follow you."

"I'm not on anything."

"What?" Mick was aghast. Ike was attentive. "I'm not online. At all."

"You're lying. Look, if you don't want to tell me it's not a big deal." Mick had gone from jolly confused laughter to a grievance tone within two sentences. He popped a Sour Patch Kid into his mouth without the teacher seeing.

"If I were on any social media sites, I'd already be following you." Ike's eyebrows rose as I spoke. "But I went off everything when I left Vermont, and I haven't found a reason to reactivate my accounts."

"That's insane." Mick stared at me as if I'd taken a vow of silence for a year. "Ballsy . . . but crazy. I want you to go back on."

"I'll think about it."

Mr. Slopey yelled toward the ceiling, "Is anyone listening? What do I have to do? Stand on my head and spit Chiclets?" He'd become one of my favorite teachers. Not because I was learning so much in physics, but because he was entertaining and his expectations were clear. I also had the sense I could reason with him if necessary. Some teachers were impossible that way, and you could tell within minutes of their introduction. "The test is on . . ."

He held his hand up to his ear, and in unison the class answered, "Next Friday."

"For the remainder of class, you're going to work with a partner to prepare for the test. I'm going to hand out the resources, so don't start calling dibs on items like you're in second grade." Mr. Slopey was always exhausted by us. I liked his predictability.

He set a copy of laminated cards down in front of Ike. When

Mr. Slopey continued down the front row, Ike faced me and said, "I choose you."

I weakly pointed at myself.

Ike smiled, which left me even more disabled, and said, "Yes. You."

"Gruff."

Ike ignored my comment and spun his chair around. He slid his legs under my desk and they were everywhere. We didn't both fit. He peeked under the table and spread my legs to allow one of his to rest between mine. His hands on the inside of my knee stole my breath from my chest. When his head rose above the table, his grin was criminal. "That's better."

"Much," I croaked out. I attempted to ignore him and spread the cards out in front of me. Each had a picture depicting a physics scenario with a problem on the back.

He leaned forward and said, "It sounds like you're hiding from someone."

"What?"

"Not being online at all. It sounds like you're hiding from someone." I stared directly into his eyes without a word. "Like you're in the witness protection program or something."

My life felt like a covert operation at times. "Something."

"Do you need help, Ever?" His voice was low. Anyone else, I would have thought he was kidding, but he wasn't. Ike didn't joke about important things. He was solid in every way.

"Just trying to leave the past in the past." I dropped my eyes to the cards because his attention was devouring me.

"Did you have a boyfriend in Vermont?" His words were light, but they fell between us like concrete. Ike Kennedy was entering new territory.

"Yes." I'd barely thought of RJ since we'd left. He was the first boy I'd told that I loved, but based on the ease in which I'd said goodbye, I'd never known what the words truly meant. Almost a year we'd been together. There must have been something wrong with me.

"Did you love him?" Ike was going rogue. We'd never spoken so openly about any subject. I wished we were alone. Anywhere other than leaning over our physics scenarios.

"No."

He sat back and gave me space to breathe. "You pick the card. Something to do with gravity," he said. Even the way he said "gravity" was hot. I rolled my head and rubbed the back of my neck. "Something wrong?" He was taunting me and fully aware of the effect he had on me.

"No." I steadied myself across from him. I pushed the card with a navy-colored moon and a falling feather between us.

"What are you avoiding? If it's not an ex."

Everyone around us was talking. Flashcards, aps, and calculators were all in use as Mr. Slopey read the newspaper in the back of the room. I let the voices insulate Ike and me. I couldn't look away from him to actually see anyone.

"I lived the first ten years of my life with my mom and my dad in Vermont."

Ike was confused, which wasn't surprising. I'd been here long enough that even Ike had heard the background of the new girls. "Where did you live after that?"

I turned over the card. "A feather is dropped on the moon from a height of two point six meters. The acceleration—"

"Where?" He put his hand over mine on top of the card. Jolts of power shot up my arm, and I forced myself not to flinch or pull away.

I stared at the card in front of me. I used the time to decide how much I would tell him. I was already painfully aware of how much I wanted him to know. "Still in Vermont." I didn't let myself look away, or maybe he didn't let me. "Without my dad. He died, and coming here has made it possible to remember him without reliving every detail of the day it happened." Ike waited for me. "I don't have to see the door the police knocked on when we didn't answer quickly enough after they rang the bell. His closet that I stood in and picked out his tie for work that day doesn't taunt me from the wall of my mother's bedroom." The feather on the physics card was drawn almost as big as the moon. The blue moon. "The kitchen counter, the squeaky stair, the light he'd shut off next to my bed every night are not here."

I'd just opened the window to my wounded soul for Ike to fly through, and I didn't care. "I want to leave Vermont in Vermont." I thought he could help me forget. Ike leaned down, forcing me to look at him. Empathy flowed from him and engulfed me. He was as kind as he was beautiful.

"I want you to, too."

Mr. Slopey told us to clean up before the bell rang.

I took Ike's sweatshirt out of my backpack and handed it to him. "Thanks again." My sight lingered one last time on it. "For the sweatshirt."

"Oh." He just stared at it, seemingly offended I'd returned it.

"I slept in it all weekend. It's warm." Ike finally took the sweatshirt from me. He lifted it to his face and inhaled. "Like you," I said, and his eyes met mine. The bell rang and everyone around us rushed to escape the classroom. Ike waited for me to pack my bag and followed me.

I could have held his hand or kissed him or lay down with him. I wanted him to know everything about me. The thought of just walking out of the building together lodged in my mind.

You're making me crazy, I thought.

Ike stood still in the hallway with a satisfied expression on his face.

My cheeks flushed, and my lack of self-control annoyed me. I walked away from him without a word.

The minutes left in the day dragged by without the possibility of seeing Ike. I wanted to get home to try to dream about him and then fast forward time to get back to physics. It'd never been this way with RJ. I'd only known Ike a couple of weeks. I needed to get some perspective, because I was becoming too close to the one person my mother had warned me to stay away from.

I couldn't get out of my house fast enough after dinner. My mother was a razor-sharp microscope hovering over me the entire afternoon. She was on edge, and instead of fearful, it made me defensive. I wanted to argue with her about Ike's integrity. I could scream that he was amazing, but I had no evidence except the way he made me feel when I was around him.

The wind was behind me until I soared upward and flipped to the other direction. Male voices traveled on top of the treetops. Ike was below. I somehow knew it before I could see him or hear him laughing. The sound of his happiness warmed me in spite of the fact that he was forbidden.

I slowed my pace at the first sense of others in the woods. The police were scattering out from two cars on the side of the road. I fell to the tree line and brushed by them. Each officer turned toward me with their hands on their guns.

Stay out of the woods.

"The caller reported them in this vicinity."

I dove forward and flew the fifty yards to where Ike, Paul, and Ty sat around drinking cans of light beer without any idea of their impending arrest. I landed in the brush next to them and rustled around heavily to distinguish myself from an animal. Someone was there with them, and they needed to know.

"What the hell was that?" Ty asked, and they all eyed the forest around me.

"I don't know, but if I get caught by the cops again, I'm kicked off the team," Paul said.

"Me, too," Ty said. "And on a school night. My mother will beat me unconscious." They were idiots. I didn't understand why Ike even hung out with them.

The voices of the officers came into range behind me. I flew up. I'd done all I could to warn them.

"You guys run out of the clearing and across the field. I'll make noise and coax them farther into the woods," Ike said.

"How are you going to get out?"

"I'm fast. Remember?"

"If you're not there in five minutes, we're leaving without you," Ty warned Ike with no apology.

"Thanks," he said without a care in the world.

I followed him from above the tree line. The officers heard his first few steps and followed as he'd predicted. Ike was fast, but there were four officers and lots of trees in his path. I wanted to pick him up and bring him with me. I could have him home before the police found their way out of the woods, but it was out of the question.

Ike tripped over a fallen tree that was camouflaged by the uneven ground beneath it. He hit his head on a branch and rolled onto his back on the ground. The cops were closing in. Their footsteps were muffled, but their words were distinguishable. "Over here." I couldn't let them see him.

I dropped, landed on top of him, and whispered in his ear, "Don't say a word."

"Ever?" He strained to look down the front of his body, but he couldn't see me.

I leaned up and rested my lips near his ear. "Shh," I whispered, and Ike disappeared, too.

"Where did he go?"

"Did you get a good look at him?"

"I saw the back of him the whole time. Big guy. He wasn't thirty feet in front of me, though."

The officers stood still just to the left of us and listened for sounds of Ike's escape. I covered him as his heart raced beneath me.

What was I doing? This would not be tolerated or understood . . . or forgiven.

He would be my only mistake.

I forced myself to concentrate on the woods surrounding us. The wind picked up and blew the trees toward the clearing, enticing the officers to follow it.

"This way," they said and ran away.

I savored the last few seconds of being near him, but the guilt of what I'd shared ate away at the inside of me. I couldn't be near him without acknowledging the danger I'd put my coven in.

"What's happening?" His whispered voice was stifled by questions. His arms lifted off me and his head brushed against mine as he turned to look for me, for himself. "How . . ."

I pushed against the ground beneath him to stand. Ike caught me by the arms and pulled me back to his chest. We were invisible to each other and the forest around us.

"Don't," he said, and everything I knew to be true dissolved. "Don't leave me."

I had to go, but instead, I melted back into him. My head rested against his chest. "Tell me what's going on," he pleaded. "Ever." He couldn't know it was me. I'd said four words to him, there was no way he would have recognized my voice.

The scent of light beer trickled from his lips and reminded me he'd been here with his friends, not me. I flew into the air above him. Ike appeared, sat up, and looked around. He stared up into the sky, and I flew home.

XII

I T WAS IMPOSSIBLE TO AVOID Ike, but I couldn't face him without losing myself in the memory of what he smelled like beneath me in the woods or the feel of his solid chest pressed against me. I scurried out of physics on Friday, seeking some distance from him in reality and in my mind.

The assemblies had been announced during first period without much information as to why we were all being gathered at different times into the gymnasium. The only thing I cared about was missing history. For that, I'd take any topic the administration wanted to talk to us about.

I found Ruby and Maya sitting next to Gwen on the far end of the bleachers and took a seat with them. Ike was sitting directly across the gym and surrounded by an army of football players. I let my sight linger on him long enough to realize he was staring at me without bothering to try to hide it.

"What are we doing here?" Ruby asked with her usual level of patience for the unknown.

As if on cue, the principal walked to the center of the gymnasium and turned on a microphone to address us. "Good morning."

There was not a word in response.

He cleared his throat. "We're going to be repeating this assembly for different groups of students throughout the day, but since you're the first, I'm sure you're wondering why you're here." He paced a few steps and turned to both sides of the gym as he spoke. "There have been some recent incidences—" The microphone screeched through the speakers, forcing most of us to cover our ears. The principal shifted it away from his mouth. "Several violent attacks have occurred in the past month, and today, we're lucky enough to have detectives from the Salem County Sheriff's Office here to discuss some things you can do to keep yourself safe."

He was joined by a man in a suit with slicked back hair. Rather than the administrative-speak version of the "recent incidences" this man worked in the business of violence. "The beatings are extensive and from what we can tell, unprovoked. The perpetrators are targeting women, and the attacks are increasing in frequency."

The girls sitting near me shifted in their seats. If his goal was terror, he was a master. "We're coordinating with local police forces and state police troops to step up patrols, but this is a rural area and each of the assaults have taken place near or in the woods. Today, we're going to discuss and demonstrate some techniques to fight off an attacker."

This should be good. Ruby smiled at me when I turned her way.

"Rule number one, do not put yourself in a compromised position." As the detective spoke at length about not going into or near the woods, never to be walking alone at night, not to stop on the side of the road, and the necessity of keeping your car doors locked even when you're driving. I hardly paid attention. All I could focus on was the feel of Ike's eyes on me.

The detective was on rule number four before I heard another word he said. I took off my sweatshirt and shoved it in my backpack. The gym's temperature, or my own, was rising. I pulled my hair off my neck and twisted it over my shoulder, seeking some relief.

"One female and one male volunteer," he said and hands shot into the air around me.

I pulled Ruby's down. Her spirits followed her arm. She wanted to torture one of our poor classmates with her strength and battle readiness. *Not today, sister.* Gwen awkwardly climbed down the bleachers to the gym floor and faced a senior from the other side of the room. She was at least a foot shorter than he was and appeared childlike. The urge to run to her side and protect her overcame me. Maya leaned back against my knees, and I touched her hair.

"Aim for the face and the groin." The detective pointed out as important areas to the delight of his audience. "A thumb in the eye or a finger in the windpipe are both attacks you can mount even when you're being choked."

Gwen and her attacker were placed in different positions to demonstrate the moves as the detective delved into each one. The heel of the hand to the chin. Fist to the nose. Car keys to the eye, cheek, and ear. Heel to shin. Foot to groin. The crowd fell silent as the detective instructed Gwen to lie on the floor. Maya stood and walked to the bottom of the bleacher. She nonchalantly leaned on the banister by the staircase, as if she were waiting for an appropriate time to go to the bathroom.

Gwen laughed nervously as the detective planted a knee on the floor and leaned over her. He described a twisting of her wrist, knee to stomach, foot to hip combo move that seemed pretty complicated for a victim to execute in the moment of an attack. When he began to review it, Gwen pulled her arm away and launched him five feet across the floor with a foot to his chest.

The crowd gasped. Gwen sat up and stared at the detective, waiting to be chastised. Ruby elbowed me in the side with a huge grin on her face.

"Wow. So that's another way to do it." The detective rose to his feet and helped Gwen stand. "Small, but mighty," he said and kept staring at Gwen as if she had flown to the ceiling.

Gwen stayed standing in the middle of the floor while the principal talked over the bell about staying out of the woods and looking out for one another. She was staring at the floor around her feet. She'd surprised herself as much as the detective.

When the bleachers filtered out, Maya said, "I'm going to talk to her."

I hung back, wanting to talk to Gwen, too. The other students all had somewhere to be, which was anywhere but in the gym.

"You should stay out of the woods." His voice near the edge of my ear set me on fire. I turned to face Ike's scrutiny. He stared into my eyes as if his inspection ended there.

"I will."

XIII

RUBY HAD THE TEN CANDLES lit and lined up on the floor. She sat with her legs crossed and stared at the mason jars as the introduction of the song played. The lyrics began and the candles brightened in unison to the beat of the music.

She was really quite good. I lay in my bed and watched as the different candles almost extinguished and then burned bright again. They were the perfect accompaniment to the music blaring around us.

"Still haven't heard from Harry?" I asked when the music and the fire died down.

Ruby shook her head, and all the candles burned bright again. "I'm waiting to hear who he's going to homecoming with."

"Oh." That was all I had for her. There wasn't a name that was going to please her, and we both knew he was going with someone.

All she could do was wait to be pissed off and set things on fire to entertain herself.

I rolled over and hugged my stuffed dog to my chest. I closed my eyes and remembered the width of Ike's shoulders in front of me during physics. His hair. His upper arm when he leaned over and pulled something from his backpack. What I wouldn't give to still be wearing his hoodie.

I'd listened to every conversation of the girls around me, seeking information about Ike's past and present relationships. It appeared there'd been many in the past, and only frustration currently. Every girl liked the bad boy. I didn't think he was bad, though.

"We're leaving," Maya called up the stairs. "Game time!"

I dragged myself from my bed and found one of my boots under the loveseat. I leaned against the wall, pulled it on, and listened to our mothers below me. They were already outside. Sloane paced back and forth and flung her hands in the air as she spoke. The three of them had been flying more and more without us as if they were an invisible security force. They had also been whispering more often. The coffee table in the family room was covered with old books and notebooks as if they were studying for an exam. None of the entries in the books made sense to us.

"I felt nothing," Lovie said.

"They're taking too many chances." My mother's voice lowered as she spoke.

"That's because they've been running amuck since we moved away. There was no one to keep them in check." Sloane opened the back door, but before walking through, she added, "They're behaving like a bunch of bored children." The screen door hit the jamb, and I thought I heard her say, "Who kill people."

Ruby, Maya, and I didn't initiate any conversations about the Virago or the woods. Instead, we rode to the packed stadium in silence. Ruby's and my minds were devoured by boys whose thoughts we couldn't decipher, and Maya was lost in whatever held her attention out the window. We should have flown.

The stadium was packed. As usual, the entire town had made it out for the game. We found Gwen and sat with her and the several people she had with her, who were quickly becoming our usual crowd.

As the game clock ticked away, more people filled the already crowded bleachers. I only needed a few inches of space. Just enough to watch Ike the entire sixty minutes of play.

The formation looked like any other. I kept my eyes on Ike as he lined up across from the offense. I couldn't see his face behind his helmet, and I couldn't imagine anything but him smiling the way he had in physics, but I assumed he had some type of game face on. Something perfectly scary for the Penns Grove offense.

The ball was snapped, and Ike pushed past the line. He practically ran them over. They fell to his feet as he blazed through. He was diving toward the quarterback when a Penns Grove player hit him mid-dive. Their helmets met in a hideous clash that seemingly reverberated through the stands. The crowd around me shouted and booed for a penalty on the head-to-head contact.

Ike didn't move. His body had rolled onto his back as he hit the ground, and there he stayed. Several players surrounded him. The coach and athletic trainer ran onto the field. A hush fell on the stadium as it became clear both players involved in the collision were unconscious.

Wake up, Ike. Right now. Wake up.

I closed my eyes. The sight of him motionless was choking me. I couldn't breathe. I left the crowd of the bleachers, found an open spot on the fence lining the field, and leaned my elbows on it before dropping my head into my hands.

Wake up.

"Wait!" someone yelled, and I lifted my gaze in time to spot

Ike's mother. She stopped next to me and turned back to a man that looked like Ike with fire practically shooting from her eyes.

"I will not wait." Icy air flew off her. She stopped as she passed by and stared at me with recognition. She warmed, but not in a kind way. It was an angry fury burning through her, and she inhaled deeply gaining power from it.

"They'll take care of him." The man grabbed her arm, but she yanked it away as if he had never touched her and walked onto the field. She pushed past the athletic director and knelt beside her son.

Wake up.

Her head whipped in my direction, her eyes narrowing as if she'd heard me.

I jerked back from the fence for more distance between us, but I didn't take my eyes away from her or Ike.

"Dad, what's happening?" Gwen ran up next to me, and her dad came and stood beside her. With his arm around Gwen's shoulders, he watched in horror as the stretchers were rolled onto the field.

"He's going to be okay," Ike's father said and rubbed Gwen's arms. "Ike's tough."

The entire stadium was silent. What was there to say? No one knew exactly what was going on except the half dozen people surrounding the boys. Mrs. Kennedy didn't signal anything to her husband and Gwen. She was on her knees next to Ike's head.

The seconds dragged into grotesque minutes. Every moment was unbearable as the boys were loaded onto stretchers. There was a collective headshake as they were wheeled off the field and both sides of the stadium could only watch.

"We're going to Salem," Ike's mother called as she followed the paramedics.

"We'll follow you," he called back, and he and Gwen rushed to their car.

Wake up! Screamed in my head, throwing every ounce of frantic desperation I had into the demand. A moment passed as I watched Ike being loaded, and then his mother turned to face the crowd, her husband and daughter gone already.

"He's awake," she yelled right before the ambulance doors closed.

I exhaled.

"Let's go home." Ruby was done with the game. She was uninterested when we'd arrived, but now that there'd been a lull in the action, the excitement was completely lost to her. I was frozen against the fence. "All this school spirit is exhausting me."

She and Maya led the way as we walked back through the parking lot to Millbrook. We wandered down the street to the railroad tracks and traversed them for several feet until we were out of sight from the street and the houses. I was the first to run. Within three steps, I was invisible and airborne. Ruby and Maya followed me.

We soared over the stadium. The lights that illuminated the field were far below us. Two hawks flew next to us until we picked up speed and they couldn't keep up. Ruby and Maya drifted to my sides, only a few feet behind me.

We landed in our backyard and remained unseen until we opened the back door to our house.

"How was the game?" Lovie asked.

"Boring," Ruby said and flopped onto the sectional in the living room.

"Two boys were hurt," Maya continued.

"Oh no. Anyone I know?" Lovie asked as my mother walked into the room.

"No," I answered and stopped them from speaking. Ruby stared at me, perfectly aware of what I was hiding from our mothers. "I'm going upstairs."

I climbed the two flights in silence and lay on my bed in the corner of the room. The tapestry that hung above my bed billowed down from the ceiling and held me in a purple and turquoise cloud.

Mrs. Kennedy's coldness returned to me, and it was almost enough to make me believe my mother's warning that Ike's family was dark. Ike was nothing but warm, though. He drew me to him in the exact way his mother's glare pushed me away.

By the time Ruby and Maya came to bed, I was snuggled under the covers with my blanket over my head and my stuffed dog in my arms. The attic was drafty. I moved the air around us until it held the warm molecules close to our bodies.

Maya was the first to fall asleep. Ruby was always the last. I couldn't remember a time in our lives that I was awake and she wasn't. She needed half as much sleep as the rest of the population and suffered in silence every night as the rest of us left her alone.

Come to me.

My eyes shot open at the familiarity of his voice. His words in my head took my breath away.

Ike?

Come to me, Ever.

It was impossible. I shook my head. My mind was giving me what I wanted. I convinced myself that I was just worried about him. He was fine, and this was ridiculous.

Ever, come. Please.

I rolled over and hid my head under my pillow. I was losing my mind. Going crazy. He couldn't tell me anything. He couldn't hear me, either. He was Ike. Only women were witches, which meant Ike was incapable of talking to me telepathically.

Ever.

My name, inside my head, invaded my bed and left me adrift in my attic in Auburn, spinning in a storm of confusion.

Ever! he yelled. I was sure of it. He was calling to me, and I couldn't ignore him. I slid out from under my covers and faced Ruby in the moonlight from her window.

"Ever?" she whispered with shock covering her face.

"I'll be back. Just an hour." I arranged the covers up to my pillow.

"Do you even know where you're going?"

"My mom said all the roads lead to Auburn, so I'll head toward Salem until I see a sign for the hospital."

"Brilliant plan."

"It's easy out here. I'll fly low."

"Keep in touch."

I slid open the window by her head and jumped out. I was flying before I reached the second story roof.

I flew southwest through Auburn and across Route 40 until I saw the sign for the hospital. It was that easy. I followed the road, knowing that was usually the least efficient way to go but not willing to get lost. Tonight was not about exploring.

I stayed invisible as I entered the emergency room. The automatic doors opened, and the woman behind the counter stared toward me. Her brow furrowed as she stood and searched the doorway for whoever just walked in, but eventually sat and returned her attention to the papers in front of her and took a bite of a green apple. I waited next to her desk for someone to exit the restricted area, but no one came. The hospital was quiet. It was late at night, and there were no emergencies in Salem County.

Ever, come.

The door finally opened, and I walked through it, avoiding the uniformed police officer that was exiting. I followed the sound of Gwen's voice. She and her father were chatting outside a curtain. The muzzled terror on her father's face at the field had been replaced by a pleasant calm. He looked like Ike. I finally saw what my mother had seen in Ike the day outside of school. This man wasn't just Ike's father; he was *Ike* twenty years older.

I wanted to show myself to Gwen and ask about her brother, but I couldn't. She'd think I was crazy. I was beginning to think it myself.

Ike's mother emerged from behind the curtain followed by two nurses wheeling Ike out on a stretcher. The realization of my whereabouts and everything I was risking set in like a dark cloud over a summer day. I would see him, and his voice would stop in my mind. I would silence it. I was just worried about him. That was all.

His family surrounded him, even in the elevator as they rode to the third floor, and when he was transferred to the bed closest to the window in his room. Ike's mother kissed his forehead as his father and Gwen watched from the end of bed. They were close, and the absence of my father hit me again. I lowered my invisible head to avoid seeing them.

I turned to leave, but the Kennedys walked by me, exiting first. The nurses teased Ike about his mother's concern as his family left him alone for the night.

"I thought she'd never leave," he said, and the nurse laughed. "Imagine if there were really something wrong with me."

I moved closer. He was, after all, the person I'd come to see. It was more than that, though. Something stronger than both of us pulled me to him. The nurse lowered the top half of the bed until his head was only slightly raised. She adjusted the pillows behind him and placed one under his arm.

"Better to sleep like this?" she asked.

"Yes." Ike scanned the room as if he still expected his mother to be there. "No roommate tonight?"

"Three sixty-five B is officially empty tonight. The room's all yours." The nurse pressed several buttons on the machine standing to the side of Ike's bed and made sure his arm and IV were comfortably resting above his blankets. "I'm going to let you get some rest." She tied the call button to the side of his bed. "Just press this button if you need anything, and we'll come."

"Thanks for everything." His genuineness flowed over me.

We were alone. His hair was close to his head from the helmet and God knows what else had been done to him since he'd left the field. His eyes were almost as dark as his hair tonight. I could only see a hint of blue in their deep pools. He was thinking, and I wanted to know what about.

I started to leave. Ike was staring out the window. When I reached the doorway, I couldn't go. Just seeing him wasn't enough. I exhaled and showed myself before tiptoeing to his bedside.

"Ever," fell from his lips. My name, barely above a whisper, sent an electric current down my spine. "Thanks for coming." He spoke as though he'd been waiting for me rather than just hoping I'd show up.

"You must be exhausted. How's your head?" I whispered.

"A mild concussion. Nothing too serious." I rested my hands on the bedrail between us, relieved. "I could hear you when I was on the field. I could hear you yelling for me to wake up."

I shook my head. "I wasn't yelling."

Ike placed his hand on top of mine, and I watched as he squeezed my fingers. "I know you weren't yelling. I heard you inside my head."

I hid my shock at his words and kept my muscles soft as his hand still rested on my own. "You sound like a crazy person," I said to diminish it. All of it.

"I heard it. I'm sure of it, and you're not going to convince me I didn't."

"It was all in your head."

"And in yours," he said, and I lowered my eyes. I searched the threads of the white blanket covering him for answers to a question I'd never thought to ask. No one had ever heard me but another witch. One that was thinking of me and open to my words at the time. It was like throwing a ball to a friend who had their back to you. If they were expecting it, they'd turn and catch it. If not, it might bounce on the ground behind them and roll right by without them hearing a thing.

"I know you like me, Ever."

I stopped mid-thought. "What makes you think that?"

"I can feel it." His gaze moved from my lips to my eyes and a wave of heat spread through me. "Every time I touch you, I can tell." My breath caught. I swallowed hard the truth in his words. I flipped his hand over and traced the E in the lines of his palm. "Can you feel it?" he asked. His touch invaded me.

I closed my eyes and nodded. I'd let him have this one truth.

"Come here." Ike pulled my arm until I was leaning over his chest. I rested on my forearm on top of him. Our faces were only inches apart. I fought the urge to close my eyes and get lost in him. Everywhere my body touched him was on fire. He lit me up, and I sank into the warmth.

His lips were pale against his olive skin. He couldn't hear me. It was impossible. I looked him in the eye again and thought, *What am I thinking now?* Ike didn't move as I challenged him. *Kiss me.*

I waited, convinced he couldn't hear me. I memorized how his chest felt beneath my arm and the way his eyes darkened in the dim light. He was beautiful, even in a hospital gown and a stark white room.

Ike pulled me closer and kissed me. He paused, and shock ran through my body, chasing emotions I couldn't quite place with my bottom lip still touching his. I held my breath and hid behind my closed eyes. He kissed me again. This time, I let myself forget the implications and responded. The frenzy he'd created flowed through my body on top of him and my tongue inside of him. My fingers wrapped around his arm. I braced myself against climbing into the bed with him.

My lips rested on his as I inhaled, forcing myself to move back and put space between us.

I heard you.

I depleted every ounce of power within me not to react. "I have to go. I've broken a lot of rules to get here. Sneaking out of my house, taking my aunt's car, driving without a license," I said and backed away from him.

Whatever you say, Ever. My pace quickened with his voice in my head. *You can trust me.*

I was unseen as I walked out the door. I flew home not following the roads. I no longer needed them. The sky was lightening. It would be morning soon, and Ike was going to be okay.

I wasn't sure I was.

XIV

I STAYED AWAY FROM IKE on purpose the rest of the weekend. My mother thought Ike's family was dangerous, and I would have believed her if I'd never talked to him again after the bonfire. I should have been afraid of him or at least, repelled by him, but even my mother's warning couldn't tarnish the strength and safety I felt when I was near him. The only thing that terrified me was how little her warning mattered. I was tiptoeing on a tight rope suspended above my mother's head. If I fell, it was going to hurt us both.

I busied myself with nothing the way I used to in the months following my father's death. I could have laid on a blanket and looked at the sky for hours. I knew he was up there watching over me. My mom would come and lay with me sometimes, but most days, I was alone.

Today, Ruby and Maya were playing catch on the grassy patch between the trees and me. They each had a glove to catch the ball, but neither of them threw it. It just left their glove and landed in the other's. It was exercise for their mind not body. I let the predictable rhythm of their throws placate me.

My mother was watching. To anyone beside Ruby, Maya, and me, it appeared she was cleaning out the flower beds on the back of the house, but we knew she was listening and seeking and observing.

I inhaled the fall air. It filled me with relief. I needed some space from Ike Kennedy. Of that I was sure, but I couldn't seem to find any solace in the separation. I just wanted to be with him.

Ruby and Maya added another ball, and two of them flew through the sky at the same time.

When I got bored with watching them play, I offered to help with the weeding, which my mother declined. Lovie let me pitch in to make lasagna for dinner, but the whole time I was lost with Ike in my head. I caught her watching me twice while I layered in the mozzarella cheese.

I needed to get out. Up into the sky. My before-dinner flights were quickly becoming my habit in New Jersey. It wasn't too cold yet, but it got dark early, and I loved flying in the dark. My mother was not as big a fan of my new hobby as I was. I licked the spatula, placed it in the sink, and disappeared into the backyard without a goodbye.

I flew until I forgot about my mother and Lovie and my old house in Vermont. I soared through the sky and let the wind steal my thoughts. It was peaceful. When I felt renewed and ready to face my family again, I dropped down behind the tree line in our backyard and landed with a thump. I was tired. Too exhausted to be as careful as I should be. Ike Kennedy had stolen my sleep and whenever I'd been near him, I feared he'd stolen my sanity, too.

I showed myself right before walking into the clearing that was our backyard. Billy Roberts was standing in front of me and staring without a hint of surprise. He was expecting me.

"What are you doing here?"

He didn't flinch. "I came to see you." He glanced past me and then up to the moonless night sky. "Enjoying your evening?"

Every muscle in my body tightened to hide the chill he sent down my back. "Yes. It's beautiful out here."

Billy's eyes traveled from the top of my head, down my body, and finally rose to my eyes again. "Yes. It is." There was something almost sad about him, but I couldn't dwell on it because I was too busy managing my instinct to flee.

"Do Ruby and Maya know you're here?" Surely, they saw his car when he drove in, but if they had, they never would have let him near this area when I was flying.

Billy laughed a little. He found some humor in the absurdity of my question. "No." He shook his head. "They don't know."

"They didn't hear your car?" I took a few steps toward the house and kept the distance from Billy and me the same.

"I didn't drive." I looked at him confused. "I was out for a run and thought I'd stop in." Billy was wearing jeans and flip-flops.

"A run?" The light demeanor drained from him. "You don't seem like a runner."

He closed the distance between us. "What does a runner seem like, Ever?"

I didn't back away. Billy didn't scare me, and he should be clear on that fact. "Why are you here?" I asked again.

He smiled broadly. He enjoyed my challenging him more than my being cordial. Billy liked a fight. "I wanted to see if you're going to homecoming." My eyebrows rose before I could contain my shock.

My answer to this question suddenly seemed very important. Whatever Billy was thinking about him and me at the dance, I wanted him to stop. "Ruby, Maya, and I are going."

"Just the three of you?"

"Sam and Corey are driving us, but we're all just going as friends." I chastised myself for sharing the last part. Who I was going to the dance with was none of Billy's business.

His head bobbed in an exaggerated nod. "Nice guys." He moved closer to me until we were only a few inches apart. Billy was taller than I was, but not stronger. "I thought you might be going with Ike Kennedy."

Ike's name triggered some supernatural protective anger inside me. "You ran all the way out here—to Auburn—where you never come, to see if I'm going to homecoming with Ike?"

Billy reached behind me and separated my hair into two ponytails. I exhaled slowly to stifle the shivered reaction to his touch. "No. I came out here to see if you'd go with me." I didn't look away. I didn't smile. I'd give him nothing. "I think you and I are similar in the best kind of way."

"I don't see it." I was nothing like Billy, and his touch felt nothing like Ike's. I tugged on his wrists, but he tightened his grip around my hair. He pulled down until my chin was pointed toward the sky.

Billy leaned into me and whispered in my ear, "You will someday."

I was running through my mind the ways I was going to hurt him before he released me and stepped back. I lingered on the idea of him being hit in the groin over and over with a large branch from the tree to the right of us.

Ruby and Maya stepped into the light from the back patio and paused when they saw me talking to someone. By the looks of confusion on their faces, it was clear they couldn't see who it was.

Come, I thought, and they walked toward us. I relaxed with each step they got closer.

"I'll see you in school tomorrow," he said and left without

another word. Maya and Ruby glared at him as he passed. They stopped and watched him walk down our driveway.

"What was that about?" Maya asked when I reached them.

"Apparently, he wants me to go to homecoming with him."

"You said no, right?" Ruby crossed her arms.

"Of course I said no."

"Gwen hates him," Maya said.

"Do you know why?"

She shook her head. "I never asked." We started to walk toward the house together. "But I think he scares her."

"I think that's his hobby."

XV

TOOK OUT MY FAVORITE hoodie with the falcon embroidered on the front and put it on. As soon as I tightened the string around my neck, I was grateful I'd thrown it in my backpack. There'd been a chill in the air since last night. I spent the morning glancing around, waiting for Billy to suddenly be next to me or behind me. His frigid aura followed him instead of giving me warning. I could sense my mother, my coven, even Ike from a hundred feet away, but Billy seemed to always be a surprise.

Billy turned the corner by the office and almost ran right into me. We stopped inches apart and stared at each other. His forehead was bruised with an inch-long cut still bright red in the middle. His eyes were void of emotion, both the intrigue and dominance from the night before gone.

"What happened to your head?" I asked more out of habit than any care I had for his well-being.

Billy leaned back with a quizzical look. I waited for him to reach up and touch the subject of my question, but he just exhaled and straightened. "I didn't get home until late last night and Pops wasn't pleased."

He waited for my reaction as I hid my horror. I'd considered so many ways to injure him the night before and still the image of his own father doing just that disturbed me to the point of silence. The corner of Billy's mouth tilted up, and his eyebrows rose slightly. He liked throwing me with his candidness.

I left him standing in the hall without a word of sympathy. I wasn't sure what Billy deserved, but it wasn't to be hit in the head by his father. No one deserved that.

My morning dragged. History was the worst of it. After leaving Ike in physics, the day could end. I wished Mr. French would stop talking about Pearl Harbor and assign us pages to read. Anything to make the time go by faster.

Then, seven minutes before the end of class, the fire alarm rang through the halls. I covered my ears when we walked under the bell and out to the side yard of the school. Falling leaves floated to the pavement beneath us as we made our way to the lawn.

Mr. French walked down the line, taking attendance as he went. I was last, right behind Paul Wentzel. As soon as Mr. French returned to the front of the line, Paul took out his phone, read the screen, and handed it to me.

I just stared at it between us.

"Ike wants to talk to you," Paul said as though there were nothing surprising about the statement.

"Really?" I searched the lines on either side of us. I didn't see Ike in any of them.

"Really."

I took the phone from his hand and read the text Paul had just gotten, which told him to hand me his phone. I looked up, still trying to figure out what was going on, but then the phone buzzed with another text. Paul lifted his eyebrows and tilted his head at his phone in my hand.

The second text read: Meet me in the custard stand's parking lot when this drill is over. Paul will get your backpack from the classroom.

Mr. French stared each of us down in the same way the other teachers were policing their own classrooms. I had three minutes until lunch. If Paul grabbed my backpack, no one would miss me until Spanish. Ike's ability to formulate this plan made me wonder if the fire alarm wasn't a surprise to him.

The order of the texts I wanted to send back was something like: what, why, and how? What I actually typed into Paul's phone before hitting send was: Okay. I deleted the entire group of messages before handing him his phone back just as the bell rang and we were allowed back into the building. Paul was getting my backpack. I disappeared.

I stood still while every student filed back in. Several teachers faced away from the building, watching for stragglers, but they couldn't see me. I looked for Ike, but he was nowhere to be found, either.

I walked across the side lawn to the front of the building and waited for two cars on the horseshoe drive to pass me before crossing it and descending the hill on the other side. The traffic on Route 40 was busy since it was lunchtime. No one stopped for me, even in the crosswalk, because no one knew I was there.

I'd never skipped school before. I couldn't think of a single time I wasn't exactly where I was supposed to be. When I was almost to the custard stand, Ruby was frantic in my head.

Where are you?

I'm at Cream Valley.

I knew that wasn't going to be the end of it, but stating it in a matter-of-fact way calmed my nerves.

Huh? Maya chimed in.

I'm skipping lunch and meeting Ike.

There was nothing but silence from either of them. It was almost as unnerving as walking behind the custard stand and seeing Ike astride his motorcycle waiting for me. He was holding a helmet in his hands. I stopped and let my eyes linger on his thighs and his thick waist before I realized I'd stopped moving.

Don't worry about me. I'll be back before lunch is over.

I walked over and stood next to Ike. His forever-stern expression broke, and a small smile warmed me. It reminded me of how different he seemed carrying mums for his mother.

"I want to take you out to lunch," he said, and I realized I was half-expecting him not to be here when I showed up.

"That's perfect."

He raised his eyebrows at me and asked, "Why's that?"

"I want you to take me to lunch." He handed me the helmet, and I climbed on the back of the motorcycle. Something else I'd never done before. It was safe to say that if my mother drove by and saw me skipping school and riding on a motorcycle, she'd never believe her sight.

Ike handed me his backpack, and I put it on. I leaned in tight against him and wrapped my arms around his stomach. Instead of grabbing my wrists, I rested each hand flat against him.

He took off east on Route 40, and I searched for a way to feel the wind on my face with his enormous body in front of me. Ike drove the speed limit. After a few minutes, he made a left onto Avis Mill Road and turned into a driveway. There were no cars parked on the gravel. No windows open in the house. He stopped the motorcycle behind an out building that was neither a garage nor a barn.

Ike leaned back against me and said, "We're here." I'd never been more disappointed to reach a destination. I could have held him close to my body in this exact position until the sun set. He put the kickstand down, and I stepped off.

Inside the small structure, there were three pieces of furniture that appeared to be midway through refurbishment, a tractor that looked to be in the middle of repairs, and a couch, chair, and coffee table off to the side.

Ike slid the backpack off my shoulders. His closeness was confusing me. I reveled in the loss of thought and in Ike Kennedy. "I bought a ham and cheese sandwich with mustard and an Italian sub," he said and took the sandwiches out of the bag and placed them on the coffee table.

I stopped scanning the room and faced him. "I'll take whichever one you don't want." There was not a sound in the building. Ike and I were successfully hidden from the rest of the world. "Where are we?"

"It's Ty's house. This is his dad's workshop." He sat on the couch and moved the ham sandwich in front of him. "We hang out here sometimes."

I was frozen in my spot until he looked up at me. "Do you bring a lot of girls here?" It mattered. Without my knowledge, I'd developed a relationship with Ike that hinged on his answer to this question. I couldn't be just one of the others to him, because he was already far beyond that for me.

He stopped opening the bag of Doritos and stared at me as if I should know the answer, but I couldn't let myself assume anything. "Pleading the fifth?" I asked and tried not to let him hear the disappointment in my voice.

"I've never brought anyone here." He was quiet. Serious. "I wanted to take you to my house. I live on a lake and I wanted to go on a canoe ride, but I didn't think we'd have enough time."

Satisfied with his answer, I sat. I unwrapped the Italian sub he'd picked up at Heritages and tried to digest the fact that Ike and I were having lunch together. We ate in silence until I finally asked, "So why did you bring me here?"

"I wanted to see you away from physics . . . or a party." He faced me. "I needed to be alone with you." His words were attached to a thick air that weighted down each syllable as they entered my body and touched me everywhere.

"To tell me a secret?" I teased him. His eyes covered every inch of me as if searching for the answer to a question he hadn't asked. It was only after he smiled that I remembered to laugh and contribute more than just words to the conversation.

Ike leaned into me until his face was only inches from my own. I held my breath and my eyes open. "Actually, I was hoping you'd share one with me." His voice was almost desperate. "Ever."

I froze. I wasn't sure how far he was going to go with this. He'd returned to our innocent discussions of nothing since the hospital. It was our safe place. My security. The only way I could continue to see him was if he dropped the questions of what I was or the things that I could do.

He reached up and ran the backs of his fingers down the side of my jaw. I closed my eyes to hide from him. Ike held my face in his hands, igniting my senses as he moved. I could have let him take it all from me. He inched closer to me and said, "You can trust me." My head fell to the side in his hand, and he kissed my neck. His lips trailed down. My back arched at the sensation as I inhaled deeply at the touch. There was such gentleness from the enormous grizzly beside me.

I couldn't shake the need that consumed me.

I treaded there until my eyes opened, and reality snapped me back.

I couldn't do this.

My mother would kill me.

He was forbidden.

"I need to get back," I forced out.

I shocked him. He thought we were together. I assumed he was trying to figure out where I'd left him.

"Go out with me Saturday night." Ike's voice soothed me, immediately. He was unfazed by my intention to leave. His hands returned to his sides. My gaze followed them there.

"Saturday night is homecoming," I absently said.

"I know. I want you to skip it and go somewhere with me." He wasn't joking. His voice was rough. The words had been buried and were finally clawing their way to his surface.

"Where?" I was only going through the motions. I'd follow him anywhere. I just wasn't ready to admit it to him.

"I want to show you something before it gets too cold."

I waited for him to continue. I needed him to explain why tomorrow night was so important, and why he wasn't going to the dance. When it was clear he was done sharing, I asked, "That's all?"

"That's all." Ike leaned over and kissed me again. It was a peck, but his lips rested against mine. It was my choice if I wanted this to go further, but I knew that if I did, I'd be lost to him, so I reluctantly pulled back.

"Should I pick you up?" he asked, and I opened my eyes.

A million scenarios ran through my head. All of them ending with my mother saying no and locking me away somewhere because he was at all times to be avoided.

"I need to check on a few things and get back to you. Ruby, Maya, and I were supposed to go to the dance together." Ike stared at his backpack on the floor at our feet dejectedly. "I want to go with you," I said and willed him to believe me. I wanted there to be no question of who I'd rather be with on Saturday night. "I just have to figure it out. My mother is . . . strict."

He looked confused, which made sense since I'd been out every weekend I'd lived here. Seemingly with barely a curfew or questions being asked. The reality was I had only one rule, and it was to stay away from him.

"About certain things she's strict," I admitted.

"Go to the dance. I'll pick you up there."

"I'll be in a dress. You can't pick me up on your motorcycle."

"I'll borrow Paul's truck."

"Why?" I wanted him to get down on one knee and profess his love to me. I was insane. Knowing him and wanting him were unraveling the fibers of my being.

"I'll explain everything Saturday. I'll meet you behind the school at eight."

"It isn't that easy. They watch the doors. You have to have a note to leave the dance early."

He shook his head in frustration. "Why do people go to these?"

I leaned into his body and tilted my lips toward his ear. "Because it's nice to dance with someone once in a while." He stopped breathing. "I'll figure it out. Pick me up behind Wawa."

"Wawa? What if someone sees you?"

"No one will." I sat back. "Just park behind it and wait. I'll be there at eight."

XVI

BESIDES FUNERALS, I NEVER GOT to dress up with Ruby and Maya, and I'd never worn a dress like *this* to a funeral. Our mothers had been more excited than we were to go shopping. They reveled in the day as if they were the trio attending the dance and not us. I half-expected them to start trying on dresses themselves.

Maya's dress was my favorite. It was electric blue, tight, and stunning next to her dark hair. She belonged somewhere other than Woodstown, New Jersey, but that went for all of us no matter what we were wearing.

A scream rang out from the attic. Even through the shrill voice, I knew it was Maya. I followed our mothers as they flew up the two staircases to our room. Ruby was staring at Maya who was holding her dress in her hands. Tears ran down the sides of her face as she turned the dress toward us. The front was shredded and covered in hideous red stains that appeared to be blood.

Oh, my God. Lovie's words echoed the solemn pit in my stomach. *How could they?*

Ruby, Maya, and I stared at her.

"They haven't been in Auburn in a hundred years. At least. What makes them think they can come here today?" My mind swirled, trying to make sense of what Sloane was saying. "They've come too close." Her mouth was pursed as if she might spit on the dress. "And they've gone too far."

"The protection spell should have outlasted all of us." My mother's eyes never left the dress in Maya's hands. "Regardless of who moves in or out of Auburn. This land is sacred."

"Says who?" Ruby asked.

"Our great great grandmothers." Sloane's voice was filled with disgust. "The last time there was a war with the Virago."

Small nods of heads, dips of foreheads, and one disgusted snort came from our mothers as they went back and forth in silence.

"We'll get you a new dress," Lovie told her daughter. "I promise."

Our mothers left us alone in our attic. We checked every inch of it for anything else that had been touched. I leafed through the pages of the books stacked on my nightstand until I noticed the page missing from my journal. It was ripped out clean except for a tiny corner that had been left behind. I ran my fingers down the thread of the binding as Maya's cell phone rang. No one ever called us. The ringing was ominous in our breached castle walls.

"Hello," she said with an easy tone after seeing the caller's name. She mouthed "Gwen" to us.

"Oh nothing. Just cleaning my room." Maya kept moving books as she listened. She stacked the last one and looked back at Ruby and me when she said, "No. We're fine, but thanks for checking on us."

When she hung up, Ruby asked, "What was that?"

"She knew," Maya said. "Not what happened or who we're afraid of, but she said she just had a weird feeling." I let go of the dress I was inspecting in our closet. "Probably the same way I knew she was in the bathroom last Tuesday crying over Dave."

"You didn't tell us about that," I said.

"It wasn't a big deal."

"Until now. What do you think it means?" But Maya and Ruby just looked at me, none of us had the answer and none of us slept that night. Our fortress had been invaded and we didn't feel safe.

"Wretched" was the first word I heard after the sun rose. I opened my eyes to the sounds of our mothers still going on about Maya's dress. Unbelievable, appalling, disrespectful, disgusting. The list of adjectives was long and perverse and included many words I'd never heard my mother say before. They were utterly beside themselves that someone had been in our house. Lovie made us breakfast. We ate in silence. Each of us appearing more exhausted than the witch to her right.

"We'll go to the mall today and look for a new dress," my mom told Maya.

"It's okay. My friend, Gwen, is going to bring one in that she said I can borrow."

"Who's Gwen?" Sloane asked. Our mothers gave high alert a new extreme.

"She's fine. Just some girl about my size in my algebra II class. If the dress doesn't work, we can go shopping."

I liked Gwen's dress even better than Maya's original one. Somehow, Gwen had dug through her closet and picked out the one frock that suited Maya more than anything in the stores. As Maya hugged her with gratitude, love washed over me. The Kennedy family could not be dark. Not even if my mother said they were.

I'm not going into the dance, I thought as I examined myself in the mirror.

Ruby stopped applying her mascara and stood to face me. She tilted her head to the side. I knew she was gauging me. She had the patience of a cat.

"Where are you going?" She must have been satisfied with my excitement. "Do I even have to ask?"

"No. You don't."

Maya stepped into the bathroom and caught on immediately. "You're not going?"

I shook my head. The less I said aloud, the better. My mother had backed off the surveillance detail and seemed to believe I was respecting her wishes and staying away from Ike. I'd never disobeyed her before, not once in the sixteen years I'd been alive.

"As long as you two are okay going alone."

"To the high school? I think we'll survive." Ruby was insulted.

"I'm not sure you should take this lightly. My mother hasn't stopped mumbling obscenities since they were in here."

"Yeah, well you're lucky because my mom doesn't mumble."

"I hope you know what you're doing," Maya said with nothing but concern in her voice.

"Me, too." I braided one side of my hair and clipped the end to the matching braid on the other side.

"What is it about him that makes you do this?"

I let go of my hair and stared at Ruby in the mirror. "I don't know. He makes me forget how sad I am. How sad I was." In the mirror, I could see the blush rushing to my cheeks. "He replaced a piece of me that was missing. I'm whole." The thought of Ike was making me hot. I fanned myself. "And I've been lit on fire."

I relaxed in Ruby and Maya's closeness and realized they had only understanding. They were the only two that ever would. We'd known the same torture of losing our fathers and moving to

Auburn, but we also knew we were meant for something different than what we had. With Ike, I could feel myself coming into it.

"Stay in touch. Corey is supposed to be bringing us home so you'll need to time your arrival perfectly."

"I know. Ten thirty, right?"

"It ends at ten thirty," Maya said.

"How are you going to pull this off?"

"I don't know."

For a person who could literally disappear, removing myself from the homecoming dance was proving to be a daunting endeavor.

Corey and Sam picked us up in Corey's father's SUV. Corey and Sam's parents came, too so they could snap their own sets of pictures. Our mothers tried to appear of this earth. They wore jeans and sweaters and didn't have any makeup on, but even in the way they moved it was clear they were ethereal beings living together in some sort of spiritual awakening the rest of the world hadn't discovered yet.

The other adults were gracious. There was the brief examination of how they all knew each other. Our mothers were a few years younger than their parents, but of course, they could place each other. Corey's father gave him a stern warning about drinking and driving, to which he scoffed at because everyone entering the dance was given a breathalyzer test. I wondered if Ike knew that little detail. He could add it to the plentiful reasons he'd already collected for *not* attending school dances. Pictures were taken. It felt like three thousand, and then we were released to have fun at the dance.

We parked on Millbrooke. When the rest of my group took their first steps toward the school, I bent down and disappeared.

"Where's Ever?" Sam asked.

"She changed her mind," Ruby said, and when he looked behind them and started to ask more questions, she winked at him and said, "It's nothing for you to worry about." Ruby slipped her arm around Sam's elbow, and he forgot all about me.

It was already after eight, but I'd texted Ike on the ride over that I'd be a little late. I ran three steps in my heels and flew to the other side of town where Wawa was lit up and full of people.

I found Ike parked in Paul's truck out back with the passenger door away from the convenience store. It was perfect. *He* was perfect. I opened the door and appeared as I climbed into the truck.

He jumped in his seat and settled into a stunned expression. My dress became tiny and fragile in the pickup, or maybe it was in Ike's stare. The magenta brocade flowers and the short hem felt ridiculous next to Ike in his jeans and T-shirt, which were at place in Paul's truck. I wished I hadn't come. The sudden urge to apologize overtook me.

"You're beautiful." His words paralyzed the self-doubt running through my mind. A warmth spread over my thighs and up my chest. I raised my eyes to meet his stare. I exhaled and did the only thing I could do. I smiled at him.

The traffic in and out of Wawa was endless. Everyone needed gas, milk, cigarettes, or some other item of convenience. The store was more central to our town than a church. I was beginning to understand it was somewhat of a religion in the area.

"We should go," I said, not wanting to be recognized. Actually, I didn't really care. I just didn't want my night to end before it even started.

Ike put Paul's truck in gear and headed back toward Auburn. The bench seat felt seven feet wide as we rode in silence. I could move next to him. Just unbuckle my seatbelt and slide over as if he'd invited me to. I clasped my hands together in my lap and fought for some control.

"Where are we going?"

"It's close. Right up here." He kept his eyes on the road, and I didn't move from the safety of my seat against the window.

He pulled into the old Laurel Hills development and drove toward the back. There were no sidewalks and all the houses were surrounded by woods throughout most of it. It was difficult to even know where some of the homes were except for the entry to their driveways. I'd flown over the area before. We were coming to the end because the creek that ran next to my house was coming up. There was no way to cross it from inside the development.

Ike turned onto a dirt lane, which was barely visible between two driveways a quarter mile apart from each other, and down a steep hill.

I leaned my head against the window and stared at the trees above us. In the moonlight, their orange, and red, and yellow hues were less of a contrast. *DO NOT GO INTO THE WOODS,* beat against the inside of my head.

Still, when Ike pulled to a stop, got out, and walked around the front to my side, all caution I had fled. He opened my door, and the sweet gesture threw me a little. I wasn't used to him making an effort to impress anyone, or maybe it was the gentleness of it that was hard to place.

"Good call on the motorcycle. You definitely couldn't have ridden in this dress." He held out his hand, and I took it as I slipped off the seat to the ground in front of him. I wanted to kiss him. That was what a normal girl would do.

He closed the truck door and walked away from me. After three steps, he whirled around and faced me with his hands on his waist. "I brought you out here to show you something, but also to tell you a few things."

This sounded like a lecture. "What kind of things?" The night air chilled me. I crossed my arms at my chest.

Ike ran his hand through his hair and stared at the sky before zeroing in again on me. "When I was lying in the woods, about to be arrested for drinking, you came to me and held me so the police couldn't see us."

My breath caught. There was no way he could know that for sure.

"Ever." My name from his lips brought me back to him. "You were on top of me, and I wanted us to stay that way—hidden from the rest of the world. Together." I shook my head. Slowly at first, but almost violently by the time I could speak.

"I don't care how we disappeared or how you found me in the middle of the woods. None of it matters, Ever." He lowered his voice and said, "But before I had a chance to convince you that you could trust me, you were gone."

Ike moved closer to me. My mind raced around the image of him in front of me. I couldn't separate the honesty in his voice from the impossibility of his words. "So, I was left wondering if I was losing my mind." He was unbearably close. In every way. "Monday in school, you returned to acting as if you hardly knew me. As if it'd never happened."

"It didn't."

He almost laughed. He was toying with me. I stepped back because that was what you did when danger was near you. "And then I got hurt on the football field." I stopped moving and focused. I searched his eyes for the darkness my mother had warned me about, but all I saw was Ike. "And I heard you, Ever. I *heard* you yelling for me to wake up in my head. I didn't imagine it. It was you." I shook my head in denial, but tears were filling my eyes. "You came to the hospital, and you knew I could hear you, but you still didn't trust me there."

"You're wrong." About that he was. I always trusted him, even when I shouldn't have, but witchcraft wasn't only my secret to share. His not being allowed to know had nothing to do with him and me. It was a secret that belonged to the beginning of time.

"And then I kissed you . . . and I decided you had to be mine. I wasn't going to share you, and I wasn't going to lose you." I stood in shock at every word. "I don't care what you are or how you do the things you do, and I know I'm not crazy. I can tell by the way you look at me, even in school, that you feel the same way about me that I do about you."

"What do you want?" My jaw barely moved as I spoke. I was clinging to my sanity as he professed his own.

He held my face in his hands and tilted it to him. "I want you to kiss me tonight and not disappear." I closed my eyes. This was impossible. "I want you, Ever."

I stepped away from him and the cold washed over me. The ground around me was covered with fallen leaves already. They'd all be gone in a few weeks. If I told my mother about this, we'd be gone, too. I opened the truck door and grabbed my purse.

Ike stared at me. The anger in his stare echoed the betrayal of my actions. He was dangerous. He had to be. I closed my eyes and hid myself from him.

"Ever," he pleaded. I took three steps away and flew into the night. I let my tears fall to the ground beneath me. I had to tell my mother all of this. She was right. There was no other explanation. Ike had to be something or else he wouldn't be able to hear me and feel me. I followed the creek until I reached the bank by my house.

I flew low until I heard his voice in my head. *Ever.*

The night air swirled around me, but all I could feel was Ike. I wanted him to be good so I could have him. So I could keep the warmth forever. Maybe I'd created the Ike I wanted in my mind. If my dad were here, he would have liked Ike. My dad would talk to my mother. He'd make her understand. He'd help me convince her that Ike was good.

I landed at the back of my house and remained invisible. My mother and Sloane were at the kitchen table reading books and taking more notes. Sloane said something to my mother, causing her to toss her notebook on the table in disgust.

Ever. I never told a soul. I'll never tell anyone.

His words stabbed through the center of my chest.

He hadn't even let on that something was amiss, but this entire time he'd been watching me, or waiting for me. I hated my mother for making it so I couldn't talk to her about him. About *this*, but she'd kill me if she knew I was anywhere near him, and I couldn't stay away. He made me happy, and I trusted him. Even if I shouldn't, I did.

Come back to me.

I stared at the tree line behind my house. The truth I always knew, but had been unable to face, struck me.

I didn't care what Ike was.

I launched and flew east at full speed. Ike was staring into the night sky as I flew over him. He was waiting for me with the same patience he'd had all these weeks he'd known a secret that history wouldn't let be told. I landed in front of him and showed myself. I pulled him to me with my arms wrapped around his neck and pressed my lips against his. He pushed me against the side of the truck and kissed me until I forgot everything except how much I needed him in my life. I felt him against my thighs, and a new need coursed through me. I'd never been kissed that way before. I'd never known the force of Ike Kennedy before, either.

"I'll never tell," he said.

No one knew. Only Ruby and Maya, and they were like me. Ike was just a boy. I almost laughed at the thought. He was far from *just* anything. He watched me as I calmed. He kissed me once more.

"There's something I want to show you." He took my hand and led me farther into the woods to a tree twice the width of me with wooden stairs nailed to the side of it. My gaze followed the stairs up to a tree house twenty feet above us.

"It's so high."

"I know. It's easier going up than coming down."

"Especially in heels."

I spun around and stepped back until I was standing directly in front of him. I inhaled and reveled in his closeness before reaching down and taking each of his hands.

"What are you doing?" he asked as I positioned his arms around my shoulders. He held me tight against the front of him and kissed my cheek.

"Hold on," I said and moved my face away from his lips. We disappeared.

It was as if we were cemented to the ground. I'd launched before without a running start, but with Ike, I didn't move at all. I bent my knees slightly and inhaled. When I released my breath, I shot us into the air and landed on the wrap around porch of Ike's tree house. His breath drew in and his arms locked around me. His excitement infiltrated me. Ike liked to go fast. His heart raced against my back, and I wanted to feel it beating next to me forever.

"Wow," he said breathless, and I turned in his arms and held him tight to me as we reappeared. Impressing him filled me with the pride I'd buried with my father. It also unhinged me. I already trusted him to keep my secret, and the fact that I did made me question whether I should trust myself. "Was that hard?"

"Much harder than I'd thought it'd be." I'd never flown with someone else attached to me before. "No running start."

"Is that how it usually works?"

Not once in my life had I ever explained an element of my power. "Do you mind if we don't talk about it right now?"

Ike searched my eyes for some other answer, an explanation as to why I didn't want to share, but I'd already revealed enough for one night.

"Come inside."

There was an actual door. The last tree house I'd entered was in Vermont on my neighbor's property. I'd been there once while their oldest daughter babysat me, but she wouldn't let me climb the tree to see the inside, which was ridiculous considering I'd been flying into it without her since I was five.

Ike's tree house was about eight feet by six feet. There was a three-sided table in the corner with bug spray, a lighter, and a deck of cards on it. There were a few gallons of water next to the table and a lone candle in the middle of the floor.

"A candle? In a tree house?"

"I know. I'll light the candle in a minute. I want to show you the best part first."

He unlatched wooden panels in the ceiling and let them fall toward us. He hooked each one to the edge of the ceiling. The sky was exposed and every star in it shone like diamonds.

"Wow." I let my head fall back and watched the stars above us.

"The first time I saw you, I wanted to bring you here."

I faced Ike. "Why?"

"I don't know . . . but now that you're here, I don't want you to leave." He kissed me again. I pulled him closer as I fed off the strength I felt when I was with him. I stood on my tiptoes until he lifted me up. I could have stayed in his tree house forever.

He lowered me to the floor with the gentleness of breeze, but I wouldn't break. He walked over to the corner table and picked up the lighter. He tested it above the candle. Behind him, carved in the wall by the floor, was *H + I*.

"Did you do that?"

He turned to see what I was talking about. "What?"

"The initials?" Ike plus someone.

"No. It was there since my dad's time." I stopped running through every girl I'd met at Woodstown whose name started with an *H*. "This was his tree house when he was young. My grandmother still lives on the property."

"Interesting."

"Yeah, especially since my mom's name is Gisel." Ike winced in a funny way, as if he'd just told his mother that his father was in love with another woman.

I swallowed hard. The truth was rising and choking me.

"What?" he asked.

Gisel, my mother, her hatred of his family, the Virago, Auburn, it all rang through my mind. I was swarmed by glimpses of memories trying to fit together as the truth. I was so close. I could almost touch the words, and then my phone alarm rang on the floor next to us.

"I have to go." I found my phone in my purse and shut off the alarm.

"When can I see you again?"

The question, and my alarm, brought me back to reality, the one that didn't include Ike because my mother had made him off limits. "About that. My mother seems to feel strongly that I should stay away from you." I could barely get out the last word. It sounded even more absurd telling Ike in his tree house than when my mother had first said it.

"I got the same speech from my mother."

"What?" I stepped back so I could see him. He was completely serious and as forlorn by the situation as I was. "She told you to stay away from *me*? What have I done?"

"What have I done?" He chuckled at me as he asked.

"Well, you're Ike Kennedy. Dark and brooding, motorcycle-riding rebel. You're a mother's nightmare." I exaggerated the words and stood on my tiptoes to kiss him near the ear. "But me? I'm an angel."

"Is that what you are?" I held my breath. He still didn't know that much about me. Just that I wasn't like him, but if he could hear me in his head, he wasn't what I thought he was, either.

Why do you think you can hear me? I asked.

Maybe because I love you.

You barely know me.

"I know more than anyone else," he said, and a lost sense of security covered me with his words. He was dangerously close, and that was exactly where I wanted him. "And I'm a lover."

"I have to go." The weight of my words were crushing me.

"I have a lot of questions."

"Me, too." I reached down, blew out the candle, and disappeared. The smoke from the wick billowed into the air, and I flew out the roof with it. When I cleared the trees, I looked down and Ike was staring into the night sky. *See you soon, Lover.*

XVII

"I THINK WE SHOULD GO," Lovie said. I heard her, but I was barely listening. Ike was talking to me inside my head and every word was critically important. I clung to him and the fact that he truly knew me. The secrets between us were intoxicating.

"I'm just not sure it's fair to them," my mother said.

I love you, came through. Ike kept telling me, but I never responded the same. It wasn't because I wasn't one hundred percent certain that I loved him more than anyone I'd ever met before in my life, but because . . . it was hard to love someone my mother hated. I sighed and thought back, *You're a lover.* Ike was never insulted. He was amused.

"We would do it for them. We *have* done it, and our mothers before us. The Virago is a common enemy."

The word Virago caught in my mind. "What are you guys talking about?"

All three of them turned and faced Ruby, Maya, and me. "There's a . . . party," my mother said and then looked at Sloane and Lovie for approval. They nodded as if party was as good a word as any. "In the next county up. There will be a lot of witches there, and we want to ask them what this area has been like since we left."

"Been like?"

"What's going on with the Virago."

I'd never been around a lot of witches. In fact, I'd never actually met a witch outside the women in this room. "Really? Like how many?"

My mother shook her head. "It's hard to say. A witch from Kingsway, Tara Jane, and her coven host it every year. It's been a part of their family for a while."

"Have you guys been before?"

All of our mothers stared at each other with dulled facial expressions. "Once. When we were almost your age. Our mothers brought us."

"By the looks of you guys, it was a great time." Ruby said what we were all thinking.

"It was," my mom said in a way that should have ended the conversation.

Sloane chimed in with, "The Kingsway coven is *always* a good time." She leaned back and smiled at the ceiling as if remembering a specific night that she wasn't going to share. I wondered if there were going to be witches there our age. If they were attending Kingsway while we were surviving Woodstown. If their mothers looked like ours and if they too had lived their entire lives afraid of an invisible group of witches called the Virago.

We drove to the house on High Street in Mullica Hill. From the outside, it looked like any other house decorated for Halloween. We parked on the street and followed our mothers as they passed the cars in the driveway to the front walk. Sloane and my mom moved to the side, letting Lovie stand between them. She turned to look at both of them and then knocked. Lovie would be my first choice, too. She was always the sweetest.

The door opened and the music wafted outside and met the smoke from the fire burning out back.

"Lovie," the woman said with an enormous exhale. "Why, it's been forever."

"We were wondering when you guys would come by," another woman said as she peeked over the shoulder of the one in front who was waving us in.

"Get in here before they see you."

It wasn't necessary to explain who "they" were.

We entered a large room with dark wooden floors. Henna tattoos were being done by a woman seated on the piano stool, and the sign hanging above her head said: 1,417th Annual Goddess Gala. Our mothers were engulfed by women dressed in casual clothes, flowing dresses, and costumes befitting a Halloween affair. Ruby, Maya, and I stood back and took it all in.

"Would you like a program?" The woman who asked carried a stack of booklets in her arms. She was tall with a collusive grin.

"Sure." I flipped through the papers. There were twelve in all, listing ten different sessions of performances, teams, hometowns, warm-up times, competition times, and room locations. "What is this?"

"First time?" the woman who handed us the pamphlets asked, her warm brown eyes welcoming.

"Yes."

"Well, let me go over the program with you."

Ruby and Maya watched over my shoulder as the woman waved her hand in front of the first page. The paper changed from white to black and the words were no longer a concise type. They were cursive and written with a silver pen.

"Perhaps this will make more sense."

"No." Ruby shook her head as she spoke. The woman only laughed at the three of us.

"It's simple really. The competitions take place throughout the night. There's flying for both speed and distance, weight lifting with your mind, of course, telekinesis and archery."

"Archery?" Of all things, why archery?

"I know. We just all really like it, so we put it in. You're not allowed to use any powers, though." She flipped through until we reached the end of the archery section. "These last few pages tell you the courses that are offered and give a description of each." I saw Group Messaging, Flying in Bad Weather, Using Aerial Cues, History, Politics, The Earth Witch, and finally my eye caught on Relationships with Witchcraft.

"What is the Earth witch?" Maya asked and leaned farther over my shoulder to read the program in my hands.

The woman's eyes narrowed just a hint as her head tilted to the side. She scrutinized us as if she were listening to something or to someone. She might have been smelling us. I wasn't sure what was going on. "None of you." We looked at each other and back at her. "You're missing your Earth witch. Did something happen to her?" Sadness overtook her. It fell from her eyes like tears. Her sympathy was misplaced on us.

We weren't missing a thing. "Nothing." Maya finally spoke on all our behalves.

"Well, something did."

Someone called, "Jennifer" from across the room.

"One minute," the woman standing in front of us yelled back.

"I need you *now*."

Jennifer rolled her eyes. "Are you guys married? No. You're too young to be married. These witches are sometimes like husbands . . . a pain." The woman who yelled widened her eyes and tilted her head reiterating her emergency. "Don't get married young. Your friends will be enough for a while."

"Jennifer!"

"If you don't kill them." She laughed a little.

I looked between the two of them, trying to make sense of their exchange and every picture on the wall and each person standing near them.

"Enjoy yourself," Jennifer said and walked away.

"This place is bizarre," I whispered never taking my eyes off her.

"In all the right ways," Ruby added. "Let's go see what's outside."

The backyard was a bright, beautiful, unbelievable attraction with screams and cheers, objects floating, and women chanting. My attention drifted in every direction, trying to take it all in. Instead of sticking together, we split up. It was the most efficient way to see and hear as much as possible. We promised to meet by the food in an hour, but as I looked around the living room where people were floating in the air above us, I knew stopping to eat would be a challenge.

I went to several classes, which were held in different areas of the house. My final of the night was Relationships with Witchcraft. If Ike and I were ever going to be more than a girl staring at the guy in front of her in physics, I was going to have to figure out how to have an actual relationship. As a witch.

Based on the attendance of the class, I wasn't the only one who struggled with the subject. How much do you tell someone? Who can you trust? It wasn't as if we could erase a person's memory for the past ten years if a marriage didn't work out. Witches in general were a loyal bunch. Both because of the tremendous necessity for keeping our secrets and because we were raised in such close circles of friendship. The coven was regarded higher than family. This commitment to relationships transferred to our marriages. The incidence of divorce for witches was below four percent, which was much lower than for the rest of the world, but there were still break ups to manage.

I sat in the downstairs bedroom as the others filed out. There was so much swirling around in my head, I could barely halt it long enough to solidify a question, but with every detail I'd gathered, the one constant on my mind was Ike.

I approached the lecturer as she slid folders into her bag. "Excuse me," I said, unsure if I was allowed to talk to the speakers.

"Yes. Ever."

"How did you know my name?"

"It's one of my gifts."

"Can we all do that?"

She studied me for a moment, making me feel like an eight year old. "No. We're all only humans, and we each have different gifts. Some people are Olympic caliber runners, some have perfect pitch, and others can multiply multi-digit decimals in their heads. We can fly and move things with our minds." I was sure I appeared confused, but her words made perfect sense. The explanation situated my family within the rest of the world in a way that was comforting. "Our covens are our team, and on our team, we have some players that are better at some things than others."

"I'm a flyer."

"Yes. I know." She was fully smiling, and I assumed it wasn't because she'd caught my earlier competition. "We all have the potential for different abilities, and some can be cultivated through practice, but there's no guarantee on what each of our gifts will be."

"Can I ask you about something else?"

"Yes." For the first time since she'd noticed me, she appeared confused.

"Who are the Virago? The dark witches?"

She stood perfectly straight. "No wonder I couldn't sense your question. They're far from understood."

"I'm learning that."

"Have you encountered the darkness?"

"I don't know." Fear for what Ike's family was bore down on me.

"You'd know. Lost witches can be clever, but to another witch, they can't completely hide. Just like when you meet any other witch. You just know."

"Tonight's the first time that I've met another witch."

Her head tilted in surprise. "Really?"

"Yes. We recently moved here from Vermont."

"How is it there? I've barely been out of New Jersey."

"Huh?" I must have heard her wrong.

"I've never been to Vermont or practically anywhere else. Philadelphia, Maryland. We went on a class trip to Washington D.C. when I was young, but never as far as Vermont."

"It's nice, but I didn't meet any witches up there, and my mother always said there was no Virago to worry about."

"Well then it sounds divine. They're a mess down here."

"What makes them dark?"

She led me to the edge of the bed and scanned the room to confirm we were alone. "Every witch is born into a coven." We sat at the same time. She lifted her eyebrows and I nodded my understanding so far. "They are our families, and like all families, it's tragic when something happens that tears them apart."

"Like what?"

"The reasons are as varied as they are heartbreaking, but they are never taken lightly. Dismissing someone of your own bloodline is paramount to losing a limb."

"Okay."

"When a witch finds herself without a coven, she is alone for the first time in her life. I'm sure it's bewildering." She looked down at her hands and the hurt of her own memories saddened me as well. "They are doomed to live the rest of their lives alone."

"That makes them dark?"

"That makes them lonely. When their solitude is the result of a coven disintegrating rather than death, the witch is an outcast, and to counteract their predicament, some witches join the Virago. The Earth witches are the most vulnerable, because without a coven, they have no powers. Other witches join in hope they will be given a coven and increase their strength."

"But how can they be given a coven?"

"The Virago is made up of shunned witches, but under certain circumstances a member of the Virago can regain her coven."

"How?"

"If every witch in the member's original coven dies, regardless of their current relationship, she becomes a coven of one. Her abilities are reborn including the capability to cast spells. That lone witch can create a new coven." My mouth fell open. "It rarely works out. The witches were not born into it. They can't get along well enough to support it usually. It's unnatural, but the Virago has become very powerful in this area. The women have lost their grounding to the earth. They're irresponsible, selfish, and angry. It's very dangerous for everyone involved."

"Are they more powerful than the rest of us?"

"Their powers are almost the same, but a dark witch has nothing to lose, no love to behold. No moral compass to follow. They are willing to cross lines we are not."

"I've met someone that I'm afraid is dark. Or his family is." Ike hearing me call to him lodged in my mind. "Or he is something else. I don't know."

"Ike?"

The shock hit me again. Could my mother read my mind like this? "Yes."

"I'm not sure what he is, but you'd be incapable of completely missing the darkness. He isn't connected to the Virago."

I lowered my head and choked back tears accompanying my enormous relief. The terror of losing him had been overwhelming, but I just got my first piece of ammunition in the argument against my mother. He wasn't dark. I'd always known it, but I'd doubted my own instincts that told me I could trust him.

Ruby, Maya, and I found our mothers huddled with four other women in the kitchen. They each had bottles in their hands as if they were pouring drinks, but the liquid stayed still. "We're sorry to ask, but they were in Auburn."

"It's unbelievable," the petite woman in the seventies attire said. "I'm not even sure how it's possible. Since you've been gone, it's been incredibly dangerous." She took a wine glass from the cabinet above her head, and I wondered if she was Tara Jane.

"I wish we had known. We'd have come back sooner," Sloane said as we sank into a couch below the window of the kitchen and didn't say a word to each other. Ruby, Maya, and I didn't need words, we needed help, and that was why we were here. The image of Maya's dress and the thought of some monster in our bedroom still haunted each of us.

"They killed that Earth witch from Upper Pittsgrove. Maryann, what was her name?"

"I think Tanya. It was horrible. They found her body on the side of the road. She was missing an ear."

"Despicable."

I stood to see them again. Two full covens of witches my mother's age. Never had I even imagined such a thing in Vermont. The seven of them together formed a solemn unit of understanding. The petite one with the kind brown eyes held my attention. Why did the Kingsway coven have four witches? I studied each of them. Their appearances were no more similar than my mother and Lovie and Sloane's, but their connection was palpable.

"It will be a war." My mother finally spoke.

"It doesn't have to be. Just a clear message that there are still boundaries," the witch with the piercing blue eyes said.

"I pray you're right, Maryann," Lovie said.

They picked the night before Halloween—Mischief Night—to deliver their message. The Kingsway witches dispersed, and our mothers filled in the chairs around us.

"So hey, what's an Earth witch?" Ruby nonchalantly threw out. Our mothers stopped talking and eating and smiling. They all stared at Ruby from their seats across from us. "Right. Seems important," she continued.

"An Earth witch . . ." Lovie began, and her counterparts stared at her. "Is like any other witch in a coven, except she is the closest to the Earth and needs her sisters for her powers to be present." We'd all been apart for years and still had our powers.

To keep her talking, I asked, "Am I an Earth witch?" Jennifer had already made it clear there wasn't one with us, but any information was better than none.

"No, sweetie. You're all air. I've never seen anyone who can fly like you." Sloane and my mother's eyes tore through Lovie, and the excitement drained from her face.

"An air witch?" I stared at my mother. "Why is this the first I'm hearing of this?"

"Ever, you know how I hate labels. Just because you can fly better than most doesn't mean I want you to live by society's expectations of a pre-defined designation." I fought to keep my eyes on her and not let them roll back into my head. Sometimes she exhausted me, especially when she dismissed Ike's entire family as dark without ever having spoken to him and then lectured about stereotyping.

"What am I?" Maya asked her mother.

Lovie looked to her sisters for permission, and they stayed completely silent like a heavy door that was being pried open a centimeter at a time. "You're a water witch."

"Oh, that totally makes sense."

"Which makes me . . . a fire witch?" Ruby asked the group. "That is so cliché. Make the fire witch the red head. Seriously?"

"Fire witches are not necessarily red heads, and you should be proud of your hair. It's gorgeous."

"I'm about to burn this place down."

"Don't say that. Don't ever say that. Especially not here. Tonight."

"Has there ever been a man who's a witch?" I asked. I needed to know what Ike was more than understanding my own existence.

"Why do you ask?" My mother's eyes bore through me with the question. Her sisters followed her lead.

"I'm just going through the eight hundred and sixty-five questions that have popped into my head since we arrived."

"The short answer is no."

"What's the long answer?"

"Just like gender issues in the non-witch world, we still have some things to figure out. Witches, as a group, are much more open to differences than the general population, but we still do not accept that a witch might have been born into a male body. We're struggling with the idea that it occurs, and it isn't a mistake. We don't know how to place the notion based on our history so we're exploring whether *it* or our past should be redefined." As usual, my mother's input was unhelpful when it came to Ike.

When the belly dancers began their performance, Maya, Ruby, and I moved from the living room to the backyard and found three seats by the fire pit. Our mothers were finishing the weight lifting competition to the side, which basically entailed participants lifting heavy objects without touching them. The competition seemed like nothing our mothers would generally be attracted to, but they were adamant that they wanted to try.

I knew it had something to do with the elderly woman in the pale pink floral dress. My mother had spent the last hour glancing at her. When the woman was present, and the rest of us free, my mother's interest in weight lifting became almost obsessive.

The woman's hands were knotty knuckles covered by freckled skin. She rubbed them together, suggesting they ached as much as they hurt to look at. She was the first person at the party—or whatever this was—that didn't greet us warmly. Our mothers approached her with great reverence. When I heard my mother say, "Please," I knew they needed her help for something, and I wasn't going to miss a word of it.

I hunched over the side of my chair with my head hidden in my arms and focused on their voices.

"We're desperate, and they're strong," Sloane said. The agony in her voice rattled me.

"Unbelievably strong," Lovie chimed in, but the witch only shook her head.

"They can do it. We just don't know how. We've tried ourselves a hundred times, but we can't break it."

"A witch's spell is not meant to be broken," she said definitively. A group of boulders lying next to each other immediately piled together without anyone touching them.

"Please . . ." Lovie's voice was tragic, and I looked over my shoulder to make sure she wasn't crying. Ruby and Maya were watching our mothers as well.

"Bring them here," the old witch said.

Without direction, the three of us walked over to our mothers. They moved us in front of them to face the old woman's inspection. She walked past each of us, leaning in as if suggesting the knowledge she sought was somewhere between our scent and our aura.

"Hold hands," she said. We reached out and took each other's hands standing in our line. "Exactly. They should be a circle. These girls have never known what it feels like to be whole." There was an underlying disgust in her voice, and it was directed at our mothers. "All three are completely unaware of how deficient they are." She glared at our mothers behind us, placing the unspoken blame on them. "You should be ashamed of yourselves. It's one thing to live a full life having been born without an arm, but why would you cut one off if you have two?"

A chill slipped across the back of my neck. I tightened my grip on Maya and Ruby's hands and braced myself for her coming words.

"They're missing their Earth witch. And somewhere out there is a witch that has no idea how powerful she is." The old woman stepped away from us. "You can't change the future by ignoring the past. Buried secrets will always rise again."

XVIII

MISCHIEF NIGHT BEGAN WITH A series of private conversations between our mothers, hushed words, and texts between them and the Kingsway coven. The evening ended with our mothers flying away and leaving the three of us safely stuck in our house.

"They can't just leave us here," I said.

"They just did," Maya responded while loading the dishwasher.

"I know where they went," Ruby chimed in while she put her shoes on. "I read it off my mom's phone."

"You did?" Maya was appalled. What would we do without her conscience?

I was already slipping my boot on one foot and hopping toward the door on the other. "They're going to kill us."

"They'll never know we're there."

"They always *know* everything," Maya said, and neither of us argued with her.

The farm wasn't hard to find. It was the only house on the entire road. A few buildings clustered together in the middle of nowhere. We stayed near the road until we heard voices near the barn. The three of us flew until we were close enough to make out words, but far enough away to fly home and not get caught.

"We'll hold them back," Maryann from the Kingsway coven said. They formed a circle and held hands.

"You're going to let them see you?" my mother asked.

"The point is for them to know we're here," she responded and all three of our mothers appeared to.

My nerves knotted with the sight of our mothers standing behind the other coven. The Kingsway witches chanted rhyming lines as clear as a song while our mothers flew into the air and circled the barn. The witches' voices strengthened as the winds whirled around us and the moon disappeared in the sky. Maya and Ruby moved until their bodies touched my sides.

"Sloane!" Lovie chastised her, but for what we couldn't see. "Of course we're letting the horses out."

The barn doors swung open and our mothers disappeared inside. Nine horses and a dog ran out and toward the house. The house's second floor windows opened and the front door swung toward the inside. Three women flew outside and straight toward the barn. One woman was in her robe and screaming obscenities, but they all froze. Suspended in the air and trapped in an invisible wall.

Holy, Ruby thought beside me. *We have got to learn how to cast a spell.*

The trapped witches flailed their arms and legs, but stayed helpless in the sky. *It's incredible.* A man came to the window of the house, but he was thrown away from it as the front door and all the windows slammed shut.

"We're back, witches," Sloane said, and the barn burst into flames behind her. The wind picked up, increasing the flames, and our mothers floated above it.

Tara Jane glanced our way, but never stopped reciting her verse. I flew back a few feet taking Ruby and Maya with me. The central figure returned her attention to the enemy imprisoned by her words.

Maya tugged on my arm and pulled me toward the road. We flew home, showered, and climbed into our beds. There we stayed still in shock from what we'd seen until our mothers returned filthy, exhausted, and reeking of smoke. That night we slept under the promise their message had been received.

We went to school the next morning without asking our mothers a question. I thought it was smarter to seem curious, but I couldn't form a thought beyond what I'd witnessed the night before. News of the barn fire spread through town and every student in school was talking about it. It continued through the day and infiltrated every conversation around me at the football game. No one guessed that the barn burned because the farm's property straddled the line between Salem and Gloucester Counties, which made it the perfect place for two neighboring covens to unite. The Kingsway witches had proven to be greater allies than our mothers had hoped.

The fourth witch of the Kingsway coven still bothered me. The one named Tara Jane was the last one to enter their circle during their spell casting, and the group practically ignited when she did. If I had to guess, she was their Earth witch. On this topic, I had plenty of questions for our mothers, but an eerie silence fell over them. They mourned the visit with the elderly witch the same way they'd grieved for our fathers. Sloane forbid us from ever mentioning the Goddess Gala again.

I focused on the back of Ike. He was standing on the sideline and waiting for the play to end. It did, and the crowd counted down the last few seconds of the game. Players and coaches engulfed him. The entire team was crowded around him when he stopped moving and looked back into the stands where I was sitting. The music and cheers muted. The fans leaving the stands disappeared. He captured me in his stare.

I love you, I thought. I'd never told him before. I should have waited for a time when we were together, but I couldn't stop him from knowing right that minute. It was almost urgent. Probably because I'd spent the last few hours staring at the back of him, or more likely because I could finally trust myself that he was good.

Ike's lips broke out into a wide smile and he answered with a simple, *I know.*

Ruby wrapped her arm around my shoulder. *It's scary, the way you look at him.*

It terrifies me.

Maya chimed in with, *In a good way?*

The best kind of way.

Does he know? Ruby already knew the answer. They both did without my having to tell them. *We trust you.*

I wanted to be at his motorcycle the minute he came out of the locker room. I left Ruby, Gwen, and Maya, and cut through the woods to the side street where he'd parked. When I could almost see the clearing in front of me, Billy stepped out from behind a tree and made me jump.

"Well never, ever, ever." His words were loose but not quite a slur.

"Billy."

"Didn't think I'd find *you* in the woods. Or maybe I did."

I didn't roll my eyes. I also did not say, "Whatever" which was exactly what I was thinking.

"What? No smart answer?" He moved closer to me, and I could

smell the rum on his breath. "Am I not even worth speaking to anymore?"

I looked to the top of the hill where I'd rather be. "Of course." Whatever it took to get this conversation over with. "I've gotta go, though. See you later."

"You're not going anywhere."

I stepped to the side of him, and he grabbed me by the shoulders and threw me on the ground at his feet. A branch tore through the fabric of my shirt and scraped my collarbone in the process. Before I could reach up and touch it, Billy was on top of me with his lips on my neck. Repulsion ripped through me.

I pushed against his shoulders and screamed, "Get off me!"

Billy took my wrists in his hands and held them against the ground near the sides of my head. His full weight rested on my chest.

"I know exactly what you are, Ever."

I stopped moving and stared into his eyes. He was evil and bulging with misplaced confidence. My stomach churned beneath him and his perceived power over me.

"I find that hard to believe."

He ground his body against me. I shifted so his legs fell to the outside of mine.

"Why's that?" he asked smugly.

"Because if you knew, you wouldn't be on top of me."

His laugh was venomous. It rang in my ears until the tree beside us fell on his ankle, a sickening *snap* sounded right before Billy screamed out in pain. I pushed him off me as Ruby, Gwen, and Maya ran into the woods. Ruby helped me up as Maya rolled the tree off Billy's ankle.

Once I was standing, Ruby turned and kicked Billy in the face until blood gushed from his scalp. She leaned down until they were almost eye to eye and stared at him until Billy closed his eyes.

"Look at me." The world seemed to stop as the three of us watched her in silence. She gripped his hair in her fist until he winced. "You shouldn't be alive. Do that again, and you won't be." She pushed his face away. Billy rolled on his side clutching his leg in agony.

What now? Maya turned to me as she thought. Billy was lying on the ground beneath us writhing in agony and glaring at Ruby with death darting from his eyes.

Gwen stared at Billy with the same hatred that boiled inside me.

What are you doing here? How did Gwen even know where I was?

"I don't know," she answered me, and Ruby's attention shot toward her. "This awful sense of dread came over me. It was choking me and forced me to my feet. I started walking away from the stadium and saw Ruby and Maya running into the woods. I followed them to you."

Gwen, can you hear me? I held my breath and waited for her answer.

Yes. She thought back as her gaze took in the trees and Billy on the ground and each of us watching her. *What's happening?* Gwen spread her fingers out in front of her body and rocked back and forth on her feet as if she was testing her body.

First her brother, then Gwen. *I'm not sure.*

What the—

Ruby, it's important we stay calm. Maya kept an eye on Gwen as she spoke. *This makes perfect sense.*

Really? Even Ruby's sarcasm didn't quell my anxiousness.

Gwen began to shake. I looked to Maya for help. She slipped her arm around Gwen's elbow and led her out of the woods and away from Billy. Ruby cast one last scathing look down to Billy before turning and walking away. I followed as we climbed the hill to the school.

Why didn't you scream for Ike? Gwen turned to me, still appearing dazed when we approached the locker room.

Because I didn't need him . . . and I wanted Billy to live.

The four of us stood in a circle staring at each other and waiting for one of us to share an explanation.

I have to go, Gwen thought when her ride pulled up. Her eyes darted from the car to each of us and back toward the woods where we'd left Billy. She wrung her hands as she took a step back from us. Gone was her carefree smile and lighthearted words. Terror poured off her, and I didn't know how to explain it, or convince her she wasn't crazy and we weren't some evil villain squad.

Everything's going to be fine, Maya told her.

Ike came out of the locker room as Maya and Ruby walked away discussing Gwen in their heads. He kissed me without saying hello. It was dangerous. Someone could see us and tell my mother. When he laid his hand flat on the side of my neck, I realized I was trembling.

"What's wrong?" He stood straight. "I thought you were meeting me at my bike." His attention focused solely on me.

I inhaled deeply to calm myself. "Nothing." *Cerium, Ce, number fifty-eight. Europium, Eu, number sixty-three.*

His fingers fell down to my collarbone where he pushed my shirt to the side and exposed a fresh cut. "What happened?"

My eyes filled with tears. "I fell." I breathed through my nose and touched his fingers. "In the woods. Just now." I pressed his palm to my lips and kissed his hand. "I feel stupid."

"It's a nasty cut." He pushed my shirt back again with his other hand, but instead of examining my collarbone, he was staring into my eyes and willing me to tell him every detail.

I shook my head. "It was more embarrassing than anything."

It was so much more than embarrassing. It was infuriating, and I had to get out of this conversation before Ike sensed the rage.

"I love you," he whispered and let go of my shirt as if he knew exactly what I needed from him.

"I love you, too. I'll see you tomorrow." I exhaled. Even with him letting me off the hook, I was thankful for the Virago-induced curfew as Ike walked away. I hated lying to him, and thoughts of Gwen were consuming me as I raced to catch up to Ruby and Maya.

The three of us feigned boredom and made excuses for why we needed to get to sleep early. When I turned out the light in our bedroom, I whispered, "We need to talk about Gwen."

Maya sigh. She rarely liked subjects that we *needed* to talk about.

I sat up in my bed. "Did I ever tell you guys that Ike's mother doesn't want him to see me?"

"You?" Ruby was offended on my behalf.

"I know. Me. What's wrong with me?"

"Besides the fact that, if you get mad at him, we could possibly curse him."

"One. I would never do that. Two, I'm not even sure that we can. And three, she doesn't know any of this."

Ruby was lost in thought as she tiptoed across our room and climbed under the covers with me and Maya lounged across the foot of the bed. "How do we know she doesn't know?" Maya and I both sat still as Ruby's words sank in. "We are what we are because of our mothers."

If Gwen were our Earth witch, then her mother would have to be a witch, too. "Her mother's name is Gisel," I said. "*Our* mothers had a best friend they loved named Gisel. We're missing our Earth witch. The last time I checked, our mothers were down one witch, too."

"It's impossible." Ruby's words were dismissive, but her head shook from the details. She couldn't deny my logic, and none of us could forget the way Gwen spoke to us in our heads, but Ruby still trusted her mother. My blind faith had been diminished by my mother's unreasonable ban on Ike.

"What if it isn't? What if Gwen and her mother are witches?"

"I love Gwen," Maya said. "I've loved her since the first time I saw her."

"There's no way," Ruby said. "All they've talked about our entire lives is the power of the coven. They wouldn't keep her from us."

"This is terrifying," Maya said before sliding off my bed and crawling back into her own. "Let's sleep on it."

I lay in the dark and thought of Gwen until sleep finally found me. I was flying through the sky. I was dreaming, again. Ruby was next to me, holding my hand.

"Ever?" she said, but it wasn't Ruby's voice. It was Gwen.

"Gwen?" I was sure it was her. I needed Ruby and Maya with me, but they were nowhere nearby. "I can't see you when we fly."

Gwen let go of my hand, and when I landed, she was standing next to Billy. I woke. My panic wouldn't let me go back to sleep.

The rest of the weekend, I mulled over every emotion I felt while Billy had been on top of me. The most prevalent was abhorrence. Maya thought I should tell our mothers, but I just wanted to forget it ever happened and avoid the lecture about being in the woods after they had repeatedly warned us away.

At school, I avoided Billy in the halls. I didn't look at him in the class we had together. I moved to the opposite end of our lunch table. I couldn't be far enough away from him, but I didn't want to draw attention to us, either. The thought of his voice in my ear still kept me up at night. Without witchcraft, what would have happened to me?

I utilized most of physics lab to think of all the things I would do to Billy. I wanted to witness him feeling the same type of fear I'd felt when he threw me on the ground and climbed on top of me. I took two giant breaths before the end of class. Ike was with me next period, and if he sensed I was upset, he'd start asking questions. I was never going to tell him about Billy because Ike's reaction wasn't hard to predict.

Mick placed three Starbursts in front of me with a sympathetic grin. The bell rang, and I slid my binder into my bag and walked out the door.

"Ever," Billy's voice ripped through my serenity. "Ever, wait."

The people surrounding us stopped talking and looked over. Some even stopped walking completely. We were the morning showing of a film they'd been waiting to be released. I stopped, not wanting to make the exchange even more dramatic for their viewing pleasure.

Billy hobbled on his crutches until he was standing next to me. I moved against the wall, and he came closer. The traffic in the hall returned to its normal speed with the lack of a scene.

"What?" I said making it clear this conversation would be short.

"I'm sorry." Billy leaned down until we were eye to eye. "I'm *really* sorry. I'm embarrassed and ashamed." He was saying all the right things and yet, something was missing. "Ever, I'm sorry."

"Why? What is *wrong* with you?"

Billy's laugh was disturbing. It sent a chill down my back. "Oh, Ever. I could give you ten reasons for why, but they're all poor excuses. It never should have happened." He stood straight and gave me some room. It was an appropriate gesture. "I need you to forgive me."

"I need you to stay away from me," I said.

Gwen walked up and stood to my right as if she'd spent her entire life there. "Everything okay?" she asked me while staring at Billy.

"Fine," he said. "You two have been spending a lot of time together." He tilted his head, waiting for some explanation. "You two, Maya, and Ruby. You're a bit of a galère." Gwen eyed him confused. My mother had used the word when talking about her coven. They loved the sound of it. The fact that the French word from the seventeen hundreds had come from Billy's mouth sunk down to the pit of my stomach. The coincidence was unlikely innocent.

"We are," I said and led Gwen away.

"I'd expected a visit from your boyfriend."

My blood boiled in my veins. I could have thrown him out the window. I stormed back to him and threw my finger in his face. "Don't even talk about him."

"I'm just surprised that he didn't come rushing to your side. The way he looks at you makes it obvious how he feels about you." Billy's apology turned baleful as soon as Gwen had walked up. He no longer wanted forgiveness—maybe he never really did to start with. He was taunting me.

I calmed myself. I wouldn't let him know how close he was getting to my weak spot. "You're lucky he didn't," I said and walked away.

XIX

WHATEVER WE THOUGHT WE KNEW about Gwen was confirmed over the next few days. Ruby, Maya, and I watched as Gwen struggled to figure out what was happening to her while she enjoyed her newfound gifts. Things moved around the school without being touched, but only when Gwen was in the room. She was giddy whenever she used her magic to unplug things, and drop the fire extinguishers from the walls, or transform the water fountains into actual fountains. Anything to derail the teacher's lesson plans and cause class to end a few minutes early. It was obvious she hadn't been raised in a depraved home by the Virago.

We didn't intervene and just observed her. She was her kind, generous self, who was also a bit unpredictable and seemed happy to avoid us and the subject of our voices in her head. I tried to send her messages. Ruby and Maya did the same, but if she heard anything, Gwen was not letting on. Once I said, *Good morning*, and she stopped walking and looked at me, but she hadn't responded. She was avoiding the truth. Probably out of fear.

"Do you think we should talk to her?" Maya asked at lunch.

"And tell her what?" Ruby raised her eyebrows as if it were the most absurd thing we could possibly say to a person. It was right up there with we're from Mars, and I eat insects instead of food.

"I don't know." Maya's head shook as she spoke. "I caught her flicking the lights on and off before algebra today. It was thundering, so everyone thought it was the storm."

"Maya's right," I said. "We can't just let her go on the way she is. Someone's going to notice besides us."

"And if she's a witch, that's kind of an important thing to know about yourself. I like apples. I'm into art. I'm afraid of heights. I have magical powers . . . all part of discovering your truths in your teens," Ruby said under her breath.

"That's the problem. We've all had this our whole lives."

"Has Ike mentioned anything?" Ruby took a bite of her apple.

I shook my head. "Only that something's different about her, but he said the same thing about his mother."

We decided to catch Gwen after school and tell her. Maya was supposed to do most of the talking. She was the gentlest of the group, and she and Gwen seemed to have a special connection since the first day we'd met her.

Gwen was across the street from the school when we found her, and she was crying. It didn't go unnoticed that the sky was about to open up and unleash fat raindrops on us. I tightened my hood up around my neck as we closed the last few yards between us. Gwen was too busy watching the clouds roll overhead to notice us.

"What's wrong?" Maya asked.

"Dave is hooking up with Lydia."

"What?" I asked. I had English with both of them and besides her laughing at every word he said, I'd never noticed a thing.

"I found her in his top contacts. I knew something was going on."

"Top contacts?" I'd been off social media for three months, and I already had no idea what she was talking about.

"I asked him about her, and he got defensive and called me 'clingy'."

"Oh. No." Ruby shook her head in complete agreement with Gwen.

"I know! I could kill him."

Dave's car was stopped on Lincoln Avenue, waiting for the police officer who was directing traffic. Gwen stared at his car with vengeful spite in her eyes.

"Okay, we need to talk," Ruby said, and Gwen snapped out of her hateful trance. "Now."

Thunder roared above us as we walked to the Farmer's Exchange where Paul's truck was parked. The sky had darkened more in the last few minutes. The wind moved the clouds above us. They swirled and broke apart but didn't let the sun shine through. We lowered the tailgate and Gwen hopped on it.

"Besides . . ." Maya began. She chose her words carefully. "Has anything seemed different lately?"

"Like how?" Gwen asked. She was sincere. It was easy to forget how illogical our reality was.

"Like, things you'd like to happen do," Maya continued.

Ruby rolled her eyes and added, "Or you can move things with your mind?" She was much less gentle. Thunder rumbled in the distance.

Or you can suddenly hear us inside your head, Maya added and Gwen turned to her with wide eyes.

"Or when you're with the three of us, you feel more . . . alive than ever before?" I added. I could feel it myself. I'd always been stronger with Ruby and Maya, but the four of us together sent a tingling beneath my skin.

"Yes . . ." Gwen's gaze fell to the ground as she digested our questions. She shook her head. "I don't know what's happening, but it's amazing."

"We're different," Maya said. "And we think you're different in the same way."

"Special." Ruby nodded, encouraging Gwen to believe us without being pushy about it.

Never in the history of witchcraft had I ever heard of this happening before. We were all born this way. So was Gwen. An ominous growl of thunder erupted above us.

"Gwen." She dragged her eyes up until she faced me. "We think we're a coven. The four of us." I took her hand in mine to ease some of the tension spraying off her. "Your powers weren't known to you until the three of us found you because you're unique." She was concentrating on my every word. "You somehow work because of the three of us."

"And you make each of us stronger." Maya held Gwen's other hand.

"But what are you?" Gwen looked each of us in the eyes and the clouds opened up, dropping a deluge of water. The drops bounced off the car roofs and windshields and hammered the tree's last golden leaves until they dropped from their branches and swirled against the storm drain next to us. Cars pulled over, and people ran for cover under awnings and overhangs.

Gwen stared down at herself amazed. The four of us were completely dry.

"We're the witches of Auburn."

GWEN HAD TAKEN THE NEWS like a warrior. She hadn't missed a beat when we'd told her what we were. "I knew it!" was all she'd said. She'd stumbled upon us running in a marathon, and instead of considering any of the ramifications, she had just fallen right in next to us and matched our strides.

She was . . . not negligent, but impulsive. Maya, Ruby, and I had been raised with the knowledge of power. Gwen woke up one day with it, and she was drunk on the excitement. Doors opened. Lights switched off. We entertained most of it as long as no one got hurt. We tried to be understanding of what Gwen was going through while still keeping the rumors that the high school was haunted from running rampant.

The student body was split. Half were realists that preferred a conspiracy theory to any ideas of the supernatural that the other half insisted was the case. When Chrissy fell off the top of the cheerleading pyramid, Ruby yanked Gwen out of the grandstand. I knew they were outside the stadium, talking but not speaking, about how Gwen could not use her powers in that way. When they came back, Gwen swore to me and Maya that she hadn't done a thing. We chalked it up to karma and prayed Gwen was telling the truth. She was fun, but she didn't dwell on consequences, if she took them into account at all.

I stared at the computer screen in front of me. The brownies Lovie had insisted on baking were making it difficult to concentrate. I could barely hold my head up as I typed. Exhaustion was taking over my thoughts on *A Tale of Two Cities*. Really, it was my thoughts of Ike that excluded every other piece of knowledge. I'd snuck out the last two nights to see him. Both times we'd met at his tree house and somehow squeezed into his sleeping bag together. I wanted to get him a second one for Christmas so we could lay one on the floor and another on top of us.

"Ever, we're going to Maine." My mother was excited.

"Great," I responded without a hint of actual enthusiasm. "When?"

"This weekend."

"I can't go this weekend." Panic shot through me. It was Gwen's birthday party. I was actually going to see Ike's house. Maybe even the inside of it. I wasn't going to miss the chance for a trip to Maine or anywhere else.

"How long does that paper have to be?" She came and read over my shoulder. "I feel like you've been working on it for days."

"The teacher answer is, 'it should be as long as necessary to convey our well-written insights,' but he also mentioned that it would be impossible to thoroughly express all of our thoughts in under five pages." My mother's forehead scrunched up. "You're the one who wanted me to take Honors English."

"You're good at it. I'm also the one who wants you to come to Maine. It's Mrs. Fields' wedding."

"Mrs. Fields that we lived next to in Vermont?"

"That's the one. She's getting remarried."

Lovie and Sloane came into the room with gloves on their hands. They'd been raking leaves all morning. I couldn't understand why they didn't move them with their minds and chose to actually pile them up and drag them to the woods. They washed their hands and poured two cups of coffee.

"Take these two," I said completely joking.

"Take us where? Yes! Take us," Lovie pleaded. Her eyes lit up with hope, and I turned to my mother. Lovie made it easy for all of us to forget she was in mourning.

"I've been invited to a wedding in Maine this weekend. It's completely casual."

"I'll go pack," Lovie said and walked out of the room.

"I think she needs to get away," Sloane said and drank her coffee.

"The girls have these awful papers to do."

Sloane placed her cup on the counter behind her and stared at my mother. I knew they were talking without words, going back and forth with their thoughts.

"I'm right here," I said.

"Of course you are." Sloane laughed as she spoke. "Where you'll be all weekend with Ruby and Maya. Do you think you guys can handle that? Two nights alone?"

I wasn't sure if I was hearing her right. "The three of us?"

"I don't know," my mother said.

I stifled my excitement. *Copper. Cu. Number twenty-nine. Ruthenium. Ru. Number forty-four.* I had to act nonchalant so I could put them at ease. Letting them know I was jumping for joy inside wouldn't get them out the door any faster. I focused on the computer and forced myself to think of Lucie Manette.

"They'll be fine, and it'll do Lovie good to get away." Sloane came and sat on the edge of my desk. She looked me in the eyes and pointed her finger at me. "No parties. None. No boys in the house, and the three of you are to be together at all times. Got it?" I was still too shocked to respond. "Don't screw this up."

"We won't." I might have offered too fast. *Silver. Ag. Number forty seven.* I shrugged to downplay it. No. Big. Deal.

Before school on Friday, we stood in the driveway and waved as our mothers drove away to start their long journey to Maine. It was hard to judge who was more excited—us or the three of them.

I forced myself to go to school. Actually, the fear of the school calling my mother's cell phone and her immediately returning kept me in my seat during every class of the day. Ruby and Maya were going to a bonfire at Sam's house. Ruby was finally showing some signs of life when it came to guys. Sam was the first person to replace her endless conversations about Harry. He'd come along at the perfect time. She'd kissed him the day before Harry's picture was online with a girl Ruby used to hang out with in Vegas.

"These things happen," she'd said in what I thought was a very calm and fair way, especially for Ruby.

Ike arrived right before Maya and Ruby left. I didn't hear them say goodbye, I wasn't sure what they were wearing. I couldn't take my eyes off Ike. He had on jeans and a Woodstown Wolverines T-shirt that barely fit him. I swallowed hard at the sight of him.

Ike was leaning against the kitchen counter directly across the room from me. He smiled in his notorious way. I felt like we were about to rob a bank together or steal a boat from a marina and set sail to nowhere.

"It's just us?" Either he was gauging the situation or he was nervous, which was ridiculous. Ike was never afraid of anything, certainly not of being alone with me. We'd been sneaking around together for weeks.

"We—" I started to say something and stopped. It was a collection of useless words. Beneath him. Beneath me when I was with him.

I crossed the floor between us and pulled his face down to mine. I kissed him without holding back a single cell in my body. They all wanted to be with him. He lifted me off the ground in front of him, and I wrapped my legs around his waist. I would have climbed inside him if I could. He turned and rested me on the counter.

"I love you," he said. His hands cupped my face, and I fell into his navy eyes. I wanted him. I kissed him again, trying to calm myself, but it only sent my body into a frenzy I couldn't manage. "Show me your bedroom," he said.

I inhaled Ike and slid off the counter. He followed me up the stairs, both of us walking in silence the entire first flight.

"This is my mom's room." I pushed the door open a little farther so Ike could see in. We passed the bathroom. "And Ruby's mom's." Ike had no interest. I walked faster past Lovie's door to the second flight of stairs in the guest room closet.

"This is our room," I announced with my hands displaying the space. I followed Ike's gaze across the four corners of our room. "Or our attic."

"It's nice." Ike walked over to my bed. He ran his hand over the pale blue comforter and picked up the stuffed dog from the center of my pillow. He held it up to his face and inhaled. "This bed is yours." It wasn't a question.

I met him there and pushed him down so I could straddle his lap. He was the most beautiful thing I'd ever seen, and he was in my bed. I kissed him and pressed myself to him until not even a speck of air could fit between us.

Ike lifted my shirt over my head, and I shifted just enough to let him. There was no embarrassment or timid hesitation. His strength and power invaded me. I squeezed my legs together around him to quell the energy. He kissed me again and caressed my breast until my nipple hardened beneath the lace.

I lowered my head and found the strength to admit, "I've never *been* with anyone before."

Ike lifted my chin and my eyes found him. "I know."

My heartbeat deepened with relief. "How do you know?"

He kissed my lips again and held my face in his hands. "Because since I first saw you, I knew you were meant to be with me."

"I won't be your first, though." I knew the answer. I knew it at the bonfire when Grace was throwing up, and I knew it by the jealousy of the girls who glared at me when we walked down the hall together. Admiration was one thing, but these girls wanted him because they'd already had him. Theirs was some ugly form of defeat, and it was a competition I didn't want to participate in.

Ike shook his head. My sight followed my fingers down his chest to his stomach. They rested there, where they always loved to be. The other girls whose hands had been there before me broke through my need and left me cold.

Ike held each of my arms, grounding me to him. "I can't change that, Ever."

"I know." I did know. "Imagine if it were me instead of you."

He kissed me. Gentle at first, but his need pressed against me until it verged on violent. I couldn't remember what I wanted to be different. He forced the thoughts from my mind and replaced them with a deep throbbing I'd never felt before.

Ike lay down on my bed with me still safely in his arms. He pushed my hair off the side of my face and kissed me there. His lips near my ear sent chills down my body. "I can't think about that. It's impossible to imagine." His voice was dry as it left his mouth. His words were rough. Ike understood.

We lay there until I almost forgot I would never be his first. There were so many things we couldn't change. His prior girlfriends were just a fraction of the history that would forever surround us.

I slept with Ike's heavy arm draped across my back. I don't think I moved once the entire night until I heard, "Wake up. Yoo hoo," and sat up in bed. It wasn't Maya or Ruby's voice. It was Gwen's. "Ike and Ever."

I shook Ike, who was still asleep next to me. "Gwen's here."

"Ike, get up!" Gwen yelled again.

I climbed on top of him and kissed his neck until he was fully awake. He pulled the comforter over my head as Gwen walked into the room.

"Wake up! It's ten thirty. Are you guys going to sleep forever?"

"No," Ike said and kissed me again under the covers.

"We have work to do." Ruby was there, too. I peeked out from under the comforter. Ruby, Gwen, and Maya were standing at the foot of my bed, practically tapping their feet. "Last night, while you two were 'visiting,' we discovered some of Gwen's powers, and today we're going to see what else we can figure out."

"Really?" I sat up and wrapped the blanket around my chest. "Like what?" I turned to Gwen. "What can you do?"

"Show her," Maya said with pride oozing all over Gwen next to her.

Gwen focused on the floor next to my bed. She stared at Ike's boot until it flew straight up in the air.

"Well done, Gwen," I said as the boot hovered above me.

"You have five minutes to get downstairs," Ruby said.

Ike stared at me dismayed as the three of them practically skipped out of the room.

Gwen was part of us. Maya knew it the first time she'd met her, and I thought it when the witch in Mullica Hill told us about our Earth witch. *Gwen* was our Earth witch.

"What's going on?" Ike leaned up on his forearms with a stricken expression while I found yoga pants and a hoodie to put on. I stopped in his stare. It was easy for me to forget how little he could comprehend since he seemed to understand me completely.

"Gwen's like us." I let that sink in and put my sweatshirt on. "I think she's one of us."

"What does that mean?"

I leaned down and kissed him. "I think she's the fourth member of our coven. She's our Earth witch."

His confusion was obvious in his perplexed gaping mouth and the lack of feeling in his kiss. "Does this mean we're related somehow?"

I laughed. "No, but your sister and I are sisters in a sense." His brow furrowed. "We're still figuring it all out. Just be supportive of Gwen. This is probably frightening for her."

I brushed my teeth and found my boots. Ike followed me through my morning routine, and we met Gwen, Maya, and Ruby outside. Power flowed through my veins being in their presence.

I inhaled the cool fall air. "Man, it's unbelievable." I ran my thumbs over the pads of my fingers as energy flowed through my body and threatened to ignite there.

"I know," Maya said.

"You called it," I said to Maya and then to Gwen, "Maya knew you were special the first day of school."

"Let's get started. We have a lot to go over." Maya was taking the lead. "Invisibility." She tipped her head to me. "Ever, would you do the honors?"

I stepped into the center of our circle and said, "It isn't that we really disappear; it's that we're no longer visible to people who are trying to see us. We block the image before it hits the eye's lens, or any other lens for that matter. That's why, when we're invisible, we can't be recorded, either." I inhaled and let myself go.

"How did you do that?"

I reappeared and thought through the steps in my head that had become second nature. It was like explaining to someone how to breathe. I'd been born with it. "You have to quiet your mind and focus on losing your image. It should be your only thought. Close your eyes, and you'll go, so to speak."

Gwen stood next to me. We all watched her in curious silence. She inhaled and stared at the cloudless sky above us, and then she disappeared. As quick as she left, she returned.

"What happened? Why didn't it last?"

"You just have to practice," Maya said rubbing Gwen's arm.

"Once you get it down, you'll be able to also hide anything in your arms." With a come hither face, I summoned Ike to me with my finger. He walked over and circled my shoulders with his heavy arms. I wrapped my hands around his waist and looked behind me at Gwen. "You ready?"

She nodded, and Ike and I disappeared together. I stood on my tiptoes and kissed him. We were the only two people left on the planet. A tiny moan slipped from his lips, and I stood down and showed us again. Ike was blushing.

"You two are getting hard to be around," Ruby said. Somehow, she kept from rolling her eyes. "Let's try the group chat thing I learned at the gala." She faced Maya and Gwen. I walked over and stood next to them. Ruby concentrated with her eyes closed.

So Gwen, how about that time Billy Roberts attacked Ever and ripped her shirt—

Ike's face turned red and his eyes found mine.

"No!" I screamed, trying to stop Ruby, but it was too late.

"Ever?" Ike demanded.

"What have you done?" I yelled at her.

Ruby stared at me as if I were crazy. "What? He can't hear me."

"He can," I said and ran to him.

"What the . . ." Ruby said, but I ignored her.

"Ike." I touched his chest, which was heaving through labored breaths. "Ike, listen to me. It was not a big deal. I can handle Billy Roberts."

"When?" The word was pushed out through gritted teeth, and I wasn't sure if he was more pissed at Billy for touching me or me for not telling him. "When?"

There was no escape from his question. "The night of the last football game." My voice had never sounded so small. Ike looked at me as if I'd betrayed him. Maybe in some way, I had. "But he was drunk, and he apologized. It really was nothing."

"How could you keep this from me? I asked you how you got that cut, and you told me you fell."

"That wasn't a lie." I remembered barely missing the branch in the eye as Billy pushed me down. "Ike, please." I rested my hands on his chest, and he grabbed my wrists.

"Okay." Ruby stood next to us letting her words fall between us. "Billy's an idiot. It really was nothing. Ever dropped a tree on his ankle, and he rolled off her."

I lowered my head, knowing Ruby divulging Billy's location on top of my body would not be overlooked by Ike. Ike stormed out of my yard, leaving me lost without him. I walked into the house, climbed the stairs to my bedroom, and covered myself in the blankets Ike and I had slept in. They still smelled of him.

Come back, I thought. Over and over again, I thought, *Come back*. He didn't return.

He didn't speak to me.

I withered away in his silence the rest of the day.

XXI

RUBY AND MAYA CONVINCED ME not to follow Ike and to let him calm down. The best way to fix it was to go to Gwen's birthday party. We'd left out the last name of the birthday girl when we'd told our mothers about it. After the way my mom had reacted to just the sight of Ike, and the discussion of our Earth witch at the Goddess Gala, not mentioning the last name Kennedy seemed like the way to go.

Gwen greeted us in the driveway. She did so without speaking. *Hi, girls!*

"Hi," Ruby said and leaned into Gwen. "I know you're excited, but it's important to actually speak at times when people are watching and expecting us to speak." She rocked her head back and forth nonchalantly at Gwen. "Make sense?"

Total sense. Ruby glared at her. "Just kidding."

"She's a kidder," Ruby joked and moved out of the way for each of us to hug Gwen.

"Happy birthday," I said and squeezed her tight.

"Ike's been watching the driveway for an hour." Regret and longing overwhelmed me. I tried not to spread it all over the birthday girl. "I finally made him go out back to the lake. He was scaring people."

"He's good at that," I said, and Gwen shared a smile with me at her brother's expense.

It was November and finally cold enough to wear sweaters and parkas. I had on my typical uniform from my Vermont days. Maya looked as if the cold air actually injured her as it blew across her face. She wasn't used to it not being a perfect eighty-two degrees every day.

It was hard to tell what Ruby thought. Her sarcasm encapsulated every word, making it difficult to decipher what had the greatest impact on her well-being. She wandered through the crowd in Gwen's backyard and stopped when Sam grabbed her arm. Her expression softened. Ruby lowered her chin and peered through her eyelashes at Sam who put his arm around her shoulders. She held on to his hand. It was a rare version of peace surrounding her, and she deserved it.

Jim Dodge came up and asked me if I was inviting him back to my house for a party that night. I barely had time to judge if the question was serious when he poked me with his elbow.

"No party."

"I just overheard Ruby tell Sam that you guys are home alone. Sounds like a party to me." Jim chatted on about a party he wasn't invited to because it didn't exist. "It's kind of strange that you three are all the same age and live together. Do you find it odd?"

Gwen's father stepped out of the back door and hugged her. She stood on her tiptoes and said something in his ear. If it were my dad, I would have said something like, "Thank you," or "I love you."

If I had one more day to say things to my dad, I'd beg him not to leave me. I'd cry until he promised me he wouldn't die. I was only ten the night he didn't come home. I'd lost a tooth and I couldn't wait to tell him. That, and the fact that I got an A on my Biomes test in science. I kept checking the clock, waiting for him to walk through the door. He was always home on Fridays by six.

Six had come and gone. Seven. Eight. My mother had wilted in front of my eyes. By the time the doorbell rang, she could barely stand to answer it. Looking back, she'd known at breakfast that he was never coming back and had been mourning the entire time I was waiting.

"Is it odd?" Jim asked.

I inhaled. "Is what odd?"

"Living together? The three of you."

"It's great actually. There is always someone to talk to." Maya was across the fire from me. She was staring at Gwen and Mr. Kennedy, looking alone in every way as she wiped a tear off her cheek. "I'll be back."

I made my way to Maya, took her by the hand, and led her behind a tree. Her shoulders shook as she sobbed. "Oh, Maya," I said and hugged her. "Shhh."

"It isn't fair."

"It isn't." I shook my head against her. "It's absolutely not fair."

"I love Gwen. Really, I do." She was pushing her words out and gasping for breath.

"I know you do. This has nothing to do with her."

"I wanted my dad to be here today. Everyday."

I held Maya's face in my hands and made her look at me. "He isn't. It's nobody's fault. It's never going to be okay. He's just not here." I held her tight against my body. "But everything you're feeling right now is okay. You're going to get through this. All of us will."

"He died, and instead of grieving, I was packing to come to a state I've never been to in my whole life. I swear, Ever, if it weren't for you and Ruby, I'd run away and fly back to Hawaii. My mom's crazy. This isn't going to make me forget him. It isn't helping."

Maya was on the verge of hysterics. I played with her hair and rubbed her back until she quieted. "I don't think they brought us here to forget," was all I said. I knew my mother well enough to know there was a reason, and it was starting to feel like our lives depended on it.

I held Maya until she was her pleasant self again. I needed to talk to Ruby about keeping an eye on her. Maya always had a cheerful visage, but she was hurting. It was fresh pain, and no one was talking about it for fear we'd injure her further, but there was nothing that could make it worse.

Ruby found us and without a word, hugged Maya, too. Gwen's father had an adverse effect on all of us. As long as we stuck together there were no fathers around to make us jealous, but Gwen's was right here. A huge part of her life, and she loved him. As she should.

I thought of Ike. The huge part of my life.

Meet me at the dock, I heard in my mind. He sounded almost calm.

Ruby's arm was still around Maya's shoulders as Maya pulled it together. She waved to the girls she loved from chorus and said she was hungry. Both good indications that she was moving through her current wave of grief.

"I'll be back."

Ruby looked past me at the lake behind the house. "Going to slay the beast."

"You got us into this."

"Well, maybe if you'd shared that one very important detail about your boyfriend."

I didn't want to argue with Ruby and definitely not with Ike.

Gwen and Ike's house was situated on a small hill that fell into the lake. It had a dock in the backyard and kayaks and a canoe resting against the slope. Ike was facing the lake. He was waiting for me. The moonlight shone off the water's surface and surrounded him, making him seem even bigger than he actually was.

It was cold without the fire next to me. I crossed my arms at my chest and approached him. The moon went behind a cloud and darkness surrounded us.

I love you, I thought.

Ike slowly turned around. "I know."

"I'm sorry I didn't tell you." I moved closer to him. It wasn't that I thought that would appease him. I had to be near him. Wherever we were. "But I was afraid of your reaction."

Ike stiffened in front of me. "He should have been afraid. Not you." I wasn't sure what to say. I pulled him toward me and rested my face on his shoulder. "Ever." Ike leaned back and raised my chin so I couldn't hide in his chest. He kissed me, and a peace filled me that had left when he'd stormed out of my yard earlier in the day. "I need you to promise. Right here. Right now. That if someone or something hurts you, you'll tell me. I need to know."

"Why? I was fine."

"You were on the verge of tears that day, and you didn't fool me for a minute. I knew something was wrong. Even if I didn't suspect something, I need to know because I love you, and I'm not going to let anybody hurt you."

"Ike—"

"You're so tough? Not scared of anything. What if someone attacked me? Would you want me to tell you?" My stomach clenched at the thought of him being hurt. He held me close to him again and ran his hands up and down my back. I unknotted there. "If you tell me tomorrow that you never want to see me again, I'll still spend the rest of my life making sure you're safe."

I shook my head. "I'm never going to say that."

"I know." Ike kissed me again.

I swore to myself I'd never keep another thing from him. I moved back and held his hand in mine. His knuckles were bruised. One had a fresh scab covering it. I ran my thumb over the damage. "I don't even understand what happened that night? Billy'd never been anything but seemingly kind to me before."

"Seemingly?"

"Yeah. Everything he does is nice, but it never feels nice." Ike huffed a bit. "Did he say anything today?"

"I wasn't going to let him speak. I'd heard enough at your house, but when I found him in his backyard, he was on crutches. It's hard to beat a guy to death who only has the use of one leg." I moved closer to Ike. "I still wanted to."

I shook my head. "I was fine," I tried again.

"So was he. I explained to him that he's never to *think* about touching you again. I was willing to let him live since he was already hurt thanks to the tree you dropped on him."

"But . . ."

"But when I went to leave the piece of—" Ike shook the thought from his mind.

"What?"

"He started mouthing off . . ." Every muscle in Ike's body flexed against me. "About how your neck tasted." I cowered in repulsion. Ike swallowed hard before continuing. "And I dropped him right there on his lawn."

"You could have gotten arrested."

Ike stood frozen in the memory of his anger. "I tried to walk away."

"How hard?" I ran my fingertips down his chest.

The club music was replaced by a slow song, and the noise of the party died down. We were completely alone in the dim moonlight. I disappeared with Ike in my arms.

Dance with me.

He didn't argue or make a joke. We were invisible to the world around us. Ike held me against him. His hands rested on my back. With my wedge-heeled boots on, I was much closer to his height, which I preferred so I didn't have to reach up for him all the time. I realized that was why I loved lying down next to him. We were equal.

The front of our bodies met and everything around us was gone but the drum's solemn rhythm and Ike's heart beating against my chest. I rested my head on his shoulder. My lips found his neck, my breath caressed his ear, and my hands threaded in his hair as we moved back and forth to the rhythm of the song.

Ike angled his head so he could kiss my lips, and when he moved to pepper kisses along my jaw, I tilted my face to the sky for him. I melted into the warmth of Ike. It spread down my chest to the center of my body. My heart let me forget where we were and that we weren't alone. I rested a hand on his chest, and he covered it with his own before lifting it to his mouth and taking my fingertip between his teeth. The need I felt for him almost hurt.

Breathing was difficult, but who needed air. I had Ike. He pulled me back to him and my head found his shoulder again. By the time the song ended, I was sure we were going to run away together that minute. A fast song replaced what would forever by my favorite song.

That's why people like dances. I kissed him again, but it wasn't a chaste kiss. No, I kissed him as if he were leaving with his battalion the next day. I couldn't let him go.

"It's time to sing happy birthday," Ike's mom yelled across the yard. We both heard her, but neither one of us let go right away.

When we did, I dropped the magic that was hiding us and took his good hand in my own.

"Come on, before she sends a search party." He smiled at the thought and then let me lead him back up the hill.

The lights were out in the garage. The inferno of a cake in front of Gwen and her face above it were the only things I could see. I pushed Ike toward the front, knowing his parents would want a picture of him and Gwen together. I leaned against the wall. Gwen was turning seventeen, and so would Maya, Ruby, and I over the next twelve months.

Maya came and stood beside me. She rested her head on my shoulder.

"You don't ever have to be strong around us," I whispered, and she wrapped her arm around my waist. "We know how hard it is. Fall onto us when you need to. We'll always catch you."

I know.

XXII

"SHE'S HERE." MAYA'S EXCITEMENT TRAVELED with her words up the stairs to the attic and forced my eyes open. "The birthday girl's here."

My hand reached across the empty bed, searching for Ike. He'd slept over but must have left early to go to work. Without him, there seemed to be little reason to actually wake up. I rolled over and pressed the home button on my phone. Eight thirty. I'd barely slept. Ike and I had stayed up until almost three talking.

"Ever, Ruby, come down!" Maya was ready to begin our day. I had to admit I was a little excited, too. Gwen's powers were the first hint at an actual reason for us to be in this state.

"Why does everything have to start so early?" Ruby asked and buried her head under her pillow.

I walked over to her bed and ripped her pillow away. "We only have today. They'll be home after dinner." She covered her head with her arms. "I'll send Maya up here, and you'll wish you'd gotten up in the first place."

"I'm coming."

I threw the pillow at her and stepped far out of her reach. Maya and Gwen walked into our room. They both beamed as if Gwen had just been born to us and it was the happiest day of our lives.

The sight of my empty bed depressed me. "I miss your brother," I said and fell back onto my covers.

"It's crazy," Maya said and shook her head. "I mean. You love him. He loves you. Why can't you guys be together?"

"It has something to do with *them*," I said and rolled onto my stomach.

"Who?" Gwen asked.

"Our mothers."

Gwen was lost in thought.

"Gwen," I said to bring her back to us.

She looked straight at me. "They've been fighting a lot."

"Our mothers?"

"No." Gwen shook her head. "My mom and dad. My mother and my grandmother. Everyone seems to be fighting." Ike had told me his mother wasn't on board with our relationship, either, but he still had so much more freedom, which was ridiculous because I could fly and disappear.

"About what?" Maya asked.

"I don't know. They always stop talking as soon as I get anywhere near them."

"Does your mom ever mention our mothers?" They must have meant a great deal to each other at one time. We'd found our Earth witch, which meant that Gisel had been theirs. I wanted to know what happened.

"If she does, I don't get to hear about it."

I wanted to press for any more information she may have, but Gwen was still so new to me, and I didn't want to overstep.

"I wonder if anything special happens when we turn seventeen," Ruby said, breaking the lull in conversation.

"Like what?" Gwen asked.

Maya was already catching on. "Like we get new powers or they get stronger."

I shrugged. "I don't know. One of the women at that conference could read my mind. Like not just hear me talking to her, she knew my thoughts."

"That would be awesome." Ruby finally rose from her bed.

"I'm not so sure." It would be useful, but I assumed some people's thoughts were better left to themselves. Even without the ability to read minds, I could see how much a few girls hated me when I walked down the hall with Ike. Their words might actually wound me.

"Let's try a spell," Ruby said. Maya and I stared at her while Gwen held her hands to her chest in utter enchantment.

"I don't know." We'd only ever tried it that one time, which was an epic failure, and our mothers had been painfully clear on how serious spell casting was. "Maybe we should wait." The three of them had no hesitation, not one moment of doubt. "We should go to church."

Ruby's eyes rolled back in her head. "Why?"

"Because we always go." Theoretically, that should have been enough, but this was Ruby. "And because our mothers thought it was important before the last spell we tried."

Ruby took a deep breath as Maya relaxed next to her. She loved it whenever we calmed down. "If we go to church, you'll be okay with this?" Ruby asked.

"Okay might be overstating, but I'll do it." The idea still left me tense.

I dragged them up the hill to church. Maya and I walked in front of Ruby and Gwen as if we were pulling them on a leash. Church was exactly as it had been every other week since we moved here—pleasant, peaceful, and brief. Mr. Turnbull complimented us on attending church even without our mothers, and Mrs. Schrufer asked where they were. I caught Ruby glaring at me out of the corner of my eye when I reached for a second sugar cookie. "Gotta go," I told Mr. Turnbull and followed my coven out the door.

As soon as we entered our house, the three of them started talking about what spell we should cast. Ruby was still fixated on her hair, but after how against it her mom was, we all decided it was a bad idea. "Let's just do something small," I suggested. "Like the bird. Maybe a frog." I surveyed our room.

"How about this guy?" Gwen held up the stuffed dog from my bed and then hugged him as if he belonged to her. Maya and Ruby turned to me.

He was my dog, and I wanted to snatch him out of Gwen's arms. My dad had given him to me. The night he had, I couldn't decide if I was happier my father was home or that this stuffed dog had come with him. I looked between all their expectant faces, not really wanting to risk something from my dad. Then I remembered the bird and how nothing happened, and I sighed. "Okay."

Gwen set the stuffed animal on the floor in front of me as Ruby began jotting notes down for a spell for us to use. The four of us held hands staring at it.

"Wait," Maya said. "Remember at the party the old lady told our moms we should be holding hands in a circle?"

We moved into a circle and stood around the dog.

I started with the words our mothers had said to us. "Focus. See it alive. Believe what you can do to change it." I squeezed Gwen's hand in mine. "Breathe in your power." We all focused on the stuffed animal. It would soon be alive.

"Now recite the spell until it becomes the new truth of the world," Ruby said and chanted the spell she'd written for my dog.

One sweet dog as still as can be
Bring him to life to play with me

One sweet dog as still as can be
Bring him to life to play with me

On the second time, we all joined in. My eyes were closed. We'd barely gotten through the second verse when the dog barked at us.

My breath caught.

"We did it!" Ruby dropped our hands and jumped around the room. "We really did it."

It was unbelievable. I couldn't stop looking at the dog that was staring up from the floor in front of me and barking. I sat next to him, and he climbed onto my lap and licked my face. It would've been a sorrowful moment, one of recognition of the man I'd lost too many years ago, but this crazy sweet dog wouldn't let me be sad. He inched up until his paws were on my shoulders and he was able to properly hug me.

"Holy cow . . ." Ruby said, and her calm, quiet demeanor bespoke of the enormity of what we'd just accomplished and what else the four of us might be capable of together.

Gwen was staring at the dog and me in utter shock. I thought she might pass out. I tried to decipher whether she was amazed or petrified, but I was a little of both, so it was hard to help her. "Gwen," I gently said. "Are you okay?"

Her movements were slow. She was in a trance. "We, we . . . we did that?"

"Yes," Maya said and put her arm around her. "Together. We couldn't have done it without you."

"But how?"

"How does any of it work?" Ruby said matter-of-factly and shrugged. "We're blessed." She knelt down and petted the dog. "What's your name?" she asked him.

"Carl is what I've always called him."

"Carl?"

"It's short for caramel."

"No it isn't." Ruby shook her head, giving me a sideways look.

"It is if you're three years old."

She seemed to accept the explanation. "Carl it is."

"How are we going to explain this dog?"

"We'll tell them we got a dog," Ruby said, sounding as if the answer should have been obvious as she pushed to her feet.

"They're going to know. I had the exact dog on my bed almost my entire life. They're *mothers*. They're going to figure it out."

"Calm down." She paced as she thought. "We're going to do what any other normal teenager would do when faced with a situation they're unsure about and, admittedly, in way over their head."

"We're going to ask an adult for help?" Maya said.

"No. We're going to lie."

"It isn't going to work." There was no way we were going to get away with turning a stuffed animal into our new household pet.

"We'll say . . ." Ruby was working out the details in front of us. "That Ike bought it for you."

"Wrong." I shook my head. "Ike's out."

"Right, right, right. Ike's out." Her face lit up with a new plan. "We'll give the dog to Gwen as a birthday present."

The dog settled back onto my lap, looking almost affronted. "He's my dog. He's slept with me every night since my father brought him home from Portland for me." My voice cracked at the end. He was my dog.

"Okay." Ruby knew that idea was a non-starter. She put her

hands up in front of her. "We'll say that I ruined your stuffed animal somehow. I don't know exactly how yet. Spilled something on him maybe, and that the guy who sits next to me in Spanish was giving away puppies from a litter. So I got one for you as a peace offering." I sighed. The dog nuzzled in closer.

I avoided considering what a horrible plan it was by playing with Carl the rest of the day. The dog's energy was boundless. He loved to be outside as long as I was there, too. Ike came to my house as soon as he got off work on the Hitchner farm. He was dirty and exhausted, and I'd never seen a more striking human being in my life. He parked on the street and was walking up the driveway as Carl caught his ball in the air and ran it back to me. When he noticed Ike, Carl ran up to him with the ball instead.

Without hesitation, Ike pried the ball from Carl's mouth and threw it in the direction we'd been playing. "Who's this guy?"

"That's Carl. He's my new dog." Ike raised his eyebrows at me. "We've been busy today."

"Adopting dogs?"

I took a deep breath before admitting to my boyfriend what I was still trying to come to terms with myself. "*Creating* dogs."

Ike's mouth dropped open in shock as he turned his attention back to Carl. "You mean . . ." His eyes jumped to me. "Is that the stuffed dog you keep on your bed?"

I felt the small blush of embarrassment on my cheeks as I nodded. Yes, I had slept with a stuffed animal, but I didn't care. It had reminded me of my dad.

"Well, that's not going to be easy to explain to your mom."

"I know."

Ike stared toward the trees at the back of the yard. "The night of the bonfire. When we were pinned against that tree, what was that?"

My mind drifted back to my suspicions. "At first, I thought it was you."

"What?"

"But then I realized it wasn't." I kissed him.

"Well, for the record, I never thought it was you causing it."

"Not even for a second?" I searched his eyes for the truth.

"No. Was it Ruby or Maya?"

"I don't think so. They never said anything about it."

He watched Carl with a thoughtful expression before asking, "Where's Gwen?"

Ruby, Maya, and I had grown up with our powers. They were a part of us. They'd made as much sense as the ability to blow a bubble with gum or open a combination lock, but for Gwen, everything had to be overwhelming. Gwen was holding up better than I probably would be. "She's getting a drink."

"So, we're alone out here?"

"Yup." My smile was slow and knowing as Ike pulled me to him and kissed me again. "I don't want this weekend to end."

"Neither do I."

"It's time to fly," Maya said as she walked out the kitchen door with Ruby and Gwen behind her. I took a step away from Ike, and he waved to them. "Ever, this is yours to teach. You're the best flyer out of all of us."

Ruby stopped next to Ike and studied him. "What else can he do?" she asked me.

I looked him up and down, thinking of all the wonderful things he could do with his hands and his lips, and his—

"Like a witch," Ruby interrupted my thoughts. "What else can he do that's like us?"

"Oh. The only thing we know of is his ability to hear."

She concentrated as she continued to watch him. "Interesting."

"Tell me if you can hear this." Ruby stared at Ike.

He shrugged. Ike hadn't heard a thing.

"Very interesting." She turned back to Maya, Gwen, and me.

"I'm going to try that group chat thing again. That's how he heard last time." Her voice trailed off with her words.

Ruby regarded each of us and then closed her eyes.

Can you guys hear me?

Gwen thought, *yes.*

Maya thought the same.

I can, I thought.

Yes, Ike thought and all our stares darted in his direction. It was incredible. All of it.

"Wow! You're special. It must only work in a group." She shrugged.

Or when I'm listening for you, Ike thought as he stared at me. It appeared I was the only one who heard it.

Ruby walked toward the clearing. "Okay, time for flying."

This was the first thing we were going to show Gwen that could easily kill her. Hearing our voices and casting spells were not to be taken lightly, but flying through the air was more physically dangerous than anything else we could do.

"Okay. Let's start with takeoff." I stood in front of the rest of them. "I like to take a few steps and then launch off my left foot."

"Really?" Ruby asked. Her face was scrunched in thought.

"Yeah. How do you take off?"

"Always on my right."

I focused back on Gwen. "Once we get you off the ground, you can change this to however it's most comfortable for you." She nodded. "I like to take running steps, and I always become invisible on the first one."

"How are you going to show her if you're invisible?" Maya raised a good point. Our yard was private, but not secluded. We had neighbors here in Auburn, and no one would ever forget seeing us fly.

I waved Gwen over to me. When she was close, I took her hands and positioned her against the back of me. I wrapped her arms around my neck and had her clasp her own wrists.

"You can do that?" Ruby asked, realizing I was going to fly with Gwen draped over me.

"The hardest part is getting up there. I obviously can't run with her on my back."

"How did you figure it out?"

I tipped my head toward Ike. "I flew with the big guy before."

Ruby was indignant. She turned to Ike, "You flew with her?"

"Yeah. Why?"

"I don't know. It's so . . . intimate. I've never flown with anyone, and I've never heard of anyone flying on someone's back before." She was studying him. "What else have you two done?"

Gwen saved me with her plea of, "Can we please not? He's my brother."

"Of course." Ruby backed off. "Understood." She held up her hand for me to continue with the flight lesson, but I knew she'd revisit this topic before the weekend was over.

I quieted my mind, and Gwen and I disappeared. I bent my knees and Gwen followed. Another breath and we jetted into the air above my yard. Gwen screamed out, "Ahhhh," as we ascended, and I told everyone on the ground that we were fine. I thought to Gwen, *You have to be quiet, especially in the air.*

We flew over the creek and into Gloucester County. We crossed the railroad tracks and flew over the post office. When we reached the woods on the other side of Swedesboro, I slowed and dropped us down to the ground.

You don't want to go in too fast. It's kind of like getting off one of those people movers at the airport, but not really.

That was amazing.

I know.

We showed ourselves to each other.

"How about we hold hands?" I was starting to get nervous. "And only fly a few feet off the ground." She was bouncing her head up and down. Gwen wasn't afraid at all.

We stared at each other until we disappeared, and I gave her hand a squeeze, letting her know I was ready. Together, we ran three steps before diving up into the air.

The shock of flight hit her, and she stopped concentrating. I pulled her toward me, afraid she'd plunge to her death, but she recovered and soared next to me.

I'm doing it!

You are.

She flew faster beside me. *You make me brave.*

No one can make you brave. You're born with that power. I answered her back.

I could hear encouragement from Ruby and Maya, but Ike never thought a word. We flew over the creek and past the outskirts of Woodstown before heading back toward Auburn.

I'm going to let go. Gwen thought.

Are you sure?

Yes. She dropped my hand. I moved in to fly even closer to her.

On the heels of Ruby and Maya telling Ike not to worry and that she was safe with me, a cold, hard air surrounded us. It pressed against our backs. I'd never felt anything but the wind in the sky. This was a hard wall, a cage that had somehow trapped us.

I reached for Gwen, and pulled her close to me right before I banked left, pulling her along. I assumed it was some type of current, but even though that was logical, I knew it was something evil. The air remained against our side.

Hold on to me! I practically shouted in my head at Gwen. I dove down, and the air pressed us closer to the ground. I pulled Gwen onto my back and darted toward home.

I was just about to call Ruby and Maya when I heard, *We're on our way*, in my head.

My arms were tight against my sides and Gwen was solid against the back of me. We flew with the stale, dead air chasing us, but it didn't interfere with us until I felt what I could only describe as fingertips running down the side of my arm. Chills flowed through me, and I flew faster than I ever had before.

I could feel Ruby and Maya approaching. The familiar sensation of their closeness surrounded me before Ruby and Maya were on each side of us.

What is it?

I don't know.

I can feel it.

Them. It's them, Maya said. *We're surrounded.*

Who?

We banked north, and the air cleared as soon as we hit the boundary line of Auburn. I inhaled and exhaled forcing my panic away until I was finally able to breathe.

Gwen, who had no idea what had just happened, held my hand in a tight grip and shifted off my back. She flew on her own safely between Maya and me.

Take Gwen back, I thought to Maya.

Ike growled in my head. *No!*

I wasn't going to argue with him. I needed to find out who or what had been with us and if I waited, they'd be too far away. Ruby and I watched until Gwen and Maya reappeared safely next to Ike on our back lawn.

Without a word to each other, we flew back toward Woodstown. When we got there, we didn't find anything but a gentle breeze in the air.

Ever, come back here. Right now.

I ignored him.

Ruby was quiet, more evidence she was concerned. We flew the entire perimeter of the town and then straight over the center of it.

Nothing. Not one sign of anything we'd just experienced.

I let Ruby lead the way home so I could focus on the air around us. I waited for the hard wall to erect next to us, but there was nothing but the usual wind blowing. We landed at the back of our property and faced each other. Neither of us had answers to the questions we hadn't been able to form yet.

Ike stormed toward us. Without a word, Ruby walked away, knowing he was my next dark force to deal with.

"How's Gwen?"

He stopped three feet from me. His expression was a glare infused with fear. Rage was an easy emotion for him, but his girlfriend and his sister in danger at the same time had mixed things up for him. "Confused," he said through a tight jaw.

Adrenalin coursed through me. I couldn't slow my heart rate any more than I could stop myself from walking up to him and pulling him down to me for a kiss. Ike responded without argument. I threaded my fingers in his hair and moved even closer. His anger melted away. He lifted me, and I wrapped my legs around his waist.

I kissed him until the only thing I felt from him was love, but when he placed me back on the ground in front of him, I knew this moment wasn't as simple as a kiss.

"I needed you to come back."

"I was fine."

"Maya said you didn't know what it was."

"It doesn't matter what it was. I was fine."

He pointed his finger at me and poked it into my chest. "It's that attitude right there that makes me crazy."

I kind of loved that he was concerned, but I couldn't let him think it was okay to order me around. With a soft touch, I wrapped my fingers around his much bigger hand. "You have to go before my mom comes home."

"Promise me you won't go back out there." I sighed. I wouldn't lie to him, but I wasn't sure if I was going back up there tonight. "I will hold you down here. Don't forget you might be invisible and able to fly, but if I get my hands on you, I'm still strong enough to hold you here."

I leaned in and kissed him again, letting him believe that was the truth. "You don't need your strength to hold me here."

"Promise me, Ever." Ike's expression was stern. He wasn't swayed.

"I promise."

XXIII

WE MADE EVERYTHING LOOK GOOD, but not too good, which wasn't hard to achieve with Carl running around. He barely left my side to eat, but he was warming up to Maya and Ruby.

I felt our mothers nearby before the minivan drove by the kitchen window and parked behind the house. Lovie was the first one to walk through the door, and I wished it had been just her.

Carl ran from my side to Lovie and jumped up on her. His paws were on her thighs. His tail was wagging furiously.

"Down," I yelled. "No jumping." I gently urged him back as Sloane and my mother walked in.

"Hi, girls," Sloane said before her attention fixed on Carl. "What is that?"

My mother pushed past her and stared at the dog. Carl jumped all over her, already knowing her better than she knew him.

"Carl! Get down." I stayed focused on him so I didn't have to face any of them.

"It's Carl," Ruby said answering her mother's original question as if it weren't a big deal that there was a dog in the house.

"Carl?" my mother asked. The name's significance was not lost on her. I assumed she was examining the dog and concluding he looked exactly like the stuffed animal I used to have that was also named Carl.

Sloane stood in front of Ruby. "Was it necessary for me to spell out not to get a dog when I gave you the list of rules? Because, until I just saw this, I considered the three of you to be pretty smart."

"Of course not." Ruby knelt down and pet Carl. He was hard to resist. "And we are smart."

"Then why am I looking at a dog in my kitchen?"

"So, you know the stuffed dog Ever has slept with since she was little?" Sloane was searching her mind for the memory. "Her dad brought him back to her after a work trip. Aunt Helene, you know the one I'm talking about." Ruby was good. I sensed nothing but the truth from her. She'd said she was going to stick as close to the actual events as possible.

My mother nodded but didn't say a word as she continued to look at Carl.

"Well, I was throwing it around the other day, and it got caught on a door knob and ripped." This made no sense, but Ruby thought something completely inconceivable might be the most believable. "Really badly ripped."

Our mothers were now all staring at her, but Ruby didn't let their scrutiny faze her. "This guy, Bob, in my Spanish class has been bugging me to take a puppy from his dog's latest litter. And . . ."

"And?" Sloane was not appeased.

"And Ever was so devastated, I called him and he brought one over."

"We didn't let him in the house, though," Maya said and then added, "I swear," for good measure. "He gave us some food to get started, but we need to go to the pet store."

"I'm sure there's one in a neighboring state."

I glared at Ruby. This was not the time for her thoughts on the lack of shopping options in rural South Jersey.

"So, *Bob* gave you this dog for free?" Sloane asked.

Carl ran over to her again. He was our only hope. It was a terrible plan, but we couldn't think of a better one.

The name Carl slipped from my mother's lips, and the situation became critical. She would kill us for casting a spell and then grill us about how we had managed it. I could feel her putting the pieces together. She was currently working through the impossibility of the three of us being so reckless, but she would arrive at the only logical conclusion momentarily.

I panicked. "We need to talk to you about something serious." All eyes in our kitchen fell to me where I was still kneeling on the floor with my dog. "We were flying earlier and encountered something."

My mother stood straight. "What?"

The dog was forgotten. I stood, too. "We aren't sure. It was a force of some kind."

"It surrounded us and pushed us toward the ground," Ruby joined in.

"Oh." Lovie walked to each of us and touched us one by one in some way. "Are you all right? When did this happen?"

"A few hours ago. We're fine," I said and tried to keep my voice perfectly balanced between curiosity and reverence. "We just didn't know what it was."

Everyone forgot about Carl.

"What did you do?" Sloane asked, but she was watching my mother.

"We stayed together and flew home," Ruby said.

It was close to the truth. I added, "They were gone when we reached Auburn."

"They?" my mother, who'd heard every word I'd ever said, keyed in on that one.

"It was just a feeling."

Our mothers were in shock. I felt for signs of fear, but I couldn't decipher any in the cacophony of emotions that were pouring off them. Nothing was simple all of a sudden.

My mother nodded at Sloane. It was just a slight tip of her head. The motion you'd make at the end of a statement, but they'd silently shared the words. "I'm going to change, and then I'm going to fly."

"I'll go with you." I wasn't staying behind.

"No."

"But I can show you where they were."

"You're staying here." My mother's eyes narrowed, ready to fight me and whatever was in the sky.

"What is it? You know."

"I don't know, but it could be the Virago, and I don't want you anywhere near them."

"I'm the strongest flyer," I said. There was no arguing that. My mother only stared at me. "By far."

"How about the four of us go?" Sloane said. "Maya and Lovie can hang back in case we need help."

My mother stayed quiet. I didn't know if she was talking to Sloane. They'd had twenty more years of practice silently speaking to each other. I couldn't always tell what they were up to. "Okay, but if I say you're to go home, you have to turn back immediately"

"Fine."

"I'm serious, Ever. Not one word of argument. If I say 'go home,' you're to go."

"Got it." I put my hands up in front of me.

Sloane and my mom went upstairs to change while I slipped out back into the cold night and called to Ike in my mind.

Ike.

Miss me? He responded within seconds. He was playful. Just the way I loved him.

Horribly so.

The moon was out. It lit up the sky, making it seem much earlier than it was.

I'm going up in a few minutes. These words were met with complete silence on his end. *My mom's coming and Ruby and her mom.*

Your mom?

I know. I just wanted to tell you.

Make it so I can hear you.

I can't or she'll hear you, too.

"Ready?" Ruby said as they all stepped outside.

Ever, be careful. Let me know the minute you're back on the ground.

I will. I love you.

I thought of the periodic table of the elements. *Co, Cobalt, number twenty-seven. B, Boron, number five . . .* I ran the abbreviations through my mind to clear it before facing my mother. My feelings for Ike would be as obvious to her as my delight at my first birthday cake.

The four of us walked to the tree line behind our house, stepped behind it, and took off into the air. Ruby and I flew shoulder to shoulder with our mothers on either side of us. I led the way around town and into Gloucester County. There was nothing but the crisp night air and the moon. It was so peaceful that I almost forgot the reason we were flying.

Our mothers fell back and flew behind Ruby and me. We soared over the turnpike and back toward Auburn. Lovie and Maya walked out the back door as soon as we landed behind our car.

"Anything?" Lovie asked.

"Nothing," my mother said and then added, "No one flies alone, and no one flies without us knowing."

More rules.

"And if you're flying and encounter whatever it was again, you're to call us immediately." Sloane looked at Ruby and then at me. "Even if you're somewhere you shouldn't be. Do you understand?"

The three of us nodded.

"Let's get some sleep," Lovie said and rubbed my shoulders. "Tomorrow starts another busy week." She turned to Maya. "Did you get your paper done while we were gone?"

I left them all behind and climbed the stairs to our attic. I fell flat on my bed and stared at the ceiling.

I'm back. Safe and sound.

Now I'll be able to sleep. Anything out there?

Nope. Perfectly fine. I love you.

I love you, too.

COURAGE

Helene

IN THEORY, SINCE THE GIRLS were at school, I should have been able to relax, but I knew Ever saw Ike there. At least I was reasonably confident of her location and that there was some supervision. Seeing Ike Kennedy on the side lawn of the high school had stolen any security I'd felt upon my return to Auburn.

The sight of him had done more than that. It almost killed me. Of course, I'd heard. Trish couldn't wait to tell me the day we registered the girls for school about Gisel and Isaiah's shotgun wedding. Gisel *never* considered consequences. There was miniscule amount of satisfaction surrounding the news she'd gotten knocked up and her baby had been a boy, but I had to feign a coughing fit to end Trish's walk down memory lane because I knew I couldn't take any more information.

I'd wondered no less than a thousand times over the years who'd they'd gone on to marry, if they had kids, if they were happy in spite of being without me, but I never dared asked a soul for information. I knew it would wound me the exact way it had when Trish told me, but when Ike looked at my daughter, terror set in. Protecting Ever eclipsed any of my former feelings for his parents.

Woodstown was huge compared to Auburn, but it was still a small town. Each graduating class was under two hundred kids. Sometimes as few as a hundred and seventy, but that should have been enough to keep Ever away from him.

Sloane sang as she hung the new curtains in her bedroom that she'd ordered two days before and paid express shipping for because she had no patience. "I'm ready to hang them now," she'd said and hit the button to confirm her order. The curtains were white with a subtle metallic swirl pattern that reminded me of the set her mother had hanging in her living room when we were young. All the women in her family had a similar panache to their style. The windows were open and the autumn breeze billowed the fabric around her legs before she affixed the rod to the brackets.

"Need help?" I leaned against the wall as Sloane stood on a stool in front of her window. Ever couldn't understand why we didn't just use our powers to do everything, but there was something to be said for completing a task the conventional way.

"Nope." Sloane tightened the screws that would hold the bar in place and spread the fabric out evenly across the sill. "Did Ever say anything else about the weekend?"

"No." Sloane half-laughed at my defeated response. She'd expected my denial. Our girls had officially reached the age when they told each other more than they told us. "I'm worried about her."

The humor drained from Sloane's face. "I know. We're all worried."

None of this had to be said, but I needed to talk about it. "Was it this obvious when I was in love?"

Sloane pulled the final few centimeters of a joint out of her nightstand drawer, lit it, and said, "No one knows your daughter better than you. I suspect you knew before she did that she was in love." I examined the family portraits on Sloane's nightstand of just her and Ruby as Sloane blew smoke toward the ceiling. There was only one that included her late husband, but it'd been taken when Ruby was just a baby.

"Do you think there's any hope it isn't Ike Kennedy?" I asked.

"No." She offered me the joint, but I waved it off.

This was killing me. "Not even a second of hesitation?" She couldn't have at least pretended to think about it a little more?

"I mean, there's always hope." She stood back from the curtain and examined her work. "But history's a hellion."

I left Sloane's room feeling worse than I did when I got there, and passed the bathroom.

Lovie'd been in there with the shower running for at least forty minutes. I knew she was crying, masking her sobs with the running water. Based on my own mourning, Lovie might cry in the shower for months. I left her alone because no one knew better than Sloane and me that there was nothing anyone could do.

I walked out the back door of the house and was in the air before the screen door slammed back against the doorjamb. I flew straight up until the air that entered my body replaced the utter sadness of my existence. I'd flown in this exact spot with my mother until she died before I was old enough to drive. If she were here, none of this would've ever happened.

I wouldn't blame her, though. There were so many others to condemn. I'd spent the last twenty years dwelling on them—hating them—while I searched for a way out. I was exhausted from it, and I moved back to Auburn only to have the first boy Ever loved be a Kennedy. May that whole family drop off the earth. I banked east toward Woodstown.

I flew high and basked in the memories of us flying through the summer nights when Lovie, Sloane, and I were teenagers. We'd take off just as the lightning bugs filled the darkening sky and fly for miles before landing and watching the stars take over the night. I wouldn't have survived my life without them, but even with their boundless support, I still found myself looking around or listening for the other piece that made us whole. The nagging feeling of loss wouldn't let me rest. It was always right there in the back of my mind, blocked by the urgent need to find a new future for Ever and Maya and Ruby. This tragic life couldn't be theirs, too.

I flew low over the football stadium. The parking lot was full of students' cars. The stands were empty, but I could still hear the band playing *Louie Louie* if I concentrated hard enough. The Chestnut Run Pool was just to the southwest. Our mothers had taken us there for summer swim team when we were little. By the time we were fifteen, we never went, but we'd fly over the fence and swim in the moonlight every Wednesday night. We called them our Aqua Eves.

Even then, it was impossible to keep Lovie dry for very long. I sped up and flew toward Alloway, dipped low at the lake and let my fingertips run across the top of the still water. The fish jumped out and dove back in as I passed. Alloway Lake was the second place I'd ever caught a fish. Oldmans Crick had been the first.

The flying relaxed me. I swirled through the air, pivoting with the wind to head back toward Auburn. I took the long way, not wanting to leave the air, and I crossed over Laurel Hills. It was stupid. I was over-confident. The leaves had fallen to the ground and the treetops were visible, as was the tree house.

My chest tightened at the sight of it. Love washed over me as if shot from a cannon perched on its balcony. There was desire and obsession and utter despair coursing through me and releasing my tears. I flew straight up, higher than I'd ever flown before, to distance myself from the little hideaway.

Ever cannot love Ike Kennedy.

I inhaled, solidified my thoughts on the subject, and told myself it had nothing to do with me. It was my past that made it impossible, but I feared it also made it inevitable.

I flew with the Woodstown Auburn Road and veered right toward town, or "street" as the girls called it. I no longer suffered from the urgent need to escape this hill that my mother loved. The firehouse, the church, and every residence between them and the crick reminded me of the time in my life when laughter was free and friendship was forever. I needed to come home probably years before I did.

I landed in our backyard and stepped through the tree line, visible to anyone who was watching.

When I walked inside, the house was warm. Sloane had lit a fire, and Lovie was baking banana bread for the girls' snack after school. Love replaced the damaging emotions inside of me. I took a deep breath and held it, letting it fill the empty gashes of my soul.

"I'm choosing to forgive them," I said. Sloane turned to me with wide eyes. Lovie put her coffee cup on the kitchen table and waited. "All of them." Tears lodged in my throat. I wasn't sure I could, but I was going to try. I hadn't wanted to be the cause of Gisel losing her powers, but I had been young and devastated when I'd made my choice. The craft was as much a part of her as she'd been a part of me. "Even Clara," I said. It'd been twenty years since I called her anything but a disgusting curse word. "The solution doesn't exist in hatred."

Lovie's eyes welled with tears. "Only in love," she said. It took coming home to Auburn for me to realize it.

Sloane winked at me and returned to sorting through the mail on the kitchen table. A quiet calm surrounded us while we waited to pick up the girls from school. Things would change now. We'd find peace where I'd left it. In Auburn.

We all went to the high school in Lovie's minivan to pick up the girls. Carl, too. He loved to ride, especially if Ever was the destination.

"We're probably going to need another car when the girls turn seventeen," Lovie said.

"Ever isn't even excited about it. All she wants to do is fly." I left off, *and probably be with Ike Kennedy.*

"Let's go to the park and let Carl run around," Ever suggested when she climbed into the third row with her dog. No one protested, so we made the short trip. Sloane, Lovie, and I hadn't been to Marlton Park since the night we graduated from high school. That night, Gisel had been with us, too. This time, we'd take our daughters back there without her.

It was warm for early December, but when the car doors swung back against their hinges as the wind caught them, Lovie pulled her coat collar up around her neck. "Whoa! I see why nobody's here."

"This park is possessed by the wind," Ruby said, and Sloane and I stared at her, but she just climbed from the van and said, "What? How come a bunch of witches don't believe in ghosts?"

Carl ran past us and frolicked on the open lawn as Ever grabbed his ball from the floor of the van and threw it to him. He brought it back and nudged it against her thigh. Sometimes, I thought he was actually smiling at her. She pried it from his mouth and threw it again before she, Maya, and Ruby ran to the far side of the park, laughing as Carl chased after them with the ball in his mouth. Lovie, Sloane, and I stood in a line, leaning into one another. We were more solid than we'd been the day before.

Ever's scream rang out across the lawn, and all three of us sprinted in her direction. Horrified, I watched as Carl was flung into the sky by invisible hands at the same moment as an icy wind hit me in the face. The puppy crashed into the lawn and yelped. Ever ran toward him, but before she reached him, she was shoved backward and slammed into ground fifteen feet away from me. Blood throbbed behind my ears. I would kill the witch that touched her.

"Mom!" Ever screamed as tears tracked down her cheeks and her eyes widened in terror—Carl was above her, his legs were being pulled in different directions.

Anger seared through me before I disappeared into the air. I thrashed through the energy, circling with my hands fisted straight out from my sides. I could feel their traitorous bodies and hear their screams as I hit them.

Carl fell to Maya's waiting arms.

Go north, Helene. It was Sloane. She and Lovie would circle back behind me. As soon as their words entered my mind, the wind slowed and the calm returned, but I wasn't letting them get away. I soared forward until the bitter darkness coated my mouth with the knowledge that they were in front of me. I reached for an ankle and grabbed it, but was kicked in the face for my effort.

A noxious laugh pricked at my ears as I withdrew, and then there was nothing. Not a sound, a scent, or a sense that anyone else was in the air. Sloane jetted up beside me.

Where's Lovie?

She went back with the girls.

I held still, searching the air for clues of where they'd gone, but we were alone. We flew back to Marlton Park in silence. Ever ran to Carl and held his head. I dipped low above them. His front paw was bent in a way I'd never seen before. His breaths were short.

"He's going to die," she cried. The pain in her words incited hatred I hadn't felt since her father left this world.

"No he's not," Sloane said and appeared next to her. She wrapped her arm around Ever's shoulders and helped support the dog's head. "Take him to the car. Keep him steady. Move him as little as possible."

The girls fled with Carl.

I'll take them to the vet. Sloane followed the girls to the car, but I could sense the anger swirling around her. *If you find them, call for me.*

Do you feel anything? Lovie seethed as she flew toward the end of the parking lot.

No. Nothing but utter hatred.

They're going to kill someone.

Themselves, if that dog dies.

Besides the crisp breeze, no one would have believed evil had just departed Marlton Park or that it'd ever existed there in the first place.

Sloane, the girls, and Ever's beloved dog returned from the vet only minutes after Lovie and I got back. His front leg was in a cast and one side of his face hung lower than I remembered.

"He's a little loopy from the pain medicine," Sloane said and put a prescription bag down on the counter. "I might take some of it myself."

"Are you three okay?" I was asking all of them, but my sight was locked on my daughter.

"Who would hurt a dog?" Ever asked.

"Someone trying to make a point," Sloane said and reminded me of how we'd saved the horses from her.

"What made you scream the first time, at the park?"

Ever closed her eyes and swallowed. When she opened them, she stared at her dog. "He was giving me the ball, wagging his tail, and nudging my hand to take it from him. I was petting him, and they yanked him away from me. They threw him into the sky while he cried out. He was crying for me to help him." She shook her head to release the images from her memory.

"Ever, they're evil, but they're not unstoppable."

She sat on the floor with her dog curled in her lap. She stared at his cast and rubbed his head until I feared she was retreating to a place buried inside her mind. "Ever . . ."

She finally looked at me. "I wanted to go home," Ever said, but I didn't understand. "To Vermont." My heart broke. *This* was her home. "*None* of this existed there." She started to cry. "I wanted to leave and never look back." For the first time since we'd returned, I questioned what we'd done to our daughters by bringing them to Auburn.

"But?" Sloane was the only one brave enough to speak.

"But then I thought about Mr. Turnbull and Edna Schrufer and the Kingsway coven and my chess partner and all the other people I've come to love and the fact that Carl is with us because we're here . . ." She looked around our kitchen and finally fixed her steely gaze on me. "I want to kill them."

We all did. After today's attack, we could spend the wee hours of the night ridding this town of every member of the Virago we could get our hands on, but that was not our nature. "We can't kill them," I said without making light of Ever's decision. The remaining members of my coven already knew we couldn't. Our daughters did not. It was one more lesson a young witch had to learn. "A witch cannot kill another witch. It's the essence of the code we live by."

"How can the Virago be killing all those women then? What about the Earth witch they killed that the Kingsway coven told us about?" Ruby asked. She was ready to fight.

"The Virago have no honor. They live by no code."

"Then we shouldn't treat them as witches." Ruby always saw things as black and white, and in this moment, her clarity was intoxicating.

"We won't let them change who we are," Lovie said, ending the conversation.

Ever

S LOANE DROPPED US OFF AT the front entrance and pulled away as we ran to the overhang for shelter. I hated to leave Carl home alone for anything these days, but the storm made me especially nervous. He wouldn't be allowed in the high school and none of us could miss tonight. My mom asked Mrs. Schrufer if he could stay with her while we were out, and she couldn't say yes quickly enough. I was actually worried that she wouldn't give him back.

"Let's go," Maya said, nervously eyeing the dark clouds above us as lightning streaked between them. She loved the ocean. Hated storms. Ruby was the opposite from her, and as usual, I was somewhere in between.

We walked through the auditorium and backstage where everyone was busy getting into their robes and warming up their voices.

According to my fellow chorus members, this was the most popular concert of the school year, but I thought the winter thunderstorm outside might keep people away. I shook my head, knowing nothing would keep the people of this town away, not even a storm strong enough to wash away cars.

We lined up and filed onto the stage and then up onto the risers. Ruby was in front of me. Maya was to my right, on the other side of Gwen, who seemed thrilled with the storm. Energy burst from her, making my skin tingle just from being in her presence. It reminded me of the strength I always felt when I was near her brother, but it was different with Gwen. Her eyes closed as she inhaled and let her head fall back.

I scanned the audience and found Ike sitting next to his mother. He was watching me like I was the only person in the room. I let the corners of my mouth tilt up slightly, knowing only he would see. Sloane and Lovie were in the side section of the auditorium a few rows back from Ike. I smiled widely at them and searched for my mother, but there was only an empty seat.

I finally found her standing in a doorway to the right and talking to the security guard who'd asked me about her the first day of school. The giggle she let out before slapping his arm was made decades ago when a joke was told that was so funny it would still amuse her. She hugged him and walked into the auditorium as the lights dimmed, alerting everyone to take their seats.

The beginning stanza of "Oh Holy Night" fell from my lips, but there was something unholy about the night around us. With each step my mother took, something churned inside me. It wasn't just me. Gwen was on edge next to me. Ruby leaned back, and I touched her hair to calm her. We were all poised to ignite in some way we'd never felt before. It was the first time the four of us, and our mothers, had been in the same place.

I found Ike. He would ground me. He'd silent the chaos inside my body. His eyes darted between his sister, me, and his mother, who was leaning forward with her head in her hands near her lap and her shoulders shaking.

I sang and tried to make sense of everything around me. The storm raged outside. The thunder almost drowned out our voices. Mr. Carey pleaded with overt arm motions for us to continue and to use our "strong" voices.

Ike's mother stood as we began the final words of the song. The people immediately next to her watched her while they clapped. One man stood as if she'd initiated a standing ovation. Gisel looked directly at my mother, who was staring back at her. Even from the top row of the risers, I could feel the love between them. It was deeper than the earth and harder than a rock. It was the kind that can only be found after years of being buried.

With a crackling sound, the window to my right broke, leaving a spider web crack in the glass. The noise stopped the singing. The piano halted. The lights flickered above us, and my sight found Ike's mother again as the riser fell beneath me. Maya and I grabbed Gwen and hovered above the wreckage for a half second before placing her on the ground. The entire row had collapsed, leaving students on the floor everywhere around us. Some from the row below us had fallen in shock. They were moaning on the ground and rubbing various parts of their bodies in near darkness.

Even in the chaos, I didn't take my eyes off Ike's mom. When she covered her mouth with a hand, turned, and ran for the door, I didn't miss it. My mother followed right after her, and a minute later, so did I.

The hallways were electrified in their wake, and the trail led right through the side door, which was where I watched them from. Ike's mother waved her hand above her head and the tree across the street uprooted and fell on its side.

She raised her arms high, and the rain stopped falling upon her.

"Gisel," my mother yelled.

Tonight, her name fell from my mother's tongue as familiar as my own. Ike's mother spun around and stared at a truck parked on Lincoln Avenue.

"Gisel, stop!"

"Don't you dare tell me to stop!" she screamed back at my mother. Her anger hit the door in front of me like a car crashing into a wall. "Twenty years I've been without my powers. Twenty years!" Her voice was a barely a shrill by the end. She refocused on the truck and flipped it on its side with a twirl of her hand.

"Gisel, you have to calm down."

"What do you care?" she asked as she spun around to face my mother.

"I never stopped caring about you. None of us have." I thought Ike's mom might cry, which for some reason was more disturbing than her uprooting trees and throwing vehicles.

"That isn't true." She shook her head denying my mother's words.

"Your powers would only come back with our love." Tears filled my mother's eyes. I couldn't look away from her. "I forgive you."

Gisel dropped her head back and stared at the raging sky. She raised her arms above her head and clasped her hands before disappearing. I could feel her flying over the school.

"Gisel," my mother yelled into the black sky as rain continued to fall above her. Sloane and Lovie ran out another door and worked together to lead her back inside. I was frozen in my spot, staring out and trying to process everything I'd just seen. Only a broken heart could cause destruction like this.

"Ever." I settled into Ike's voice saying my name from behind me. It moved me to him where he held me against his chest before I could exhale. "Ever?" He leaned back and ran his hand down the side of my face. "Tell me. What's wrong?"

"Nothing," my mother said from the doorway to the hall. Her voice had never been so cold. I closed my eyes and lowered my head. "Move away from him, Ever."

My insides were breaking apart and falling to my stomach. I couldn't swallow. I couldn't breathe. They were my everything and they were at odds. "Mom."

"Ever." My name was a sledgehammer she wielded through my chest. "Move. Away. From him."

I rested my hand on Ike's stomach as I took one step back. I lost myself in the navy pools that appeared black in the dim light of the stairwell. He took my hand in his, and I held it tight.

"Ever—"

"Don't speak to her."

"Mrs.—"

"Don't speak to me, either. For all our sakes, yours especially, I want you to stay away from us."

"What?" Ike faced my mother without an ounce of fear in his body.

I was ready to collapse on the floor. "You forgave her. I heard what you said. Why can't you see who he is? How good he is?"

"Go get in the car, Ever."

"Mom—"

"Now!" She'd never yelled at me that way before. I'd never given her a reason to.

Go, he thought, and I prayed my mother couldn't somehow hear him. *I love you.*

I took another step back and released Ike's hand. It slipped through my fingers and rested at the side of his body. I watched it hang there as if I'd never touch it again.

I walked to the car with my mother a half-step behind me. I could feel her furious breaths on the back of my neck, but I didn't care. Nothing could penetrate the feeling of loss that leaving Ike had inflicted upon me. That she had just forced upon me.

"I told you to stay away from him."

I turned on her ready to fight. "That's all you told me! You moved me back here with nothing but questions and expected me to just conform." Gisel and Gwen were her secret. They were supposed to be my sisters. I barely knew the woman standing before me. "You don't get to control everything."

"I've told you everything you need to know, and that is to stay . . . away . . . from him!" By the end of her sentence, she'd practically lost all composure.

"Why?"

The rain drove harder upon us. "He'll hurt you."

I continued walking while I shook my head.

"Ever." She jerked my arm and twisted me around.

"I love him." My mother froze in front of me. She inhaled and straightened her posture until she was at least an inch taller than me. "I love him, and there isn't a thing dark about him."

"You're never to see him again," she said and watched me crying in the rain. "He'll destroy you." It didn't sound like she was talking about me, though.

We drove home in silence. I didn't care if my mother ever spoke a word to me again. I hated her. Silently, I walked to my room, changed for bed, and crawled between the sheets. Ruby and Maya, my two pillars of strength, lay on either side of me, making sure to leave enough room for Carl to curl at our feet.

They didn't say a word—hadn't asked me a single question about what happened outside the concert. They just sensed it was devastating because they knew me better than was humanly possible.

My mother poked her head in the door to our room. She looked around and finally found all of us huddled together on my bed.

"Can I talk to Ever," she addressed the coven she'd brought me home to. Ruby and Maya didn't move. None of us were listening.

"I love how you guys protect each other, but no one's trying harder to keep her safe than I am."

I sighed at her words. Ruby and Maya left me to my mother. I sat up and faced her. I held my knees to my chest and covered my feet with my comforter as my mother sat on the side of my bed.

"Do you trust me, Ever?"

I'd always trusted her. Without a second of hesitation, I'd taken every word she said as the truth, but that was in Vermont. She wasn't right about Ike's family. I knew she wasn't, and I think she knew she wasn't too. There was something she wasn't telling me, and for that, I wasn't trusting her.

"Yes." I didn't care anymore if I told her the truth.

"Then why don't you trust that I know he isn't good for you?"

Rage ripped through my chest. He was more than good for me. He was a part of me. "Because you don't know how *kind* he is or how incredibly *strong* he is." I steadied my voice. "And you don't know how powerful he makes me every minute I'm near him."

She rubbed my legs. I could feel her compassion, but it was void of any understanding. She'd come here to convince me, not to hear me. "You're right, Ever. I don't know him, but I know where he comes from . . . Who he comes from." Gisel and my mother staring at each other in the auditorium flashed through my mind. "And I know this relationship will never work. You'll be hurt."

I shook my head and closed my eyes. "This has nothing to do with Ike and the Virago. It's about his mother, isn't it? You've kept me away from him so I wouldn't find out who she really is? Why? Tell me why you'd hide that from me . . . from us?" My question was met with pursed lips and no answers, so I pushed on. "Ike can't hurt me. You're the only one who's doing that."

"Ever. The Virago is on the attack. You're young. You've been raised in the safety of the forests of Vermont, but we're in New Jersey now—"

"What does any of that have to do with my being with Ike? If things are so dangerous here, why did we even move?"

She sat up straight and returned her hands to her lap. "You have to stay away from Ike Kennedy. If you fall in love with him it will end tragically."

"I already told you. I love him."

"And that's what's terrifying!" She calmed into a steely realization. "You're naïve . . . and you're forbidden to see him or anyone else. Your nights out are over for a while." She stood and faced me.

"I'm not going to live under your rule forever."

My mother walked out of my room, leaving me fuming as hot tears raced each other down my face and dripped onto my knees. I shut off the light next to my bed and lay in the darkness.

I loved him, and nothing she could say at this point could change that. Maybe she never could. I was completely empty. I couldn't see Ike. I didn't want my mother, and nothing I'd ever believed in seemed true in the dim light of the night.

When I thought I could hear his voice without crying, I listened for him. His words were filled with despair. He was scared for me. *I love you, Ever*, he thought over and over again. I thought of other things. I ran through memories of Vermont in my mind and every moment with my father. I remembered him waking me up on my birthday, every single one that I could recall, and I remembered the day he left us.

He was standing in the kitchen, packing a banana in his bag to take to work with him. My mother kissed him on the lips and told him to stay. Her desperation upset my stomach. I couldn't eat anymore. She'd been frightened in a way I'd never seen.

"I'll be back before you know it," he'd said and kissed her again.

"I'll love you forever," was the last thing my mother had said before he stepped out the door.

When the police knocked on the door, she'd steadied herself

behind it before she'd opened it. She knew he was gone.

I love you, Ever, Ike broke through, and the tears flowed down my face again.

I'll love you forever, I thought back. I knew I would, but unlike my mother, I wasn't letting Ike go.

Helene

THE FIRST CHRISTMAS AFTER EVER'S father died was hard. Ever had clung to me, so terrified I would die, too. She was the saddest little girl I'd ever seen. So, Sloane and Ruby and Ever and I had flown to Hawaii, and Lovie's husband took on the fatherly role for all the girls, which made it easier. Still, Ever had described the time as quiet. I knew what she'd meant. The chaotic energy, the excitement of the holiday had slipped away and had been replaced by the two of us trying to survive each day.

This Christmas had been even worse. I was crumbling inside, and she hated me because I forbid her to be with Isaiah and Gisel's son. Carols were being sung in every corner of the town. The houses were drenched in lights on the insides and the outsides, and everyone—except my daughter—was joyous. She brought the whole house down with her.

I wondered if Gisel was being tortured as much by her son. *Helene.* With the thought of her, her voice entered my mind. I sat up straight in my bed. I hadn't heard her in twenty years, but with forgiveness came her powers and her voice inside my head.

Helene, I want to see you. I need to talk to you. Her voice was the same ethereal tone it'd had been decades ago, and I wondered how many times she'd tried to reach out to me over the last twenty years.

I raised my hands and covered my mouth. This was really happening. Gisel was restored as our Earth witch. My coven was finally intact, even if my heart was still a bit broken.

Helene . . .

Gisel wouldn't stop. She was the most stubborn out of the four of us. She and Sloane used to lock horns whenever they found themselves on opposite sides of an issue.

Yes, I thought.

Yes you'll see me?

Yes. Not here, though. Not in Auburn . . . and not there. Going to the house she shared with Isaiah was completely out of the question.

Meet me at the winery tonight at six o'clock.

I exhaled. *Okay.*

I'd go alone. The way I should have faced her the morning after Isaiah told me they'd had sex. Maybe none of us would be in this mess if just Gisel and I had talked, but having Sloane and Lovie standing behind me gave every word out of my mouth the weight of the coven when it was really only my heartbreak speaking.

I thought about not even telling Lovie and Sloane that I was going, but there'd already been enough secrets for six covens. We needed the truth. When I finally emerged from my bedroom, I was showered and dressed in jeans and a sweater.

"Well, look at you," Sloane said.

I must have looked like hell the past few weeks. I certainly felt like it. I missed Ever more than I thought possible. Her room was right upstairs from mine, and I longed for her more than my mother. It was a horrifically tragic existence, and based on Ever's current disposition, our situation was torturous for her, too.

I still could not relent. She couldn't be with him.

"I'm meeting Gisel at the winery tonight."

Sloane placed her coffee mug on the table and took a seat. "Really?"

"She invited me this morning." *In my head.*

Sloane's lips puckered with a question she couldn't voice. Her head tilted to the side as if she had a good ear she needed to hear from.

"I know."

"Wow." *That's incredible.*

"Which part?" I asked.

"What forgiveness can do." Her warm expression confirmed meeting Gisel was the right decision.

I should have suggested breakfast or lunch. That way I wouldn't have had it looming over me all day. The girls came home from school, and Ever went to her room without looking at me.

I followed her up, searching for any subject she'd talk to me about. She was lying on her bed staring at the tapestry hanging from her ceiling.

"Now that the holidays are over, it's time to start thinking ahead." I sat on the edge of her bed, and Ever continued to study the fabric above us. Carl left his position at her ankles and snuggled up next to her neck. There wasn't a thing in this world that dog loved more than Ever. I knew exactly how he felt.

"We need to make a plan for Ruby's birthday and yours."

"I'm good." Her gaze never left the ceiling.

"This is a big one, Ever. We should celebrate. Maybe we can have a combined bash." I worried she was becoming depressed. A celebration might be just what all of us needed. Something to focus on that was happy. Although, Christmas had failed miserably. She was young. She'd bounce back and get over this.

She sat up and faced me. "You know what I want for my birthday." Carl moved his head to Ever's lap.

"Why do you have to make this so difficult?"

Tears welled in her eyes. "He's all I want."

God help me. "Ever, that's crazy. It can't be."

She lay back down and stared at the ceiling again. I wanted to argue, to scream, "What's so great about Ike Kennedy?" After all these years, and in spite of the fact that loving him nearly killed me, I was still tortured by the memories of Ike's father. I knew better than anyone how difficult it was going to be to leave Ike behind, but there was no other choice.

Five o'clock came, and we ate in silence the same way we had for weeks. Lovie and Sloane and their daughters talked and joked around us, and I sat and wondered what this would be like if Ever and I were alone. What would we do without these women in our lives?

When the girls had cleared the table and gone into the family room to watch television, Lovie and Sloane sat at the kitchen table with me in silence.

I'm proud of you, Lovie thought.

How is that possible?

Since you found a way to forgive Gisel, anything is possible.

They were right. We were going to find a way to move past this. I grabbed my purse before walking out the back door to the car. I didn't have to lie to Ever about where I was going. It was the only advantage to her not asking me any more questions.

The winery hadn't been here when I'd left twenty years ago. It, the golf course, the Dunkin Donuts . . . they were all new in an area that valued nothing more than history. The enoteca and most of the vineyards were on the Sharptown Auburn Road. "All roads lead to Auburn," my mother had always said. I parked next to the white BMW with the Woodstown paw print magnet on the trunk. Gisel had wanted a white BMW since before she could drive, and what Gisel wants—

I pushed down the bitterness rising in my throat before opening the door.

I could do this.

Gisel was sitting at the table closest to the fireplace. She looked up immediately when I walked in, but instead of smiling, she appeared to be in shock. With unsteady legs, I walked to the table as she poured me a glass of wine from a bottle labeled: Good Karma.

"I can't stay long."

"Leaving is your specialty," she said without a hint of anger.

My own emotions were not quite so in check. "How's your mother?"

Gisel's head drooped toward the table. No one could hurt a person as adroitly as their best friend.

She took a deep breath and faced me again. "I'm sorry," she said. I sat in the chair across from her, but didn't respond in any way. "I hated you for leaving me. I'm grateful you came home. I love you. I need you." Her eyes filled with tears, and I fought not to feel her pain. "I—"

"I forgive you," I said. I let her words steal the bitterness from me. I wanted to hug her, to love her again, but that emotion couldn't break through the wall I'd erected twenty years ago to save my sanity.

Gisel wiped away her tears and rested her face in her hands. This was the most fragile I'd ever seen her. The time apart had affected us both. "Thank you." She looked up. "Not just for me, but for my daughter."

I nearly choked on the word. I'd only heard about Ike, but the elder witch at the Goddess Gala had made it clear that a daughter existed.

"What's her name?" I asked.

"Gwen." Gisel's expression burst with pride at the mention of her daughter. We were all blessed to have them.

"Have the girls met her?" I ran through my mind searching for the name Gwen in every detail they'd told us about their new school.

"Of course. They were at her birthday party."

"Of course." I nodded while questioning where else the girls had been since we moved them back to New Jersey. "Do you think they know?" I didn't have to say, "About their coven" or "how they belong to each other."

"I knew when Gwen was born that she was a witch, but her powers didn't fully emerge until she found her coven."

"I'm sorry, Gisel." I'd always teased her for never considering the consequences of her actions and now I was discussing the second generation who suffered because of my own lack of forethought.

"What now?"

What now? I felt like screaming into the sky. My God, what were we going to do?

"Ever is grounded. She isn't allowed to see your son." Gisel sipped her wine. "And the Virago does not condone forgiveness."

Her calm expression changed at the mention of their name. She practically sneered as she shook her head. "They've been running wild since you guys left."

"I'd assumed you'd be one of them by now."

Gisel's head snapped up. She stared at me in disbelief. "I would never." She shook her head, willing me to believe her. "They tried, but I'd rather live alone."

"You weren't alone, though." She had Isaiah. The Virago should have tried to come for me.

"I'm so sorry, Helene." She twirled her wine glass by the stem between her fingers. "I'm ashamed." Her gaze fell to the table as she shook her head in self-disgust. Gisel swallowed. Her eye tightened shut, and the muscles of my heart clenched. "That night—"

"I can't." I couldn't go back there. Not yet. Maybe not ever. "I need to just move forward. Okay?"

"You know that will never work. If you didn't know it before, you realized the day you chose to come home." She was right, but I was paralyzed.

"I'm going to go. I'm glad your powers are back."

"I'm alive again. It's as if the only things real from the last twenty years are my children. The rest was half a life without you and Sloane and Lovie." My mind was drawn to the questions I'd ask about her husband if he wasn't Isaiah. What about him? Wasn't he real? "I love you, Helene."

I tried to smile. It looked as awkward as it felt, I was sure. I left my best friend of the first eighteen years of my life. I'd officially lived longer without her than with her, but that was somehow going to change.

Ever

WE BARELY SPOKE—NOT ABOUT Ike, not about the weather, not about Christmas cookies, the New Year, Martin Luther King Day, and most notably, not about Gisel. I was too depressed by my own loneliness to feel anything else. I no longer cared why we were in New Jersey. I just wanted to know when Ike and I could get out.

Winter was always the longest season. I used to think it was because I lived in Vermont, but it was long no matter where I was. This particular winter had a wartime feel because of the hole in my heart.

Ike was wrestling, and it took an act of God for me to actually see him compete. I convinced my mother I should manage the boys' basketball team. The conversation went something like:

"Do you care if I manage the basketball team?"

"Boys?"

"Yes."

"Ike Kennedy?"

"No."

"Sounds good."

Just like that, I was the team manager, which basically meant I kept the stats at the games. It also meant I was in the gymnasium across from where Ike was practicing, and if I timed it right, I could see him wrestle some other enormous human being in the heavyweight division.

On Friday, Mick, armed with a mouthful of bubble gum, asked Maya to the prom. It was sweet. He'd made her an animated card on the computer with a bunch of chess pieces moving and talking. He acted as if he were just showing it to her for fun, but when the king invited the queen to the prom, he put his hand over the screen and said, "Maya, will you go to prom with me?"

I hadn't realized how much she liked him until she practically floated across the room with joy. Maya said yes before her mother could say no. She assured *all* our mothers that she and Mick were just friends, but if I could sense how Maya really felt about him, I assumed our mothers could, too.

Ruby, Maya, and I kept moving. There was talk of dresses and flowers and transportation, and of course of who Mick was related to and how our mothers knew his entire family already.

My mother's relationship with the security guard at my school had suddenly become close enough for him to watch me while I was there. I had no privacy and no time to be alone with Ike. Mr. Slopey's class wasn't exactly a sanctuary for forbidden romance. I was wilting away, and my mother still preferred it to my being in love with Ike.

I caught myself imagining Mick was Ike as he sat across from me considering his next chess move. Next year, Ike would have to join the chess club. Even the notion of that conversation made me laugh.

"What's so funny?" Mick asked, abandoning his train of thought.

"Not much these days."

Mick leaned back in his chair and studied me instead of the board. "Did you and Kennedy break up?"

Did we ever have a chance to be together? "Kind of. I don't know." The words almost hurt me physically. "As far as my mother knows."

"Ah, sweet Juliet."

"Please don't."

"Okay." Mick returned his concentration to our game. One of us should have been paying attention.

I had three moments of seeing Ike, a thousand silent sentences to savor in my mind, and my memory to get me through the school day without seeming like I was *with* Ike. It was easier at home, where there was no chance of him popping up around a corner or meeting me on the stairs.

As for my birthday, March sixth, I turned seventeen with little fanfare and was still a prisoner. Lunging toward the finish line of convincing my mother I was yielding to her demands, I agreed to play rummy with the rest of my house and blow out a candle on a cupcake. Carl was at our feet or on our laps at all times. He was pure love without consequence. The perfect addition to a house full of witches.

The moment was light. I even caught myself laughing at Sloane, who was making fun of my mother for having icing on the tip of her nose. I realized the dark cloud my and my mother's discourse had everyone living under. I wasn't the only one grounded. Everyone joined in my misery because we were constantly connected. I couldn't hide an emotion from the five of them.

When Maya, Ruby, and I said good night, our mothers looked at us with relief. Things were going to get back to normal, or our normal, but what they couldn't have known was that I'd let normal back in to find a way to get out.

My mother's staying at my grandmother's, and my dad's clueless. Come stay with me. Ike's voice rang through my mind. Even just the idea of sleeping in a bed with Ike was enough to warm me under my comforter.

In your room? He was insane. I'd never even been inside his bedroom. I'd flown over his house every time I could escape from my prison, but I'd only been as far as the bathroom at Gwen's party.

Just for a little while. Please, Ever.

I inhaled and let the idea sink in. By the time I let the air out of my lungs, I knew I was on my way to him. I tiptoed to Ruby's bed and shook her arm. "Ruby," I whispered. When she opened her eyes, I said, "I need you to cover for me."

She nodded without thinking. There was nothing I couldn't ask of her. As she regained consciousness, she sat up and faced me. "I think you're crazy, and your mother will kill us both."

"I know."

"Are you sure he's worth risking everything?"

"Even more."

"Ever . . ."

"I'll only be gone for a little while. If my mom comes in, tell her I went flying. That I couldn't sleep and I just needed to feel the air in my lungs from high above the earth."

Ruby voice softened as she said, "That sounds like you."

"It is me."

"She'll still kill you."

"But not as painfully as she will if she knows I'm with Ike."

I lifted the window by Ruby's pillow and stuck one leg out. I couldn't take a few steps. I had to just fly, and that was exactly what I did.

I'm here, I thought when I was almost to the lake.

Ike's house was a contemporary rancher. One window facing the lake opened and the screen was raised. I hovered above until Ike took a step back, and I flew right through. Ike closed the window behind me, and as soon as I showed myself, he tackled me onto his bed. He rolled on top of me and kissed me until I forgot we'd ever been apart. When his weight began to crush me, he leaned up on his forearms. I reached up and threaded my fingers in his hair as his lips stayed on mine. All I could feel was the penetrating warmth of Ike. *This* was worth the risk of my mother's wrath.

"Thanks for coming," he whispered in my ear. I tilted my head as a chill ran down my neck. He kissed me there, following it to my collarbone. He knew my body.

"I should thank you." I rolled over on top of him and sat up straddling him. His hands circled my neck, and I let my head fall back to the ceiling exposing it to him. Silence enshrouded us. Time had stopped, and the only sensation I had was the touch of his hands on me.

Ike sat up and pulled me closer. He kissed me again, this time with the need we'd attempted to ignore the last few weeks. A heavy weight sank down on me and nestled right where I sat on top of him. My whole body was alive for him.

"Ever, I want you," he breathed the words into my chest. His fingers brushed across my breast as his voice penetrated my skin.

I fought to inhale. "I know."

"Tonight."

My legs tightened around his back, his lips on mine stole every thought I'd ever had that didn't include me lying in his arms with my clothes off. The word "yes" was forming on my tongue, but the footsteps in the hall snapped my head up. I disappeared.

"Everything okay? Why are you up so late?" Ike's dad said as he opened the door. Ike was still sitting up near the edge of his bed.

"Fine." His voice was rough. "I couldn't sleep."

"Do what your mother always said when you were little, 'Think happy thoughts.'"

Ike nodded a little too fast. "I'm going to try that. Thanks." Ike's dad shut the door and took the light from the hallway with him.

I appeared again and climbed off Ike's lap. I sat next to him and wallowed in the fact we'd never be alone again. He must have guessed what I was thinking because he leaned over and kissed my cheek. He was gentle and kind. He was Ike.

"I have something for you," he whispered.

"What?" I searched his face for joy, or playfulness, or regret.

"Your birthday present."

Sadness and guilt fought for space inside of me. "I . . . I . . . didn't even have a chance to get you a Christmas present." I hadn't been allowed out of my house since the holiday concert.

Ike leaned back and took out a tiny box from the drawer by his bed. He lifted me on top of him the way I'd been when his dad had walked in. "You being here, right here"—he looked down at my thighs on top of his—"is the only gift I'll ever need." He kissed me again and made me forgive myself for everything I'd ever done wrong in my life. "Here." He held the box between us. "Open it."

I did as I was told and removed the red shoestring from the box that was covered in aluminum foil. My fingers gingerly slipped under the tape and released the box from the wrapping without a sound. It wasn't the first gift a boy had ever given me, but it was the first one that really mattered. I lifted the lid and the square of cotton under it to find a thin, rose gold ring with an open heart on top.

"Ike . . ." I couldn't find any other words. I loved it as much as I loved him.

"It's my heart." He slipped the ring on my middle finger and held my hand flat against his chest. His heartbeat was strong and pounding against my palm. I left my hand exactly where he'd put it and kissed him again. "Take good care of it, Ever."

"I promise." Only I could ruin this moment. I inhaled my annoyance with myself. "Ike?"

He almost laughed at me. His shoulders shook a little as he raised his eyebrows. "Yes?" He stretched the word out as if he knew what I was going to ask. I lowered my eyes, and Ike dipped his head down to still see them.

"Have you ever told anyone else that you loved them?" It was stupid. I didn't want to know the answer unless it was no.

Ike shook his head and said, "I haven't loved anybody else." I let that statement and his love in to the very center of my being. I was never going to let it out.

I wanted to stay in his arms until I was out of high school and somewhere far enough away from my mother that Ike and I could be together, but I knew I had to go. Dawn was racing toward us, and I had to be in my bed when my mother woke me for school the next morning.

"I have to leave."

"I know," he said and ran his fingers across my leg.

I stood and lifted the window next to his bed. I forced the levers on the old screen toward the center and raised it, too. It screeched and somehow cut me on its way up.

"Ah," I said, and inhaled through clenched teeth.

"What happened?" Ike was next to me, examining my hand, before I had time to look at it. "Oh, Ever. It's bad." It felt bad. I fly through the dead of night and somehow manage to hurt myself climbing out of a first-floor window. I shook my head in disgust. "Come in the kitchen with me so we can wash it and get a Band-Aid." I stayed completely still. His kitchen would be near his father. His father would tell my mother.

Blood dripped from my hand to Ike's below it. "Okay." I swallowed back my fear.

He opened his bedroom door, and the house was completely

dark. A television sent muddled words from the room at the end of the hall. I wasn't sure Ike even heard it.

He never let go as we tiptoed to the sink in his kitchen. The modern space that appeared to have been recently updated was a stark contrast to the kitchen in the cliffside farmhouse I was living in.

I braced myself for the water to run on my hand. The cut was between my thumb and finger and somehow sliced from the back to my palm. Had it been deeper, it would have severed my thumb.

Ike's fingers brushed against my skin as he washed the blood off. "You okay?" I overflowed with his touch.

The lights turned on, and the kitchen filled with questions.

Ike's dad glared at his son. His gaze then landed solely on me as silence fell on the room. He tilted his head as his examination stalled while he stared into my eyes. What he found there was lost in his head. There was something I should say, but I didn't know what.

"Dad—"

"Don't 'Dad' me. What the hell is she doing here? Your mother's going to lose it."

"Ever, this is my dad." Ike rewound the entire conversation. He took it back to a civilized point. "Dad, this is Ever."

I smiled weakly at Mr. Kennedy. He was handsome in his pajama pants and T-shirt. Something was intriguing about him that had been eclipsed by his wife the few times I'd seen him. Mostly, I noticed he was warm like his son.

"You two are going to start a holy war." He sighed. "Did you hurt yourself?" Blood dripped from my hand. "Let me take a look."

Ike retreated, letting his father take his spot by the sink next to me. Mr. Kennedy reached across me to a light switch that lit up the area and the gruesome cut. "You're going to need a few stitches."

"No stitches." My voice was low. I shook my head slightly.

"It's going to scar," he said.

"That's fine."

Mr. Kennedy lingered on my words, half-smiled, and said, "You're just like your mother." Regret followed his words.

"That's what my dad always said." I examined my cut trying to get lost in it and forget the tears that were welling up in my eyes. He wrapped paper towels over my hand and held them firmly against it. "How well do you know her?"

"Ike, go in the closet outside my bathroom and get me the basket with all the first aid stuff." Mr. Kennedy looked at me as he spoke. I felt the need to follow Ike with my eyes, but I stayed still in his father's stare.

He switched his focus to my hand. "Everyone around here knows each other."

"Do you know why she's afraid of you?"

At this, he laughed. Loudly. "It'd take a lot more than me to scare your mother." He dried the cut with gentle dabs of the towel. "I imagine she's worried you'll fall in love with my son."

"Why? He's wonderful."

Ike returned with the basket and dug through it for gauze pads. He opened several and stacked them on top of each other. Mr. Kennedy placed them over and around my hand as Ike tore off pieces of tape. "There's a lot of history between our two families. Most of it was happy. The rest should remain forgotten." He finished bandaging my hand. "I'll take you home."

I examined every inch of his face for evidence he knew of our powers, but he gave nothing away. I turned to Ike seeking guidance, and he nodded.

"Thank you," I said.

I leaned against Ike's chest in his kitchen while Mr. Kennedy went to change his clothes. I memorized every inch of Ike and inhaled the scent of his soap.

"He likes you," he whispered.

"How can you tell?"

"By the way he listens when you talk."

The look in his father's eyes haunted me. Like he knew who I was before I even knew he existed. Ike kissed the top of my head and tightened his arms around me. "I love you."

"Okay. We ready?" Mr. Kennedy asked. I moved a step away from Ike and followed them to his truck.

Ike and I rode in silence in the back seat. He held my cut hand in his lap and ran his fingers across the skin not covered by the bandage. I rested my head on his shoulder and wished his father was driving us to the airport.

When we drove into Auburn, I leaned up to the front seat and said, "Um, Mr. Kennedy? My visit wasn't exactly planned. Do you think you could drop me off on the street instead of my driveway?" I winced while I spoke. I knew it was asking a lot. Most parents would ring the doorbell and deliver me back to my irate mother, but I felt there was a chance with Mr. Kennedy. If he knew my mother as well as he seemed to, he must have known this would be ugly.

"I will, but I want to know you made it in the house."

I scrutinized my home. Ruby's window was the nearest to the street. "I'll turn the light on by the window in the attic. That's where we sleep."

He put the car in park and looked up at the top of my house. "You and your mother?"

"No. Me and my sis—friends," I said and kissed Ike on the cheek. I stepped out of the car and shut the door as quietly as possible. I walked up the steep driveway and around the tree at the top of it. From there, I disappeared and flew up to the attic. I listened for sounds of life. The house was unconscious. According to the clock by Ruby's bed, it was four forty-five. I switched on Ruby's light, waited a moment, and then turned it off. The sound of Mr. Kennedy's car driving away was the signal I could exhale.

Helene

THE INK ON MY HAND wouldn't come off—no matter how many different soaps I tried. I rinsed the lather away with scorching hot water again only to find the blue blotches had barely faded. I wasn't even sure where it'd come from. There was probably a pen in my purse oozing permanent liquid onto the contents as I stood wondering. I finally gave in and moved the particles of ink from my skin.

A black extended cab truck pulled in the driveway and drove past the kitchen window toward the back of the house.

I stopped breathing.

There were several reasons I'd avoided returning to New Jersey. The memories of my mother, the betrayal by Gisel, and even the slightest chance I might have to face Isaiah. There was little hope any of my hesitations could be avoided, but I'd clung to the possibility the universe would protect me.

I shut off the water and listened to his truck door close and his footsteps in the snow that I hadn't shoveled yet. I closed my eyes as the memory of his voice late at night slipped down my neck and landed between my legs. Twenty years had passed, and I still couldn't control my thoughts of him. I inhaled to keep from disappearing inside the memories.

The back door opened. A chill rushed into the room as Isaiah kicked the snow off his boots against the doorjamb. My back straightened.

How dare he just walk in?

Each boot dropped to the floor before he stepped into the kitchen. Without turning around to face him, I willed a plate to shoot off the table and toward his head. Even though I didn't have the pleasure of seeing my target, the maneuver calmed me. Inflicting pain on him was therapeutic in many ways.

The plate hit the wall, and remnants scattered over the floor near my feet. I steadied myself and turned to find Isaiah still crouched over with his hands up for protection.

My God, he was beautiful.

"I'm sorry."

But then he spoke and reminded me of how much I hated him.

"Why are you here?" I removed every emotion I could identify from my voice. I might have forgiven him, but that didn't mean I had to be nice to him.

He took a step closer, and I eyed the water pitcher on the table. Isaiah paused and threw his hands up in surrender. He laughed a little. The sound of it pierced tiny cracks in my armor. "Easy."

"You are. Now what do you want?"

Isaiah stood at his full height and forced my mind to recall every inch of his body in my mind. Heat swirled in my joints and settled in my cheeks before I could contain his effect on me. "When

I left my house, I thought I was coming here to somehow fix this mess . . ." He took a step toward me, but I backed up and sought protection from the wounds he'd already inflicted. The pain in his stare told a hundred versions of our demise. I didn't want to relive any of them. He sighed before saying, "But now . . . that I'm here, I realize the *only* reason is I wanted to see you."

The width of his shoulders, the strength in his hands, the way he stood with his feet a few inches apart, all took me back to the night I returned from Vermont. I swallowed the twenty-year-old tears. "You should go."

"Helene, you're the strongest person I've ever known." He took another step toward me forcing me to lean against the countertop behind me.

"How could you?" The question had run through my mind no less than a million times since the last time I saw him. He winced at my words. "How could you?" I asked again and let the anger drain from my body.

"I was terrified of you leaving me." I dropped my head and closed my eyes. I couldn't see him and hear him at the same time. "The thought that I'd never be enough to keep you happy here, stole my sanity every night until I did the unthinkable. I hurt you before you could leave me."

My breakfast churned in my stomach. "Were you that selfish? Could I have missed it? All the times we were together. The way you treated me after my mother died. Every breath you took, each word you said to make me laugh." The memories absorbed me. "Every single time you touched me, I clung to. How did I not know you were capable—"

"It was one night, Helene. Not who I am. One mistake."

"You married her! Was that a mistake, too?"

The tortured look in his eyes broke my heart all over again. "I've been dead inside since the day you left. I'd lost hope. You wouldn't see me or talk to me."

As if this were all my fault. As if I had been the one who cheated. Who had broken his heart. I swallowed all the anger. "Enough. It's done. We were finished before I went to Vermont. I just wish you'd told me instead of sleeping with her."

"I'm sorry, and I miss you more than I can explain."

"I don't care how you're feeling."

"You're lying. You never stopped caring."

I couldn't listen to this. "Stop. Please . . ."

"I didn't come to hurt you."

I faced him and all we'd been through. "Just the sound of your voice hurts me."

Isaiah stared at the floor between us. It might as well have been a thousand miles. There was too much distance to travel back. "They love each other," he said, and I knew he was talking about Ike and Ever.

I turned back to the counter and dried my hands again on the towel that hung from the oven door. "It's impossible. You know as well as I do they can never be together."

"They're probably together right now." I threw down the towel in disgust. "She's beautiful, Helene." He walked farther into the room. His steps were small, testing whether I'd injure him. "And strong like her mother."

"When did you meet her?"

"With Ike."

I shook my head at his son's name. "I forbid her to see him."

"Would you have ever stopped seeing me if your father had forbid you?"

I walked over to him. He was the same height I remembered standing beside and dancing with and lying next to. Heat poured off him and invaded me with the need I'd abandoned for Isaiah. I stopped only inches from him and admitted, "I would have spent

every minute of my life with you, no matter what anyone said."
My reminiscence was replaced with the frigid edge to my voice. He
leaned away in fear. "But I have buried my mother, my father, and
my husband. Don't think for a second that I'm the same girl you
knew twenty years ago." I forced myself to calm down. I would not
lose control with this man ever again. My voice softened. "Ever, is
my entire life . . ."

"They're in love, and no matter how much you don't want that to
be the case, it is." My traitorous lip trembled, and he reached for me.

"Come here."

I shook my head and forced shut my eyes in pain. "I can't touch
you."

"I can't *not* touch you." He pulled me to him. "I don't care if
you're about to set me on fire." He wrapped his arms around my
shoulders and held me close to his body. "It's worth whatever pun-
ishment you inflict on me."

I rested my head on his chest and let go of the burden of hating
him that I'd carried with me for two decades. My heart raced at his
touch. I was eighteen again. I was almost whole. I tilted my head
until my lips were near his neck. Not a day had gone by since the
last time I'd rested there.

There had been many days, though.

I stepped back from my first love. "You should go."

Ever

THE FAKE MEETING FOR THE yearbook staff and next year's football team had been put on our parents' calendars over a week ago. The weather had finally broken. We could go to his house, or out on the lake, or even to the tree house, but instead Ike took me on his motorcycle to a field overcome with flowers and sprouting from the green swarm of various plants surrounding it. Wild didn't describe the patch at the edge of the woods in Upper Pittsgrove.

"This is . . . chaotic," I said.

"It's dead field."

"It appears more than alive to me."

Ike swung his heavy arm over my shoulders. "No one can ever build on it, so the flowers have taken over."

"Why can't they build?"

"As the story goes, it was an orchard, and the pesticides used deposited dangerous levels of arsenic in the soil. It's kind of a legend around here. The land that can kill you, grows the prettiest flowers."

I stepped into the flower patch and moved the soil with the toe of my shoe. There were more flowers sprouting from the ground. Dead field made no sense. It reminded me of how Lovie used to say, "Everything can be explained by magic." I reached down and let my hand caress the tops of the tallest plants. They swayed beneath my touch.

"Take me flying," Ike said from behind me.

I didn't respond. I hadn't been flying much myself lately. There were so many rules associated with it. It was the most freeing experience I had and it'd been shut down with parameters such as no one flies alone, no flights without prior permission, and absolutely no night flights. I still snuck out and flew to see Ike, but it was less often and less enjoyable because the consequences of getting caught were daunting.

"I know you heard me," he said and smiled. He was doing it more and more and it made him completely irresistible.

"I don't think it's a good idea."

"I thought you said whatever it was that day wasn't dangerous."

"I said I didn't know what it was."

He nodded his head a little put off. "Well, you made it sound like it was nothing."

"And Carl . . ."

"Carl was playing on the ground. If something was going to hurt us, they could do it right now."

"Why do you want to fly so badly?"

"Because you love it. Because out of all the things in the world your family could have given you for your birthday, they gave you a necklace with a flying bird on it. It's a part of you, and I'm left out of it."

"You couldn't be left out of a part of me."

"I am. I have no idea what it feels like. I've only been a few feet up in the air." I leaned into him and reminded myself to focus on the words he was saying and not his chest beneath my hands. "Last night, I made Gwen tell me all about it. She says she can't take me because she isn't strong enough."

I backed away. "She shouldn't take you."

"I know." He was gentle but serious. "Gwen said you're the strongest flyer. Better than any of the others."

Some ridiculous pride my father used to instill in me came flooding back. I basked in Ike's admiration. "I want Ruby and Maya to be with us if we ever go."

"I want it to be just us." He kissed me until the tension disappeared and I was left with only Ike pleading near my ear, "Please."

I exhaled my defenses. "Okay."

"Really?" His shock made me think I'd had a choice. "Okay, let's go." He marched me away from his bike. "Tell me what to do."

"I love you."

Ike stopped moving and studied me. "I know you do."

"Hold on to me." I twirled around, and he moved close to my back. He wrapped his arms around my shoulders, up near my neck but not choking me. "You know you're enormous, right?" He was everywhere on top of me.

"But you love me." He kissed my cheek.

"Don't let go."

"Never."

Ike and I disappeared near his bike. Without a running start we were slow to clear the trees, but when we finally reached a good altitude, I'd adjusted to the weight and we were able to soar above them.

This is incredible, Ike thought.

I know. I love it.

I see why.

I took us over the Woodstown Lake and Marlton Park. I slowed above the pastures and the rodeo. I dipped down and up again, showing off for my boyfriend attached to me, and when there was nothing but field in front of us, I flew forward faster than I'd ever gone before.

I slowed slightly to rest before speeding again, and a force pressed against us from the side. I let it push us west to feel what it was. The only thing I knew for sure was it was the same as the first time I'd taken Gwen flying.

Ruby, Maya.

From what I could tell, it was only on one side of us. It was resting against us but not trying to stop us. I sped up, and it pushed harder, not falling back. It was fast, too. Whatever *it* was.

Ruby!

No one answered.

What was that? Ike felt it.

I don't know. We're going back.

Maya!

I pushed back. Adrenalin took over as it surrounded us. It thrust above us and on each side. It was pushing us lower to the ground. Either Ike was getting heavier or whatever was on top of him was.

I pulled ahead and tried to land, but it moved below me, and then I felt it. A punch of some kind in my ribs. It flung me with Ike on my back against the wall of energy next to us, which pushed us away. We were going to crash if I couldn't break free.

Mom! Terror was taking over.

Ever, where are you?

Flying. I need you!

Come back toward Auburn. I'm on my way.

I slowed almost to a stop. Just before the point of us dropping to the ground.

Hold on, I thought to Ike before bolting in the direction of Auburn. I was ahead of it, but I could feel it pressing against my feet, gaining on us.

By Auburn Farms.

We're here. I could feel my mother, Lovie, and Sloane careening toward us. The sense of them nearby gave me strength to fly even faster.

Ike is with me. I heard a gasp. *Don't fall in line. Stay scattered,* I thought ignoring their shock.

It's a sweep, Lovie thought.

Followed by Sloane practically yelling inside my head, *I'm going straight in.*

We dipped low to the ground. Air whooshed by me twice, but I couldn't tell who or what it was. My mother was flying in circles around me creating a tunnel to keep whatever it was away. On the edge of the breeze, I thought I heard a man's voice say, "Helene," but that was impossible.

Sloane! The fear in Lovie's voice intensified my own terror. There was a thud below us. A woman rolled across the road and into the field before the Turnpike overpass. She rose up on her hands and knees and looked to the sky before disappearing again.

We reached the outskirts of Auburn, the air cleared. I could breathe, and I could move. The weight lifted. I landed in my backyard with my mother breathing down my neck. Lovie and Sloane flew back in the direction we'd just come. I showed Ike and me to my mother at the same moment she became visible to us.

"My God, Ever." She was livid. "He could have been killed." Her voice rose. She never yelled. She raised her finger to me and shook her head. "You think every hit and run is a car accident. That every tree falling is the wind. Every house fire is a candle too close to a curtain." She was barely stopping for air. "Things—awful things—are happening around you every day. You have no respect for the dangers that are out there."

"I made her take me," Ike said, and my mother turned her anger on him.

To my utter shock, she calmed in front of my eyes. She stared at Ike until she said, "No one *makes* Ever do something. I know that better than anyone after the last few months."

She turned back to me on the verge of tears. Her anguish was tying me in knots. "What if we couldn't get to you? Haven't I lost enough?" She glanced at Ike and stared back at me. "Haven't you lost enough?"

Without a word to defend myself, I stayed silent. She left us standing at the back of our yard and stormed into the house letting the screen door slam behind her.

I faced Ike and let the four feet between us anchor me.

"I found something I'm afraid of," I said, and tears filled my eyes. "Losing you . . ."

Ike's arms were around me before the dam broke, but there was nothing he could do to erase the fear of my life without him.

Helene

"**MY GOD, THEY COULD HAVE** been killed." Even after three glasses of wine, my blood was still chilled. Lovie filled my glass again while the three of us sat around the kitchen table.

"They weren't though," Sloane said, but I couldn't calm down. Ever took too many chances. She'd never had enough fear. She was always hanging from the highest tree branch and running off the high dive. Her father'd loved it. I was terrified by it.

"I think she gets it now," Lovie said. "I heard her upstairs crying." Losing Ike scared her more than losing herself.

"I don't think I'm capable of raising a teenager."

"I think everything that's happening is developmentally appropriate for her age." Lovie's face scrunched up as if I might lash out in response. "I'll make some hummus." Her eyes widened suggesting my sanity was in the tahini paste. She stood and moved so she was standing behind me. "You're a wonderful mother of a brave and willful young woman," she said as she wrapped her arms around my shoulders and gave me a hug.

"I'm exhausted. I don't know how much more of this I can take." I sighed and downed the rest of my wine. The empty glass I left sitting in front of my empty chair as I dragged myself upstairs and sank under the covers in my dark room.

Every detail of our flight home ran through my head. I slowed the thoughts down and tried to pinpoint any information we could use to defend ourselves the next time. There would come a time when one of us would fly alone. One of our daughters.

My body finally surrendered to sleep, but it wasn't a restful night. I didn't dream, but my mind wouldn't stop. I kept waking up and changing positions until I faced my window and realized it was open a crack even though it hadn't been since before Thanksgiving.

The moonlight hit the old glass and cast a milky sheen across my pillow. It was the same muted tone as the hint of honeysuckle that surrounded me. The memory of him returned instantly. I stopped breathing and listened to the warm air blowing through the ductwork and the gargled words from the television in Lovie's room and the complete silence near me. Without moving, I dragged my sight through every inch of space around me that was visible in the dim light.

"Don't be afraid," he said, and the voice of the man who'd carried me home so many years ago brought back every emotion of the last time we were together.

I sat up, still searching for the exact origin of the words, and said, "I never got a chance to thank you for carrying me home the night I hurt my shoulder."

He didn't respond. I reached out to the side of my bed I thought the voice had originated from and flinched when he grabbed my hand before it touched him.

"Thank you," I said. His palm was rough and his hand covered mine completely. He was big, I remembered. "Tell me your name."

"Xavier, and you're welcome, Helene."

The way he said my name hit on a more recent memory. "Xavier, were you flying yesterday?" He sighed loudly. "There was a disturbance when my daughter was out. Some type of force."

"There used to be a level of creativity." A sinister tone swelled in his words. "No one cares about the arts anymore. Just throw witches out of the sky. Civilization is declining, don't you think?"

"I thought I heard you say my name when I was in the air."

"That would be strange." His words were light. The ending of a joke neither of us laughed at. "How would I know it was you up there?"

We were all invisible. "I was wondering the same thing."

"Perhaps I was with you when you took off, and that was how I knew."

Before Ever had called to me, I was cutting vegetables in the kitchen with Lovie. Sloane was wasting away watching reality television in the family room.

"Xavier, who are you? What are you?" He wasn't a witch, but he could fly. He was an outsider but hadn't hurt me, and he was with me much more often than I knew.

"Helene, I hate labels. I don't think we were meant to live by society's expectations of a pre-defined designation." He threw the words I'd said to my daughter at the Goddess Gala back in my face. I moved my hand from his and rested it on my lap.

"How often are you with me?" A chill ran up my arms and down my back. "Xavier?"

"I have to go." His voice was softer. I'd hit on something between us that I wasn't sure he'd ever wanted me to know.

"Stay. Are you hungry?"

A light chuckle came from near the window. "No, Helene. I'm good."

"I want to see you."

"That isn't possible, especially not here."

I didn't push. I wanted to know more about him, but the tiny pieces I already had disturbed me. The window opened wider as well as the screen and the honeysuckle scent disappeared. I left the warm covers of my bed and closed them both. I looked up at the moon as I locked the window that apparently didn't actually keep anyone out.

I stared at the antiqued glass until the sun rose.

Ever

I MISSED IKE. THE WAY his chest felt beneath my fingertips. The sound of his voice spoken aloud. The way his steel demeanor fell away when I walked up and he pulled me close to him. Nothing seemed worth waking up for since he was no longer a possibility of my day.

My mother hadn't spoken to me since she saved us. She couldn't face me. I'd broken every rule while I lied to her face, and she wasn't going to get over it easily. Or at all, maybe. I assumed I was still grounded from seeing Ike. In a rare moment of defeat, I considered breaking up with him, setting him free. The expression on my mother's face after our flight was filled with such anger and fear, I started to believe that I was a terrible person and that Ike was somehow in danger just from loving me. That moment lasted from my eyes opening in the morning until a few seconds later when I heard him say in my head, *Good morning, beautiful.*

I regretted moving to this hellish place where I fell in love and then had it ripped away by the only other person I loved more than myself—my mother. I couldn't look at her. Hatred for her was boiling below the surface of my existence. She could feel it. At first, I'd tried to hide it, but it was clear she was never going to be reasonable about Ike, so I let it flow freely whenever she was around. Our home was in an endless state of misery, and our whole family was trapped in it.

I listened for him constantly. I couldn't focus on anything besides the possibility of hearing him. My entire day revolved around the forty-three minutes we were together in physics. My homework was a nuisance. Chess club was a joke. I lost every game because I was listening for his voice from the minute he arrived at school. The second I awoke. The breath before consciousness. I was empty without him.

Go to the prom so I can see you.

What?

I didn't expect to hear from him again until after first period. I'd ridden to school in the back seat of Mick's car. He drove us now that he and Maya were "just friends." They all left me in the car in the student parking lot and walked to school. I was dead inside. They were nice enough to drive me around.

Go with a friend, but let your mother think you like him. Then come to the shore for the weekend. We can be together.

There were moments of weakness, times when it hurt more than I could comprehend, that I thought it was only in my head. Surely, he didn't feel as strongly about me. He wasn't suffering the way his absence was killing me, but then he'd connect with me and melt every thought like that away.

His voice gave me the strength to exit the car and walk toward the school.

No one will ask me. They're all afraid of you.

To anyone watching me, my humor at that thought would have appeared deranged.

They should be.

I laughed a little. He would forever be gruff to everyone but me. That wasn't true, though. Someday, it would be someone other than me. A girl who was allowed to see him. I wounded myself with my thoughts.

I'm going to see who Paul's taking. He's about the only guy I can trust with you.

I don't want to go.

My mind was consumed with his silence. I stopped walking near the other side of the bridge and stared at the creek below me. I never wanted to be with anyone but him, and every time I stopped to realize that wasn't going to be our future, it made me cry.

I don't want to see you there with someone else. I was choking up. *I don't want to dance with someone else.*

Are you crying?

No. I lied. I wouldn't make this worse for both of us.

Don't move.

Ike rode down the hill and stopped at the edge of the wooden bridge I was standing on. He took the extra helmet out from under the bungee cords on the back seat and handed it to me without a word.

I buckled it under my chin and climbed on behind him. I didn't care who saw us or where my mother was when she received the call that I'd skipped school. My arms around Ike were all I could fit in my mind. When we cleared the boundary line of the town, Ike opened it up, and we rode fast. Fear gripped me as we rode toward my house. I was afraid he was taking me there to talk some sense into my mother, but all I wanted was to be alone with him. I wanted him to take me to the tree house.

He made a right onto Laurel Lane and made it clear that was what he wanted, too. He rode as far down toward the creek as possible on the bike and parked it next to a tree. I got off first and hung my helmet on the handlebars.

"This isn't working." Ike's stare stole me from my spot on the earth away from him. He got off the bike and pulled me close.

"No."

His lips found mine, and with just the touch of them, every fear I had on my way to school disappeared.

He brushed the hair off my face and studied me. "I'm not going to lose you," he said.

"I don't know what to do. She's never been like this."

"*You've* never been like this." His words broke through our impossible situation.

"No." I shook my head. "I've never loved anyone the way I love you."

Ike lifted my chin and forced me to face him again. "Run away with me. We'll go somewhere we can be together."

"How?" He was crazy. I couldn't even miss a few hours of school with him.

"When you graduate, we'll go and we won't look back."

"Ike, that's a year away."

"In September, I'll be in a dorm in Glassboro. You can come stay with me whenever you want."

"I can't even see you and I sit next to you in physics!" I took all my frustrations out on him. I stepped away from him, stared into the forest around us, and then turned and met his eyes behind me.

"You're seeing me now."

"This is impossible."

"I'm not letting you give up."

His love infiltrated me and stomped out all the doubts I had about us. "I'm not giving up."

"That's my girl . . . or whatever you are." He focused on the tree house high above us. "Let's go up." Ike put his arms around me. I closed my eyes, hid us, and flew over the rail and onto the balcony. "I'll never get used to that."

I pushed him into the tree house and backed him up against the wall. "Can you stop talking?"

Ike held me tight against him, and I lost myself there. He was still generous and respectful, but there was something desperate about the way he kissed me. Then he lifted me on top of him and held me there for hours as he played with my hair. He didn't even ask to make love. We didn't speak. There was no music. Just us and the animals outside his tree house to protect us. It was perfect, but it wasn't forever.

I leaned up on his chest and kissed his chin and then his lips. "I think I have to go back."

"No." He shook his head, dismissing the whole idea.

"I should at least listen to what she has to say."

He stared at the ceiling and finally said, "It isn't going to be good. I don't want her to upset you."

"I'm sure I've done my share of upsetting today. What time is it?"

Ike turned his phone on and the time lit up the screen. It was four fifteen. I sighed. The carved initial on the wall caught my attention. *H + I.*

"Ike, what's your dad's name?" The pieces were fitting together in my mind.

"Isaiah. Why?"

"My mother's name is Helene."

"What?" he asked.

Only a broken heart could cause hatred like this.

I shut my eyes and listened for my mother.

Ever, come back. Talk to me! Her voice was a tortured cry in my mind.

Mom.

Ever, where are you?

Mom, the way you're feeling right now. The fear, the uncertainty, it's the way you'll feel for the rest of your life if you don't let me see him.

Ever . . . I thought she might cry.

I'll leave. Forever. I swear, I will.

Come home. She was gentle again. She was my mom.

Tears filled my eyes as I rested my head back on Ike's chest. He tightened his arms around me and kissed the top of my head.

I'm not coming back without him.

Bring him. His parents are here, too.

My head shot up.

"What?" Ike asked and held me as he sat us both up. "What? What did she say?"

"Your parents are at my house."

Ike looked the way I felt. Distraught.

I held on tight to him as we rode to Auburn. The idea of just riding away kept jumping into my mind. I squeezed Ike between my thighs to ward off the jitters that were taking over with each mile closer we got to my house. When I slid off the back of his bike in my backyard, Ike had returned to his rock-solid self. I fed off his strength. I inhaled deeply and walked in front of him to the back door of my house. Inside, my mother, my aunts, Ruby, Maya, Gwen, and Mr. and Mrs. Kennedy were all waiting in our kitchen.

Air forced itself into my lungs. My senses were on high alert. My gaze shot around the room. I inhaled the ham and pickle smells from an earlier lunch. Wafts of brownies infiltrated and calmed me. Everything was more acute. I fought to control the energy overwhelming me and turned toward Ruby for answers.

"I know," she said. "It's like we've been running on forty percent."

Sloane rubbed her daughter's shoulders and said, "If Clara were here I'm not sure I could stand to be inside, but man it feels good to be this powerful again." She shook her head with satisfaction covering her face.

Ike's father was staring at my mom. His jaw was clenched shut, but his eyes held nothing but pain. My mother glanced everywhere around the room except at him.

"You two were in love?" I asked Mr. Kennedy. He only stared back at me.

"Dad?" Ike asked from behind me. His mother ignored his father. Her attention never left my mother.

"A long time ago," he said. My mother finally looked at him, and the room electrified. It soared from their stare and pushed me a step back toward Ike.

"None of this matters," Ike's mother broke through the energy. She pointed at us. "You two are done."

Ike moved from behind me to my side. He tilted his hip to stand slightly in front of me. His protective stance wasn't lost on his mother or anyone else in the room.

"Oh my God." Mrs. Kennedy sat as she spoke. "You love her." She looked from us to the center of the table. She stared there until she snapped her head toward my mother and demanded, "How could you let this happen?"

"*Let?* I have forbidden her to be anywhere near him."

Ike's mother sank into defeat in front of us. With a much quieter voice she asked, "What are we going to do?"

"We're going to tell them, and then we're going to get rid of it," Sloane said and sat across the table from Mrs. Kennedy.

It was as if they were alone in the room. Ike's mom stared at Sloane. "We can't change the spell. It was cast by a full coven. To change it, even if we could, *which* we *can't*, would interrupt the entire universe. We'll set into motion horrors we can't even predict."

A fierce cold darted off Sloane as she fixed her eyes to Mrs. Kennedy. "That's easy for you to say as your husband sits at the table with us."

"I begged her not to!" Mrs. Kennedy yelled. "I have searched the world for a way to reverse it. Read every piece of information and talked to every witch that would speak to me."

Lovie came and rested her hands on the table as she stood above all of them. "This isn't helping."

Mrs. Kennedy inhaled loudly. When she exhaled, I thought she might cry, but she was as steady as her son. In a calm voice she said, "You can't just stop a spell. You'll unhinge this whole town."

"What spell?" I asked.

Everyone but my mother, who was too busy staring at Mrs. Kennedy to realize I'd said something, turned to me. When Ike's mother faced her, my mother said, "You should tell them." I knew the offer was significant.

Mrs. Kennedy moved in her chair to face Ruby, Maya, and me. "Our families' history has not been an easy one. Your grandmothers and Gwen's grandmother were also a coven."

She wrung her hands before placing them flat on the table in front of her. "Lovie's mother died when she gave birth to Lovie." Mrs. Kennedy paused to look at Lovie. "When Lovie was born, there were three remaining members of the coven. Gwen's, Ruby's, and Ever's grandmothers." She surveyed the kitchen we stood in. The house had been a part of all of our families for generations. "And then, one day when we were in high school, Sloane and Helene's mothers—Ruby and Ever's grandmothers—went to the shore." My mother's head dropped. I wanted to hug her, but I couldn't move for fear Mrs. Kennedy would stop speaking. "Their car was hit head on by a tractor trailer, and they both died."

I'd heard the story before, but today I realized my mother was about my age when she buried her own mother. I understood what it meant to be without a parent, but I couldn't comprehend what it must have been like to lose her mother.

"My mother was alone for the first time in her life," Mrs. Kennedy continued. "She never got over it. She felt abandoned. The loneliness without her sisters ate her alive inside." Gisel's eyes found each of our mothers. "Our last year in high school was turbulent. Between the four of us, we had one mother, and she was angry. A lot happened." Mrs. Kennedy's words trailed off as she looked at my mom. "Some terrible things that I regret every day. When Sloane and Helene and Lovie were planning to leave me here alone . . . without my powers, my mother became enraged. She took out all her anger on the three of them. She wanted them to feel the same pain she saw inflicted on me."

I reached up and placed my hand on Ike's back. I needed to feel him.

"And she cursed them," Mrs. Kennedy said, and I stopped breathing.

"Mimi?" Gwen wailed. Her mother only nodded her head at her.

"What was the spell?" Ruby demanded. She was ready to lunge at someone.

Mrs. Kennedy paused for what seemed like ten minutes. I waited for her to walk out of the room and leave us with only questions, but she finally said, "That death would hunt their children's fathers."

"I don't understand," Maya whispered next to me. She broke through the rage inside my head.

Maya's father's funeral. The dress I'd worn to my dad's. His favorite tie. The sound of the doorbell when the police came . . .

"Yes you do," Ruby said, and Maya began to shake. Her hands were clenched into fists at her side as her chest gasped for tiny breaths. I reached out to her, but she ran past me and up the stairs to our attic.

Ike turned around. He blocked out my view of every other person in the kitchen. He took my face in his hands and gently ran his thumbs across my skin, but all I could think was that his grandmother had killed my father.

Ever, it wasn't me. I closed my eyes and listened. *I would never hurt you.*

"Ever." My mother's voice was forceful behind Ike. "Do you understand why you can't see him?"

"He didn't do this."

"It's as much about him as it is about us," my mother said, but I still didn't understand. "The spell is meant to carry to our daughters, too. If you and Ike continue seeing each other, get married . . . if you ever have a child, Ike will die."

"And you'll wait for it to happen," Sloane said. I tried to comprehend what they were telling me. "You'll wait for the day your daughter will bury her father every day that he's still alive."

"That's why you never came back? Vermont, Hawaii, Vegas? You tried to outrun it?"

"Yes," my mother said. "We tried everything."

"And that's why it seemed like you were expecting it?"

I'm sorry, my mother's voice in my head quenched some of the need inside of me.

"How did you live that way?" I asked all three of them.

"With hope," my mother said. "Always with hope, but when Maya's father died, we knew we had to come back here. The three of you were starting to fall in love. You've already lost your fathers. We can't watch you bury your husbands."

"But there's no way to stop it," Ike's mother said, and no one argued with her.

"If we need a full coven to cast a spell, how could Ike's grandmother curse us?" I asked.

"She's a full coven. Her sisters died." My mother said and then added with great effort, "She hadn't been denounced or left, Clara being alone was a natural part of life. Her powers remained completely intact." She stood straight. "Dangerously so."

"She couldn't just kill you."

"Even in her bitterness, Clara was still a witch. In her head, she was an honorable one. She would never impact another witch's mortality. Not even the ones she cursed to live a life in hell."

"Oh."

"She did the next worst thing. She tortured us by taking away someone we loved." She stared back at Ike's father.

"Well, we're going to figure it out," Lovie said. Everyone's attention fell on her. "Together. We're a coven—two covens." She considered Ruby, Gwen, and me like she'd given birth to each of us. "And we're not leaving here until the spell is broken." She was nodding her head, willing us to commit. When the room calmed, she said, "We need to eat. I'll bread some eggplant."

Helene

I T WAS A STRANGE REUNION of sorts. The first floor of our house filled with witchcraft and Isaiah and his son. Lovie searched for ingredients in the pantry and refrigerator as Gisel and Sloane sat at the kitchen table reviewing every time we'd each already tried to break the spell. They'd found and interviewed every Earth witch that would talk to them about Clara's specific powers, but every witch was different and the incidence of curses within a coven were practically nonexistent. Ruby settled in on Sloane's right with a notebook. She didn't say a word, just furiously scribbled notes as they plotted through the last twenty years of our efforts.

Gisel lost her powers when she'd lost her coven. She was our Earth witch and without us, she had no powers to utilize. The only thing she could do was convince her mother that she'd made a mistake, and after twenty years of attempting to do just that, she'd finally given up hope.

When Clara had first cast the spell, Gisel furiously tried to block it or break it. She'd written careful notes during that time and sent Ike home to get her notebook.

I needed some air. I needed Ever's father. He'd always been the voice of reason. Even without knowing about the curse, I'd hoped he'd be able to overcome it. I searched the world to find a man as strong as he was. He wasn't just physically foreboding but mentally invincible as well. If there was a man that could stand up to Clara's evil will, I thought it would have been Owen, but in the end, he died, too.

Maya and Gwen followed me outside. They were showing off Gwen's new powers. I sat on the Adirondack chair and watched as they went through everything Gwen knew.

"It seems the girls have done a wonderful job teaching you."

Gwen beamed with pride. "They did. Look what else I can do." A branch near her head bent almost completely to our feet. The tree's roots were beginning to break through the ground.

"Gwen, no." She stopped and stared back at me again. "You've learned your power, but you still need to study the craft."

"What do you mean?"

"We're witches for a reason. It isn't just a carnival game. We believe our powers have been bestowed as a gift."

Gwen's eyes focused on the ground between us. She was concentrating on my words. There was so much for a young witch to learn. Lessons that began the minute they could talk and walk would have to be reviewed for a seventeen year old. It was a tremendous task for Gwen and the rest of us.

"Why you?" I continued. "Why not the girl in your English class? How will you protect the Earth when no one else will?"

She looked from the tree to me. "I see."

"It's our place in the *world* first and then it is us." My intention was not to scare her, but she reminded me of her mother in our youth—a bit wild.

"Of course," she said. She was lost in thought, as if she were going over some mistakes she'd already made. "Your mother will teach you everything you need to know. Until then, discretion is the utmost priority. Sharing our secret exposes all witches to danger."

"If I'm an Earth witch like my mother . . . that means if Ever, Maya, and Ruby ever get mad at me I'll lose my powers. Isn't that what happened to my mom?"

My heart broke for her. No young witch should have to worry about such a thing. "Don't think about any of that. They'll never leave you."

Ruby came outside carrying a tray of iced tea that I was sure Lovie had sent. Somehow, she could always sense when there need-ed to be a breath in time. I left the girls to their seventeen-year-old selves and made my way back into the house. I thought I'd lie down for a while. Take a break from everything and everyone, but when I reached the doorway to the living room, Ever and Isaiah were locked in conversation.

"I was too young to love your mother the way I did. I was a boy trying to navigate the emotions of a man." Isaiah's eyes were fixed on the old pictures on the table next to him. "She'd been accepted to every college she applied to, and I was going to commute to West Chester."

Ever stayed quiet, petting Carl who was sprawled out next to her.

"She always wanted to leave. To travel. She'd go anywhere, but I liked it here." He reached out and touched the picture of me in my wedding gown that was under the old lamp beside him. "It was never a question that she'd move." I'd told him over and over again that I wasn't leaving him. "I think she was running from the memory of her mother, but I couldn't comprehend what her death had done to Helene." Isaiah raised his hands in defeat. "My mother's still alive today."

His head shook slightly as he looked around the room at nothing in particular. "All Helene thought about—all she *talked* about—was getting away from Auburn. It felt like she was escaping me, too. Me and Ike's mother. Gisel wasn't going away to college, either, and out of the four of them, she was the only one who still had a mother." Ever hung on his every word. "It sounds crazy, but it separated them in a way they'd never experienced before."

"It isn't crazy. Out of the four of us, Gwen is the only one who still has a father." Her voice broke on the word "father" and tore my heart apart with it.

"When your grandmother and Ruby's grandmother died, it was a scary time. It should have brought us closer together, but it tore us all apart. The whole town surrounded them with love, but they were so shocked, all they could feel was pain."

"It's probably none of my business," Ever started, and I braced myself. "But were you always in love with Mrs. Kennedy, too?" I stopped breathing and waited for Isaiah's response.

"No." He regarded my daughter with pride as if she was his own. "Ike's mother and I got together a few years after your mother left town. We were all each other had left."

Isaiah looked over his shoulder and stared at me. Ever turned and noticed me, too, but all I could see was the boy I'd left in New Jersey when I'd escaped to Vermont. He was now Gisel's husband.

"I don't think I can do this," I said. The whole, *We're one big happy family now and we're going to get through this together*, was too much. For the last twenty years, some of them were more together than I was.

Isaiah didn't move, not even a twitch of his hand, as Ever's eyes flicked between us.

He finally said, "You can do anything."

Ever

I LEFT MY MOTHER WITH Ike's father and walked into the kitchen. Sloane, Ruby, Gisel, and Lovie were all lost in a chaotic mix of words.

I stood at the head of the table until they dropped their conversations and waited for what I had to say. "With Gwen, we can cast spells. We changed my stuffed animal into a dog, so I'd say we're pretty good at it."

"You cast a spell?" Sloane asked in complete disbelief.

"We created life. I think we can come up with something to overturn this."

"You can't change a spell." Ike's mother was adamant. "The universe has accepted it, to even try to reverse it will create havoc. It could destroy us all."

I was convinced we could come up with a spell that would enable my husband to survive, one that would stifle Ike's grandmother's curse. I knew Maya and Ruby would cast one with me, but we needed Gwen. Gisel was in the way.

Before I could push it back, I thought how much easier this would be if she'd die. I was a horrible person. She was Ike and Gwen's *mother*, but . . . my mother's coven would be intact and strong with only the three of them. It was in that moment I realized why a witch couldn't kill another witch. The balance of power and love is a delicate one until goals were at odds. Then it's an impossible one.

I left them all in the kitchen and went to find Gwen, who was cuddled up next to her father, telling him all the things she could do. All the things I'd told my father flew into my mind and hurt me one by one. Mr. Kennedy asked her what she liked best about her powers the same way my father used to, and I started to cry.

It was ridiculous. I'd had ten years with my father asking me what was my favorite or what I liked best about life. I should be able to see a friend bask in her father's attention without crying, but apparently, I couldn't.

I disappeared and walked out the back door. I didn't want to explain myself, and I didn't want anyone to make me feel better. I wanted my dad. The trees swayed above me in the evening breeze, and the crickets chirped endlessly. They were almost able to block out my atrocious thoughts.

"What's wrong?" His voice, his words of concern, warmed me. I showed myself to him, tears and all. "Ever, what's wrong?" Ike's arms around me healed me. I rested against him.

"How did you know I was out here?"

"I could hear you crying, I think." I shook my head. I hadn't made a sound. "Or maybe I could feel it." He held me tighter. "It hurt." I pulled my arms to my chest and let Ike engulf me. I would sometimes lay the same way against him when we were snuggled together in the tree house. "Now tell me what's wrong."

"I'm jealous you and Gwen still have a father, and I'm disgusted at myself. I would never wish this on either of you." My chest shook with a sob as I began to cry again.

"Shh. Ever, this is a really bad situation. You guys and your mothers have been through so much. My grandmother did this . . . to you."

I leaned back to face him. "I'm scared that someday it's going to be you. That you're going to die. That the curse will come full circle and your grandmother and mother will be tortured by all of this, too." Sobs tore through me. I wasn't jealous. I was terrified. "I get it now, why they wanted to keep us apart. I can't lose you, and I can only imagine what it would do to our moms."

"You won't. We're going to figure this out. Together, like Maya's mom said." He held me until I believed him.

I looked past his shoulder at my kitchen, which was still lit up and bustling with activity. "There's a lot of history in there."

"Not ours," Ike said. He kissed me, and the trees swayed harder above us. I held on tight to Ike, but no one knew what to do.

❧

Gisel and Gwen were at our house every night for a week straight. They read, they researched, and they took notes. Our mothers called every older witch they knew. It always came back to casting a new spell, and Gisel was still against it.

"What if we just don't have children," I said over breakfast Friday morning. Ruby and Maya shrugged. *Not* getting pregnant was most high schooler's goal, we'd just extend it into the rest of our lives.

"We'd never want that for you girls," Lovie said and sat next to us. "One day, when it's the right time, the four of you are going to make exceptional mothers."

"And we're going to be the perfect grandmothers." Sloane

laughed as she flipped pancakes. The thought of any of them as grandmothers was hysterical.

Ruby was unusually quiet. "Ever's got a point. If we never have a baby, the spell shouldn't be set into motion. We just won't have kids."

Sloane came over to the table, spatula in hand. "Witches don't have that luxury. The universe will demand a baby from you." Maya, Ruby, and I sat back in our chairs and stared at Sloane. We'd never heard a word of this. "At least one of your children will be a girl, to carry on the world." Our mouths fell open. "When the next generation's coven is created, you'll all have daughters born within a year of each other."

"But . . ." Ruby began.

"What? It isn't that different from regular society. Believe me, it isn't easy *not* to have a baby as a woman in your late twenties and thirties."

The next time we were alone at school, I mentioned the idea of not having kids to Ike, and he hated the idea as well. He was already imagining himself surrounded by kids and throwing them around in the lake by his house. He was a big, giant, romantic.

"They said I wouldn't have a choice. That I'd get pregnant when the universe was ready for me to."

"I guess it's best we're not doing anything that could make that happen then."

I kissed him. "I know how happy that makes you."

Ike didn't come back with his usual quips on the subject. "I think we should go see my grandmother."

My eyebrows rose to the top of my forehead. "Clara?"

"Yeah. She started this whole thing. Maybe if she knows that I'm possibly in danger, she'll reverse it."

"I thought she was sick."

"She's dying. So let's go after school."

The day dragged by. No one thought visiting Clara was a good idea, but we were out of alternatives. She scared me. The woman cursed her daughter's coven to a life lived in hell waiting for their loved ones to die. She was a horrible person, but she was also capable of spell casting all by herself. Something I didn't have the luxury of.

I didn't tell my mother about the meeting. All of our mothers had already, at length, debated how to handle Clara. According to Mrs. Kennedy, she was incorrigible and still dangerously bitter. There was no question my mother wouldn't let me go.

Ike pulled up to the nursing home on the other side of town named the Friends Home where Clara lived. How fitting, I thought, to visit my archenemy at the Friends Home.

Ike held my hand as we signed in at the desk and were given visitor's passes. We followed the hall to Clara's room. She was lying in her bed and facing the window when we walked in. The skin on her arms was hanging off the bone. Her eyes were covered in a milky white film.

She brightened at the sight of Ike. The corners of her mouth tilted up the same way Ike's did when he wasn't being abrupt. The similarity softened me to her until she noticed me standing behind him.

Clara sat up straight in her bed much faster than I thought possible for a woman who appeared so frail. Pulling herself back against her pillow as power oozed from her.

"Hi, Mimi," Ike said and kissed her cheek.

Her eyes never left me. "What is *she* doing here?"

"I want you to meet her." Ike turned to me. *It's okay*, he thought. "I love her, Mimi."

"No." Clara's head shook violently, and there was a lash of power that almost forced me back a step.

"This is Ever. We're in love. Do you know what that means?" he asked, and Clara finally released me from her stare of death and focused on her grandson.

"Do *you* know what it means?" She dipped her head and stared at him.

"I do. I know everything, and I'm here for you to help me end this."

Clara's head shook back and forth as if it weren't connected to her body. "No," she said, but it was barely audible.

"I'll die." The words from Ike's mouth tightened my chest and pushed the air from my lungs. Tears filled my eyes.

Clara glared past him at me. "Leave her." She grabbed Ike's hand and held it between her own. She stared at him, but Ike didn't falter. Her jaw fell open. Her breaths were labored. "Even without a curse, she'll leave you and break your heart."

"That isn't going to happen, Mimi. None of it." Clara huffed and dropped his hand in disgust. "I want you to cast a new spell that will end this."

A force flew from her fragile frame and this time I did take a step back. Ike's hold on my hand never relented. "You have no idea what you're asking. You'll unleash the hounds of hell if you reverse a witch's curse. Even her own." She leaned back in her bed, dismissing the conversation. "There's a simple answer to this and that's for you to never see her again."

Ike stood up straight. "I'd rather die."

With that, he turned and led me into the hallway. A cold breeze swept past me from Clara's room.

It wasn't until later that night that Ike called my phone to tell me his grandmother had passed away sometime before dinner. We'd left at four thirty.

I told my mother and aunts of her death. I expected some version of "Ding Dong! The Witch is Dead" to be sung, but there was nothing but silence and sorrow. Clara took with her the hope that she'd fix this.

Lovie was the only one who still believed. My mother, Sloane, and Gisel went through the motions every day of trying to find a solution, but their expressions were grounded in defeat. Gwen, Ruby, Maya, and I—my coven—were beginning to lose faith as well. The Virago had retreated. At least we hadn't heard from them. Billy was leaving me alone, and our mothers were finally letting Ike and me be together, but I felt no relief. The curse wore on all of us more than anything else combined.

Our prom dresses hung from the doors of our closet in the attic. All four of us were going. Ike and I were riding in a limo like most of the other students in our school. I'd be in a dress with flowers woven into the lace. He'd wear a tux. No one would talk about dying.

The dress became a symbol of how fleeting Ike and I were. Our future was limited unless we wanted to risk his life. It was an impossible amount of responsibility for a seventeen year old. It was the death of our future hanging over our heads every time his lips touched mine, which to my delight was frequently.

When he went to work Saturday morning, I went to his house. I rang the doorbell and waited for his father to answer, but when the door opened, Gisel was standing in front of me.

"I need to talk to you." My heart was breaking with every word from my mouth.

Ike's mom sensed it, and her face crumpled in concern as she grabbed my arm and gently led me inside. I followed her to the kitchen. "Sit," she said and pulled out a chair for me. "Can I get you something to drink?"

I shook my head and sat in the chair she'd pulled out for me. Water splashed across the closed windows behind us. It sounded like a fire hose dousing the house. Gisel sighed. "It's Gwen," she said. "She's enamored with her influence over the elements. She's been having water fun all morning and she's very unpredictable. She soaked two carpets before I got all the windows shut."

I laughed at the thought of Gwen outside. She was a delight to be around even when she wasn't experimenting, but the thought of her powers left me cold. I stared at the table between Ike's mother and me.

"What is it, Ever?"

I inhaled and faced her. I had to get it over with before I lost my nerve. "I thought . . . maybe because you barely know me . . . and because—" I choked a little on my own words. "He's your son who might die, that you'd help me."

Gisel reached out and held my hands. "I am trying to help, Ever. I swear I am."

"I know." I wasn't talking about trying to stop the curse any-more. I wanted her to make it so I wasn't a part of it. "I actually was hoping you'd help me change myself to stop it."

Gisel tilted her head and furrowed her brow. "Change? How?"

"If I wasn't a witch anymore, I wouldn't be part of the coven. And without the coven, the curse won't apply to me." A lump lodged in my throat. I inhaled through my nose. "And it won't apply to Ike."

Gisel released my hands. "Does Ike know you're here?" She sat up straight in her chair and leaned back annoyed. I wasn't sure at what.

I shook my head. Ike would have fought me about this until he fell over dead from arguing.

Gisel moved her chair until she faced me and held my hands in hers. "I do know you, Ever. You are my sister's daughter, and I love you like my own." Tears fell from my eyes, and Gisel wiped them away the same way my mother would have. "But even if that wasn't true . . . *never* give up your powers for a man. Never." The water drenched the window again behind me. "Any man worth such a gesture would never allow it."

"It's the only way." My voice cracked as I spoke.

"Ever, I don't know what you not being a witch would do to this coven. Our family. But you can't do it. Would you ever give up Ike?"

Tears filled my eyes again. "No."

"Then why give up yourself?" I lowered my head and she pulled me to her. Gisel held me until I had calmed enough to stop crying and breathe normally.

"Mrs. Kennedy, I love Ike more than the air and the sky and the sun and the moon. I love Ike more than I love being a witch, and if I have to give that up to save him, then I will." My voice was steady. Ike gave me strength. "I can't lose him."

Mrs. Kennedy searched my eyes for something I couldn't give her because I had nothing more to share. She lowered her head as though I'd wounded her somehow. "Come with me," she said and stood. She grabbed her purse and keys off the counter by the sink.

"Where are we going?"

"To unleash the hounds of hell. God help us."

I stood back, unsure if I was getting what I had asked her for or if she had something else in mind.

"Hey, crazy Earth witch!" Gisel yelled as she walked out of her garage with me right behind her. "Let's go."

"Where are we going?" Gwen asked as she jogged over to join us.

"To Auburn," her mother said.

I stepped out from behind her mother and Gwen's expression filled with love. "For what?"

"To change history, and we're going to need you."

"I'm in," Gwen said and climbed in the back seat of their car.

We're driving? Since when did we drive places we were in a hurry to get to?

Mrs. Kennedy said, "You can sit up front, Ever."

Right. Up front. With Mrs. Kennedy. My, how things have changed. I leaned my head on the window and watched the clouds swirl in the sky. I was thankful for the car. We could fly through bad weather, but it was functional rather than enjoyable.

"Was it supposed to rain today?" Gisel asked. I shrugged. I hadn't noticed the weather since I found out Ike was going to die if we had a child. Day-to-day information fell into the background of my life.

"It was supposed to be sunny." Gwen was disappointed. She had plans. "Ever, you should see how good I'm getting." She took her seatbelt off and leaned over the front seat. "Today, I lit a fire, added air until it was raging, then moved water from the lake and put it out."

"All without burning down our house," her mother said proudly.

"Mostly. The corner on Ike's side doesn't count."

I wanted them to keep talking. It calmed my nerves. I felt responsible for whatever was about to happen even though it'd been set into motion long before I was born. Mrs. Kennedy made Gwen rebuckle but they continued chatting about Gwen's powers. No one seemed to be listening, not even the person speaking.

My mother and every other member of my household were waiting for us in the yard when we arrived. I turned to Gisel, wondering if she'd been in contact with them.

She shook her head. "Something like this, they could sense."

"Oh."

We piled out of the car and walked straight to where everyone was standing. Mom, Lovie, and Sloane all watched Gisel expectantly. "I'm willing to try if you guys still want to," Gisel said and there was a collective release of tension. Her decision was something they had all been waiting for but weren't willing to push her on.

"Are you sure? You might be completely right. This could destroy us all," my mother said to Gisel, giving her the final say again.

Gisel looked over her shoulder at me. "It will definitely destroy us if we don't. We have no other choice."

"We'll need a spell," my mother said to Sloane.

The wind kicked up, swirling around us. It was a warning, and we all ignored it.

"I already have it." We followed her into the house. "I wrote it twenty years ago and have been tweaking it since we moved home."

Lovie and Sloane removed the leaves from the kitchen table and pushed it to the side leaving about six square feet in the center of the kitchen for us.

"When you guys created Carl, how did you do it?" Sloane asked us.

We still weren't used to telling the truth when it came to Carl. Gwen jumped right in. She hadn't broken any rules the day he was born. "We stood in a circle, held hands, and recited the spell."

"What spell?" Sloane asked.

"Ruby wrote it." Sloane looked proudly at her daughter.

"I pretty much copied the failed bird spell."

"I'm still proud," her mother said.

We all moved into a circle facing out toward our mothers and held hands. Ruby's were clammy, which was another warning that this was a dangerous idea. "I'm going to give each of you the spell to begin. You are the future and you're innocent." I wondered how I was going to hold hands and the piece of paper and had opened my mouth to ask, but Sloane clarified. "I'm going to give it to you in your minds."

We all nodded and then closed our eyes so we could focus. The spell appeared in my mind. It was written on a black piece of paper with silver ink. "Cool!" Gwen yelled.

"How did you do that?" Ruby asked.

"Magic, of course." Sloane laughed, but the thunder rumbled above us followed by streaks of lightning illuminating the dark room. The world outside was a dark charcoal color. The new leaves on the trees threatened to all blow away with the branches holding them.

"Okay. Let's start with you guys. Close your eyes. Concentrate. Believe what you can do to affect change." I lifted my chin toward the ceiling. Every element of my body acutely focused on Sloane's words. I could do this. "Breathe in your power." I took a deep breath.

"Now recite the spell."

What once was four, can never be three
A force united to set them free

The unspoken truth of loss and fear
Hidden by hope, the answer lies here

Forgiveness and love, repair the tragic past
Betrayal, desertion, the spell that was cast

Twenty years apart. Too long to mourn
Now right the wrong that hatred had born

Maya, Ruby, Gwen, and I held hands and spoke the words of the spell to the universe. We repeated it, letting thunder punctuate each line.

"Don't stop!" Gisel yelled over the noise of the storm.

What once was four, can never be three . . .

The front and back doors flew open, and the wind blew around us. I squeezed my eyes shut and focused on the words as I held Ruby and Gwen's hands tighter. Ike would survive this, even if I didn't.

Forgiveness and love, repair the tragic past . . .

I could hear collisions of large objects behind me and feel debris splinter off and soar around the room. The storm was inside with us. Our mothers formed a circle around us, each of them facing their daughter as they joined in the chant of our spell. Two full covens. The walls shook. Broken glass and dishes swirled at our feet. My hair blew above me, and the wind slapped across my face. The howls of the wind and dark bass of the thunder drowned everything but the spell that kept falling from our lips and lifting to the wind on our combined voices. I wasn't frightened. I was fierce.

What once was four, can never be three
A force united to set them free

The unspoken truth of loss and fear
Hidden by hope, the answer lies here

Forgiveness and love, repair the tragic past
Betrayal, desertion, the spell that was cast

Twenty years apart. Too long to mourn
Now right the wrong that hatred had born

Then, almost as quickly as the storm took hold, it was gone. The wind stopped blowing and the sky calmed. The house was held in a heavy silence. Not one of us moved.

I opened my eyes and looked into my mother's. She began to cry and said, "We did it. It's gone. I can feel it's gone."

"I can, too," Lovie said a moment before Sloane and Gisel's confirmations came as well.

The house was in shambles. The front door was hanging off the hinges. The couch had flown against the doorway to the kitchen and pictures of our mothers were lying on the floor in broken frames.

"Ike," Ike's mother said to no one. "I have to find Ike." He was working on the Hitchner farm. If he was outside when the storm came through—"

He was already talking to me in my head. "He's okay," I told her. "He went in the Hitchner's basement. He said the damage isn't too bad over there."

Gisel's mouth dropped open and she stared at me with wide eyes "Ever, how did you talk to him?"

I glanced to my mom, who was probably going to be livid that I kept this little detail to myself, and spoke, "Well . . . see . . . Ike seems to have some powers."

"What?" They all stopped what they were doing.

"He can hear me . . . in his head. He can also talk back."

"How?"

I raised my shoulders and shook my head. "No idea. It's never happened to me before, but I'm guessing it has something to do with his mother being a witch."

"And it has something to do with you." Gwen waved her hand in my direction. "He can't hear anyone else unless you're involved. It's something special between the two of you. I've tried it on Dave Anzaldo a hundred times, and he never hears a word I say." I loved Gwen. "Of course, that's when I'm actually talking to him, too."

"Did you check on Isaiah?" Lovie asked, and Ike's mother looked at my mom, but Lovie was talking to her.

She shook her head and seemed disgusted with herself. "I was only worried about Ike." Gisel was lost in thought until she said, "I have to go. Gwen, stay and help everyone clean up. I'll be back if I can."

My mother grabbed her arm. "Are you okay?"

"I'm better than I've been in twenty years."

She pulled Gisel into a hug. "Geesey."

Gisel sank into her embrace. "I love you, Helene."

I picked up the photograph of my grandmother with my mother. There was a perfect crack down the center of my grandmother's body. I ran my finger over the line, but there was no sharp edge.

"What else can we do?" Gwen's voice rose from the rubble. Our mother's heads snapped up and stared at her. Gwen scared them.

She was new and unpredictable.

"Nothing without my permission," Gisel said, and my mother faked a laugh.

The fire whistle blew from down the street. The power was gone. Through the open back door I could see half the trees were lying on the ground. Lovie's car was flipped on its side.

"We've done enough," I said.

Helene

I T TOOK FOUR DAYS TO clean up the yard, and that was with using our powers as often as we could get away with it. Gisel and Gwen spent the days with us as we pitched in to help the rest of Auburn undo the damage the storm had inflicted on their properties.

Our neighbors expressed condolences to Gisel over Clara's death, and with the curse lifted, I could almost empathize with Gisel's loss. Her and Clara's relationship had always been a difficult one. Gisel was a glorious handful in our youth, and Clara was a bitter shell of the woman she'd been before her coven had died.

I surveyed my family, all eight of us working together with love and respect and gratitude. So many people never got a second chance the way we did. "I'm grateful."

Lovie was the first to notice. She stopped collecting sticks from

Mr. Chew's side yard and stood straight facing me. "We all are."

"No one more than me," Gisel said as she moved to my side.

Sloane, who was watching the girls shovel debris away from the storm drain in front of Mr. Crawford's house, turned and smiled over her shoulder at us.

"We have to make sure this never happens to them," Lovie said. "They've been through enough. They need each other."

No one had ever blamed me for the split in our coven, but the guilt crept in at night. I wondered if Gisel ever lost sleep over her part in it. I would do anything I could to teach our girls that no matter how angry they got or how hard things seemed, walking away was never the answer.

Sloane looked back at me as if she'd heard my thoughts. "They're good."

Somehow, I knew she was right. "I'm going back to start lunch."

"Make sure it includes wine," Sloane called out to me as I stepped onto the now cleared sidewalk.

I climbed our steep driveway with tired legs and a sore back. Isaiah's truck was parked next to the house. He was taking several pizza boxes out of the passenger side. When he saw me, he stopped moving.

"Hello," I said. Words and thoughts churned inside me, wanting the freedom to be heard, but I still couldn't face the great wealth of emotions attached to Gisel's husband.

"Hi." He lifted the pizzas a little. "I, uh, brought you guys some lunch. Ike said you've been working nonstop to put the town back together."

I took two boxes off the top. "It's the least we can do."

Isaiah followed me through the back door and into the kitchen. We put the pizzas on the counter and found ourselves next to each other. Too close for me to breathe normally.

"Will you leave now?" His voice was low. Just above a whisper.

It caressed my ear and traveled down the side of my neck.

I could no more leave Auburn than I could drop Ever off at a bus station. Even though she was driving me insane. "I want my family back."

Isaiah only stared at me. The air surrounding us was too thick to navigate through. "You'll forgive her, but not me?"

Letting go of the past with Gisel was easily explained. By forgiving her, I got her back. The love, the friendship . . . all of it.

Things could never be the same with Isaiah. By forgiving him, I was finally letting him go.

"I've forgiven you both."

"It doesn't feel that way."

I inhaled the strength not to look away. "What else are you asking for?"

He moved next to me and rested both hands on the counter in front of him. His head hung low. I couldn't watch him, the sight was making me weak, and I'd never give my strength away for him again. I stared forward at the table in the middle of the room.

"Do you remember the first time I kissed you?" He was a ruthless man. The heady smell of the wood pile burning in the center of the crowd that night surfaced in my mind. Fear of how far he'd take this tightened my chest. "You were leaning against the trunk of Ben Keen's car at Stoners Lane, surrounded by Gisel and Lovie and Sloane."

I turned to see him watching me. A tiny piece of me knew that it wouldn't hurt this badly if I didn't still love him, but that wasn't something I was willing to consider, maybe ever . . . and he was married to Gisel. My feelings for him had no business here. "Isaiah—" I took one step away from him, and his fingers laced around my wrist.

"Ben handed you a cup and started talking to you." Isaiah tightened his grip. "But I couldn't let that happen, so I walked up in front of everyone and kissed you." Every muscle in my body tensed at the memory. A first kiss that twenty years later still captivated my body. "I had never felt that way about anyone." He had to stop. "Before or since."

"I hate you."

He was undaunted. "I can't get you out of my head, Helene. I've been trying for half of my life to let you go, but I can't."

"What are you doing?" My voice sounded as tortured as the rest of me felt.

Isaiah took a step closer and whispered in my ear. "I want you back, too."

"You've left none of me to have back." I spat at him. His words could never mean a thing. "And you're married."

He stood shaking his head. "Don't you understand? It doesn't matter. This marriage means nothing to Gisel or me."

"Your relationship is not my concern." I couldn't listen to another word. "I want you stay away from me."

"That's impossible." I left him as Ever and Ruby walked in. They were covered in dirt and so lost in their conversation they barely realized Isaiah and I were in the room. I swallowed back the devastation the same way I'd done when I left for my first semester in Vermont and searched the cabinet for paper plates. The rest of my family arrived, and we ate our lunch together. I wouldn't let Isaiah, or anyone else, ever ruin this again.

Ever

RUBY'S PROM DRESS WAS NOT red. It was poppy. She corrected each and every person who commented on it. I warned her when she chose it, but the plunging V-neck that practically met the slit up her thigh was irresistible to her. Secretly, I thought she really loved red, but she just couldn't reconcile it with the commonality of a girl named Ruby who loves red. She existed to challenge the ordinary.

She'd made fun of my white gown.

"Ivory to be specific," I'd corrected with an ironic smile.

Even Ruby had to admit my dress was beautiful. It was simple, and soft, and if I had to fly in the spaghetti straps and fabric that hung straight to the floor, I could.

"You look like a virgin," she'd said and held out the dress to examine the lace overlay that was covered in peonies.

I only winked at her, which drove her insane. She asked me at least twice a week if Ike and I had done it yet, but I had no new information to share.

Ike made me promise no witchcraft. We were going to be a normal couple on prom night. Two people who met and fell in love. He was an amazing athlete. I was good at chess. That was all. Just two kids with nothing to worry about, but what to do first when school let out.

He picked me up in his mother's car. My mother and aunts watched as I pinned his boutonniere to his dark gray tux. I stepped back and let my sight linger from his navy eyes to his shoulders, to his waist, and back up again. I'm not sure what expression was on my face, but Ike was laughing at me when I met his eyes again.

"It's like the first day I saw you," I said.

"What is?" He touched my elbow. A simple gesture that bound me to him further and forced me to breathe deeply for air.

I exhaled. "You're beautiful."

"I should be telling you that." Ike leaned over until his lips were near my ear. He paused, and his breath slipped across my lobe and down my neck before he whispered, "You're the most beautiful thing I've ever seen." I reached out and grabbed him to keep my balance. "And you're mine." I could feel his lips tilt into a smile against my cheek before he kissed me there.

I couldn't face anyone. Being near him flustered me, and I knew I wore my feelings for everyone to see. I was sure I was blushing. "We should go," I managed to get out.

My mother followed us to Ike's house, where my entire family convened to take pictures by the lake. Gwen, Maya, Ruby, and I stood side by side as the sun dipped low behind us. We were finally exactly where our lives had brought us—together. I ignored the tingling I felt in their presence and resisted the ever-present urge to soar into the sky. Ike and I were just two high school students tonight.

I love you, I thought, and he peeked at me from behind his father.

Mr. Kennedy hadn't said a word since we'd arrived. That wasn't true. He'd said hi to me and even hugged me. He hadn't said a word since my *mother* had arrived. I followed Mr. Kennedy's line of sight to the dock my mother was standing on and it dawned on me, they must have gone to prom together. I swallowed back their dark past that I didn't know much about.

"Okay, now let's have all the boys stand behind their dates," Mrs. Kennedy directed. She was animated and happy. She appeared weightless and unfazed by my mom and Ike's dad history. She'd regained her powers after twenty years. They'd reclaimed their pasts. Sam, Mick, Ike, and Dave Anzaldo all stood behind us.

Ike's hands rested on my hips. I stood straight for the camera instead of leaning back against him the way I wanted to. The pictures were endless. The high temperatures from the afternoon still lingered, and I knew Ike was too hot in the late sun.

"Thanks for taking me to prom," I said and kissed him on the cheek.

"Are you kidding? I can't wait to dance with you again." I lost myself in his eyes. We'd been through so much to be able to stand together in front of our families without hiding anything. Ike rubbed his thumb over the top of my hand, knowing exactly what I was thinking.

"What's this?" Gwen said as she pulled an envelope out of her silver beaded purse. She read the paper as we all watched. Gwen looked up into my eyes. A cold breeze blew between us. "It's for you."

"Aw," Maya said and slapped Ike on the shoulder.

I stared at the envelope in Gwen's hand. I didn't want it. Without touching it, I knew Ike wouldn't have left a note for me in his sister's bag. He would have handed it to me or left it somewhere I would find it. Gwen approached me, and the cold air swirled around my head. I swallowed hard and took it from her extended hand.

My name was scrawled across the front of the envelope. Ike leaned over my shoulder as I opened it, and my instincts told me to hide it from him. To protect this night that we were just Ever and Ike.

"Open it." His voice near my ear wasn't gentle. It was a reflection of the grotesque emotions building inside me. I stepped away from him. His displeasure with my movements lodged in my chest. I faced him. It was just us. We were going to the prom.

I ripped open the envelope and unfolded the paper inside. It had a single feather as a watermark, exactly like the pages of the journal I kept by my bed. The page had been torn out and was missing the bottom corner by the seam.

I remembered to breathe when I looked back at Ike. He was watching my every reaction.

The note said:

I meant it when I said you were perfect.

I *let* your boyfriend hit me to see how strong he is.

You'll be the first to know when I hit back.

"What's it say?" Maya asked.

Nothing was going to ruin tonight. Ike and I deserved it to be perfect. I removed the ink from the page as I recited the elements in my head to calm me. *Neptunium. NP. Number ninety-three. Strontium. SR. Number thirty-eight.* I shrugged as I held the paper in the air.

"Nothing."

BONUS MATERIAL

The Witches of Auburn

Ever	Helene	
Ruby	Sloane	
Maya	Lovie	
Gwen	Gisel	Clara

The Kingsway Coven

Jennifer

Maryann

Riley

Tara Jane

Please see the next page for a preview of the
next installment in The Witches of Auburn series.

THE WITCHES OF AUBURN
A NOVELLA

HAZEL BLACK

1

This would be my only mistake.

Twenty years ago . . .

ISAIAH'S BODY TOOK UP MOST of the doorway. He leaned against the dingy white molding and rested his head on it. Without the doorjamb as a gauge, I'd never have believed he was the same height he'd been a few weeks ago. He certainly hadn't shrunk, but he still seemed smaller. His loss of stature wasn't physical, though. The emotional blow he took when Helene left seemed to cut him off at the knees.

He'd been here every day since that day, but I didn't know why. Maybe it was because he needed to talk to someone about her or maybe he just drifted back to the last place he'd seen her. From my house you could see up to her bedroom window and into her kitchen. Perhaps, Isaiah was as attracted to the memory of her as he'd been to Helene.

"Did you find her?" I asked, but I didn't really need to. If he'd been able to fix things by following Helene to Vermont, he wouldn't be standing in my kitchen in New Jersey right now. Based on the tortured look on his face, none of his possible answers would bring either of us any peace.

He nodded with his sight fixed on my mother's sun hat and gardening gloves, which rested in the center of the kitchen table. They were covered in soil and were out of place on the table. On a different day, she never would have left them there.

I filled two glasses with ice and poured vodka halfway up into both. The only juice in my refrigerator was orange, and I used it to top off the toxic concoctions. The glasses were freebies from McDonalds, and the colors had faded into an almost gray picture. I stirred the drinks and handed Isaiah the glass with the Hamburglar on it. He was the criminal in my head.

"Where's your mom?" Isaiah asked and took a big gulp from his glass. She was obviously gone. We wouldn't be standing around drinking in front of her. She would end our eighteen-year-long lives with a stare.

"My dad's in the hospital again. She's with him."

Isaiah didn't say, "I'm sorry." Those words we'd never say to each other again. Not for anything.

I focused on my mother's gloves and tried to move them with my mind. I bit my bottom lip as I willed the glove to fly across the room, but it stayed perfectly still and out of place.

"Helene was talking to some people . . . other students, I think." His gaze fixed on the contents of his glass. "She was standing in the hallway outside a lecture hall." He took another long sip.

I abandoned my efforts to move the gloves and sighed. He was going to hurt me. Whenever he mentioned her, he inflicted pain. I let him keep coming back and doing it over and over again because it hurt less than being alone. The inside of my head was more terrifying than my reality these days.

"Some guy was talking to her, and Helene was laughing as if he was hilarious." Isaiah stared back at me, waiting for me to say something that would repair this, but I'd accepted weeks ago that this was our new reality. "Like she could be happy. Like she *was* happy." He wasn't angry or yelling. The two of us were too pathetic for that type of display.

"Did you talk to her? What did she say?" Why couldn't she just talk to him?

"She stared right at me and stopped laughing. Like a fireball had flown across her face. She didn't just stop smiling. She died in front of me. Every sign of life drained from her expression."

I'd told him to stop holding out hope a million times since Helene had moved to Vermont early for college just to avoid us. "Then what happened?"

"I thought she was going to talk to me, even if just to yell at me, but she excused herself and walked out." Isaiah's shoulders slumped farther. His head fell back as his empty stare connected with the ceiling. He might stand in my kitchen like this forever because he had no idea how to move forward without her.

"And?" I couldn't take it anymore. The silence screamed at me from everywhere, but mostly in my head where the voices of my sisters no longer spoke to me. It didn't matter how often I called out to each of them every day or begged them to answer me—there was nothing.

"She disappeared. I sat outside her dorm like a criminal for three hours, but she never came back. No one would talk to me about her." He stood straight. "She must have already warned them that if I ever came by they weren't supposed to tell me a thing about her."

"Of course, that's the only explanation for a girl not telling you exactly what you want."

Isaiah downed his drink. I followed his lead. We'd drink ourselves through our first semester at college and forget about the loves we'd lost. I refilled our glasses, but there wasn't enough vodka in the world to make me forget Helene and Lovie and Sloane.

We escaped the kitchen—the scene of my second crime against my coven—and sat on the plastic chairs perched in my backyard, which was where we drank three more screwdrivers. I made all the drinks, but I couldn't tell you how we finished the bottle. It'd seemed like only an hour ago I'd cracked the seal on the bottle, and now I handed it to Isaiah to hide behind the seat in his pickup. Mama hated alcohol, especially when Daddy drank it.

"Let's go for a ride, and we'll throw it out at Wawa." There was nothing better to do. The isolation was drilling a hole in my soul.

Isaiah barely stayed on his side of the road, but there were no other cars to demand his composure. We drove out past Upper Pittsgrove and swung back around through Woodstown. When the darkness finally replaced every glimmer of hope in the sky, he pulled behind hay bales, which were stacked two stories high on the edge of a field. They formed a wall between Isaiah's truck and the world outside that had rendered us angry and bitter.

"Did you bring me here thinking I'd have sex with you again?" I was practically slurring. I sat straight in his truck to mask the effects of the vodka.

"Are you kidding?" he asked. His expression held nothing but hate. I couldn't tell if it was directed at him or me. "I can barely stand the sight of you." He pursed his lips together.

The memory of his hands touching me, pulling me down against him while his lips pressed so hard on mine I thought I'd bleed ran through my mind. It was followed by the familiar guilt scraping my insides in its wake.

"Let's climb the wall," he said and got out of the truck.

I stayed still in my seat. The hay was stacked straight up with an uneven amount on each row, creating a staircase on one side.

No one should climb it. I could have flown. I swallowed down the longing for the gifts of my old life.

Isaiah opened my door, leaned against it, and stared at me until I rolled my eyes and followed him to the hay. By the third row, the bales beneath us were unsteady. Each row was designed to support the one above it. Not me and my best friend's enormous ex-boyfriend.

Isaiah held each bale above me as I climbed before him. He was a gentleman and kind and had no business being anywhere near me. He'd ruined my life. I'd ruined his. The liquor clouded my judgment. Again.

The breeze picked up on the top row. I stayed in the middle of the stack and let my hair blow across my face. It was as close to flying as I'd come in months. The farthest I'd been off the ground. My intoxication morphed into adoration for the sky and the air and the night. It was my home. I'd owned it with my coven, but it was lost to me.

"Gisel . . . what are you doing?"

I could barely hear him; I was fixated on the night around me. "Maybe they'd come back if it was a life-or-death situation." *Once a witch, always a witch.*

"The girls? Are you talking about Helene and Lovie and Sloane?"

I'd given up on them. There was nothing left to say. Not a word they'd hear. They may as well have been dead. I'd be better off if they were. "No. I'm talking about my powers." I leaned farther into the breeze and stepped to the end of the bale. The straw gave way at the edges and released from the tightly knotted rectangle. I played with the frayed straw with the toe of my shoe. "I've never been without them."

"Or the girls."

"It's so sad." I didn't feel like crying, though. My anger kept me alive. It would make me fly again. "All of it. Incredibly tragic. My entire life gone in one day."

Isaiah stared at me as I spoke. The moonlight barely lit his face enough to see the pity. I was pathetic. I turned away from him and my old life, bent my knees, and swung my hands into the air. I—

Isaiah tackled me onto the hay beneath us. He landed on top of me and held me there. The weight of him, the length of his body, and the memories of the last time he was there, forced a tear to break through my frozen interior.

"You still have power, Gisel," he whispered in my ear. "You weren't just a witch, and you're not just a girl now."

"You're only being nice."

"I'm being your friend."

He rolled to my side, and I sat up facing him. "You should have been my friend that night."

"I know."

"I absolutely *hate* you. The only person I deplore more than myself is you, Isaiah Kennedy. You're the worst human being to ever walk the face of this earth."

"You repulse me, too." He lay back and stared and the night sky.

"I mean . . ." My head shook. Something in my core was breaking free. It was either because of the vodka or his touch. "What were we thinking? How could we?"

"I can't talk about it or I'll jump myself."

The thought of him erased from the situation pleased me. "I should push you. Helene will forgive me if I kill you."

"No, she won't."

"We should give it a try."

Acknowledgements

I rarely include acknowledgments, even though there are always many people I need to thank, but this book was special . . . to say the least.

Thank you to Charlie for stopping what you were doing and getting lost with me in the details of witchcraft, pushing me not to be typical, and being patient when I didn't understand what you were talking about. I spend so much more time in reality than you do. It's one of the many things I love and envy about you.

Thanks to Vivian for creating the writer Hazel Black. It fell off your tongue with your other option, Jupiter Young, and I laughed, but it is creative and captivating and fun. Like you.

This book would not have been published without the following people:

Maryann Morris and Nicole Warner for being obsessed with these women before you read a word. You can't buy that kind of support in this business or in life. I'm lucky to have you both.

Michelle Mann, Tricia Steiner, and Michelle Ottaviano for reading it and telling me you loved it many, many drafts ago. You saved it from being a Christmas present for only my daughter and my mother.

My editor, Ashley Williams. You are incredible. I wanted to throw this manuscript at you many times over the last year, and every time it was because you were amazing at your job.

Rose & Evelyn for giving me a glimpse into the secret society teenagers exist within. It's crazy how quickly I forgot.

The tiny town of Auburn, you still enchant me every day.

And finally, to Jill Kugler and Kate Waters, thank you. You are the best kind of coven. May our daughters protect theirs, the way we have our own. *Geesey* . . .

HAZEL BLACK

HAZEL BLACK GRADUATED FROM RUTGERS University and returned to her hometown in rural South Jersey. Her mother encouraged her to take some time and find herself. After three months of searching, she began to bounce checks, her neighbors began to talk, and her mother told her to find a job.

She settled into corporate America, learning systems and practices and the bureaucracy that slows them. Hazel quickly discovered her creativity and gift for story telling as a corporate trainer and spent years perfecting her presentation skills and studying diversity. It was during this time she became an avid observer of the characters she met and the heartaches they endured. Her years of study taught her that laughter, even the completely inappropriate kind, was the key to survival.

Made in the USA
Middletown, DE
01 September 2017